'[A] Scandinavian crime nove
by Hans Olav Lahlum, trans
Dickson, is the second book
Kristiansen, known as K2. Set in Oslo in 1969, it is a traditional
closed-circle mystery . . . The solution is ingenious, and the
investigation, with leads stretching back to the German occupation of Norway during the Second World War, certainly
holds the attention'   *Guardian*

'The second instalment of a captivating murder mystery series
set in 1960s Norway sees Inspector Kolbjørn Kristiansen seek
the advice of Patricia, a brilliant young amateur sleuth confined
to a wheelchair, to work out which of ten dinner guests killed
a business tycoon and former resistance fighter during the
Second World War. As the inspector tries to untangle the lies
and deceit he receives a series of letters warning of further
murders. Lahlum keeps the reader guessing until a clever and
satisfying conclusion'   *Daily Express*

'This is a continually fascinating novel which not only holds
true to the spirit of Agatha Christie but also has a twenty-first
century take on themes and subjects that never would have
been tackled by the Queen of Crime'   *Waterford Today*

Praise for The Human Flies

'Locked-room mysteries used to be a staple of golden-age crime fiction. Now the Norwegian novelist Hans Olav Lahlum has revived the form in *The Human Flies* translated by Kari Dickson. The novel is set in 1968, when a young detective inspector – Kolbjørn Kristiansen, known as K2 – is sent to an apartment block in Oslo to investigate the murder of a Resistance hero. The victim has been shot in his flat but there is no sign of the weapon and the front door appears to be locked from the inside. It is the start of a brilliant investigation in which K2 is secretly assisted by an enigmatic young woman who is confined to a wheelchair' *Sunday Times*

'As the latest Scandinavian crime writer to break into the English market, Lahlum is an admirer of Agatha Christie . . . As the story carries back to the dark days of the German occupation, a subplot of treachery and revenge emerges. A Christie-style finale has the suspects gathered to hear which of them is to be given the black spot. This crime in a cold climate deserves a warm welcome' *Daily Mail*

'If you fancy a traditional closed-circle murder mystery . . . try *The Human Flies* by Hans Olav Lahlum . . . With its conscious echoes of Agatha Christie and Rex Stout, this first whodunnit by a well-known Norwegian historian and leftist politician will delight fans of both authors' *Morning Star*

'Prepare yourself for a classic whodunnit of the highest calibre, a deviously challenging murder mystery set in an apartment complex in 1960s Oslo . . . a joy to read' **Crime Fiction Lover**

SATELLITE PEOPLE

HANS OLAV LAHLUM is a Norwegian crime author, historian, chess player and politician. The books that make up his crime series, featuring Criminal Investigator Kolbjørn Kristiansen (known as K2) and his precocious young assistant, Patricia, are bestsellers in Norway. *The Human Flies* was his first book in the series and is followed by *Satellite People*. The third, *The Catalyst Killing*, will be out soon.

Also by Hans Olav Lahlum

THE HUMAN FLIES

Hans Olav Lahlum

SATELLITE PEOPLE

Translated from the Norwegian by
Kari Dickson

PAN BOOKS

First published 2015 by Mantle

This paperback edition published 2015 by Pan Books
an imprint of Pan Macmillan
20 New Wharf Road, London N1 9RR
Associated companies throughout the world
www.panmacmillan.com

ISBN 978-1-4472-3277-3

This translation has been published with the financial support of NORLA.

Originally published in 2011 as *Satellittmenneskene* by Cappelen Damm, Oslo

135798642

A CIP catalogue record for this book is available from the British Library.

Printed and bound by CPI Group (UK) Ltd, Croydon, CR0 4YY

Visit **www.panmacmillan.com** to read more about all our books
and to buy them. You will also find features, author interviews and
news of any author events, and you can sign up for e-newsletters
so that you're always first to hear about our new releases.

Dedicated to Agatha –

the queen of classic crime

Some of the characters in this book may have been inspired by people who are now dead or alive, but the events that take place during the Second World War and in 1969 are not based on historical events. Magdalon Schelderup and all the guests at his last supper are fictional characters who bear no resemblance to any dead or living persons.

DAY ONE

An Unexpected Storm Warning

I

'Good afternoon. My name is Magdalon Schelderup and is no doubt familiar to you. I would like to arrange a meeting with you this coming Monday. The reason being that one of my nearest and dearest is planning to murder me later on in the week!'

The time was a quarter past one. The day was Saturday, 10 May 1969. The place was my office in the main police station in Oslo. And the words seemed to hang in the air for a long time after I had heard them.

I waited for this particularly tasteless joke to be followed by either a loud laugh or the phone being thrown down. But the connection was not broken. And when the voice continued, it was without doubt Magdalon Schelderup's distinctively rusty yet dynamic voice, just as I had heard it many times before on the radio and television. I immediately pictured the legendary businessman and multimillionaire as he was most often photographed for the papers: dressed in a long black winter coat, his furrowed face secretive and barely visible under a brown leather hat.

'And just in case you should for a moment believe otherwise, I am Magdalon Schelderup and I am of sound mind and sober. You have been recommended to me by several acquaintances, and I was singularly impressed by your work in connection with the much-discussed murder case last year, so I thought I would give you the honour of solving this case too. The question is quite simply whether you can spare the time to meet me on Monday in connection with my planned murder, or not?'

I felt increasingly bewildered as I sat at my own desk on what I had presumed would be a very ordinary Saturday shift. It was starting to dawn on me that it was in fact Magdalon Schelderup who had called me and that he was serious.

I replied that I would of course give the case highest priority and suggested that we should meet that very same day, rather than wait until Monday morning. Not surprisingly, Magdalon Schelderup had obviously considered this possibility too.

'The truth is that only an hour ago I thought of driving into town to meet you personally. But then I discovered that three of the tyres on my car had unfortunately been slashed overnight. I could of course have taken my wife's car or used one of the company cars, and I can certainly afford to pay for a taxi, but this episode has made me strongly doubt whether the person I had thought of mentioning to you today is in fact the guilty party.'

In response to this, I asked if there were several people in

Magdalon Schelderup's closest circle who he suspected might want to kill him. There was a short burst of dry laughter at the other end of the telephone.

'Absolutely. In fact, my closest circle is made up entirely of people who might be suspected of wanting to kill me. It is incredibly difficult to be both successful and popular over time. And given this dilemma, I have always chosen success. But what is new here is that I have good reason to believe that one of my nearest and dearest not only wants to kill me, but also has concrete plans to realize this sometime next week.'

The situation struck me as more and more absurd, but also more and more interesting. I heard my own voice say that we should then at least meet as early as possible on Monday morning. Magdalon Schelderup agreed to this straight away and suggested that I come to his home at Gulleråsen at around nine o'clock. He wanted to dig a little more and would assess the situation over the weekend, but was certain that he would be able to confirm his suspicions well enough to tell me on Monday.

Still dazed, I wished Magdalon Schelderup a good weekend and asked him to take every precaution against possible danger. He assured me that there was no risk of an attempt on his life before Tuesday afternoon, at the earliest. However, he would stay indoors at home until I came to see him on Monday morning and would do everything necessary to ensure his own safety.

Magdalon Schelderup's voice on the telephone was just as it was on the radio: a grand old man's voice, calm, convincing and determined. I put down the phone without any further protest and scribbled our meeting on Monday morning at the top of my to-do list for the coming week.

II

The remaining three-quarters of an hour of my Saturday shift passed without further drama. It was impossible, however, to stop my thoughts from turning to this unexpected telephone conversation. To the extent, in fact, that I called my boss to inform him about the phone call before I left the office. To my relief, he gave his approval of the way in which I had dealt with the situation.

Back home in my flat in Hegdehaugen, I found the latest article about Magdalon Schelderup in the pile of newspapers. It had been published only three days before. Yet another front page of the *Aftenposten* evening edition was filled with his photograph, this time under the headline 'King of Gulleråsen'. It concluded by saying that if the richest man in Gulleråsen was not already one of the ten richest men in Norway, then he very soon would be. The value of his property and assets was estimated at over 100 million kroner. Only months before his seventieth birthday, the property magnate and stock market king was at the peak of his career. With increasing regularity, financial experts speculated that he was one of the twenty most powerful men in Norway, though it was now many years since he had retired from his career as a conservative politician.

Over the years, newspapers and magazines had used unbelievable quantities of ink to write about Magdalon Schelderup. To begin with, they wrote about his contributions as a Resistance fighter and politician during and immediately after the war. There was then a rash of speculative and far less enthusiastic articles about the contact his family businesses might have had with the occupying forces during the war, and why a few years later he stepped back from an apparently promising political career. Later articles about his growing wealth and business acumen were frequently alternated with other more critical articles. These discussed his business methods, as well as the breakdown of his first two marriages and the financial settlements that they incurred. The interest in his turbulent private life appeared to have diminished following some further articles in the early 1950s when he married his third wife – this time a woman twenty-five years his junior. In recent years, however, there had been more and more articles that questioned the manner in which he kept shop. Former competitors and employees more or less queued up to condemn his methods and he had regularly been taken to court. With little success. Magdalon Schelderup cared not a hoot what the newspapers and magazines said, and with the aid of some very good sharpshooting lawyers, he was never sentenced in any court.

And it was this dauntless and apparently unassailable magnate who had telephoned me today to say that someone close to him planned to kill him next week.

Thus 10 May 1969 became one of the very few Saturdays when I yearned with all my heart for it to be Monday morning and the start of a new working week. I did not know then that the case would develop very quickly and dramatically in the meantime.

DAY TWO

Ten Living and One Dead

I

The following morning, 11 May 1969, started like every other Sunday in my life. I caught up with my lack of sleep from the previous week and did not eat breakfast until it was nearly lunch. The first few hours of the afternoon were spent reading the neglected papers from the week gone by. I even managed to read the first four chapters of the book of the week, which was Jens Bjørneboe's *Moment of Freedom*.

When the telephone rang at twenty-five past five, I had just stepped out of the shower. I made absolutely no attempt to answer it quickly. The caller was remarkably persistent, however, and the phone continued to ring until I picked it up. I immediately understood that it was serious.

The telephone call was of course for 'Detective Inspector Kolbjørn Kristiansen'. It was, as I had guessed, from the main police station in Møller Street. And, to my horror, it concerned Magdalon Schelderup. Only minutes before, they had received a telephone message that he had died over the course of an early supper at his home – in the presence of ten witnesses.

On the basis of what had been reported by the constables at the scene, it was presumed to be murder, but which of the witnesses present had committed the crime was 'to put it mildly, unclear'. The officer on duty at the police station had been informed that Schelderup himself had contacted me the day before. As none of the other detectives were available, the duty officer felt it appropriate to ask whether I might be able to carry out an initial investigation and question the witnesses at the scene of the crime.

I did not need to be asked twice, and within a few minutes was speeding towards Gulleråsen.

II

When I got there at ten to six, there was no trace of drama outside the three-storey Gulleråsen mansion where Magdalon Schelderup had both his home and head office. Schelderup had lived in style, and he had lived in safety. The house sat atop a small hill in the middle of a fenced garden, and it was a good 200 yards to the nearest neighbour. Anyone who wished to enter without being seen would have to make their way across a rather large open space. They would also have to find a way through or over the high, spiked wooden fence that surrounded the entire property, with a single opening for the heavy gate that led into the driveway.

I mused that it was the sort of house one finds in an Agatha Christie novel. It was only later on in the day that I discovered it was known as 'Schelderup Hall' by the neighbours.

There were eight cars parked in the space outside the gate, in addition to a police car. One of them was Magdalon Schelderup's own big, black, shiny BMW. I was quickly able to confirm that he had told the truth: three of the tyres had been slashed with either a knife or some other sharp instrument.

The other cars were all smaller, but still new and of good quality. The only exception was a small, well-used blue Peugeot that looked as if it had been on the road since the early 1950s. I jotted down a working theory that all of the deceased's guests were overwhelmingly upper-class, albeit with some obvious variations in their financial situations.

It was not a warm welcome. As I made my way to the front door, a cacophony of wild and vicious barking suddenly erupted behind me, and I spun round instinctively to protect myself against the attacking dogs. But fortunately that was not necessary: the three great Alsatians that were straining towards me were clearly securely chained. Nevertheless, the sight of the dogs only served to strengthen my feeling of unease and my conviction that Magdalon Schelderup must have felt safe in his own home. The threat had been in his innermost circle – as he had expected, but it had come two days earlier than anticipated.

At the front door, I greeted the two constables who had been first at the scene and were now standing guard. They were both apparently relieved to see me, and confirmed that despite the death, the mood in the house was surprisingly calm.

I soon understood what they meant when, one corridor and two flights of stairs later, I stepped onto the red carpet in Magdalon Schelderup's vast dining room. At first it felt as though I had walked into a waxworks. The furniture and interior was in the style of the early 1900s. The fact that there were no pictures or decoration of any type on the walls only added to the cold, unreal feeling. There was a single exception, which was therefore all the more striking. A well-executed full-length portrait of Magdalon Schelderup filled one of the short walls.

The host himself was now laid out on a sofa by the wall, just inside the door. He was dressed in a simple black suit, and as far as I could see had no obvious injuries of any kind. His eyes were closed and his lips had a bluish tinge. I could quickly confirm that there was no sign of life when I felt for a pulse in his neck and inner wrist.

A large dark mahogany table set for eleven dominated the centre of the room. The roast lamb and vegetables had been served on porcelain plates and the undoubtedly excellent wine had been poured into the wine glasses. But none of the guests had shown any inclination to eat or drink. They also had champagne, which no one had touched.

What had obviously been Magdalon Schelderup's throne at the head of the table was now empty. The ten guests, silent in their Sunday best, had taken their seats around the table again. They were all looking at me, but no one said a word. A swift headcount informed me that there were six women and four men. I noted a degree of uncertainty and surprise in some of the faces, but saw no evidence of grief in any. Not a single tear on any of the twelve ladies' cheeks around the table.

Eight of the guests I reckoned to be fairly evenly distributed across the age group thirty to seventy. They all looked very serious and impressively controlled. There were two who stood out, each in their own way, and therefore immediately grabbed my attention, and they were the youngest in the party.

In the middle of the right-hand side of the table sat a slim, fair-haired young man in his late twenties, who was by far the most nervous person in the room. An hour had passed since the death, and yet he was still squirming on his chair, his face hidden in his shaking hands. There were no tears here either, only beads of sweat on his temples and brow. It struck me that there was something familiar about the young man. But it was only when he realized that I was looking at him and he took his hands from his face that I suddenly recognized him as the famous athlete, Leonard Schelderup.

I had no doubt read somewhere on the sports pages at some point that Leonard Schelderup was Magdalon Schelderup's son, then promptly forgotten. A year ago, I had myself stood on the stands at Bislett Stadium to watch the Norwegian Championships and seen Leonard Schelderup fly past on his way to winning gold in the middle-distance race, his shoulder-length hair fluttering in the wind. And I had been very impressed. Partly by the manner in which he allowed his competitors to pass, only then to speed up dramatically when the bell rang to mark the final lap. And partly by the almost stoic calm he displayed during the thunderous applause when he passed the finishing line. I commented to the person standing next to me at the time that it seemed that nothing, but nothing, could make Leonard Schelderup lose his composure – which was why it now made such an impression on me to see the same man sitting there, looking up at me with pleading eyes. He was only a matter of feet away and apparently on the verge of a nervous breakdown.

The situation was no less bewildering when Leonard Schelderup then broke the silence, throwing up his hands and saying: 'I don't understand why he chose me to taste his food. It wasn't me who started the tape. I didn't taste the nuts. I have no idea who killed him!'

Leonard Schelderup's outburst seemed to ease the tension ever so slightly. No one said anything else, but there were sounds of shuffling and sighs around the table.

And fortuitously, I caught the first smile in the room. It was fleeting and a touch overbearing, just as Leonard Schelderup fell silent. A few seconds later the smile was gone, and I never found out whether she saw that I had noticed. But I did. My gaze had swung almost instinctively a couple of places to the left to catch the reaction of the youngest person in the room.

At first glance, I thought it was my advisor, Patricia, who had somehow or other managed to sneak both herself and her wheelchair into Magdalon Schelderup's home and had joined them at the dining table. Then I started to wonder if it was in fact all an absurd nightmare. Only, I didn't wake up.

The ten guests who remained seated at the table were very much alive. Magdalon Schelderup stayed where he was, lying stone dead on the sofa by the door. The young woman who sat to the right of his empty throne at the head of the table was of course not Patricia, though the girl who was sitting there also had dark hair and the same deliberate movements and held herself in the same self-assured manner.

Only, as far as I could see, this young woman was fully able, and about half a head taller than Patricia, as I remembered her from the previous spring; and also somewhat younger. I had never seen this woman before entering Magdalon Schelderup's house. But somewhere, I had heard that his youngest child was an extraordinarily beautiful daughter, who left those she met awestruck.

Her gaze was no less bold when her eyes met mine. Another fleeting smile slipped over her lips.

It was in those few seconds that I stood there looking into the eyes of the eighteen-year-old Maria Irene Schelderup that I realized there was only one thing to be done. And that was first of all to gather as much information as possible about the death and the deceased from her and the other guests. Then I would have to hurry home and phone the number without a name at the back of my telephone book. The number to a telephone that sat on the desk of Patricia Louise I. E. Borchmann, the professor's daughter, at 104–8 Erling Skjalgsson's Street. I had, with a hint of irony, written it down next to the emergency numbers for the fire brigade and the ambulance service.

III

I established the actual circumstances of Magdalon Schelderup's death within minutes of my arrival. The ten statements were as good as unanimous.

Magdalon Schelderup had informed all those present, in writing, that he wanted to gather those closest to him for an early supper on the second Sunday of every month this spring. According to his manager, who was present, this had been done in a formal letter dated 2 January 1969. The food and drink would be served punctually at 4.30 p.m., and it would be considered 'extremely unfortunate' if not everyone was there, whatever the excuse. Those invited were Magdalon Schelderup's wife, Sandra, and his young daughter Maria Irene, who both lived with him at Schelderup Hall. Others who were in the family and shared his surname were his sister Magdalena, his former wife Ingrid, and his grown-up sons Fredrik and Leonard. Magdalon Schelderup's secretary, Synnøve Jensen, was also invited, as was Hans Herlofsen, his manager of many years. The last two people on the invitation list were an elderly couple, Else and Petter Johannes Wendelboe, whom Magdalon Schelderup had known since the war.

All those invited had taken the hint and arrived on time to every Sunday supper so far. The first four had passed without any drama. Today's, however, had started rather differently. All the guests were sitting in their usual places when Mrs Sandra Schelderup put the food on the table at half past four. Once they had helped themselves, but before anyone had started to eat, they were interrupted by the fire alarm, so they had all left the table and the room for a few minutes and gathered by the front door on the ground floor.

It was quickly established, however, that it was in fact not the fire alarm that had gone off, but rather a recording of a fire alarm playing on the stereo system.

Magdalon Schelderup had cast an evil eye around the table, but all the guests had categorically denied any knowledge of this humorous little prank. Their host had been unusually agitated and annoyed by what had happened, and sat for a minute at least, deep in thought, without wishing everyone *bon appétit*. Then he had barked an unexpected command at one of his guests, his youngest son Leonard, to test the food on his plate.

'I have a suspicion that the food on my plate has been poisoned. I am sure that no one would disagree it would be of less consequence if you were to lose your life than if I were!' had been how he put it. No one had protested.

Leonard had been visibly nervous and had tried to say that surely there was no reason to suspect that the food was poisoned. His father had curtly replied that in that case, there was no reason to be scared of tasting it. After a couple more minutes of increasingly oppressive silence, the clearly terrified Leonard had eaten a slice of meat, half a potato and a piece of carrot from his father's plate. When the young Leonard looked just as healthy five minutes later and said that he didn't feel any symptoms of any sort, his father had declared dinner served at six minutes to five.

None of the other guests had reacted to the food. Magdalon Schelderup, on the other hand, had had an acute reaction, whereby his throat and mouth swelled up dramatically. Unable to talk, he had waved his hands around and pointed down the table – seemingly at his two sons. His pulse had been dangerously high and racing, according to his wife, who had helped him over to the sofa after the attack. He then experienced violent cramps and died only minutes later. Magdalon Schelderup had clutched his heart in the final minutes of his life. The guests all agreed that heart failure was the most likely cause of death, though acute breathing problems were also a possibility.

The link became clear when the deceased's wife detected evidence of powdered nuts in the meat still left on his plate. Young Leonard had covered his face in horror. He was so upset that he was unable to say for certain whether he had noticed a faint taste of nuts or not, or if there had been no trace in the piece of meat that he had eaten. The fact that Magdalon Schelderup suffered from a life-threatening nut allergy was well known to those in his closest circle. And for that very reason, nuts of all kinds were strictly forbidden on the property. Magdalon Schelderup had always been a strict enforcer of this rule.

It was swiftly established that all the guests had known about his nut allergy and that nuts were forbidden. They would all have had the opportunity to sprinkle some powdered nuts on his plate in the confusion that ensued after the fire alarm. They were the only ones who could have done it. Magdalon Schelderup had given his staff time off during these Sunday soirées. The host and his ten guests were alone in the house.

The food had been prepared by the host's current wife, together with his former wife, who was also one of the guests. They sent each other scathing looks, but were in absolute agreement that there had been no nuts, in any shape or form, anywhere near the kitchen when they were making the food. And there was indeed no trace of nut powder on any of the plates other than that of Magdalon Schelderup. It therefore seemed most likely that the deadly powder had been added to the food after it had been put on the table. Which meant that it had been added by one of the guests, who had come not only with powdered nuts, but also a strong desire to kill the host.

I spent the next three hours taking down personal statements from all the ten witnesses in a guest room on the ground floor that became an improvised interview room. At nine o'clock, the deceased was collected by a police doctor, and I did not think there was much hope of getting any more from the ten survivors.

While it was quite clear to me that Magdalon Schelderup's murderer had been sitting at the table, I still had no idea of where he or she had been sitting. And fortunately, neither did I know that it would take me seven long and demanding days to solve the crime, even with Patricia's help. Nor could I have predicted that evening that any of the ten guests from Magdalon Schelderup's final supper would follow him into death in the week that followed.

IV

I decided to start by questioning the person at the table who was closest in age to the deceased Magdalon Schelderup, namely his sixty-seven-year-old sister.

Magdalena Schelderup asked for permission to smoke during the interview. Given the dramatic situation, she seemed otherwise to be remarkably calm. Her body was thin and bony, and the firmness of her handshake was a surprise. I noticed that she was wearing a thin pewter ring, which seemed oddly out of character for an older woman who by all accounts was very well off. However, I deemed what I could not see on her hand to be more significant – a wedding ring, in other words.

In explanation as to why she still had the same surname, Magdalena Schelderup told me without hesitation that she had never been married. To which she added quickly that she had never had any children either. The family had always been small, but now she was the only surviving member of her childhood home. She had grown up with an older and a younger brother. The younger brother, how-ever, had been weak both physically and mentally, and had died as the result of an illness in spring 1946. Magdalon had dominated his siblings ever since they were little. In his first two years, he had enchanted his parents so much that they decided to give their daughter a name that was as close to their son's name as possible.

Their father had also been a successful businessman, and the children had grown up in very privileged material circumstances. Following the death of the younger brother after the war, Magdalon had taken over the running of the family business and quickly expanded. Magdalena had passed her university entrance exam and taken a two-year course at the business school. However, when her parents died, she was left such a tidy sum of money that she could dedicate herself to her interests without having to worry about making a living. She still received an annual share of the profit from her parents' companies, which far exceeded her outgoings.

Magdalena Schelderup took a pensive draw on her cigarette when I asked if she had had a close relationship with her brother. Then she shook her head, slowly. They were in contact often enough and shared a circle of mutual friends, but they had not discussed anything of a more serious nature together for the past twenty-five years. She had the impression that her brother seldom sought the advice of others regarding important matters, and to a great extent followed his own beliefs and whims. He had certainly never asked his sister for advice in connection with business or more personal matters. But she did claim to know him better than anyone else, all the same, having watched him her entire life.

'If you want to understand my brother, be it as a businessman or a person, you have to understand that he has always been a player, since he was a little boy,' Magdalena Schelderup added, out of the blue.

She continued without hesitation when I asked her to expand on this.

'Ever since he was a youth, Magdalon has played with

money and people, the business, his private life; in fact, his entire existence became nothing but a great game. My brother often played with high stakes. If you were to say that he sometimes played crooked, I would not contradict you. Magdalon played to the gallery out there to gain recognition. But most of all, he simply played to win and to get whatever he wanted. Be it money, houses or women,' she concluded, with a bitter smile.

Magdalena Schelderup sat in silence for a while, lost in thought, smoking yet another cigarette. Then she continued, at a slower pace.

'You may perhaps hear from others, both inside and outside the firm, that my brother was a man with a head for money, but not for people. That is what people who do not know him or understand him often say. Magdalon's greatest gift was in fact that he had a finely honed ability to understand all kinds of people. He was exceptionally good at seeing other people's strengths and weaknesses, and could often predict exactly how they would react in various situations. But he only used this to his own advantage. I can understand that others might at times think of him as cold and heartless in his dealings with other people, including his own family. But there is actually a difference between being inconsiderate and not understanding when one should be considerate, if one bothered at all about other people.'

I gave a thoughtful nod, and followed this up with a question about his familial relations in general. His sister hesitated, and then said that perhaps his wife and children would know more about that than she did. From her place at the table, she judged her brother's third marriage, which had also been the longest, to be the 'least unhappy'. The transition from the first to the second, and the second to the third had both been difficult periods. Her brother had without a doubt expected more of his two sons, but his expectations were not easily matched. It seemed that his daughter was the child he appreciated most, but that might also be because she was the youngest and still lived at home.

As far as Magdalon Schelderup's inheritance was concerned, his sister claimed to know very little. Her annual share of the profits from her parents' companies was secured for the rest of her life, no matter who now inherited the companies. It did not really matter much to her. She already had more money in the bank than she could use in a lifetime, and she had no one to leave it to.

She did not say it in so many words, but I understood what she meant. She, for her part, had no possible financial motive for her brother's murder.

This sounded logical enough. And she seemed to be so relaxed when she said it that I almost struck her from the list of suspects. However, I did note with interest that she lived only a short distance away, and that she had been at home alone in her flat on both Friday and Saturday. The deceased Magdalon Schelderup's sister had known him longer than anyone else round the table, and in practice had had the opportunity both to puncture the tyres on his car and to put powdered nuts in his food.

V

From the deceased's sister, I moved on to his widow, having first made sure that she was in a fit state to be questioned. There was still not a tear to be seen on her cheeks.

Sandra Schelderup was a relatively slight, dark-haired woman, with a straight back and a determined face which gave the impression of a strong personality and will. She stated her age as forty-five. With regard to her background, she informed me briefly that she had grown up on a small-holding in one of the rural communities outside Trondheim, that she had trained as a stenographer, and had met her husband when she came to work as his secretary nearly twenty years ago. The marriage had been a happy one, despite the age difference, and his death had been very unexpected.

She claimed to know nothing about her husband's telephone call to the police the day before, or the fact that the tyres on his car had been slashed. She had, however, noticed that her husband had been obviously worried of late. He had been more alert, and had carefully checked that all the doors were locked in the evening. Some weeks ago, he had taken an old revolver from his collection and stowed it in his jacket pocket whenever he went out. At home, it often lay on his desk during the day, and she had seen it on the bedside table in the evening and morning.

But he had said nothing as to why he was worried. He was old-school, a man who would rather not discuss his troubles with his wife and children. She had taken the gun as a sign that her husband was getting old and anxious, but following his murder it was of course natural to see this in another light. And in autumn the year before, he had decided to buy three dogs to guard the house, he who had never shown any interest whatsoever in animals before.

As for the inheritance, Sandra Schelderup knew little more than what was written about it in the newspapers: that it was possibly worth several hundred million kroner in money, shares and property. She could find the name of the lawyers' firm that helped her husband in legal matters, but she claimed to know nothing about the content of his will. Her husband had routinely kept his estate separate in all his three marriages. When the matter had been raised on a couple of occasions, he had simply promised his last wife that she would be well looked after for the rest of her life, and would inherit at least two million from him.

The business had dominated Magdalon Schelderup's life more than anything else, and early on in the marriage he had made it clear that she should not worry herself about it. And so she had done as he advised. She added that it was possible that her daughter might know a little more about it than she did, but otherwise, one would have to ask the business manager.

When at home, Magdalon Schelderup had generally stayed in his combined office and library on the first floor, or in his bedroom, which was next door. His wife added that her husband slept at irregular times, and she had therefore preferred to have her own room, on the floor above. He could come and go as he pleased, as he had for all the years she had known him, she said, with a fleeting smile.

It all seemed to be rather undramatic so far. His wife's

description reinforced the picture of Magdalon Schelderup as a wilful man, but also the idea that he had been worried about a possible threat to his life in recent months. Her tone became sharper, however, when in conclusion I asked if she thought that it might have been one of those present who had killed her husband.

'Well, that is obvious!' was her terse reply.

Then she added swiftly, in a more passionate voice: 'And I can promise you that it was neither me nor my daughter. But as far as the others are concerned, I would not exclude any of them right now.'

When I asked whether that meant that she would not exclude even her two stepsons from the list of possible murderers, she replied promptly: 'Especially not them!'

A shadow passed over her face when she said this, fuelling my suspicions that the relationship between those closest to the deceased was not the best. I concluded my conversation with the deceased's widow there for the moment. I was now extremely curious to know what his children thought, both about her and about his death.

VI

Fredrik Schelderup proved from the outset to bear very little resemblance to his dead father, either physically or mentally. He was thirty-eight years old, above average height, with dark hair and a pleasant appearance, as well as a friendly demeanour. The spare tyres around his middle and the redness of his cheeks sparked a suspicion that

Schelderup Junior generally enjoyed far livelier gatherings than this one.

The conversation that followed did nothing to detract from this theory, and Fredrik spoke in a light, breezy tone. He opened by saying, without any encouragement, that he was more like his dead mother and had always felt very different from his father. His contact with his father had in recent years been 'correct and formal', if 'rather sporadic and not particularly heartfelt' on either part. Fredrik Schelderup explained that he had tried to put as much distance as possible between himself and his father and the business, and that was why he perhaps might seem to be unaffected by his father's death. Which, indeed, was the case.

His death had been totally unexpected for Fredrik Schelderup as well, who had no suspicions as to who might have put the powdered nuts in his father's food. He had been raised with a complete ban on anything that might resemble a nut, and had once, as a twelve-year-old, had his pocket money suspended for month because he had eaten a peanut on his way up the drive. He had since then respected the ban – to this very day. Fredrik Schelderup had come to the Sunday supper in his newest Mercedes, and had spent the last week either at or near to his home in the exclusive suburb of Bygdøy. He lived alone, but had a new girlfriend who had been with him every day last week. 'And some nights too,' he added, with a saucy wink.

Fredrik Schelderup struck me as being very unlike his father. When I asked what else he had done in his life so far, he quipped: 'As little as possible, while I wait to inherit from my father.' He went on to say that he had taken his university entrance exam and then studied a bit at the business school and university, but that he infinitely preferred the life of a student at the weekend to that during the week. He had stopped studying without any qualifications and had subsequently never been able to decide what he wanted to do. And fortunately, there was no real need to, either. While waiting for the anticipated substantial inheritance from his father, he had lived well on a more modest inheritance from his mother, and some income from various short-term jobs. Fredrik Schelderup jokingly remarked that he had loved driving ever since he was a boy – fast cars and beautiful women. In an even jollier aside, he added that when a beautiful woman asked him what his star sign was, he normally replied 'the dollar sign' – and then set about proving it. Otherwise his daily consumption was generally modest, 'certainly on weekdays'. He was waiting to fulfil his wish of seeing more of 'the world and its bars' until he got his inheritance.

When asked about how much he expected to inherit, Fredrik Schelderup was almost serious for a moment. He replied that he hoped he would get a third of his father's fortune, and it was reported in the papers that his total wealth was valued at more than 100 million. But he did not dare assume that he would get any more than the 200,000 kroner he had claim to as one of the heirs. He had been looking forward to receiving his inheritance for many years, but was in no way in any kind of financial straits and had not asked his father for money for years – knowing that should he ask, he was unlikely to get anything other than sarcasm in return.

Over the years, Magdalon Schelderup had repeatedly expressed his disappointment in his eldest son's lack of initiative and business acumen. The son was no longer hurt by this and had, on a couple of occasions, responded by expressing his disappointment in his father's treatment of his first two wives and their sons. The conversation had usually stopped there.

Fredrik Schelderup was again earnest for a moment when I asked about his dead mother. She had been four years younger than Magdalon Schelderup and had been a great beauty with many admirers, when, at the age of twenty-three, she said yes to his proposal of marriage. More than once in her later years she had told her son that Magdalon Schelderup had married her simply because it was the only way he could get her into bed – which apparently became an obsession from the first time they met. She had won over Magdalon Schelderup, but in doing so had lost herself, she often said with increasing bitterness.

Fredrik was the only child from a deeply unhappy marriage, which ended in a bitter divorce just before the war. Fredrik's mother was a Christian and had very much enjoyed being 'the Queen of Gulleråsen' at Schelderup Hall. She was strongly opposed to divorce, but her husband had found someone else and eventually threw his first wife out of the house, 'almost physically'. Fredrik had stayed with his father for several years after the divorce, 'for reasons of pure ease', but had then suddenly found it 'more comfortable' to move into his own flat once he had finished school. His mother did not suffer financially, but she never really recovered from the divorce. Nicotine and alcohol had both contributed to a permanent deterioration in her health, and she died of liver failure at the age of forty-nine.

With regard to his relationship with other members of the family, Fredrik Schelderup now declared that he liked his father's second wife marginally more than the third, but that he had never had much contact with either of them. In terms of the rest of the family, he tended generally to have the warmest feelings for his eleven-year-younger half-brother. They had grown closer when his brother entered puberty and had himself become the child of divorced parents. But any contact was still sporadic. They were very different, and his brother had 'been sensible enough to realize that I was not a good role model' when he was about to come of age. Fredrik Schelderup's relationship with his twenty-year-younger half-sister had always been distant. However, he did say that for someone her age, she appeared to be a remarkably determined and enterprising young lady.

A hint of seriousness returned once again to Fredrik Schelderup's otherwise jocular expression when he said this. And when he had left the room, I sat and ruminated on whether I had also seen a hint of respect or fear when I looked in his eye.

VII

Leonard Schelderup was an intense, gum-chewing man of twenty-seven, about half a head shorter than me. He appeared to glide into the room, with the classic light step and lithe body of a long-distance runner. He had managed to regain some composure by the time he came in for questioning, two hours after the murder, but was clearly still deeply affected by the drama in the dining room. He admitted as much himself and started by apologizing for his confused behaviour. He then added that the day's events really were quite extraordinary, and that he felt particularly exposed.

I said that I fully understood his situation, and then tagged on a comment that he and his dead father seemed to be very different. Leonard Schelderup chewed frantically on his gum for a few moments before his answer more or less tumbled out of his mouth: 'Yes and no. It's easy to understand that it might seem that way. I am very influenced by what other people think and say about me, and I actually care about other people's feelings. Neither were ever traits of my father. I am often nervous when meeting people and have never been interested in business. But there were similarities. I have a lot of my father's willpower and his competitive streak, but use it instead on the track and at university. And that was not what my father wanted. But in recent years it seemed that he did understand and respect me a little more. We have unfortunately never had a good relationship. But I hope that it was not quite so bad in the last year of his life.'

He swiftly added: 'I was eight when my father came into my room one day and told me that my mother was moving out and that I would be staying here without her. Our relationship never really moved on from there. I have long since accepted that my father is who he is and had absolutely no reason at all to wish him dead now. It still seems very unreal that he has been murdered, and why he chose me to taste his food is a mystery.'

The formulation 'had absolutely no reason at all to wish him dead *now*' immediately caught my attention. I asked, in a sharper tone, whether that meant that he had previously wished his father were dead.

Leonard Schelderup's jaws worked even harder on the chewing gum before he answered.

'I may have said something of the sort to him when I was a teenager, when I was rebelling. I thought he treated my mother appallingly both before and after the divorce, and whatever I did was apparently of no interest whatsoever to him. Shouting at my father was like banging your head against the wall. He never lost control and just looked down at me and through me, superior in every way. Even when I was taller than him. It always ended with me coming to apologize. And then he still just looked at me overbearingly. Deep down I hated him for many years, and in my youth I had some violent outbursts. But I have never really wanted to kill him and, what's more, have never done anything to attempt it.'

He squirmed in his chair and added in a quiet voice: 'Though God knows who will believe that now.'

I sympathized with him. Leonard Schelderup was indeed in an exposed situation vis-à-vis the others around the table, partly because he had been selected to taste the food, and partly because he was the one his father had pointed to after swallowing the powdered nuts. And what was more, he had no alibi when it came to the punctured tyres. According to his statement, he had been in the Oslo area in the days before the murder, tramping along the well-worn path from his flat in Skøyen to the track at Bislett, and to his office at the university.

Leonard Schelderup appeared to be as ill-informed about the inheritance situation as his older brother – and far less interested. He hoped that he would get a third of the fortune, but was fully prepared for the eventuality that it might be the minimum amount of 200,000 kroner. His older brother had wanted to discuss the issue with him several times, but he had tried to think about it as little as possible. It would make relatively little difference to his life if he inherited 200,000, a million or thirty million. He was happy working on his Ph.D. in chemistry at the university, and was getting better and better on the track. Any notion of joining the business was alien to him. If he inherited five million, two would go into his own account and three to his mother, who he believed should have got more after the divorce. But they both had healthy balances as it was. Leonard Schelderup did not have his own family and had no plans to get one. He added, without any prompting, that his experiences from childhood did not make it an attractive prospect.

As for the guests who were not part of the family, Leonard Schelderup had really only ever exchanged pleasantries with them. He did comment though that Wendelboe, behind his grave mask, was possibly a warmer person than his own father had ever been.

Leonard Schelderup told me that he had only sporadic contact with his older brother. The two of them had always got on well, despite the age difference, and there had never really been any serious conflicts between them. However, their differences had become more pronounced over the years, and they now had very little in common outside the family. Their father had on one occasion remarked to the young Leonard that his lack of interest in the business was a disappointment, but he had at least had one son who was interested in something other than the next party.

Leonard Schelderup said that he had had a good relationship with 'Aunt Magdalena' ever since he was a child, but that they did not meet very often. Leonard Schelderup did not hide the fact that he disliked his father's new wife, who he believed had used her youth and beauty to usurp his mother's place. However, they now had a formal and relatively relaxed relationship. She was an intelligent and active woman, who always asked politely about his running results and work situation whenever they met on social occasions. Leonard Schelderup grimaced when he added that, in recent years, his stepmother had in fact shown more interest in his life than his own father ever had done.

'There is one episode from last year that I should perhaps mention to you,' he said abruptly. His voice was trembling slightly when he continued. 'I bumped into my father on Karl Johan, where he was standing talking to a business contact. My father took me almost respectfully by the hand and said "This is Director Svendsen and he saw you at Bislett and wanted to congratulate you on winning the Norwegian Championships. And I would also like to do that. You really have become an impressively good runner!" I shook them both by the hand. Then I went and sat alone in the corner of a cafe and cried over a cup of coffee. I was twenty-six years old and it was the first time that I had ever heard my father say anything positive about my running. And the last time too.'

Leonard Schelderup had very little contact with his younger half-sister. Like his brother, he had the impression that she was unusually intelligent and determined. Even though she did not do any sports, he believed that his sister was also an exceptionally competitive person.

'We really only meet on social occasions, and my little sister is like a cat in the company of adults. She slips in and out without making any noise, but looks like she keeps her eyes and ears keen as a predator. I suspect that her claws and teeth might also be very sharp, without ever having tried to find out,' he concluded.

My curiosity regarding Magdalon Schelderup's daughter was in no way diminished by this remark. In fact, it led me to conclude my interview with Leonard Schelderup relatively swiftly. He appeared to be relieved and asked for permission to continue with his training and work as normal. He shook my hand with something akin to enthusiasm when I granted him this, and promised that he would be available in the event of any further questions.

Magdalon Schelderup's youngest son certainly seemed to be far less sure of himself here in his childhood home than when I had seen him at the Norwegian athletics championships at Bislett last year. I had to admit though that I still liked him and hoped that he was not the murderer. But given the circumstances I could not disregard that possibility.

VIII

With the few steps that it took Maria Irene Schelderup to enter the room, I understood immediately what her brother had meant with the cat metaphor. The eighteen-year-old floated in across the carpet, self-assured and almost silent, on light, agile feet. Her handshake was unexpectedly firm, without any of the trembling I had felt in her older brother's hand. Once she was sitting comfortably in the armchair she leaned forward with something akin to eagerness, but waited to speak until she had heard my question.

In the first part of our conversation, Maria Irene Schelderup did not waste words and gave clear, concise answers. Yes, her father's death had been unexpected. No, she had no reason to suspect anyone present more than anyone else.

Then she slowed down and added calmly that her father's dramatic death should strictly speaking not have been a surprise – given that his life had always been so dramatic.

'In a way,' she added, 'he was cut down in his prime today, at just the right time.'

I looked at her questioningly and she carried on, with equal calm: 'My father was a very dynamic sixty-nine-year-old, but he was born in the eighteen hundreds, after all. Time was starting to take its toll. Over the past few years, he has become more cautious. You could even notice it in his driving. Before, he consistently drove above the speed limit; now he drove just under. The past decade has seen a peak in his career, but I doubt that he would have been able to lead the company on to achieve new records over the next ten years. His personality and will were just as forceful, but he did not understand the new technology well enough, nor the changing demands and expectations of younger generations. He preferred to continue scaring people into doing what he wanted. Nowadays, appearing to be nice and considerate is obviously a far more effective strategy.'

I stared with a mixture of fascination and fear at the young Maria Irene Schelderup and asked what her thoughts were on the future of the company. Her reply was unexpectedly quick.

'That all depends on what we are now waiting for with baited breath: in other words, my father's will. We came to these suppers for the most part because he was Magdalon Schelderup, but also because we were waiting for him to tell us at some point about his will. But that never happened. Either he was still in doubt, or he just wanted to keep us on tenterhooks.'

She hesitated briefly, but then continued with youthful zeal.

'And as regards the inheritance, perhaps my father died a few years too early. The only one of his children who is capable of taking over – in other words, me – is still too young, in practical and legal terms, to head a consolidated company of that size. The alternative is to divide up the business, and that would not be profitable at this point. The company is on the offensive, and appears to be in the middle of several transaction processes that make the situation unclear for the next year. My father also liked to keep secrets from those closest to him. It was part of his strategy for holding the reins and keeping everyone around him on their toes. So none of us know what it says in the will. I know that my mother has pressured him to leave a company that was as consolidated as possible to me, but I have no idea whether she succeeded or not. It was not easy to persuade my father to do anything – not even for my mother. I presume that you will shortly be told the content of the will and I would be very grateful if you could telephone as soon as the mystery has been clarified.'

The latter was said with a tiny sweet smile. I registered vaguely that I was nodding in reply, and that her smile widened with even greater sweetness. Maria Irene Schelderup was her father's daughter: a player who needed to be watched. This feeling was in no way diminished when she continued.

'So, the situation is this: I may have a motive for murder, but if that is the case, it depends on the content of a will that I know nothing about. But I did not kill my father, regardless of what it says. I realized that he did not have many more years left, and anyway I wanted to study for a few years before taking over the business. So time was in my favour.'

I felt I was slightly at sea and tried to regain control of the interview by asking about her and her father's relationship with her two half-brothers.

'I for my part feel very little for either of them, positive or negative. Leonard is of course closer to me than Fredrik, both in age and personality. But the distance between us is still too great for me to have any sisterly feelings. The fact that we have different mothers who cannot stand the sight of each other has naturally taken its toll. I have grown up as my mother's only child, but have always been painfully aware that my father had two older sons.'

I resisted the temptation to ask her whether she had feelings for anyone other than herself, and instead indicated that she should carry on telling me about her brothers. And this also seemed to be a topic she had thought about a lot.

'As regards my half-brothers' relationship with our father, I don't think he ever saw much hope in Fredrik. A father who paid attention to every detail and a son who cares about nothing are not compatible. I would not be surprised if my father had not always stayed on the right side of the law, but it mattered to him greatly that he had never been convicted of anything, and that no one should be given the opportunity to do this. Fredrik, on the other hand, could have papered an entire wall with his speeding and parking fines. Father once commented that he had hoped to have a son who understood the laws of the land well enough to avoid them, but instead he had a son who did not even realize that laws existed. I am sure it was a great disappointment and, based on that alone, I do not think that Fredrik will get much in the will. But my father was an unpredictable man, even for me, and he had some strange and highly irrational old-fashioned ideas about the eldest son and the family's reputation and things like that. I may be wrong, but I would guess that Fredrik will fare least well.'

She continued with a slightly more earnest expression.

'I see Leonard as a more dangerous contender. He has never used his talents in the way that Father wanted him to. But Leonard has both talent and willpower, and it seemed as though Father felt closer to him in more recent years.

Leonard's success on the track was eventually to his advantage. Father had no interest whatsoever in athletics, but he approved of any quantifiable success that was discussed in the papers and by the people he met. So my bet would perhaps be that Fredrik receives the two hundred thousand that he has the legal right to claim, whereas the rest will be divided between Leonard and myself in some way or other.'

Now I really was staring at her with horrified fascination. It was easy to understand what her brother had meant when he said that she was a competitive person.

'So what you are actually saying is that Leonard could have a very strong financial motive for wanting to kill his father now – before time played to your advantage?'

Her smile was brief and unexpectedly wide. It made me think of a young female lion who has an antelope in her sight.

'As you yourself said, given the peculiar sequence of events, it is a conclusion that I would not dismiss. But it is hard to know. Leonard is, no matter how reliable, rather unpredictable in his own way. He is one of the weakest strong people I know – or if you prefer, one of the strongest weak people. Leonard is strongest in the places where he feels secure and is known, be it the running track or the library. However, he becomes very weak when he is forced into places where he does not feel secure, and my guess is that he is a very lonely man. So if I were you, I would hold all options open.'

I was reminded of what Magdalena Schelderup had said about her brother having understood other people exceptionally well, but having only ever acted in self-interest.

It would appear that his daughter resembled him in this respect too. She was by now positively chatty, and carried on after a brief pause.

'So, thanks to my half-brothers' inadequacies, I became, over the years, my father's favourite child, even though he actually preferred sons to daughters. I recall that on a couple of occasions when I was young, he was asked about the position of women in our time, and he cited a former Danish prime minister who had said that he for his part still liked women best in a horizontal position. But the experience of having me and my half-brothers seemed to change that somewhat. In the past year he has said to me a couple of times that despite my thin arms, I was the one of his children who had the greatest ability and strength.'

'And what about your mother?'

Maria Irene smiled again.

'I have something from them both. My mother is one of the strongest and most clear-sighted people I know, but she often reacts emotionally, all the same. So if I were you, I would keep all options open there too.'

Unlike her older brother, Maria Irene seemed to be unexpectedly at ease in an interview situation. I noticed that her tone was very familiar, and that I wasn't opposed to it. She held my eye, and was keen to carry on.

'You must understand that my father was a conservative man in many ways, but he was also a very complex character. One group of people in society that he could not stand, a group that Fredrik came to symbolize more and more, was those who had been given every opportunity in life but had taken none. Father was not a generous man. He gave small amounts to charity only when it would obviously improve his reputation. But he did have a certain respect, I might even venture to say love, for people of strong will who had worked their way up to become something despite a more difficult start in life. And I think it was that, as well as pure physical desire of course, that prompted him to start an extramarital relationship with my mother.'

Maria Irene Schelderup took a deep breath. Then she continued with determination.

'And I suppose that that was the very reason why he betrayed her nearly twenty years later with another, even younger woman. History repeated itself in a way that must have been deeply unpleasant for my mother.'

I was staring at her intensely – and noticed that she liked it.

'Did your father have a new lover in his later years?'

She was obviously relishing the situation and permitted herself to smile before continuing.

'Oh, so you hadn't heard yet . . . I thought it was something that we all knew, but never talked about. Mother must know, though we have never discussed it. It is perhaps less certain that my half-brothers or aunt know, as they do not live here. But I would have thought that they knew too. My father's history of relationships with his secretaries is well known, after all, and then last year he announced that she was going to be given her own room here on the ground floor.'

Finally I got the picture.

'So you maintain that, despite the forty-year age difference, your father and his secretary Synnøve Jensen were having a sexual relationship. Is that something you know or just think?'

She flashed a self-assured smile before carrying on.

'Something I know. My bedroom is directly above hers. The walls are quite thin, and my father was physically strong and active, despite getting on in years. His secretary was also surprisingly vocal in bed, when you consider how meek she is otherwise.'

We sat in silence for a few seconds. I studied the young Maria Irene Schelderup's face for any sign of emotion. I expected some anger towards her father for his obvious betrayal of her mother. But I could detect nothing, not even when she carried on talking, not in her face, her voice or her body language.

'So, the situation with the secretary is also an unknown now. If she has been left a substantial sum in his will, then it is possible that he promised it to her and so she also has a possible motive.'

I had to agree with her, but swiftly added: 'In other words, soon your conclusion will be that everyone has a motive – except you, who only maybe has one?'

She smiled her predator smile again.

'Your words. I suppose what I am saying in as many words is that everyone around that table has a possible motive. There was some old stuff between my father and his sister Magdalena, and the Wendelboes, and even Mr Herlofsen. Something to do with the war that was never mentioned, which I therefore know nothing about. You will have to ask those who were there about that. Depending on the content of the will, I may also have a motive, in which case I still maintain that I did not avail myself of the opportunity.'

I noted this down and said that I had no more questions for her, for the moment. She immediately stood up. In contrast to her older half-brothers, her hand was still as dry and firm when she left the room as when she had come in. With an arch smile, she said that it had been a very interesting conversation, and that I was welcome to contact her at any time, should I have any more questions.

She looked me in the eye as she said this – and it felt to me as though she saw straight through my uniform and me.

I hurried to close the door behind her, and then called in the secretary, Synnøve Jensen, as my next witness.

IX

Synnøve Jensen was slightly younger than I had first guessed. She told me that she was twenty-nine, and now that I saw her at closer quarters in a better light, it seemed possible. Her skin was young, although her eyes were serious. Her body was slim, and not without grace, but her movements were unsure. She stood gingerly by the door and did not approach the table until I had asked her twice.

I started with some tentative routine questions about how Magdalon Schelderup was as a boss. She replied earnestly and responsibly that he could at times be very demanding, but that he was also inspiring and nice as long as one did what was required. She had seen the job as a great opportunity and had thrown herself into it. After waiting a while to see how things went, he had declared himself satisfied with her work, and given her a pay rise as well as presents on her birthday and festive holidays. His death was completely unexpected and she had no idea who might have killed him. The idea had never entered her head and his death was a great personal loss to her. She did not want to say anything negative about either his family or the other employees on the day that he died.

Synnøve Jensen told me that she herself had grown up on a smallholding in Sørum and that she still lived in the small house that her parents had left to her. She had neither a driving licence nor a car, and took the bus to and from work every day. It was Magdalon Schelderup who had suggested that, during a very busy period at work, she should have her own bedroom here. She had accepted this, but always stayed at home at weekends and generally also during the week. Synnøve Jensen was single, had no brothers or sisters, and in fact had no close relatives at all following the death of her parents some years ago. After completing school and a secretarial course, she had for several years had various short-term office jobs. It was a great relief to her to have found a position that offered not only a regular and secure income, but also an employer and work that she liked.

She had thus far kept up her appearance as a conscientious secretary impressively well. But this crumbled rapidly as soon as I commented that her relationship to the deceased was perhaps somewhat closer than she intimated. She sat with her face in her hands for a short while. Then suddenly everything came out in a torrent.

'I didn't plan it! No matter what they say, it is not something I had planned when I started to work for him. I desperately needed a job and was shocked and overjoyed when he employed me. The idea that anyone in this house might have an interest in me other than as a secretary was ridiculous. I am not clever and I am not beautiful. And I never tried to seduce him in any way.'

I attempted a nod that was at once pacifying and encouraging. It all sounded plausible enough, given what I knew of Magdalon Schelderup so far.

'But he was tempted all the same – and you did not deny him?'

She gave her head the tiniest shake and sighed deeply.

'No, I admit it. It would not be easy for anyone to deny Magdalon Schelderup what he wanted – especially one of his employees who was dependent on the income. But to be honest, I am not sure that I would have stopped him otherwise. Magdalon could be harsh, but he was a fascinating and very charming man for all that. He was the first man who had ever really cared about how I was and thought that I deserved better.'

'And he had the money to give you a better life.'

She nodded.

'Absolutely, and that may have played a role. I have never had much. My father drank and my mother took out all her frustration on me. I was not going to bite the hand that fed me. So I put up no resistance when one day it slid round my waist.'

It was easy to feel sympathy for the plain Synnøve Jensen and her story, in the midst of all the rich people around the table. My feelings remained mixed, however. She clearly was not innocence itself, and she also had potential motives for murder. Maria Irene's words were still ringing in my ears. Synnøve Jensen was apparently surprisingly vocal in bed considering how meek she was otherwise – even when her lover's wife and daughter were there in the same house.

'Now that he's dead, your job is presumably in danger? Certainly if his wife knows about this?'

She nodded again.

'Which I am sure she does. She is not stupid and he hardly bothered to hide it. I assume that I will be without a job tomorrow. But that is not my biggest problem right now.'

I looked at her, mystified. She didn't say anything and for a moment again hid her face in her hands before she continued.

'You see – I no longer have just myself to think about.'

It started to dawn on me what she meant. And the picture was clear as soon as she patted her tummy gently.

'Magdalon has three children, but leaves behind four. Another one will be born just before Christmas,' she said, very quietly.

All life and sound in the room seemed to stop for few seconds. Synnøve Jensen shed a few tears and then dried them with a whispered apology.

In the meantime, I thought about the consequences of this sensational news. It took perhaps half a minute before I asked whether he had known. She nodded in answer.

'I had no idea what to do when I found out, and had thought of saying nothing for as long as possible. But Magdalon guessed himself – it was Sunday, exactly a week ago. He had come to know me very well and was good at noticing things. And I could not lie when he asked if I was expecting a baby. I was terrified that he would be furious. But not at all. 'Ha!' was all he said at first. Which was what he often said when he saw or understood something that pleased him. Then he asked if I was absolutely certain that he was the father of the child. I told him the truth, that there was no doubt whatsoever. For the past few months I had been working for him literally night and day. He was the only man who had shared my bed, not only in the past year but in all the years before that. This made him very happy and he was in an excellent mood. He laughed, hugged me and said that I need not worry – he would make sure that both I and the child had everything we needed.'

She stopped there, hesitant, until I prompted her to continue.

'But then . . .'

She gave a bewildered shrug.

'But then he said nothing more about it! I trusted what he had said, and did not want to nag. And strangely enough, he did not mention it all week. And now he is dead and I have no idea what is going to happen to me or our child!'

Synnøve Jensen looked mournful for a few seconds, with tears in her eyes, but then she continued.

'Believe it or not, I did try to warn him that it might all result in a child. But he said there was no danger of that, that he could no longer have children with any woman. He seemed irritated when he said it, so I asked no questions. I was so afraid that he might get angry. But he seemed to be

45

happy, even though making mistakes or incurring unexpected costs were not something he generally liked. So I chose to believe that he loved me and that he wanted to have our child. It is a thought that will comfort me tonight.'

I quickly interjected to ask if they had ever discussed the possibility of him divorcing his wife. Synnøve Jensen shook her head firmly, and assured me that this was never discussed. She admitted that she would not have protested if he had wanted to divorce his wife in order to marry her. But he had never mentioned the possibility, and she had never expected the matter to be raised. She had been prepared to be a single mother with no income and was more than happy with his promise to look after herself and the child. Now that he was gone, who knew what might happen, she concluded with a deep sigh and heart-rending sob. The child was his, but to prove it might be difficult. In the meantime, she was left with neither work nor income, a fatherless child in her womb and no more than five hundred kroner in the bank.

When asked if she knew what was in the deceased's will, her reply was a firm no. It was only a few days since he found out about the unborn child so he would barely have had time to make any changes, she added with a sob. He had never mentioned anything to her about how he had divided his wealth amongst his three older children.

Synnøve Jensen claimed that she did not have a bad relationship with the children of her boss and lover. She had known the young Maria Irene since she was fourteen, and had an intuitive affection for her. It felt as though they understood one another's difficulties. On the other hand, the secretary had thought at first that Mrs Sandra Schelderup was very demanding, then power-crazed, then jealous and, finally, downright hateful. It was not hard to see why the two older boys had such a difficult relationship with their stepmother.

Magdalon Schelderup's sister had always been very correct in relation to the secretary, if more than a little distant and patronizing. It was not easy to understand the relationship between Magdalon and his sister. Magdalena was often in the house, but never talked much with her brother when she was here.

There were not many people on the company staff. Magdalon Schelderup did not waste unnecessary money on wages. The manager, Hans Herlofsen, ran the office in the centre of town and was the only person who had an office at Schelderup Hall. He had the best overview of company business and was a very good businessman whom Magdalon Schelderup seemed to trust enormously, but still did not treat particularly well. Schelderup appeared to take his manager for granted, and the manager simply accepted all his sarcasm without ever threatening to resign.

Magdalon Schelderup's relationship with Petter Johannes Wendelboe seemed to be more equal, according to the secretary. Wendelboe had his own company and had long since sold any shares that he once had in Schelderup's company. But Schelderup remained in regular contact with Mr Wendelboe and his wife. And as with the sister, it did not appear to be a relationship where they talked much. The secretary had been taken aback by the frequent presence of the Wendelboes, especially as Schelderup had very little contact with anyone outside the immediate family unless for very good reason. She had simply accepted that it was because they had known each other since the war and had probably been close back then. Whatever the case, it was none of her business.

As far as Synnøve Jensen understood, Hans Herlofsen had also known the others since the war, even though he must be around fifteen years younger than Magdalon Schelderup and Petter Johannes Wendelboe. The otherwise good-natured Herlofsen had always made it very clear, though in a friendly way, that he did not want to talk about the war and the years immediately after. Magdalon Schelderup himself never talked about the war, but that was because he was so focused on the present and the future that he did not dwell on the past.

The secretary seemed relieved and stood up as soon as I said that we were finished for today. When she reached the door, she asked for permission to take the first possible bus home. She was tired and it was not very tempting to stay here at the mercy of Sandra Schelderup. I agreed once I had obtained a telephone number where I could contact her. It was perfectly understandable that Synnøve Jensen was tired, and that she had no particular desire to stay there with Magdalon Schelderup's wife. I asked her to stay in the Oslo area. She looked at me with sad eyes and asked in response where on earth she would go otherwise.

For one reason or another, I stood by the window and watched Synnøve Jensen until she was safely outside the gate. It did not take long. She left the house swiftly and walked away fast, with her head down. It struck me that she was the only one of those questioned so far who would actually miss Magdalon Schelderup.

X

The manager, Hans Herlofsen, was a slightly overweight man of fifty-five, with greying hair, dressed in a simple grey suit. I could imagine him being a jovial and kind uncle at any other time. But now he was visibly affected by the day's events and seemed to be somewhat tense at the start of our conversation.

He calmed down when my first questions were about Magdalon Schelderup's company. Herlofsen quickly proved to have an exceptional head for figures. He could reel off turnover and market shares from the 1940s, the 1950s and the 1960s without any pause for thought. His conclusion was that the Schelderup business empire was going from strength to strength. According to Herlofsen's calculations, the recent estimate of Schelderup's worth at 100 million was in fact too low rather than too high. He himself reckoned it to be somewhere between 125 and 130 million, taking into account various estimated fees and charges and the possibility that the value of the company might fall if the company and property portfolio were to be divided up.

With regard to himself, Hans Herlofsen told me in a succinct and practised manner that he was a widower and lived on his own on the first floor of his childhood home in Lysaker. His only son was now a grown man, who lived with his wife and two children on the ground floor. Hans

Herlofsen had always devoted himself to his work, and other than his son and his family the greater part of his social life was linked to work. Magdalon Schelderup had been a friend of his father's, so they had known each other since Herlofsen was a youth. Herlofsen had been employed by the company since the autumn of 1944 and been the manager since 1946.

When asked who he thought might have killed Magdalon Schelderup, Hans Herlofsen replied that the only thing he could say with 100 per cent certainty was that it was not he who had done it. As for the others, he would rather not hazard a guess. With a slightly self-deprecating smile, he added that with eleven others round the table, minus himself and the deceased, there was only an 11.1 per cent chance of getting it right.

I saw no reason, for the moment, to add to his burden by saying that I personally was operating on the assumption of a 10 per cent chance. I had not got any further and did not dare strike Hans Herlofsen from the list of suspects until I knew what was in the will.

As Hans Herlofsen stood up to leave, I realized that I should ask whether he had worked together with Magdalon Schelderup when they were in the Resistance. His answer was another surprise.

'Yes, of course. But I was more of an assistant to the senior members of the Resistance and was not there when it happened. If you think it might have anything to do with that strange episode from 8 May 1945, you will have to ask the Wendelboes or even Magdalena Schelderup.'

I nodded to show that I understood. Then made a note that I had to ask the Wendelboes about the strange episode that took place on Liberation Day in 1945.

XI

My conversation with the deceased's ex-wife was brief and without any great surprises. She had a slim body and her neck was almost perilously thin. Her hair, on the other hand, was raven black and her voice was spirited. She seemed far younger in body and mind than her actual sixty years of age.

Ingrid Schelderup was also visibly shaken by the death of her former husband, but her predominant focus was the situation of her son Leonard. She assured me repeatedly that she could guarantee he had nothing to do with his father's death, and expressed her concern that he would take this very badly, given his sense of duty and responsibility. His relationship with his father was not the best, but it was far better than it had been. And Leonard was the world's sweetest boy, who would never wish to hurt anyone. It was completely incomprehensible that his father had asked him, of all people, to try his food and then later pointed at him. The only explanation she could think of was that Magdalon Schelderup was no longer the man he had once been, even though that might seem strange to all who knew him.

The conversation dwelled on this theme for a few minutes without going anywhere. She then sat up abruptly

51

in her chair and raised her voice: 'You must forgive me if I am repeating myself and talking too much about my son. It is all too easy when you are a divorced woman who has only one child. And even though it is now many years since our divorce, Magdalon's death today was a great shock.'

I immediately felt that she was opening up and assured her that I had the utmost sympathy for her situation. Then I expressed my surprise at the fact that she still regularly visited her ex-husband's home, so many years after the divorce. She gave a sad shrug.

'That's what happened and how I am, unfortunately. I am still Magdalon Schelderup's wife – even though he threw me out over twenty years ago, and is now dead. I have never got over the divorce. Latterly my life has solely been about the son of the man who threw me out.'

I started to understand the lie of the land and took a small chance: 'So you never got over the divorce – and never stopped hoping that he would ask you to come back again one day?'

She gave a brief and serious nod.

'Yes, terrible, but true. Winters passed and summers passed, year after year, and nothing happened. And yet I could never give up hope. I continued to live in Gulleråsen, only minutes away. That was partly so that I could see my son as often as possible, but mostly so that I could be here quickly if ever asked. For ten years, I hoped that it was Magdalon whenever the phone rang. Every time I was invited here I dyed my hair, put on my make-up and arrived dressed up and on time. And every time Magdalon asked me to do something, I said yes and smiled as beautifully as

I could. In some strange way, I thought that if I could only do as he wished and come whenever he invited me, the day would then come when he would ask me to stay. And so I hoped, year in and year out, that one day he would throw her out in order to take me back – just as he had thrown me out on 12 April 1949, so that she could move in. But neither God nor life is fair.'

Any discussion of how fair God may or may not be was beyond my competence, so I said that it must have felt very odd for her to prepare the food together with Sandra Schelderup.

'She is a good cook, I will give her that. But yes, it was a rather bizarre and uncomfortable situation. It was Magdalon's idea and neither of us dared to ask why. So we just made the food together as best we could and talked as little as possible while we did it. And I can guarantee that there were no powdered nuts or any other form of poison in the food when it left the kitchen. We both kept a close eye on each other the whole time.'

I did not doubt that. But I did comment that she herself had usurped the place of an older woman here at Schelderup Hall. Her sigh was heavy.

'That was different. Magdalon and I were happy until the day she turned up here like a snake in paradise. His first wife was unhappy here, though she may not have recognized that herself, and they should never have got married. But of course it was not very nice then and it still is not nice now. Her fate was even more tragic than my own. No woman has a child with Magdalon Schelderup without the rest of her life being marred by it. And apparently no one is thrown out of Schelderup Hall without wanting to come back. It is strange, the power he holds over us. In that way he was a true sorcerer.'

Irene Schelderup cheered up unexpectedly when I asked if she knew that Magdalon Schelderup had a new lover.

'The illiterate secretary?' she said, with an almost joking expression on her face.

I looked at her questioningly. She blushed a touch and cleared her throat before carrying on.

'It was Magdalena who asked me if the illiterate secretary had moved in now, and I knew immediately what she meant. The secretary is no doubt well above the average literacy in her own family, but still well below the average in ours. So I thought perhaps he wanted something else from her and am only too happy to admit that I hoped that was the case. It certainly would have been a twist of fate and only fair if Sandra was also thrown out on the rubbish pile in favour of a younger, more attractive secretary. He once joked to me that he believed that any marriage was doomed when the average age of the partners was over fifty. And his new marriage had certainly crossed that line by a good margin.'

The corners of her mouth twitched for a moment as she said this, but it was a bitter smile that did not reach her eyes.

Ingrid Schelderup also denied any knowledge of the contents of the deceased's will. She had received less financially after the divorce than she had hoped, but had sufficient to live without any worries when she added the inheritance from her parents.

Magdalena, the sister, had come to visit regularly in all

the years that Ingrid Schelderup had lived here. And yet she had the impression that the relationship between the two siblings was formal rather than heartfelt. Others who appeared to be close to him in the time that she lived here were the three guests seated at the table today: Herlofsen, the manager, and the Wendelboes. Apparently after she left the neighbours had started to say: 'The only thing that changes at Schelderup Hall is the name of the wife and the number of children.' She thought that the relationship with Herlofsen had been close, almost friendly, in the years immediately after the war, but Magdalon had later treated him with sarcasm and scorn.

Ingrid Schelderup stopped suddenly and sat deep in thought after having spoken about her former husband and his manager. I eventually realized that she was sitting like this with her brow furrowed so that I would ask her a question. Which I then did: I asked her to tell me what she was wondering whether she should tell me.

She smiled with relief, but it felt slightly forced.

'I must say you really are very observant and quick, Detective Inspector. Yes, in the years just after the war, I once had a very odd experience with the manager, Hans Herlofsen, which I still can scarcely believe happened . . . I was passing my husband's office when the door opened, but no one came out. Then I tripped over something on the floor. Which turned out to be Hans Herlofsen. He stood up immediately and apologized profusely, but offered me no explanation. He was so pale and so frightened, I would almost say terrified, that I only recognized him because of his suit. I could feel his entire body trembling when I put my hand on his shoulder. I carried on without saying anything, and never mentioned the episode to either my husband or Herlofsen. It all seemed so very unreal, and yet I am still certain that it did actually happen.'

My interest was of course piqued and I immediately asked when this had happened. She shrugged apologetically, but thought it must have been shortly before she was forced to leave the house in spring 1949.

I was not quite sure what to think, but noted down the story with interest. Ingrid Schelderup herself seemed quite upset by the memory, and repeated a couple of times that she was quite certain that it was as she remembered. She then calmed down again when we started to talk about the others who were present.

Magdalon Schelderup's relationship with the Wendelboes seemed to be more balanced, and if there was a man he respected other than himself, it was Petter Johannes Wendelboe, she thought. But still she found herself wondering why the Wendelboes were such frequent visitors to the house, as they seldom said very much or made their presence known. But then there was hardly a relaxed social atmosphere at Magdalon Schelderup's gatherings. Laughter and jokes were not encouraged among the younger members of the family, either, with Magadalon Schelderup at one end of the table and Petter Johannes Wendelboe at the other. She had never asked about any details from the war, but had always assumed that they had both seen and done difficult things. Neither of them became any less serious or authoritarian as they got older. But whereas Wendelboe appeared to be utterly unchanged, she had the impression that Magdalon's moods had become even darker in recent years.

'There were two Magdalons: the one who was all seriousness and work, and the one who was the world's most charming man. Unfortunately, I have not seen the latter for many years now,' Ingrid Schelderup added in a quiet voice. She had had no idea, however, that her former husband felt that he was now in danger.

When I asked her who she thought might have killed Magdalon Schelderup, she became grave and thoughtful.

'If things are as you say with the secretary, well then there is an obvious motive for his current wife, in terms of both jealousy and money. But that is, of course, simply something I hope, not something I know. I can give you my word with regard to myself and my son. And as for the others, I suspect all and none of them.'

I was starting to realize that this would be a long and difficult investigation. But for the present, I had no more questions for Ingrid Schelderup. She also asked for permission to leave, and was granted this once she had given me a telephone number and a promise to stay in town.

XII

I had initially thought of calling in the Wendelboes separately. However, when he then came marching in with her in tow and seemed so determined, I did not dare protest.

Petter Johannes Wendelboe said that he was sixty-seven years old, and despite his white hair he was still a straight-backed and solid man with lithe, dynamic movements. Else Wendelboe was sixty-three, petite, and still a natural blonde. It struck me that she must have been extremely beautiful in her youth. I noted down that her maiden name was Wiig.

They said almost in one voice that they had been married since 1932, had three grown children and five grandchildren, and lived in a large house in Ski. Petter Johannes Wendelboe was a trained officer, but had changed career to become a businessman at an early age. He had held a number of different shareholder and board positions, but had now retired and left the business to his eldest son.

In terms of their relationship with the Schelderup family, he told me that it was the war that had brought Magdalon Schelderup and Petter Johannes Wendelboe together. They had continued to meet regularly through the years since the war, but were not necessarily what one might call close friends. In recent years, in fact, any contact had been entirely social and routine. Wendelboe had had shares in Schelderup's company for a while, but had cashed them in without it leading to any conflict when the company had become firmly established in the mid-1950s, following an optimistic expansion.

The Wendelboes had been in Bergen visiting their daughter for the past few days, but had flown back today and driven out here in order to make the supper. They hesitated in response to my question as to whether the Schelderups were as keen to visit them, but then answered that they had had very few social gatherings at home with people other than the closest family in recent years. But when they did have parties, the Schelderups were of course invited, and as far as they could remember had always come. And so they felt that it was perfectly natural to visit an old war comrade whenever he had invited them.

I tried to ease the atmosphere a bit by asking what they could remember of Magdalon Schelderup's dead brother from the 1930s and 1940s. They both started. Mr Wendelboe replied that they certainly could remember him, but it did not give them much pleasure. The first time they had met Magdalon Schelderup, he had confided in them how ashamed he was to have a brother who traded with the Germans and earned money from it. Thanks to Magdalon Schelderup's record in the Resistance movement, nothing more was ever really made of this. He had, however, on several occasions expressed sorrow over his brother's failings, and had, when he inherited his brother's wealth, given a sum of several hundred thousand kroner to a charity for those bereaved by the war.

The rumours rumbled on for several years, and when Magdalon Schelderup started his political career in the Conservative Party there were some who opposed it and had tried to use this against him. They had, however, not succeeded. He had been elected to the Storting in 1949 as he had hoped and had pulled out again four years later, even though he could have been re-elected.

'But something unexpected happened on Liberation Day itself, in which Magdalon Schelderup was involved,' I probed.

The Wendelboes exchanged fleeting glances before they nodded. But Petter Johannes Wendelboe's voice was still calm when he continued.

'It promises well for the investigation that you have already managed to unearth the story, though it can hardly have any connection to the murder today. It was a strange and tragic incident, but did not seem to cause Magdalon much concern afterwards. His explanation was reasonable enough and the guilty party was a mentally disturbed man, who gave an insane statement. So there was little doubt as to the outcome. But things like that are often a burden. And though I never heard Magdalon mention it later, I do think that it plagued him.'

I gave him a quizzical look, but he said nothing until I asked for further details.

'Our group in the Resistance was small, but still had a dramatic and important history. We never had any more than six or seven members, and now that Magdalon is gone, my wife and I and Herlofsen are the only ones left alive. The group was established as early as winter 1940–41 and managed to carry on operating without being caught until Norway was liberated. Magdalon joined in summer 1941. He contacted me himself. It was a very difficult year. We lost a member in the spring and another in early autumn. Both were found shot dead in their own homes. The murderer was never found, either during or after the war. We have to this day simply called him the Dark Prince. He was given the name because he only fired in the dark of night, and no one ever saw him in daylight.'

I was fascinated, in part by the story and in part by the expressionless face and controlled voice with which Wendelboe told it.

'For the remainder of the war, Magdalon and I and the

other members of the group slept in rooms without windows, with the door locked. As I understood it, he continued to do this for many years, even though he was not a man who was easily scared. The Dark Prince never made another appearance after 1941 and we never found out whether he was a German or a Norwegian defector. During the war we believed and hoped that he was a German who had either been killed or left Norway, but afterwards we thought it was perhaps more likely that he had been a Norwegian. The modus operandi was not German. They generally came in uniform with dogs in the early morning. We hoped that maybe the Dark Prince was one of the Nasjonal Samling members we liquidated later. We suspected one of them. But we still do not even know if it was a man. I would dearly like to know for certain before I die who the Dark Prince was.'

I was writing all this down as fast as I could. Fortunately, Wendelboe spoke relatively slowly. It had become a two-way communication with short questions from me and long answers from him. I vaguely registered his wife, who was sitting on the sidelines on the sofa, nodding from time to time.

'So this Resistance group also carried out liquidations?'

Wendelboe nodded in confirmation and looked even more serious when he continued.

'Our country was at war, young man, and no one could predict the outcome. We did what we had to whenever we could. Even when it cost the enemy their lives and us our peace of mind and a good night's sleep for many years to come. But we are talking about a total of five men over the course of four years, and in all cases there was no doubt about the guilt and evil of those men. I will carry those five names with me to the grave. And I will also take with me the knowledge that they all had the lives of good Norwegians on their conscience, whether directly or indirectly, and would have deserved to be shot by the Norwegian state if we had not killed them during the war.'

Petter Johannes Wendelboe had leaned forwards in his chair so that his face was now alarmingly close to mine. It was not hard to see why his presence resulted in a subdued atmosphere at dinner parties in the house, or to understand that he was a man Magdalon Schelderup had respected. I had no desire to ask Wendelboe whether the five would truly have been executed after the war. I had a feeling that he was not entirely satisfied with the treason trials.

'The names are not strictly relevant here. Now, is my understanding correct, that both you and Magdalon Schelderup took part in liquidation operations in the latter part of the war?'

He nodded.

'Yes, we both had to carry that burden. My wife did not participate in any such operations, but each and every man in the group took part in one or more. Even the young Hans Herlofsen was involved in one liquidation only a few months before liberation.'

I made some more quick notes. Hans Herlofsen obviously had a more dramatic past than his present jovial demeanour betrayed.

'And was this in any way connected to the situation on Liberation Day?'

Wendelboe shook his head firmly.

'Not at all. That was completely separate, and far more tragic than anything we experienced during the war.'

For a moment, there was silence in the room. Then there was a loud sob, which I realized must have come from Mrs Wendelboe. Her husband sent her a couple of long looks, then carried on talking when she did not.

'In 1944–5 there were three leaders in our group: Magdalon Schelderup, Ole Kristian Wiig and myself. Ole Kristian Wiig was the youngest of us, but also the most ideological and the best. During the war we often talked about it and agreed that the world would be his oyster afterwards if he only survived. And I believe so even more keenly in retrospect. Unlike Magdalon and myself, Ole Kristian encapsulated the political spirit of the time. He had a background in the Labour Party youth league and was precisely the kind of new young man they appointed to important posts in the years immediately following the war.'

I now noticed that Mrs Wendelboe had started to weep. She was crying silently, but all the more intensely for that. Within seconds the tears were flowing. And, annoyingly, it was her husband who once again had to tell me the reason.

'Ole Kristian Wiig was my wife's younger brother. So we knew each other extremely well, even before the war.'

I shifted my gaze to Mrs Wendelboe, who was sitting as still as a statue on the sofa. The only movement in her face was the tears that continued to stream down her cheeks.

I mumbled my condolences and asked whether they had had any more siblings – and immediately regretted doing so. Mrs Wendelboe's eyes blazed. Her composure in the midst of her grief was impressive. She remained seated with stoic calm for a short while, but when she then spoke, her voice was firm.

'No. There were only the two of us. He was so kind and bright that I was more than happy always to be in his shadow. Ole Kristian did not have a family himself, but instead was the best uncle in the world to my children. For the full five years of the war I lived without a thought for myself, but in constant fear that something might happen to my husband, my children or my little brother.'

There was another moment of silence. Her husband and I waited patiently until she was ready to continue.

'I remember the incredible relief that I felt on 8 May 1945 as if it were only yesterday. Ole Kristian lived close to us in Ski and had a key to our house. He was the one who came running across the lawn, overjoyed, to wake us with the news that the Germans had capitulated and that all our suffering was over. I remember thinking to myself that the sun had never shone so brilliantly on Norway as it did that morning. Ole Kristian left us for a few hours, and then the light vanished just as suddenly from my life. And it has never returned. It feels as though I have been living in a twilight ever since, even on the brightest summer day.'

Mrs Wendelboe once again fell silent and sat motionless on the sofa. It was a relief when her husband finally came to her rescue.

'It was an extremely sad and emotional experience for us all. It happened that very afternoon. We'd set about preparing a celebratory meal. Ole Kristian had gone to sort out a few things, but had promised to be back by three. It was an unusual day, of course, but we started to get a bit anxious when half past three came and went without any sign of him. At a quarter to four, we sighed with relief when Magdalon Schelderup's big black car swung into view down the road. We assumed that Ole Kristian was with him. But our joy was short-lived. We could soon see that Magdalon was alone in the car and that he was driving towards us at a dangerous speed. My wife took my hand and said that something was wrong, even before Magdalon stopped the car. We could see from his face that something ghastly had happened. Magdalon was not a man who was easily moved, but on that day his emotional turmoil was clear to all. He came over to us and embraced us, told us that there had been a terrible accident and that Ole Kristian was dead.'

Now, almost twenty-five years later, time had once again stopped for Mrs Wendelboe. Even her tears had stopped falling and she sat as if petrified. Her husband gently took her arm before he continued.

'The accident had involved a gunshot, he told us, and the circumstances were indeed deeply unfortunate. Magdalon and Ole Kristian had driven to the home of a dead Nazi with a younger member of the group, to secure his property and papers. The police arrived at the same time and there were no enemies present. However, Ole Kristian had still fallen victim to a fatal gunshot inside the house, which had been fired by the younger man from our group. Magdalon felt frightfully guilty and apologized profusely for having taken the young man with them. But I was the one who had accepted him into the group, so we were both to blame. The man had seemed so sincere and well-intentioned, but we should of course have realized how weak and mentally unbalanced he was in those final weeks of the war. It is strange to think how different things might have been had I realized that.'

Now it was Wendelboe's turn to sit in silence and his wife's to reach out her hand and stroke him. But it was he who took up the story again, his voice sharp and concise.

'The case was clear enough. The man was standing with the gun in his hand when the police came in. Magdalon himself had been in the room and seen him fire the shot, and the man's statement was so incredible that no one could believe it. He was declared of unsound mind in the court case and has apparently spent much of the rest of his life in an asylum. So we just had to accept that it was the work of a madman, no matter how odd it all seemed. But whatever the case, it was a great loss to us which has been difficult to live with.'

I nodded with understanding and put down my notebook. I had more detailed questions about Magdalon Schelderup's war experiences, but first wanted to check the police report about Ole Kristian Wiig's death for myself.

In conclusion, I asked as a matter of procedure whether the Wendelboes had reason to suspect any of those present of the murder. They both hesitated and then said that Magdalon Schelderup had been a very forceful and complex person who might have been in conflict with many of the people around him, but that the actual circumstances did leave the younger son in a very awkward position.

'If we were to point out one of those around the table as a suspect, it would, however, be his sister, Magdalena,'

Mr Wendelboe added abruptly, in a very grave voice. My surprise in no way diminished when his wife then immediately nodded in agreement.

He swiftly explained: 'We realize that it may sound strange and that she appears to be trustworthy these days, but you should ask her to tell you the story of her broken engagement. And then you should ask her what she was doing during the war, while her brother risked his life in the Resistance. We have often wondered why he continued to invite her to his parties for all these years, especially when he also invited Hans Herlofsen and us.'

His wife nodded again, in loyal agreement with her husband until hell froze over. They then left the room together, with my silent consent.

I remained sitting where I was to look through my notes and to think about what I had heard and seen. In light of this new information, I would very much have liked to talk to Hans Herlofsen and Magdalena Schelderup again, but they had both already left Schelderup Hall. I therefore ended up calling in the deceased's current wife for the final interview of the day.

XIII

My second conversation with Sandra Schelderup also got off to a good start. She asked about the contents of the will almost as soon as she came through the door. I replied that this had still not been confirmed, but assured her that I would contact the law firm as soon as possible, and that as the deceased's wife she would of course be informed. She thanked me for this and told me that the name of the law firm was Rønning, Rønning & Rønning.

After a moment's hesitation, Sandra Schelderup added without any shame that she had already called their lawyer there. However, he had said that in light of the ongoing murder investigation, it was not possible for him to give any information over the telephone as to the content of the will.

I answered diplomatically that I had been in contact with the law firm on a previous occasion and would do my best to find out as soon as possible what was in the will.

In response to my question regarding Magdalon Schelderup's relationship with his daughter, Sandra Schelderup replied thoughtfully that it had been 'better than expected'. Magdalon Schelderup had wanted a son and did nothing to hide it. He had commented several times during the pregnancy it was unlikely that he could be as unlucky with a third son. 'Better luck next time!' had been his first response when he came to the hospital and she told him that he had a beautiful daughter.

'But there never was a next time. It bothered him, and I was fearful of my position as I could not give him the son he so wanted. But in the end his relationship with Maria Irene was surprisingly good. It was not unknown for him to hit his sons, but he never touched his daughter. And in recent years he commented several times that, of all his children, she was the one who resembled him most. On a couple of occasions he even added that it was no doubt because, of all of his wives, I was the one who resembled him most. So he acknowledged more and more frequently that we were the two who were closest to him. I just hope that he was sufficiently aware of this to recognize it in the will.'

I took a deep breath and asked her whether she knew that her husband had kept a young mistress for the past couple of years.

Her reaction was unexpectedly relaxed. A shadow crossed her face, but she was otherwise in full control of her expression and movements.

'I pretended not to know, both to him and my daughter. But of course I noticed. And he made no effort to disguise it. One would have to be remarkably naive not to understand, when she more or less moved in here at his suggestion. It was terrible to begin with and for the first six months I expected to be thrown out at any moment. But over time I came to realize that this was no new great love, but rather the final physical fancy of a vigorous yet ageing man. There was no indication that he had any plans for a third divorce. After all, if he were to get married for a fourth time to an uneducated girl who could be his grandchild, it would make his life very difficult. It was bad enough when he left his former wife to marry me, and he had become more careful over the years. Of course, I did not like her or her presence here in the slightest, but I gradually came to see her as less of a threat. And now it is over. She will no longer have a job to come to tomorrow morning.'

It was impossible for me not to tell her the truth – that Synnøve Jensen was in fact pregnant.

This time the reaction was dramatic. Sandra Schelderup

leapt out of her chair, hit the table with balled hands and shouted: 'Impossible. It can't be his child!'

When I asked whether it had been medically proven that Magdalon Schelderup could no longer have children, she shook her head sheepishly, then suddenly blushed deeply.

It struck me that I already appeared to be tainted by the ruthless atmosphere at Schelderup Hall. I realized that this was a great blow to Sandra Schelderup both as a woman and a wife, but could not feel any real sympathy for her.

'That too,' she said, sitting down with a heavy sigh. 'And unborn children have the same inheritance rights as other children, don't they?' she added, quickly.

I confirmed this, but said that it could often be difficult to prove in such cases.

'And obviously that will be true here – unless he has left behind some kind of written acknowledgement that he is the father?'

I nodded.

'So Magdalon's will is even more important than ever – both for your investigation and for my life.'

I agreed with her and repeated that it was my hope that we would be informed of the contents of the will within the next day or so. As if by unspoken arrangement, we both stood up at the same time.

Sandra Schelderup commented from the doorway that I had no doubt already heard unfavourable things about her from the others. She asked me to bear in mind that there are always two sides to a story and that she had had her struggles too. She was a country girl who had had to work her way up from simple beginnings when she was young. It had not been easy to be married to Magdalon for eighteen years, nor had it been easy to be accepted as his third wife.

I found this to be entirely credible, but let the door close firmly behind her all the same before I made ready to leave.

XIV

The air felt clearer and sweeter when I finally managed to get away from Schelderup Hall and the irascible dogs. But the situation remained very unclear for all that. The next question was whether my first phone call should be to Patricia or to the lawyers, Rønning, Rønning & Rønning.

When I finally got home at around nine o'clock, I followed my instincts and called Patricia first. She answered the telephone on the second ring. To my great relief, her voice sounded exactly as it had one a year ago. And she seemed to brighten up when she heard that it was me and that I was calling about a new murder investigation. For the next half hour, she listened without saying a word while I outlined my initial impression of the case.

'And your conclusion?' I asked, optimistically.

'That I still do not know who murdered Magdalon Schelderup. There are far too many alternatives and theories that may prove to be true. But I would be more than happy to help you find out. We managed very well with seven potential murderers in the same building last year, so we will just have to see if we can extend our repertoire to include ten possible murderers in a mansion this year.'

I was very happy to hear Patricia sounding so optimistic and enthusiastic, and she hurried on.

'There are several strange and significant things that I would like to discuss with you tomorrow. But you have no doubt already given some consideration to what is currently the strangest and most significant point. Have you discovered any explanation as to why on earth Magdalon Schelderup could be so certain that there was no risk of an attempt on his life before Tuesday? After all, Tuesday afternoon is very specific . . .'

I said that I had given it some thought, but had not found any good explanation. The latter being more true than the former.

Patricia's voice sounded even more amused; I could almost see her smile down the telephone wire.

'There are several possible explanations. Now, what happens with remarkable predictability at some point late on Tuesday mornings that might be of considerable significance here? Hint: every day, with the exception of Sundays and holidays . . .'

I racked my brain, but following a longer pause for thought, declared that I was unable to solve the mystery – despite her hint. Patricia's first triumph was audible, even on the phone.

'And the correct answer is: the first delivery of post sent on Monday is on Tuesday morning. Let us imagine that Magdalon Schelderup was holding back an important announcement about his will or the future of the business, for example, and therefore did not need to fear for his life until he had let those concerned know. If he then posted this to those concerned on Monday, he need not anticipate an attack until Tuesday afternoon at the earliest. Which does not sound entirely infeasible, especially if we imagine that this was something about his will that he had planned to announce to the guests at dinner on Sunday, but that he was waiting to post until Monday, in anticipation of his meeting with you. The primary question would then be what he was going to write. The next question would be who he was going to send it to. The third question would be whether he had already written the letter, and the fourth question would then be where has he stowed it. Are you following so far?'

I croaked a 'yes', but that was already only just.

'Excellent. Then you will check tomorrow whether there are any unsent letters in his office or bedroom, and then, if necessary, ask his wife, his secretary and his manager. Find out what more Hans Herlofsen and Magdalena Schelderup have to say in their defence. Take with you anything that you find of interest in the war archives regarding the Dark Prince and the circumstances surrounding Ole Kristian Wiig's death on Liberation Day in 1945. Might a rather unromantic but possibly very interesting supper at my place tomorrow at half past five tempt you?'

I replied that unless there were any unexpected surprises in the course of the day that would be very tempting indeed. She thanked me politely, then added somewhat more discourteously that I should call Rønning, Rønning & Rønning immediately, in order to solve the hopefully more manageable mystery of Magdalon Schelderup's will.

I took the hint and put down the receiver. I needed a few

minutes to gather my wits before I looked up the number for Edvard Rønning Junior in the telephone directory. With alarmed delight I recognized the fact that I still lagged behind as soon as Patricia's reasoning accelerated, but that my investigation was already picking up pace before I had even had my first meeting with her.

XV

Following a couple of abortive attempts, I managed to get hold of Edvard Rønning Junior at home at around ten o'clock. He informed me that the deceased had requested that the will be read at Schelderup Hall, and had provided a list of those he wished to be present. However, there were no specific instructions as to when the will should be read, as had been the case with Harald Olesen. I therefore suggested that it should be the following afternoon, on the condition that as head of the murder investigation I should be informed of the most salient points in the will. Rønning Junior pointed out that officially a court ruling was required, but added that he 'had no objections per se, provided that the solution ensured that the will was read in accordance with the wishes of the deceased'. There was, however, a temporary practical problem in that the will was in his office, which was now closed for the weekend.

The practical-versus-principle compromise was that Mr Rønning Junior would be in the office by half past eight on Monday morning and would phone me immediately to let me know the contents of the will. He would then instruct his office to telephone or telegraph those people named on the list to request their presence at the reading of the will in the deceased's home at three o'clock that afternoon. I assured him that this would be easy enough to organize, as the deceased's nearest and dearest had all been instructed to stay in town and were unlikely to have made plans for the following day. I felt that we were both more relaxed towards the end of the conversation and I saw no reason to make more problems than I already had with the investigation. We thanked each other courteously for being so accommodating and even put the receiver down at the same time.

It was only then that it crossed my mind that I had yet to make a very important phone call – to the commanding officer. It struck me instantly that the case might be taken from me before it had even started. I could under no circumstances wait until the following day for fear that one of my colleagues might hear about the case in the meantime and snatch it from me. So I looked up the commanding officer's home number on my telephone list and dialled straight away.

Fortunately I caught my boss before he went to bed, and as luck would have it, he was in the better of his two known moods. He listened patiently for ten minutes to my account of the start of this peculiar case, then for another two minutes while I reminded him of my success as head of investigation for last year's most spectacular murder case. Then to my delight he interrupted me to say that it was his wish that I should also head this murder investigation, certainly until further notice. He added that there might be changes if too many days passed without a breakthrough, and that he would like a short report of the day's events every evening. He merrily quoted the former foreign minister, Halvdan Koht: 'That is my opinion, and I must respect it!' I had heard him say this several times before, but laughed heartily all the same and did not object in any way to his conclusions.

I was in bed by eleven o'clock, as I knew that Monday could well be a long and demanding day. But I lay there unable to sleep until about midnight, but still had not managed to find an answer to the Magdalon Schelderup mystery. I was barely able to pick out one of the guests as a more likely murderer than the others.

The Box That Contained
Something Strange

I

Edvard Rønning Junior was an exceptionally correct young man. He telephoned me at the office, as agreed, at precisely half past eight on Monday, 12 May 1969, and read Magdalon Schelderup's will to me from heading to signature. It did not take more than a couple of minutes, even though he read at an irritatingly slow speed. The will was dated 6 May the same year and comprised four short paragraphs. After the previous day's interviews, the content struck me as particularly interesting, although I had to admit that the significance of it remained unclear.

The first paragraph of the will was a sentence to say that the manager Hans Herlofsen, as thanks for his long and loyal service, was to have waived the 'small amount' still outstanding on his 'private loan drawn up in 1949'. There then followed a short sentence to say that 'the promissory note and associated written material' had been destroyed.

The second paragraph of the testament was one sentence

only where Magdalon Schelderup left his wife Sandra Schelderup two million kroner.

The third paragraph consisted of two sentences where Magdalon Schelderup acknowledged that he was the father of his secretary Synnøve Jensen's unborn child and left her the sum of 200,000 kroner for 'subsistence costs and necessary expenses during the remainder of the pregnancy'.

The fourth paragraph was the longest and most complicated. It stated that the remainder of Magdalon Schelderup's wealth and assets should be divided equally between his children on 6 May 1970. The three grown children would each receive for immediate payment no more than their legal minimum share of 200,000 kroner.

I thanked the lawyer for his help and assured him that I would be there for the reading of the will, and requested that the contents should remain confidential until it was read out to the deceased's family and friends.

It was only once I had put down the receiver that I realized that I had not asked whether any previous versions of the will existed, and if that were the case, what was said there. When I tried to call the lawyer back it was engaged both times, so I decided to leave it until after the reading. There was more than enough work to be done in the meantime.

II

The pathologist's preliminary report was as expected. Magdalon Schelderup had died of heart failure, caused by an extreme allergic reaction to nuts. He had been in good shape for his age, but had no chance of surviving such an attack. His heart and body were otherwise those of a sixty-nine-year-old man who had worked hard all his life, and the nut allergy had obviously been extremely severe.

The reports in the newspaper did not pose any problems, but neither did they help to solve the mystery. The Labour Party conference dominated the headlines. The communist paper, *Friheten*, had a report on the front page under the headline 'Key capitalist murdered' and hinted at a conspiracy amongst 'Norway's corrupt capitalist elite'. Other newspapers were more cautious and waited to see the consequences of the death, but instead wrote reams about the deceased's wealth and earlier profiles. *Aftenposten* was the only paper to publish a list of the supper guests and concluded its report by saying that 'we are delighted to confirm that the already famous Detective Inspector Kolbjørn "K2" Kristiansen has been assigned to the case, and wait with bated breath to see whether he can scale the heights of his previous success in this apparently very mysterious case'. I read this with great satisfaction, but also with increasing anxiety, knowing how far I could fall.

I then swiftly put the papers to one side in order to pursue Patricia's priorities, moving from the matter of Magdalon Schelderup's will to the question of what sort of letter he had thought of sending on Monday to one or several of his Sunday supper guests.

There were no unsent letters to be found in the deceased's office or bedroom. Both rooms were so orderly that it was hard to imagine that anything important or current could be hidden there. Magdalon Schelderup's office housed a bookshelf with an array of books about business, but no archives of any note.

Sandra Schelderup told me curtly on the telephone that she did not know of any unsent letters from recent days, but also that she did not often ask about any major or minor details of the business. Her husband had on one occasion joked that she need not worry her pretty head about his business drive, only his sex drive. In other words, I would have to ask the manager about any important documents related to the business, and his secretary about more trivial matters.

Mrs Schelderup sounded somewhat bitter and tense today, but I could understand that. She perked up when I mentioned the will and said that she looked forward to a swift conclusion. She hesitated for a moment, but then agreed to the will being read at Schelderup Hall at three o'clock that afternoon.

The manager, Herlofsen, was in the company's office in the centre of town and answered the telephone on the second ring. He had nothing of any interest to add in the way of unsent letters. He could confirm that any business documents were promptly sent to his office. However, there had not been anything of any significance in recent weeks, and outgoing post that was not related to business was not his department. In short, there was unfortunately a zero per cent chance that he could help me on this occasion other than recommending that I contact Magdalon Schelderup's secretary.

I promised to do this, but added that I needed to ask him

some personal questions. There was a few moments' silence on the other end of the receiver. Then I offered to come and see him in his office in town. He swiftly replied that he would rather come to see me at the police station in order to avoid upsetting the staff in the office. He asked if it would be possible for him to come during his lunch break, so that there would be no unnecessary disruption to the day's work. I immediately said yes to this, and he promised to be there at midday. Then he put down the receiver with remarkable haste.

The telephone rang for a long time in Sørum. However, Synnøve Jensen managed to pick it up on the seventh ring and sounded so out of breath that I immediately imagined she had rushed down the stairs from the bathroom to get it. Even when she managed to catch her breath, she knew nothing about any letters that Magdalon Schelderup had planned to send on Monday. She had only written two letters for him last week and both were standard letters of congratulations that she had sent the same day. If he had any letters pending that he had written himself, they would normally be left on or in his desk.

I immediately picked up on the formulation 'would normally be left' and in a slightly sharper tone asked where else such letters might be left if he did not want to leave them on or in his desk. Her voice seemed to fade as she answered. The feeling that I was on to something got stronger.

'Well, then they would be locked in the metal box that he kept here.'

She almost whispered the last words, before she mustered her courage and continued in a louder, faster voice.

'But I have not opened it and have no idea if there is anything in it right now, or what on earth it might be. He made a point that the box should always be locked and that it should never be opened unless he was here. So I have done as he said,' she added, timorously.

She was undoubtedly thinking the same as me. In other words, that the ground was about to collapse beneath her. Following a few seconds of intense silence she spoke again, with rising desperation in her voice.

'Goodness, how silly I am. I should of course have mentioned the box to you yesterday. The death was such a shock. I really did not think I might have anything important in my house, and nor did you ask . . .'

I did immediately ask, however, when Magdalon Schelderup had last been there and who had keys to the box. She replied, tearfully, that he had last been there on Friday. And, as far as she knew, there were only two keys to the box. One had been on his key ring, and she had the other one in her hand.

She offered to open the box straight away, if that was what I wished. Instead, I asked her to stay at home and not to touch the box until I got there.

III

It took almost three-quarters of an hour before I found myself outside the right smallholding in Sørum. The contrast with Schelderup Hall in Gulleråsen could scarcely have been greater. The land amounted to not much more than a potato patch in front of the house. And the house itself was small and subsiding. It looked as if it had been built by amateurs and a carpenter with an unsteady hand.

Synnøve Jensen was just as ordinary and friendly as she had been before. Having first looked out of the window to check that it was me, she then opened the door immediately and gave me a brave smile. She had put some coffee and cakes out on the small living-room table. The ground floor consisted of a small kitchen and almost equally small living room. A stepladder-like stair with ten treads led up to the first floor, where I could see three doors, all closed.

My hostess waved her hand around, as if to apologize.

'My home is not much to boast about. But it is all I have to offer my child, and all that my poor father had to offer me. He was a skilled carpenter once, or so said all those who had known him a long time. But then the bottle took him. Apparently he got the material for his own house from a building that had burnt down.'

I nodded with understanding. It was hard not to feel sympathy for this crooked little house and its pregnant owner. But all my attention was now focused on the metal box that was standing with its locked secrets on the kitchen table.

'I swear that I have not even touched it since you rang. But I did open it last week, so my fingerprints will be on it, all the same,' she added, hastily.

I lifted the metal box onto the living-room table and asked her not to look while I opened it. Synnøve Jensen nodded gravely and handed me the key straight away. Her hand was trembling when I touched it. She demonstratively turned her head away, eyes fixed on the floor, while I unlocked the box.

I don't know whether I actually expected to find a letter in the box or not, even less what kind of letter I then expected to find. But I certainly had not anticipated finding what I did.

There was a stack of letters that nearly filled the box.

There were ten letters there. All had been sealed and addressed by hand. The letter on top, which I saw as soon as I opened the box, was, to my surprise, addressed to 'Miss Synnøve Jensen'. The second was addressed to 'Fredrik Schelderup Esq.', the third to 'Leonard Schelderup Esq.' and the fourth to 'Miss Maria Irene Schelderup'. Then all the others followed in succession. The letters in the box were addressed to the ten guests present at Magdalon Schelderup's last lunch.

The temptation to open one of the letters immediately was irresistible. They all looked the same, so I started with the one on top. It contained photostat copies of two documents. One was the will that had been read to me by the lawyer, Edvard Rønning. The other was a very short letter, which said the following:

Gulleråsen, 12 May 1969

For your information, a copy of my certified will is enclosed. My decision regarding the contents is final.

Yours sincerely
Magdalon Schelderup

The few lines must have flickered in front of my eyes for several minutes. Apparently Patricia had been right. Magdalon Schelderup had planned to send an important letter on Monday, either before or after his meeting with me. He had after all written the letter and prepared ten identical copies to be sent. But I could not quite grasp what the intention and purpose was.

Knowing as I did what the contents of the will were, it seemed to me that this cast in an even more serious light the three who stood to gain most from it – in other words, Magdalon Schelderup's two sons and his mistress. Judging from what I knew, he had been afraid that one of them might try to kill him as soon they received the letter. It was therefore highly possible that someone had pre-empted him. Especially if the person had known the contents of the will, which had, after all, been lying here for three days – in the metal box to which his mistress had the key. I only had her word for it that she had not used it.

Synnøve Jensen was obviously a lady of strong will. She was still sitting with her face turned away, eyes downcast, when I closed the box and looked at her about five minutes later. Two frightened eyes finally met mine across the table and the untouched cups of coffee. I felt sorry for her if she was in fact not a cold-blooded murderer, but I suspected her of being precisely that. So I was ruthless, in the hope of being able to resolve the case then and there.

'There are several letters in the box – and the top one is addressed to you.'

There was a flicker in her eye, but she did not look away. 'I really had no idea that they were there. He had asked me never to open the box unless he was here, and I did as he told me,' she said. Her voice was choked and unclear, but loud enough to hear. She repeated her short defence twice more, as if it were an oath.

I could not be sure whether it was the truth or not. But I did realize that I was not going to get her to change her explanation. So instead I asked her to tell me about Magdalon's visit here on the previous Friday.

She stuttered and sniffled to begin with, but then gradually started to talk more coherently. He had offered to drive her home after work. He had done this before, and practically always came in when he did. They had stopped by a cafe in Sørum for dinner. When they got back to the house, she put on some coffee for him, but they went up to the bedroom without waiting for it to be ready. He had gone down again later and came up smiling with a cup of coffee for her. She had not seen him put anything in the metal box, but then he had his own key and could have put the letters there either before or after he came up with the coffee for her. She had been tired and had not got up until he had left.

This did not sound entirely convincing. But neither did it sound unfeasible, I had to admit to myself. So in the end I made the snap decision to take the metal box, but not Synnøve Jensen, with me. I ordered her to stay at home until she came to the planned reading of the will at Schelderup Hall later that afternoon.

Synnøve Jensen looked up at me, obviously alarmed, but immediately cheered up when I said that I would be there in person so she would be safe.

On the way back into town, I felt pretty sure that Synnøve Jensen would keep her word and come to the reading of the will. Any attempt to flee would be as good as a confession, and it was not easy to imagine how she would escape. I felt far less certain, however, of the possibility that she might be the murderer.

IV

Back at the police station I first checked that the other envelopes contained the same two documents. I then sent both the metal box and the envelopes for fingerprinting, with instructions that it was a matter of urgency that this should be done before three o'clock.

There was nothing much of any importance in either the census rolls or the police records about the key players involved, with the exception of Magdalena Shelderup who, in 1945, had been sentenced to pay a fine of 1,000 kroner and spend two months in jail. There was a short record of the reason: 'membership of Nasjonal Samling and financial dealings with the occupying forces'. Magdalon Schelderup had had a clean record. Of the remaining guests at Magdalon Schelderup's last supper, there was only a slim file for the elder son, Fredrik. He had been fined twice in the 1960s for driving under the influence and had had his licence confiscated. The second time, he had been charged another hefty fine due to his 'highly disrespectful' treatment of the police. He had accepted a fixed penalty and, as far as I could see from the file, had since kept to the straight and narrow.

I made a routine note that Fredrik Schelderup perhaps had more temperament than I had seen thus far.

Out of curiosity, I also checked the files of Magdalon Schelderup's brother and dead parents. His brother had two minor convictions for attempted fraud in the interwar period, and at the time of his death in 1946 was being investigated for extensive cooperation with the enemy. His father and mother had reported the theft of some jewellery in 1915, but were themselves reported by the insurance company for attempted insurance fraud the year after. The case concerned the most precious piece of jewellery belonging to Magdalon Schelderup's mother, a 'magnificent red diamond on a gold chain', according to the documents, which had been stolen in a burglary – something the thief, who had been arrested, had denied. The necklace was not to be found in the Schelderup home or anywhere else, however, and the case was eventually dropped.

In short, I found nothing of any relevance to the current investigation, but did make a note of the chequered family history.

As for the two Resistance men who were murdered during the war, I first made a phone call to Petter Johannes Wendelboe. I felt no need, however, to press him for names this time, and in the end I went through the archive of unsolved murders from 1941. The armed skirmishes from the 1940s were a thing of the past, and the fight against the occupying forces really became fierce only in the final year of the war.

I quickly found the two cases in question, but could not see of what relevance they might be. The names were Hans

Petter Nilsen and Bjørn Varden, who were aged thirty-eight and twenty-eight respectively, and lived in Bekkestua in Bærum, and Grønnegate in Oslo. Both had indeed been found shot dead in their bedrooms in the morning, Nilsen on 12 May and Varden on 5 September. Nilsen had lived alone and was found by a colleague when he failed to turn up to work. Varden was married and was found by his wife, who had been sleeping in another room with their small baby. No physical traces of the murderer were found in either case, and it was presumed that he either had keys, or managed to get in and out through an open window. The fact that both victims had been shot with the same weapon, a German-manufactured 9x19mm calibre Walther pistol, strengthened the theory that they had both been killed by the same person. The case was closed in spring 1943, however, due to lack of evidence, and there was nothing to indicate that it was ever followed up. A complaint from Bjørn Varden's wife, which had been filed without comment in 1949, was the only document from after the war. The word 'dead' was now written across both files in red letters.

The file concerning Ole Kristian Wiig's death on Liberation Day in 1945 was somewhat thicker. There was a death certificate that confirmed Wiig had died as a result of two bullet wounds to the head. There were also statements from two police constables at the scene of the crime who both said that they had been standing outside the house when they suddenly heard a shot on the first floor.

They saw Magdalon Schelderup at the window, who gestured to them that they should come up. They stormed up the stairs and found Wiig dead on the floor of the Nazi's study. A few feet away, a young member of the Resistance was standing, paralysed, with a gun in his hand. Just as they came into the room, Magdalon Schelderup had snatched the gun from his hands and then declared that he had seen the murder. Bratberg was apparently too confused to give a statement there and then and was arrested on the spot.

Magdalon Schelderup's written statement was an accurate account of his explanation given at the scene of the crime. Bratberg had seemed distressed and confused all day and had suddenly shot Wiig without warning. Schelderup had added a rather sad sentence at the end to say that Bratberg was obviously mentally disturbed and that he and the others in the group should have noticed this earlier. The gun belonged to Bratberg and had his and Schelderup's fingerprints on it, as could be expected, given that Schelderup had taken the gun from him.

Bratberg's written statement was a chapter unto itself. I did not know whether to laugh or cry when I read it. According to Arild Bratberg, Wiig and Schelderup had been arguing when he came into the room and Wiig had been waving a piece of paper furiously in Schelderup's face. Schelderup had suddenly darted over to Bratberg, snatched his gun from him and shot Wiig. Schelderup had then opened the window and waved to someone. After which he walked calmly round the table whistling, swinging the gun loosely in his hand and breaking into the popular song 'Better and Better Day by Day'. When Bratberg said in horror that Wiig had been hit, Schelderup had, in his words, initially replied: 'Yes, but that's not so strange; after all, there's a war going on out there!' He had then commented that it was not unusual to have a lie-down in the early afternoon, and added with a smile: 'And anyway, it's only a toy gun. Try for yourself!' Schelderup had then passed the gun to Bratberg, only to grab it from him again when the two policemen came into the room. As to the critical question of where the piece of paper was that he claimed to have seen, Bratberg stated that Schelderup had swallowed it before the policemen entered.

Of all the many strange statements I had read, this was the most confused and desperate. The psychiatrist appointed by the court declared that Bratberg was mentally unstable, and he was sentenced to indefinite detention. According to later attachments, he had been detained in a closed prison ward until 1954 and had then been transferred to the mental asylum at Gaustad. He was released on probation in 1960, but had then been sectioned again following relapses in 1962, 1964, 1965 and 1967. The picture of a seriously mentally ill person who had committed a tragic and meaningless crime was clear enough. It was not difficult to understand why the case had had such a devastating effect on Ole Kristian Wiig's sister and her family. But I did find it hard to see what relevance it might have to Magdalon Schelderup's death.

V

Hans Herlofsen was punctual and arrived at midday as arranged. He was correctly dressed and visibly tense, and nodded in gratitude when I closed the door to my office behind him.

I opened with a routine question regarding how he had travelled to Schelderup Hall the evening before. Herlofsen replied that he had, as usual, driven there alone in his own car, but hesitated slightly when I asked which car. He nodded reluctantly when I asked if the blue Peugeot was his. It felt as if I was getting warmer already. I took a chance and tried a bluff: 'Your relationship with Schelderup was fine for the first few years after the war, wasn't it? But then something happened that I think perhaps you should explain in more detail . . .'

I was prepared for a violent reaction, but it did not happen. It was clear, however, that I had hit bullseye. Hans Herlofsen started to tremble and seemed to sink back into his chair. He sat leaning back for a while, before he started to speak in a shaky voice.

'I hope that you appreciate how hard it is for me to talk about this. I will be honest, but I pray that it does not need to become public knowledge, unless it should prove to have anything to do with the murder. And I can guarantee you 100 per cent that it does not,' he hastened to add.

I waved impatiently for him to continue, but did give an understanding nod.

'It is an irony of fate that I, who have spent my life looking after figures for other people, have not been able to look after my own. There is one year in my life that I simply cannot account for. That year started on 12 February 1948 when I came home to Lysaker and found my wife lying dead on the sofa with our two-year-old son in her arms. And it ended on 14 February 1949 when I was met at the office by a furious Magdalon Schelderup, and was accused of defrauding his company to the tune of 107,123 kroner. I still remember very little from the intervening period. I know that I sent my son to my wife's sister and I myself drank and gambled every weekend and most evenings. I have no other explanation for it other than that it was an extreme form of grief, perhaps combined with a delayed reaction from the horrors of the war. Whatever the case, I am still not able to explain how I managed to lose such a large amount, even if I did bet on the horses and gamble whenever I got the chance. And the fact that I could do anything so unthinkable as swindle Magdalon Schelderup is even more inexplicable.'

I nodded in agreement. From what I had heard about Magdalon Schelderup thus far, he was certainly not someone one should try to swindle.

'But you do perhaps remember what happened on 14 February 1949?'

He nodded and swallowed.

'Yes, very clearly, unfortunately. Magdalon was absolutely livid in his own peculiar calm way, as he could be when he lost money or felt that he had been cheated by someone. He said he would call the police unless I could put the money on the table in the course of the working day – with interest. I confessed to him that I had drunk or played the money away. Then I got down on my knees in front of his desk, weeping, and begged him to spare me for the sake of my motherless little boy. I promised that I would pay him back every krone with interest over time. I explained that my assets were worth barely a tenth of the sum and that

I would not be able to earn the money if I was found guilty of fraud. He said neither yes or no, just told me to get out of his sight. He added that I might as well crawl out. So I did as he said. I crawled out of his office on my hands and knees and did not stand up until I was out in the corridor and almost tripped up his wife.'

The memory was obviously deeply uncomfortable and distressing. Hans Herlofsen wiped the sweat from his brow and took a short pause before continuing.

'There was absolutely nothing in the world I could do, so I went back to my own office and carried on working as best I could. All day I waited for the police to knock on my door. And eventually it was Magdalon himself who came in, without knocking, at the end of the afternoon. He put down two written documents on the desk in front of me. One was a confession to fraud. The other was a contract in which I declared that I owed him 95,000 kroner, of which 87,123 was an 'unpaid loan' and 7,877 was 'unpaid interest'. The amount was to be paid back with interest at 10 per cent, in annual instalments of 10,000 kroner. And my house and all my other assets were held as collateral in the event of any default in payment. I was given half a minute to sign or he would call the police. I signed, and he left the office holding both the documents. I have never seen them since, but I have been conscious of their existence every day of my life. Year after year has gone by without us ever mentioning the matter directly. I have been his slave – I had to carry on working for him for whatever wage he himself decided to pay me and could never answer back, no matter what bile he spat at me. My life has been an endless toil, a never-ending struggle to meet those payments on 31 December every year. And in 1964, I had to pawn my wife's last pieces of jewellery between Christmas and New Year in order to make it.'

My head was spinning. The situation was easy enough to understand, but not the profundity of it. Among Magdalon Schelderup's ten guests, there were already so many tragic fates and possible motives for murder.

'But I have managed to scrape together every single payment. And I have not touched a drop of alcohol or filled in a betting slip since 14 February 1949. I have managed to keep the whole thing hidden from everyone, including my son. He thinks that I am just extremely thrifty with my daily outgoings and that I actually have a lot of money deposited in the bank. And I tell my neighbours that I am careful with my money and happy with the car I've got. But the reality is that I can barely afford a new bicycle.'

'So, 95,000 plus 10 per cent interest a year, less annual down payments of 10,000 from 1949, leaves . . .'

He nodded gloomily.

'I'm afraid there's still 66,361 kroner outstanding. My crime is now legally time-barred, so there is no risk in talking to the police about it. But I am still indebted to the Schelderup family. If the story of my embezzlement gets out, I might as well forget trying to get another job. I have saved nearly enough for this year's payment and have 8,212 kroner in the bank. But I have nothing more than that, so if they got wind of my debt and demanded that I pay up now, I would lose my house and all my assets, and my son's family and I would once again be on the street. My suit is deceptive: I could be forced to sell it too. However, the worst thing is still the shame and grief it will cause my son.'

Hans Herlofsen looked at me with a pained expression on his face, and added: 'And I guess that is what is going to happen now.'

I made a feeble attempt to comfort the poor manager, but it was not easy. He told me he had no idea where the confession and the promissory note might be, or who else might know about them. But he should at least reckon that the promissory note and outstanding debt had been registered. If the company was broken up and dissolved, not only would all outstanding debts be collected, but his position might disappear. And if the company was not broken up and dissolved, the only possible solution would be for the daughter and wife to take control. And in the best-case scenario, there was a slim hope that he might be able to continue the current arrangement, albeit with higher interest rates and larger payments, he added with a bitter smile. His only hope was that there would be some kind of clemency in the will or some other papers left by Magdalon Schelderup. But in a whisper, he estimated this possibility to be 'under 15 per cent'.

I let Herlofsen go at half past midday. He apologized once again for not having told me everything yesterday. He said that it had felt as if the ground was opening up under his feet following the events of the past twenty-four hours, and I believed him. Hans Herlofsen steadied himself on the doorframe as he left my office, and I do not believe he would normally have done that.

VI

At one o'clock, an important part of the puzzle was solved when I received a verbal report regarding Magdalon Schelderup's metal box and the letters inside. It was in part good news for Synnøve Jensen. Her fingerprints had naturally been found on the outside of the box, but they were old and unclear. The only fingerprints on the letters contained therein were those of Magdalon Schelderup. These technical findings did not prove Synnøve Jensen's statement to be true, but neither did they prove it to be false, and that was what was most important here and now. The arrest warrant I had optimistically put on the desk stayed where it was, incomplete.

The greatest surprise at the police station, however, came at a quarter past one. A breathless constable knocked on the door when a letter arrived with the day's post.

The address was in itself striking, the constable said. And I immediately understood what he meant.

The letter was addressed to 'The head of the investigation into the murder of Magdalon Schelderup'. Of course, this was not so sensational in itself today, but became more so when it was established that the postmark on the letter was from Oslo on the day before Magdalon Schelderup was murdered.

The content was no less sensational. A simple folded sheet, with the following typewritten text:

Here, Saturday 10 May 1969

So the old dictator at the head of the table is dead.
Even the little miss to his right scarcely shed a tear when
his life was snuffed out.
How soon, I wonder, will you manage to work out who
put the powdered nuts on the roast?
If you do not soon raise that toast, there may be more
deaths and fewer witnesses to boast . . .

I looked up at the constable, who looked even paler than normal. He rolled his eyes and said that I should just say if I needed any help. Then he beat a hasty retreat.

The letter was obviously written by someone who was familiar with the seating arrangements and menu at Schelderup Hall. As far as I could see, the letter had been posted the day before the murder – by a confident murderer who had laid a plan and felt sure of the outcome. I had every reason to take very seriously indeed the threat that more of the guests from Magdalon Schelderup's last meal might be murdered. I sat and thought for a few minutes, in part about who the murderer might have in mind and in part about why the murderer had gone to the bother of sending the police a written warning.

I made a photostat copy of the letter and sent the original to be checked, without any great hope that it would help. No matter who had posted this letter, he or she was not very likely to have left any fingerprints or other clues.

So I reported orally to my boss that several of those who witnessed Magdalon Schelderup's death might be under threat and asked if the evening shift could be incremented should the need arise.

Then I rang Magdalena Schelderup and said that I needed to speak to her as soon as possible. She did not sound overly enthusiastic at the prospect. I heard a quiet 'Oh, no' when I asked if she could come by the police station. When I then offered to drive over to her, she asked if we could not meet somewhere in between. I conceded to this and we agreed to meet in a cafe on Bogstad Road at a quarter past two.

VII

The cafe was nice and the coffee was good. As we sat undisturbed in a corner with a piece of chocolate cake each, I decided that our surroundings were far preferable to the study at Schelderup Hall. But Magdalena Schelderup's face was definitely less relaxed and more aggressive than it had been during our first interview. She leant forwards in her chair, almost angry, as soon as I started to ask about her situation and stance during the war.

'Have the Wendelboes been wagging their poisonous tongues again? They have hated and scorned me for nearly thirty years now. I am sure that Herlofsen and many others do too, but those two are malicious through and through. I should, of course, have told you myself rather than allowing others the chance to say it for me.'

She took a breath and then pressed on.

'I was, like my late younger brother, a member of the NS from autumn 1940 to autumn 1942. My younger brother and I saw it simply as a practical means to safeguard the family fortune. I left the party when they started deporting the Jews and never took part in any NS events of any sort. After the war, I was given a suspended sentence of sixty days or the option to pay a fine of 1,000 kroner, which I paid in order to put the whole thing behind me and cause as little damage to the family and business as possible. The case was closed a long time ago now and really should be a thing of the past. And it is for everyone else except those hypocrites from the Resistance. Does someone really want to make it look like I murdered my brother because I was a member of the NS in the first two years of the war?'

After this outburst she quite literally sat in silence for a few moments, stewing. The first cigarette was lit, which had a calming effect.

'Apologies if I appear to be over the top, but I have been hounded by whispering voices ever since the war. It is of course a source of immense frustration to me that I could be so stupid as to get involved in all that to start with. But one, I have never been a Nazi and, two, I most certainly did not kill my brother.'

I noted that the latter was said with more conviction than the former, and that what she told me now was pretty well in accordance with what was written in the case file from the treason trials. So I moved swiftly on and asked her to tell me about her broken engagement.

This prompted an unexpected change of mood. A

shadow of a smile played on Magdalena Schelderup's lips when she replied by asking: 'Which one?'

I knew nothing about either of them and so said that I would like to hear about both.

'The second one, the one to which you are perhaps alluding, was no great loss at the time. He changed his mind only days before we were due to walk down the aisle, because of all this nonsense with the war and my NS membership. I didn't shed too many tears. I had realized some time before that he was not the great love of my life, and he was neither charming nor particularly good-looking. But he was a decent, presentable man with sound finances, who would no doubt be a good father and husband. I was thirty-eight years old when he broke off the engagement. It somehow felt too late and too complicated to start looking for a new husband afterwards. So perhaps in retrospect the loss was greater, now that I know he was my chance not to end up alone, a childless spinster.'

'And the first one?'

She nodded, and straightened up in her chair.

'That was a great loss. It was my first, greatest and only young love. A short and intense romance that lasted the summer and autumn of 1925, but which left its mark on my life for another decade. He was irresistibly handsome and charming, in my eyes and everyone else's. It was as though everything stopped the moment we met by a cafe table, one day when I was staying with a friend in Bergen. It would be safe to say that I did not see very much of my friend for the rest of the summer holiday, but all the more of him.'

A smile slid over Magdalena Schelderup's face, but soon froze to a bitter grimace.

'Apparently I later said of that trip to Bergen in 1925 that I was so comfortable on the bed, I might as well lie in it. When I came home from Bergen to Bærum wearing an engagement ring, I was left standing. I had not expected it to be easy. He was from the working class and, as if that were not enough, he was not working and did not have a family fortune. But I had not expected it to be so utterly hopeless either. They had never really bothered much before at home about what I did. Mother and Father were not too opposed to it at first. Magdalon, on the other hand, was adamant that this was nothing more than a youthful romance and that my fiancé was after the money. Back then, my older brother was the strongest in the family and has been so ever since. Within a matter of days, there was a united family front against my fiancé, without any of them, other than me, having met him.'

A sad expression flooded Magdalena Schelderup's face as she stubbed out her cigarette in silence and immediately lit another. She had definitely lost any appetite for her piece of cake, but her cup of coffee was empty. She suddenly looked far older than her sixty-seven years.

'We have time to do so many stupid things over the course of a lifetime. Every day I have regretted becoming a member of the NS during the war, but still, it is peanuts in comparison to how much I regret allowing myself to be persuaded to break off the engagement and return the ring by post. I knew that I would not be able to go through with it if I met him and perhaps not if I even heard his voice. So

I asked him never to contact me again. He was an honourable man and respected that. But then we did meet again all the same, in an almost bizarre way, in a hotel reception here in Oslo. There were sparks for a few minutes, just as there had been ten years earlier, until his wife appeared. And the worst thing was that I had been right, that he would have made a wonderful husband. He was now a successful businessman of his own making and was on the local board of the Liberal Left Party. When we met again in 1935, my family would no doubt have thought he would make the perfect husband. But by then he had married someone else and they had three children. It was a terrible feeling to go home alone that night, having met her and seen her beaming happily between him and their children.'

Magdalena blew out the cigarette smoke in a violent blast. The tears I had not seen when her brother died were filling her eyes.

'And I have never forgiven myself. It was the greatest mistake of my life, to betray him, not to dare to fight for my one great love when he was there, holding me in his arms.'

Without warning, she raised her right hand and pulled the odd pewter ring from her ring finger.

'I sent back the engagement ring in 1925. But I have always kept this. It was the first ring he bought for me. I think he got it for one krone. But it was as good as the only krone he had, and it was the first ring a man had ever given me. And as it turned out, I got it from the love of my life. So I am going to wear it until my dying day, to remind me of what was and what could have been.'

'And your brother – did you ever forgive him?'

Her sigh was heavy.

'I'm afraid I cannot say yes to that, even on the day after Magdalon's death. It has lain between us for all these years, without us ever speaking about it. After I met my beloved again in 1935, I told him about the episode when I came home. But asking for forgiveness was not in Magdalon's nature. Having heard what I had just been through, he did nothing, just sat there. He shook his head pensively, but said absolutely nothing. Then he turned back to his work and carried on in silence until I left. And I have waited and waited for him to ask me for forgiveness. He never did.'

Magdalena stubbed out her cigarette and finished her story in a determined voice.

'People want to believe that the reason why we have spoken so little to each other in recent years is the war. But my old love story from 1925 left a deeper cleft between us. And it started to come to the fore again as I got older and was left sitting my own, alongside my brother's steadily growing family. He thought he had the right to dismiss his only sister's great love, but he could take whoever he wanted whenever it suited him. That did not make it any easier to forgive, not even for a sister who only had one brother left.'

I expressed my understanding. At the same time, I concluded that Magdalon Schelderup had been very sharp and astute in his telephone conversation with me. His closest circle was almost exclusively made up of people who might have wished him dead. And it was clear that even the deceased's older sister had burnt with a deep passion.

I stayed in the cafe for some minutes after she had left and pondered the case. Then I got up, more thoughtful than ever, and went to my car, so I could drive up to the reading of the will at Schelderup Hall. This time I knew the content of the will to be read by Rønning Junior, but I was all the more anxious to see what reactions it caused.

VIII

When Schelderup Hall loomed into view at ten to three, I was the last of those invited to arrive at the reading. Synnøve Jensen arrived just ahead of me; she had rounded the hill and disappeared in through the gate. The other cars were, as far as I could remember, parked in precisely the same places as last time. And when I came into the dining room, the ten supper guests were all sitting in their usual places. Magdalon Schelderup's chair stood empty, but his rule was still evident in the house.

The bourgeois etiquette for receiving guests had been followed to the letter. Coffee, cakes and sherry had been put out on the table, but no one made any move to help themselves and no one said a word. It seemed to me that the silence was almost as oppressive as when I came into this room for the first time. I went over and stood by the window. It was almost a relief when I saw Edvard Rønning Junior park his car at four minutes to three, and then walk up towards the front door with his rolling gait, a file tucked under his arm. I had to hold back my laughter when the dogs' furious barking made him jump a couple of feet into the air. But he managed nonetheless and quite impressively to keep a tight grip on the file. In the tense and somewhat false atmosphere that prevailed in the room, the pedantic young lawyer was absolutely himself and someone I could depend on – which could not be said for many of the others present.

Edvard Rønning Junior surprised me, however, in a positive sense, when he made no attempt to sit down in the empty chair, but instead remained standing at the head of the table. As expected, he started precisely as the cuckoo clock on the wall struck three.

'On behalf of the late Magdalon Schelderup's estate, I would first of all like to thank you all for making the effort to come here today as requested, at such short notice.'

He received no applause for this, and so continued after his first forced pause.

'It is no doubt known to all those present here that at the time of his death Magdalon Schelderup was married and had three living children, and a fortune amounting to more than 100 million kroner. In this situation he was free to divide his wealth as he wished, with the exception that each of the children should inherit a minimum of 200,000 kroner, as required by law.'

The lawyer paused again and leafed through his papers to find the will. Ten pairs of eyes were glued to his every move. I personally was having difficulties in deciding which side of the table to focus on. I eventually decided to watch the person I was most interested in and about whom I had the greatest doubt: in other words, the deceased's secretary and mistress, Synnøve Jensen. She was sitting on her chair with impressive calm thus far.

'The deceased's will was clearly certified and dated by a lawyer in the presence of witnesses on 6 May 1969.'

Something twinkled in Synnøve Jensen's eyes. She straightened up, but remained sitting in silence, her face tense. I glanced quickly over at Sandra and Maria Irene Schelderup. The mother's mouth twitched when the date was mentioned. The daughter's face, on the other hand, remained expressionless and looked relaxed. Only her eyes, which were riveted on the lawyer, revealed just how alert she was.

'The aforementioned will states as follows: The under-signed, Magdalon Schelderup, born on 17 November 1899, hereby announces his last will regarding the division of his financial wealth and assets. Firstly, I waive the amount outstanding owed to me by Hans Herlofsen, my manager of many years. The promissory note and other documents relating to the case have been destroyed.'

Edvard Rønning allowed himself another pause. I promptly switched focus to Hans Herlofsen. He was also keeping his mask impressively under control. The two sentences that had just been read out saved not only his honour but also his future. All the same, his only reaction was a fleeting smile and a slight loosening of the tie. Then Rønning's drawling voice picked up the thread and continued. My eyes swung back towards Sandra Schelderup.

'My wife Sandra Schelderup shall be paid forthwith the sum of two million kroner to support her for the rest of her life.'

His widow furrowed her brow, and understandably enough her eyes darkened. The sum was undoubtedly less than she had hoped. But she stayed sitting calmly on her chair. The major blow was not to her, however, but to her daughter, who was sitting beside her, just as composed. My gaze slid over to Synnøve Jensen.

'I hereby acknowledge that I am the father of my secretary Synnøve Jensen's unborn child, and request that it be given my surname upon birth. It is my wish that Miss Jensen shall forthwith be paid the sum of 200,000 kroner from my estate to cover all costs in connection with the pregnancy and birth.'

If Synnøve Jensen had known this beforehand, she was a better actress than I had imagined. In the few seconds before she covered her face with her hands, her expression changed from great surprise to tremendous relief. The tears in her eyes were visible even from where I was sitting.

Another, more visible twitch passed over Sandra Schelderup's face. The other faces around the table were, as far as I could see, still tense and expectant when the lawyer once again spoke, this time to read out the final and longest paragraph of the will. The fact that the secretary was the deceased's mistress did not seem to have come as a shock to any of them.

'It is my wish that the remainder of my wealth is divided equally between my four living children as of 6 May 1970. This because my youngest child must first be born and given a name, and because any immediate dissolution of my companies would give rise to inordinate financial costs. In anticipation of the later dissolution, my companies will continue to be run by a board comprising my three grown children, my wife Sandra Schelderup, my manager Hans Herlofsen and my secretary Synnøve Jensen.'

Now all the waiting was over. This time the surprise around the table was tangible, even though they all maintained a stiff upper lip and avoided any emotional outbursts. Fredrik Schelderup smiled broadly and mimed his applause. Ingrid Schelderup also smiled with relief. Her son, on the other hand, chewed ever more furiously on his gum and looked just as serious and pensive as before. Mrs Wendelboe looked around in confusion and even her husband's stony face showed signs of surprise. Synnøve Jensen still had her face buried in her hands, but the tears were falling, round and ready, down her cheeks now. Sandra Schelderup sent both her husband's sons and his secretary a less-than-loving look, and clenched her hands.

The only person at the table who appeared to be unruffled was, incredibly, the youngest. Maria Irene Schelderup's face and body were both still completely relaxed. Her charming young girl's hands lay open and still on the table.

'However . . .'

A tense silence fell in the room as soon as the lawyer's voice was heard. This time, I also stared at him in anticipation. This was not something he had mentioned on the telephone.

'However, an earlier version of the will exists, which Magdalon Schelderup gave orally and which he wanted to be read out with his current will. It was written on 12 August 1968 and was then annulled when this new will was formalized on 6 May 1969. The annulled version is far shorter . . .'

He took another short, dramatic pause while he looked for the second sheet, and then apparently checked three times that it was the correct one.

'The annulled will stated the following: With the exception of two million kroner to be paid to my wife Sandra Schelderup, 200,000 kroner to be paid to my son Fredrik Schelderup and 200,000 kroner to be paid to my son Leonard Schelderup, I hereby leave all my financial wealth and assets to my daughter Maria Irene Schelderup.'

Suddenly all the dammed-up emotions in the room broke loose. Audibly.

Hans Herlofsen heaved a sigh of relief, clutched his throat and loosened his tie further.

Fredrik Schelderup's smile was even broader this time and he raised his glass with a jovial: 'Here's to the new will.'

Leonard Schelderup hid his face in his hands, but judging by the movements in his neck, he was chewing more frantically than ever on his gum.

Sandra Schelderup looked daggers at him a couple of times and then lost all composure. The atmosphere was electric and everyone, including Mr Rønning Junior himself, started when she flew into a rage, first slamming her fist down on the table and then shaking it threateningly at her two stepsons.

The only person who appeared not to be affected by this outburst was the very person my eyes were trained on.

As the annulled will was being read, I thought I saw the very tip of her tongue in the left-hand corner of her mouth. But afterwards, Maria Irene Schelderup was just as impassive as before.

I had to ask myself how I would have reacted in a similar situation, where a new will drawn up four days previously had cost me roughly 90 million kroner. Even though she was still to inherit 30 million or so, it was almost impossible not to be impressed by the eighteen-year-old's self-control.

It was in that moment that I realized that I was, if not in love, certainly hugely fascinated by the late Magdalon Schelderup's young and seriously wealthy daughter.

IX

The gathering soon broke up once the will had been read. Having downed his sherry, Fredrik Schelderup excused himself as he had 'celebrations to attend'. He left the room and no one made any attempt to congratulate him.

Herlofsen and the Wendelboes were more polite in their retreat, but almost as fast.

Ingrid Schelderup embraced her son, who was still visibly shaken, and helped him, it would seem, to regain his composure. Schelderup's former wife showed a new, sharper side when she thanked her hosts for their hospitality, despite not having touched a thing. It was almost possible to see the sparks in the air between Magdalon Schelderup's two wives. Maria Irene saved the situation by clasping Ingrid Schelderup's hand, quick as a flash, to thank her and wish her a good journey home. Her mother then pulled herself together enough to shake her guest's hand and to whisper goodbye in a manner that was not too spiteful.

Leonard Schelderup had apparently still not regained the power of speech, but, he too did his best to smooth over any conflict by giving an apologetic shrug before leaving the room, and then the house, on light feet in the wake of his mother.

Edvard Rønning Junior the lawyer and I were suddenly left on our own with four women: the deceased's wife, daughter, sister and mistress.

It was only now that I discovered that Magdalena Schelderup was sitting there with an inscrutable expression on her face and more than ever resembled an old owl. I would have given a lot to know what she was thinking. It struck me that there was something different about her but, rather annoyingly, I could not put my finger on what.

Synnøve Jensen sat as though frozen on the other side of the table in her plain clothes, with her face in her hands, only now her future and that of her unborn child had been secured.

You could almost touch the ice that chilled the air between the deceased's wife and mistress. Again it was Maria Irene who suddenly saved the day – and this time without saying a word. She calmly put her hand on her mother's shoulder and more or less pulled her from the room. Magdalena Schelderup followed them with her eyes but stayed seated, her face still thoughtful. She poured herself a cup of coffee. We watched her drink it in almost breathless silence, and waited for a message that never came.

It was Rønning Junior who first stirred to action. He informed Synnøve Jensen in a sombre tone that if she came by his office with her bank book tomorrow or the day after, he would arrange for her to be paid the 200,000 kroner as soon as possible. He then gave her his business card, and shook hands with those who were still there before leaving the room.

I thought I caught a hint of triumph and irony in the lawyer's eyes when he shook my hand. But it was fleeting and I saw no reason to further complicate the case by starting an argument with him. Formally, there was nothing to quibble about. I had only asked him about the content of the current will and he had answered correctly. Strictly speaking, it was my own forgetfulness that was to blame as I had not asked whether there were any previous wills and, in that case, what they said. And in any case, I now had the answer to my question only a matter of hours later. But I would have liked Rønning Junior more if he had taken the trouble to tell me earlier about the other will.

The sound of Mr Rønning's voice and steps appeared to have woken the until now paralysed Synnøve Jensen to life. She lowered her hands from her face, put the business card in her pocket and left the room with a quiet apology for something or other.

Magdalena Schelderup and I sat and looked at each other for a minute or so. The only thing to break the silence was the outbreak of barking as first Rønning and then Synnøve Jensen passed the dogs – by which time I was on my feet and looking out of the window. Rønning jumped just as much this time as he had on his way in, whereas Synnøve Jensen was obviously used to the noise they made. She walked past them unperturbed, and then on down the driveway, alone in the world, but, it would appear from my bird's-eye view, with courage.

'And now what do you think?' I asked Magdalena Schelderup.

A gentle smile crept over her wrinkled face when she replied.

'Now I am thinking the same as you. In other words, how on earth does this all make sense and who on earth put the powdered nuts on my brother's plate? And what is going to happen to those of us who are left?'

Then she stood as well. I wanted to ask her something, but could not think of a meaningful question. And to my irritation I realized that I still could not work out what it was about her that had changed since we last met. I was left with the feeling that the older Miss Schelderup was not only a wiser woman than she might at first seem, but that she also knew more than she was saying.

I had been sitting on my own in the room for a couple of minutes when there was a sharp knock on the door, and in came Sandra Schelderup. She had come to apologize for her earlier outburst, saying that the situation was obviously difficult and extremely emotional. She also wanted to ask if there was anything more she could do to help me.

I had a couple of questions about relevant details. I asked when the dogs had come the year before and who was responsible for tethering them. She replied promptly and without any fuss that her husband had bought the dogs in the middle of summer. She had known nothing about them until they stood barking at the steps. She, her husband and one trusted servant were the only ones who knew the dogs well enough to handle them. Everyone else, including Maria Irene, kept out of their way.

I soon understood that there was something she wanted to tell me, but had no idea what. So I eventually asked whether she had any new thoughts, in light of the day's events. She beamed and replied that one thought had struck her with renewed force. Given that Magdalon's son, Leonard, and his mistress both had so much to gain from his death, and that he pointed to his son shortly before he died . . . And that, as we knew, his mistress was pregnant, even though Magdalon had been convinced that he could no longer have children . . . Well, then perhaps it was not so unthinkable that maybe they were in a relationship and had conspired together?

She admitted that it was perhaps no more than wishful thinking on her part. But maybe it was worth looking into all the same.

I did not like Sandra Schelderup any the better for this, but had to admit that her theory was not something that could be ignored. But I disliked her a little less when she once again apologized for her display of temperament, before adding that she and her daughter would now leave the case in my safe hands. They were certain that I would manage to solve the apparently inexplicable murder mystery. Her husband had no doubt known what he was doing when he contacted me. He had followed the case regarding Harald Olesen's murder day by day and had sung my praises at its conclusion. I must of course just call or drop in at any time should I have any more questions.

We finished the conversation by exchanging a few

words about the continued police presence at Schelderup Hall. We quickly agreed that a police constable would remain on guard that night but would be allowed to leave the next day, unless anything unexpected happened that might give cause for concern. Sandra Scheldeup promised to call me straight away if she remembered anything that might be of importance and dutifully wrote down my telephone numbers in case she needed to get in touch quickly.

At ten past five, I slowly descended the stairs that led to the front door. My progression was slow, partly because the situation had given me a lot to think about, but mainly because I hoped that I might bump into Maria Irene.

And this, it turned out, was not difficult. She came out of one of the side doors on the ground floor just as I reached the bottom of the stairs. It was of course no coincidence that I was walking slowly down the stairs or that she came out into the hall at that moment. I think we both understood that the moment we stood face to face. Neither of us had anything in particular to say, so it was a brief, pleasant encounter. She also assured me that she had full confidence in my investigative skills and dutifully noted down my telephone numbers in case she needed to contact me.

I took the liberty of commenting on how impressed I was with the maturity she had shown in the face of such disappointment, given the strange story of the two wills. She replied that she of course wished it had been otherwise, but that 25–35 million was still an extraordinarily fortunate start in life for a young woman.

I was uncertain as to whether or not to give her a hug when we parted, but wisely offered a firm hand instead.

I noticed her mother standing like a silent statue a few feet away from the top of the stairs. There was now no doubt in my mind that I liked the daughter better than the mother. I still had conflicting feelings for the daughter, but had to confess to a growing fascination for the beautiful and serene young woman.

I had an hour-long stopover at my office prior to departing for Patricia's, but all I did was sit there looking through the case documents without becoming any the wiser. The mysterious letter that had arrived in the morning post lay on top. At half past five, I put it and the other papers in my briefcase. If I had not already needed advice and illuminating comments from Patricia, I certainly did now that I had received the letter. Unless somehow there was a rather well-informed and sardonic joker behind it, the letter entailed not only a sarcastic dig at the police, but also a threat of more murders.

The faces of the ten guests who had sat round the table at Magdalon Schelderup's last meal and during the reading of the will flicked through my mind as I drove to Erling Skjalgsson's Street. It was not clear to me which of them might have written the letter, or who the letter's threatening last line might be referring to.

X

After my experiences that day and the growing sense of unease at Schelderup Hall, it was a pleasure to enter the familiar and safe surroundings of 104–8 Erling Skjalgsson's

Street. The rooms were just as spacious and the stairs just as long as I remembered from the year before. Patricia's father, Professor Director Ragnar Sverre Borchmann, was just as impressive and reliable but, if possible, even friendlier, when I met him at the front door. Either he had not been told about Patricia's stressful experience during the dramatic conclusion of the murder case she assisted me with the year before, or he was doing an extremely good job of pretending to have forgotten.

Once again he informed me that he had not seen his daughter as alive as she had been during and after last year's investigation since the accident that had left her paralysed from the waist down. She was now already showing the same keen interest in the mystery surrounding the murder of Magdalon Schelderup and he had high hopes that she might be able to give me valuable advice. I thanked him heartily for letting his daughter be involved with the investigation, and he shook my hand for the third time when we parted. His goodwill had been rather a surprise. Talking to Professor Director Ragnar Sverre Borchman always took time, even when you said very little yourself. It was already a quarter past six and the starter was on the table when the maid showed me into the library with a small understanding smile.

To my enormous relief, Patricia appeared to be unaffected by the strain that last year's events had put on her nerves. She sat radiant by the table, ready to hold court, and showed no sign of having taken up smoking again as she had in the final stages of the our first case. The air was clean and Patricia's face was as bright as the summer sun. I could neither see nor hear any changes in the now nineteen-year-old Patricia, compared with the eighteen-year-old with whom I had shared ten intense days of investigation the year before. The pile of books she was reading at the moment included a detective story by the American author Rex Stout, a Russian book with several chessboard diagrams on the front cover and a thick English book about the great battles of the First and Second World Wars.

As had been the case when we first met, we made no attempt to shake hands. Now that I was once again in the middle of a murder case, it felt quite natural to be sitting here, asking for advice.

Patricia listened with intense concentration and made copious notes, while I used the time it took for us to eat the asparagus soup and half the beef tenderloin to tell her about the day's events. As was her wont, she listened patiently until I had finished my account of the facts of the case. She finished her last slice of tenderloin and washed it down with a glass of iced water, deep in thought. And then she took off at speed.

'First of all, I should congratulate you on another good day's work. The case is clearly very complicated, but you have already managed to draw out an impressive amount of information that answers a number of my questions.'

She pointed casually to the detective novel in the pile of books.

'Your talents are indeed greater than those of Archie Goodwin in Rex Stout's novels. So I for my part, despite being well under half the size, will have to try to surpass

Nero Wolfe's ability to spot brilliant connections without physically leaving the safety of my home.'

Despite Goodwin's popularity with the opposite sex, I was not entirely happy with the comparison. Nor was I comfortable with being reminded of what had happened, or what could easily have happened, when I persuaded Patricia to leave the safety of her home for a few hours during the last case. So I hastened to ask what she had to say about the case so far.

All of a sudden, Patricia became very serious.

'That this case is not likely to be any easier to solve than the last one, but that it may be even more gruesome. Although many things from Harald Olesen's past were revealed in the course of the investigation, this Magdalon Schelderup already appears to be a man with some very unsympathetic sides – indeed, a man who might therefore leave an even more indelible mark on the people around him. We are obviously dealing with a rather unique murder in terms of Norwegian criminal history. I am starting to believe that we are also talking about a remarkable murder victim, for better or worse, but mainly for worse. So my first observation is that we will find an exceptionally strong connection between the murder and the victim's life and personality. It is far too early to have an opinion as to who might have put the powdered nuts in his food. I can imagine several options that would imply that all ten guests could be murderers.'

I nodded and ventured something myself.

'I have also thought that there are similarities between

this case and last year's, and that your human fly concept could also apply to several of the potential murderers here.'

Patricia shook her head thoughtfully.

'Yes, that's true, but I would be inclined to say rather that we are dealing with ten *satellite people*.'

She smiled at my confusion and quickly continued.

'I'm so sorry, without thinking I used a term that I coined myself and have used so frequently since that I forget it is not an established concept for other people . . . Human flies are people who have experienced something so dramatic, not to say traumatic, that they continue to hover and fly round this event from the past for decades. Satellite people are very similar, but not quite the same. They are individuals who for whatever reason move in a more or less fixed orbit round another person. It is a phenomenon that can be found in many relationships and at all levels of society. For example, it might be a kind mother who even when she is a very old lady herself continues to circle round a sick child, or a son who though grown still gives his all to his father. It could easily be argued that our longest-serving prime minister Einar Gerhertsen's editor brother was a kind of satellite person to his sibling. And the wife of the current leader of the Labour Party, our next prime minister, also only orbits her husband.'

I noted that Patricia obviously knew a lot about Norwegian politics, but was keener to hear her explain the relevance of this new concept to the investigation. I did not have to wait long.

'The phenomenon is in fact particularly evident in the wealthy upper classes, as is the case here. Many strong and powerful people, intentionally or unintentionally, encourage other people to orbit them like satellites. Magdalon Schelderup was undoubtedly such a person, and obviously had nothing against it. As a result, these ten guests have moved round him in their various individual orbits for years. And now it would appear that one of the satellites has broken loose from its path in a very dramatic fashion and crashed into the planet it was orbiting. This has sparked a highly unpredictable situation. All the fixed orbits have been broken and chaos threatens a universe that has lost its centre point and organizing force.'

Now I understood the relevance of the concept. Patricia caught the fascination on my face and smiled.

'As you see now, a little knowledge of geophysics can be useful in an investigation. Though things are possibly somewhat simpler down here on earth. There are also examples of countries where millions of people continue to circle round one dominating person for decades and decades. One can only wonder what will happen to a country like Yugoslavia, where the pull of ethnicity and religion is so strong, the day that Tito is no longer there as the unifying force. My guess is the country will no longer exist twenty years after his death.'

Much as I found Patricia's predictions for the future of Yugoslavia fascinating, if somewhat exaggerated and utopian, I was at that moment impatient to get on with my murder investigation.

'So, you believe that even Petter Johannes Wendelboe is nothing more than a satellite person?'

Patricia smiled.

'Fair point. Petter Johannes Wendelboe is definitely a big enough character to be his own planet, independent of Magdalon Schelderup. But he has chosen to stay in his orbit year after year all the same. And he took his place at all these Sunday meals. The question as to why is therefore of great interest. Do you have any suggestions?'

I shook my already dazed head briefly.

'Sunday suppers like that are more often than not studies in boredom. However, there are six possible reasons why one might choose to go to them. For example, you might go for fear of risking a negative reaction from the host in the form of a change in the will or disinheritance. Or you might go because there is a strong positive motivation to meet someone else who is going, usually because you are in love with them and hope you will end up in the sack together. Or you go there to eat, drink or chat. However, none of these would appear to be relevant to Wendelboe, so that leaves the sixth possibility . . .'

I sent Patricia a questioning look, to which she responded triumphantly: 'He went there to listen. Wendelboe went there time after time in the hope that Schelderup himself, or perhaps one of the other guests, would finally divulge something that it was very important for Wendelboe to know. And, as Herlofsen would perhaps say, I am 99 per cent sure that the something Wendelboe hoped to hear about is something to do with the war. Hence my great interest in the three mysterious deaths from back then. I do have some theories about possible connections but they are still very sketchy, so let us come back to them tomorrow. In the meantime, I would like you to check with the Wendelboes, and possibly also Herlofsen, exactly when the murders of the two members of the group took place, and the circumstances around them, and when Magdalon Schelderup joined the group.'

I promised to do this. 'The other incident from the war, the one that took place on Liberation Day, is somewhat clearer, is it not?'

Patricia shook her head. 'That one is also very interesting. And I would be surprised if you had not already noted one very striking detail. But again, let us leave that until tomorrow. Even though I do not have high hopes of what he could or might want to tell us about Magdalon Schelderup, you should try to talk to our foreign minister, Jonas Lykke, as soon as possible.'

I nodded eagerly. The legendary Conservative politician, Jonas Lykke, was Norway's former prime minister and a great driving force behind the Conservative coalition government of the day. He had played a central role in the Resistance and in the treason trials after the war, and then went on to become a politician. He was definitely someone I should talk to about Magdalon Schelderup's life during the war and later as a politician. And I had to admit that the idea of talking to Jonas Lykke was very appealing to someone who had followed his progress over the years on the television and radio and in the papers.

I ventured to say that in criminal cases, it seemed that satellite people functioned in much the same way as human flies. Patricia nodded at first, but then shook her head.

'Yes and no. Both could obviously give motives for murder, but there are significant differences. Satellite people are often bigger and harder than human flies. They move faster. And it can get extremely cold out there in the highest spheres, especially on the far side of larger planets. And that is precisely where we find ourselves, high up in the spheres on the cold far side, in Schelderup Hall, in the middle of an inheritance dispute regarding Magdalon Schelderup's fortune. The person behind our last murder case was a very strong person, but I must warn you that the person or persons behind this case may be even more calculating and dangerous.'

We were interrupted by the maid, who came in to clear the table and serve dessert. And although the rice cream was beautifully prepared and delicious, both Patricia and I were losing any interest in food. Patricia had truly picked up pace and raced on as soon as the door closed behind the maid.

'You have no doubt already reacted to several striking similarities. The first that struck me was the reading of the will, with even the same lawyer. It can hardly be coincidence, and nor is it. From what Sandra Schelderup and Magdalon himself have said, the explanation seems to be clear enough. Magdalon Schelderup followed your last case in the media with great interest, no doubt because it was obviously an exciting game that struck a chord with him. When he then decided to write a will shortly thereafter, he chose a similar format and the same firm of lawyers. So far, so good . . .'

I nodded; there was nothing that surprised me so far.

'And even though we are now most interested in the man's second will, the first one is also of interest. Why did

Magdalon Schelderup suddenly decide to write a will in August last year? If the decision had been directly inspired by the Olesen case, he would hardly have waited until four months after it had been solved and closed. The possibility of a connection here is underpinned by the fact that he also got the guard dogs, without any prior warning, at around the same time. So it is likely that something of interest happened here last summer. I would urge you to contact Schelderup's doctor tomorrow and ask if he knows anything more about this. We may then also get the answer to another important question that struck me . . .'

She stopped for a moment, but continued with a mischievous smile when I impatiently waved her on.

'That is, the method of murder chosen. Serving nuts to someone who is allergic of course has its advantages; for example, if there is a risk that you yourself might be asked to taste the food. But it is far less certain than using cyanide or any other lethal poison. Unless Schelderup's health might otherwise indicate that a small dose of nuts would mean certain death. And if that was the case, who else other than he himself knew about it? That would be very interesting to know . . .'

I agreed with this and promised to contact Schelderup's doctor the following day.

'As for the motive, it is perfectly understandable that Sandra Schelderup would want to cast doubt on his stepson and mistress. Equally, it is not unthinkable that her conspiracy theory about the two being a couple might be true. However, I think it is a dead end that is leading us in entirely the wrong direction. Quite literally, I would say.'

Patricia laughed her withering teenage laugh without explaining why. Then she was serious again and started to summarize the situation and, fortunately, her preliminary conclusions were very similar to my own.

'In short, the last will gives both sons, the secretary, the manager and the ex-wife all a clear motive. But the previous will, which may have been the last one that anyone knew about, gives the daughter and her mother an even stronger motive. Of those sitting around the table, that leaves the Wendelboes and the deceased's sister, who all could have reasons for wanting him dead that have nothing to do with money. So, for the moment, we certainly do not need to worry about any lack of suspects or motives.'

I had to agree with her, but quickly asked what she thought about the letter. The colour seemed to drain from her face instantly.

'I do not like it one bit. I find the implied danger of further deaths in the letter very troubling indeed, especially as it was posted before Magdalon Schelderup's death. The letter is one of the most alarming elements in this case so far, and it may well be a crucial clue. But for the moment, it is impossible to say where it might lead. It is highly likely that the letter was written by the murderer. And if that is the case, the only things we can deduce are that he or she for some mysterious reason wants to give the police some hints, and that he or she has only average talents when it comes to poetry. And given what we know so far, that basically would not exclude any of the guests.'

After the maid had collected the dessert bowls, Patricia asked suddenly whether I was still in touch with any of the people involved in our last case. I shook my head and looked at her, puzzled.

'No contact with any of them?' she repeated, with a careful smile. I replied 'no', and asked why she wondered about that. Patricia was obviously taken aback by my question, and answered abruptly that it was a good thing that I had nothing else to think about and could give my full attention to this new case. To which she swiftly added: 'And I would strongly advise you in this case, too, to be wary of all those who were in the building at the time of the murder and to keep them at arm's length until the case has been solved. It is possible that fewer of them have lied in their first statement than was the case last time. But that being so, there are more who have not told you details that might be of crucial importance to the investigation. In fact, I suspect that all ten are guilty of withholding crucial secrets.'

I nodded eagerly. 'So you have no doubt that we will be able to solve the case?'

Patricia smiled. 'But of course. There is always only one truth in a murder case. And it always comes to light when you have the skills to gather the right information and interpret it correctly. And we both have just that. Continue to delve for the information we do not yet have and give me some time to think over what we already know, and very soon we will have some breakthroughs. We already have far more interesting information now than we did at the same point in the last investigation. If it continues in this way, well then, my hope is that we may achieve our goal within about a week.'

I let myself be reassured by this, but already had an unexpected amount to think about. So I hastily thanked Patricia for the food and left, having made a preliminary arrangement to meet her again for supper the following day.

XI

When I got home I immediately phoned the main police station to say that I needed to speak to Jonas Lykke as soon as possible in connection with the ongoing murder investigation. My boss agreed that this sounded wise and, without hesitation, promised to call the Ministry of Foreign Affairs regarding my request.

At a quarter to nine I attempted to unwind by watching the Monday film, which was the German classic, *The Blue Angel*. And even with Marlene Dietrich on the television, my thoughts continued to whirl around unfolding events and the Gulleråsen murder mystery in Oslo. And then the phone rang for the first time that evening. It was by then five to ten. The voice on the other end was female and friendly, but with a tone of underlying anxiety. It was Sandra Schelderup. She was calling to tell me that a revolver had disappeared from her husband's gun collection. The one he had kept with him in the bedroom and office in recent weeks was still where he had last left it, in the locked drawer of his desk. But another, older, revolver had now disappeared from the gun cabinet in the hallway. She did not know if it was loaded, or whether any ammunition had been stolen. It was impossible to say whether the revolver had disappeared in the course of the day, yesterday or some days before. But it was clearly not there. For many years the cabinet had contained two rifles, two pistols and two revolvers. And now the older revolver was missing. According to the contents list, it was a Swedish-produced 7.5mm calibre Nagant revolver.

I asked her who might know about the gun. She paused, said quite clearly that she and her daughter knew nothing about where it might be, and then added in a hushed voice that those who knew the house as well as they did were her stepsons and the secretary. She managed to curb herself in time and added that any one of their visitors might of course have known about the revolver and taken it with them. The cabinet had been locked as it should be, but the lock was not very advanced and a key from the neighbouring cupboard could be used to open it.

Sandra Schelderup sounded tired and frightened, which I could well understand. So I thanked her for calling and asked her to contact me immediately should she discover anything else of importance. She promised to do that and again stated how glad she was that I was the one leading the investigation.

XII

I was about to sign my first report to the commanding officer at around a quarter past ten, when the telephone rang again. This time it was Leonard Schelderup's voice on the other end, sounding even more upset than I had heard it the day before.

'I do apologize for calling you so late. But I have just had a telephone call from someone who did not identify themself advising me to confess to the murder of my father. I of course replied that I was innocent, but the caller hung up immediately. It was a deeply unpleasant experience!'

I agreed that it must have been and asked straight away if he had recognized the voice. The tension in his own voice was even more audible when he replied.

'No. The voice was distorted and in any case only said a few words. But it did sound familiar all the same, as if I had heard it before, but I would not dare to say where and when that might have been. And that only makes things worse.'

My attempt to pacify Leonard Schelderup by saying that it might just be some prankster who had read about the case in the newspaper was of little avail. He thought this highly unlikely, as his telephone number was not listed in the telephone directory and was only known to his close family and friends.

I had to concede that this was a fair point, and immediately offered to send a constable round to stand guard outside his front door. At first he accepted this offer, but then abruptly changed his mind and asked that no one stand guard before tomorrow morning at the earliest. He repeated this twice. He promised to think some more about the voice on the phone and to call me immediately if he had any idea of who it might be.

Leonard Schelderup sounded slightly calmer by the time we finished our conversation around eleven o'clock. 'Thank you for taking the time to talk to me this evening, and hopefully we will talk again in the morning!' were his last words before he hung up.

I did not take the opportunity to ask about his relationship with his father's secretary, Synnøve Jensen. It was clear from Leonard Schelderup's mood that it might be best to leave it until tomorrow and to discuss it in daylight.

After I put down the receiver, I sat for a further ten minutes speculating on yet another small mystery within the greater mystery of Magdalon Schelderup's murder. Even though the day had brought to light a lot of new information, the answer did not feel any closer when I finally went to bed at a quarter past eleven.

The day's events had also taken their toll on me. I lay there until well past midnight, my mind churning over what had been said, half expecting the telephone to ring again. Then I finally fell asleep, only to be woken by a very odd nightmare. I imagined that Leonard Schelderup had rung me again and begged for a constable to be put on guard as soon as possible.

At a quarter past two I stumbled over to the telephone, annoyed with myself, and dialled the number of the police station to ask if it would be possible to station a police officer outside Leonard Schelderup's flat in Skøyen. I knew that resources were tight and that posting an officer overnight was limited only to exceptional cases of imminent danger. But I suddenly had the feeling that this was precisely one such extraordinary and dangerous situation. There were a couple of men on duty in case of emergency and they promised that one of them would be outside the address given in Skøyen by three o'clock. I lay tossing and turning for another ten minutes, castigating myself first for having been overcautious and calling out a policeman in the middle of the night, and then for not having done it sooner.

The alarm clock glowed a quarter past three by the time sleep overpowered my tired brain. I then slept heavily until the morning, unaware of the drama that had taken place under cover of darkness.

DAY FOUR

On the Trail of a Lonesome Horseman

I

Tuesday, 13 May 1969 was another day with an early start. My telephone rang at twenty-three minutes to eight, just as I put a cup of coffee down on the breakfast table. When I answered 'Kristiansen, how can I help you?' there was a couple of seconds of heavy breathing on the other end before a woman's voice pierced my ear.

'Is that Detective Inspector Kristiansen? If it is, please can you come immediately? There has been another murder.'

The voice was trembling, and yet impressively controlled and clear. I recognized it immediately as one of the voices I had heard at Schelderup Hall. It took a couple of seconds more before I realized it belonged to Magdalon Schelderup's former wife, Ingrid. She spoke quickly and was remarkably informative.

'I am in Skøyen, in my son's flat. I came to see him this morning, but someone has been here before me. Leonard is lying on the floor with a bullet wound to his head and has obviously been killed. If you come, you can see for yourself!'

The choice of words was rather odd, but her voice was still impressively clear for a woman who had just found her only son murdered. I vaguely recalled Patricia's words about the hard and strong satellite people involved in this case. Then I mumbled my condolences and asked her to stay where she was with the door locked until I got there. She promised to do this, but added that it was too late to save her son's life or to catch the murderer.

So Tuesday, 13 May turned into one of the very few days when my breakfast was left untouched on the kitchen table. It took me less than thirty seconds from the time I put down the phone to when I slammed the front door shut behind me.

The drive to Skøyen, on the other hand, felt incredibly long. I remembered what a great experience it had been to watch Leonard Schelderup sail across the finishing line with rare majesty, his long fair hair flowing, to win gold in the Norwegian Championships at Bislett the year before. I also remembered only too well his frightened face at the reading of the will, and his terrified voice on the telephone last night. Now that Leonard Schelderup had in one fell move gone from murder suspect to murder victim, my sympathy welled up.

Alone in the car, I cursed several times the fact that I had not come out to see him last night. For the second time in three days a Schelderup had phoned me and for the second time he had died before I could speak to him. My only defence was that I had offered to station a policeman outside and he had said no. This time I had even ordered a constable to go there several hours later. But the facts of the matter were still brutal: Leonard Schelderup had telephoned me yesterday evening to say that he was frightened and this morning he had been shot and killed.

The investigation seemed to be more complicated than ever. I had never truly believed that Leonard Schelderup had murdered his father, but no more than a day ago he had been the only one of the ten who had stood out as a natural suspect, in addition to Synnøve Jensen. And now that he had become a murder victim himself, it felt as though the mystery was getting deeper, despite the fall in the number of possible suspects. Apart from Synnøve Jensen, I could not pick out any one of the nine remaining as a more or less likely double murderer than the rest.

The first person I met at the scene of the crime was the constable who had been standing guard. He immediately came forward when he saw me on the pavement outside. He was a down-to-earth, good police officer who gave a down-to-earth and good report, according to which he had driven here as soon as he had been asked last night and had been standing guard, with a clear view to both sides of the building, since ten to three in the morning. There had been no sign of life in either of the flats in the building at that point. No one had come or gone from either of them, until an older lady, who it turned out was the deceased's mother, had rung the bell at around twenty past seven. The light in the neighbour's flat had come on at ten past seven, but there was still no sign of life in Schelderup's flat by that time.

Thus there was only one clear conclusion, and that was that if Leonard Schelderup had been murdered during the night, the murderer must have done it and left the building before ten to three in the morning.

Ingrid Schelderup stood patiently by the window in her son's flat while I talked to the constable. She waited to unlock the door until I rang the bell, but then took only a matter of seconds.

The first thing I saw when I stepped into the flat was Ingrid Schelderup's taut face. The second was her pale, shaking right hand, which was pointing to the floor. And the third was a revolver on the floor where she was pointing. The gun was lying on the carpet just inside the door. With a quick look I could confirm that it was an old Swedish-produced 7.5mm calibre Nagant revolver.

And so one of the small mysteries was solved. The revolver that had disappeared from Magdalon Schelderup's cabinet had been found again. But that left another, deeper mystery. And that was who had taken it from Magdalon Schelderup's gun collection in Gulleråsen a day or two earlier, presumably with the intention of aiming it at his younger son?

Leonard Schelderup himself was nowhere to be seen in the hallway. He was lying on the floor in the living room beside an armchair that was facing the television. His body was intact, clean and whole, apart from a bullet wound in his forehead from which the blood had poured freely. One look was enough to confirm that any hope of life was long gone. The flow of blood from the wound had already started to congeal. I quickly estimated that Leonard Schelderup had died in the early hours of the morning, at the latest, and perhaps even late in the previous evening.

With as much sensitivity as I could, I asked Ingrid Schelderup the one question that I needed an answer to here and now: had she found both the body and the gun exactly where they were lying now? She dried a tear before answering, but then gave a decisive nod. She had not touched the revolver and she had only gingerly touched her son on the neck and wrist to feel for any sign of life. The front door was unlocked when she arrived, she told me. When she discovered that, she was almost paralysed by fear. Then she had opened the door and seen the gun without hearing any sounds of life from the flat and had immediately realized that he had been murdered during the night.

It was easy to draw some conclusions, having looked around the flat. Leonard Schelderup had obviously been shot, presumably with a revolver that someone had stolen from his father's house and brazenly left on the floor after the murder. Given Leonard Schelderup's intense fear the night before, it was unthinkable that he might have forgotten to lock the door before going to bed. He must therefore have been murdered by a guest who either had a key or whom he had let in. But there was little more to deduce from the scene of the crime. Even if the list of potential murderers was limited to the nine remaining guests who had been at supper in Schelderup Hall when his father had been murdered two days earlier, it was impossible to exclude any of them.

I looked at Ingrid Schelderup without saying anything. She looked back at me, equally silent. Her eyes were not only sad, but frightened. I got the feeling that we were thinking the same thing. Namely, that it would seem

Leonard Schelderup had been shot in much the same way that members of his late father's Resistance group had been, but twenty-eight years later.

II

One detail in Leonard Schelderup's flat quickly caught my attention. The two chairs on opposite sides of the kitchen table did not give away much in themselves, even if he did live on his own. But the kitchen table was set for two. The coffee cups served to reinforce the impression that young Schelderup had sat here the night before with a guest. When he called me at around ten o'clock, the guest had not yet arrived, or he had chosen not to tell me. There was not much more to be drawn from it. One of the cups had been used, but the cup and plate on the other side of the table were untouched. I was fairly convinced that Leonard Schelderup's guest had been sitting on that side.

However, the most remarkable discovery was in the bedroom. It seemed unlikely that Leonard Schelderup had gone to bed, only to get up again and get dressed before being shot in his living room in the middle of the night. And yet it would appear that there had been considerable activity in his bed the day before. The pillows and duvet were in a tangle and the sheet was half pulled off the mattress. It might of course be the case that Leonard Schelderup had simply not made his bed when he got up yesterday morning, but his mother insisted that he was a very tidy and good boy who always made his bed as soon as he got up. There were no visible physical traces of sexual intercourse on the covers. The crucial proof that someone else had not only been in the flat in the past twenty-four hours, but also in the bed, lay on the pillow. The forensic team found two curly blond hairs that clearly came from Leonard Schelderup's head, but also three longer, darker hairs that were quite obviously not his.

As I stood there looking at the three dark hairs, it seemed to me that the case had now leapt forwards towards a possible solution. I felt a stab of sympathy for the dark-haired Synnøve Jensen, but the evidence was certainly stacking up against her.

Ingrid Schelderup held her poise and control throughout our conversation and the examination of the flat. But then the tragedy apparently struck her. Sitting alone on the sofa, she suddenly broke down and collapsed in a sobbing heap. I managed to coax her back up into a sitting position. It was of course no easy thing to comfort a woman who has just found her only son shot and murdered. In the end, the constable offered to drive her home and to stay with her until she was given some tranquillizers.

At half past eight, I was sitting on my own in Leonard Schelderup's flat, with my dead host lying eternally silent and cold on the floor in the living room. My eyes rested on him while I used his telephone to call the main police station, who promised to send down some more forensic scientists to examine both him and the flat. His body was now finally released from the tension of the past few days. But his face was tense and frightened, even in death.

I sat there looking at the dead man. There seemed to be

no way around it; all circumstances now seemed to point to Synnøve Jensen. Though why she should kill her other lover and fellow conspirator, if that was what Leonard Schelderup had been, was very unclear. But the hairs on the pillow were a strong indication that that was the case.

III

I did not need to go far to question my first witness. Leonard Schelderup's neighbour was the obvious starting point and as luck would have it, she was at home.

Halldis Merete Abrahamsen was, in her own words, the seventy-nine-year-old widow of a successful pharmacist. She was well off and her mind and all her senses were still in perfectly good working order. And I could absolutely believe that. It was also obvious, however, that her social life and horizons had shrunk somewhat since her husband had died and the children had moved out. The pictures, books and furniture were all those of a woman who spent an increasing amount of time at home, with her thoughts drifting further and further back in time.

This was a sad situation for Halldis Merete Abrahamsen, but very good for the investigation, as she seemed to have developed a keen interest in her neighbours instead. A small pair of binoculars placed to hand on the windowsill in the kitchen confirmed my suspicions in this regard. And the young Leonard Schelderup held a special position amongst the neighbours. This was due no doubt to the fact that he lived in the flat next door, but perhaps even more to his name and family fortune. Mrs Abrahamsen proved she had an impressive memory when she rattled off her neighbour's family tree and the most recent estimates of the family's wealth.

'One still reads the papers and takes an interest in those around one,' as she put it.

The widow first of all expressed her shock at the news about the 'handsome young man's tragic death', and then proceeded to tell me everything about him. As a neighbour he had been very considerate and never disturbed her in any way. He left for work early in the morning and often came home late at night, because of his training sessions. Other than his mother, he seldom had visitors, and on the rare occasions that he did, the guests all left early without making any noise in terms of music or other boisterous behaviour.

She then lowered her voice discreetly and confided in me that a mysterious man had come to see him in the evening several times this autumn. As she remembered him, he was a young, dark-haired man, but she was a little uncertain of his age as he had a beard, and was wearing a hat and a winter coat with the collar turned up. 'As if he was doing his best not to be recognized by anyone. Isn't that rather odd?' she added in a whisper. The only thing she could say with any certainty about the guest was that it was a man, and that he was above average height.

I dutifully noted down all the information about this apparent stranger. It was clear that her description did not fit any of the guests from Magdalon Schelderup's last supper, unless it was Fredrik who had come wearing a false beard. On the other hand, it seemed unlikely that the murder of Leonard Schelderup had nothing to do with the murder of his father the day before. With the exception of his family and their fortune, Leonard Schelderup appeared to have lived a quiet life.

I pressed on and asked if there were ever any lady visitors.

Mrs Abrahamsen leant in towards me and lowered her voice even more. It turned out that Leonard Schelderup had lived there for 'more than four years and seven months', but she could not ever remember seeing a woman come here, other than his mother. 'But then last night,' she whispered with glittering eyes, 'last night of all nights, I think he had a visit from a lady! Now isn't that a coincidence?'

I had to agree with her and made a quick note.

Halldis Merete Abrahamsen had unfortunately been in the bathroom when the mysterious lady arrived. So she had only heard the clicking of her heels when she arrived at a quarter to eight and then the door closing behind her. She left again at twenty-five to ten, just as it was starting to get dark. But the widow had managed to catch a glimpse of a mink coat, small red hat and high-heeled shoes. The visitor had walked quickly down the path without looking back and then disappeared from sight. A woman of 'good social standing', that was obvious, but Mrs Abrahamsen was unfortunately unable to give any more details about her age, hair colour or appearance. But she categorically dismissed my suggestion that it might have been Ingrid Schelderup who had popped by to see her son. She knew the mother's footsteps too well. This was a lighter tread that she had not heard before.

The first part of the story only served to strengthen my

suspicions regarding Synnøve Jensen, to the point that I nearly drove straight out to arrest her. But then I hesitated when I heard that the visitor had a mink coat. I could not imagine that Synnøve Jensen would possess such a garment and had certainly seen no sign of anything resembling that in her humble abode. This was followed by another cold shower when I realized that Leonard Schelderup had telephoned me after the woman had left. So it was difficult to imagine anything other than that he was still alive.

When I asked about any later visits, Mrs Abrahamsen was evasive and apologetic. As she was not expecting any further drama that evening, she had gone to bed around ten o'clock; she had slept soundly, as she was suffering from a cold. She had woken up around midnight and thought that she heard some hasty steps outside on the stairs, but had then fallen asleep again without hearing any more. The doorbell had not rung, because then she would have heard it. When I asked whether the footsteps she heard later on that night could have been the same, only this time perhaps without heels, she was ashamed to say she did not know. She had only been half awake, and did not dare say anything other than that the footsteps she had heard around midnight were hasty.

This could undoubtedly still be combined with my theory so far, that it was Synnøve Jensen if not both times, then certainly the second time, and it was she who had shot Leonard Schelderup in the early hours. It could well have been out of desperation because he had got cold feet and wanted to confess that he was the father of her child and that it was they who had killed his father.

The theory was in no way idiot-proof, I had to admit. It grated even on my ear. But still it grated less than all the other theories I could think of, so in the end I got into my car and drove out to Sørum.

IV

Synnøve Jensen sat at the kitchen table and cried.

For a long time. Her tears dripped onto my hand when I eventually reached out to put it on her shoulder. Either she was a particularly good actress with a talent for crying when the situation so required, or she was telling the truth when she maintained that she was very sad to hear about the death of Leonard Schelderup. She had never really had the chance to get to know him properly, but he was, after all, the brother of her unborn child and he had always seemed like such a quiet and good person, so she had not a word to say against him. And he had most certainly not had an easy life, caught between his divorced parents and in relation to his new stepmother. And another murder only two days after the first was an even greater shock. So Synnøve Jensen continued to weep.

It seemed pretty pointless after all this to ask if Leonard Schelderup had been her lover and if she had shot him. So I settled for saying that I had to ask them all to account for their movements yesterday evening. Synnøve Jensen dried her tears and mumbled that she had been at home alone all evening and gone to bed early. She had never been invited to Leonard Schelderup's home and had definitely never gone there. She had once heard his father phone him from the office, but she could not recall ever having spoken to Leonard Schelderup on the telephone. She had no idea where he lived in Skøyen or which bus to get there. None of this sounded improbable but, on the other hand, there was no one who could confirm it.

Synnøve Jensen's wardrobe was by the door and it did not take much time to look through it, limited as it was. It did in fact contain a pair of shoes that might with some goodwill be called high-heeled, but nothing that resembled a mink coat, even seen through an old lady's eyes. It struck me that the generosity that Magdalon Schelderup had shown to his mistress in his will did not seem to bear any relation to the generosity he had shown her when he was alive. I did not quite trust the idea that everything he had ever given her was now hanging here.

I drove away from Sørum with the feeling that Synnøve Jensen would definitely end up in hell if her fingerprints were found anywhere in Leonard Schelderup's flat. And if not, I almost believed her already when she said that she had never been there. And in that case I had no idea who the dark-haired woman from the evening before might be.

V

Back at the police station, I was told that the results from the fingerprint analysis were not ready yet. So in the meantime I telephoned Hans Herlofsen and Magdalena Schelderup. Both were composed and seemed to be surprised by the news of Leonard Schelderup's death. Both denied categorically that they had either called him or been to see him the day before. Both denied, even more vehemently, any knowledge as to who might have killed him. Magdalena Schelderup said that she had been at home alone, but had nothing to back this up. Hans Herlofsen had an alibi until ten o'clock: he had been in the office in the centre of town, in a meeting with three other members of staff about the future of the companies. But after that he was, in his own words, also home alone.

I spoke to both Sandra and Maria Irene Schelderup as soon as I could and the answer was much the same. Unlike the others, however, the two ladies at Schelderup Hall had a reliable alibi. Sandra Schelderup had been on the telephone to me about the time that the mysterious woman in the mink coat had visited Leonard Schelderup, and the police outside Schelderup Hall could confirm that both the mother and daughter had stayed at home. They had appeared in the windows at various times during the course of the evening and no one had left the house. The dogs had been quiet all night.

I breathed a sigh of relief at this news and patted myself on the back for having maintained a police presence at Schelderup Hall overnight. The terrifying thought that young Maria Irene might be involved in the murders in any way receded, even though last night's alibi did not mean that either she or her mother could be excluded from having taken part in the murder of Magdalon Schelderup.

Sandra Schelderup also seemed pleased to have an alibi.

In light of this, I then let her decide whether she felt it was necessary to keep a police guard at Schelderup Hall or not. She thought for moment or two and then replied that as they had the dogs and since there was really nowhere to hide in the garden, the officers could perhaps leave the following day, unless of course there were any signs of danger in the meantime.

I had just lifted the receiver to call the Wendelboes when I suddenly remembered the questions that Patricia said I should ask about the war. I also needed to get hold of Fredrik Schelderup to tell him about his brother's death, and to pay him a visit. So in the end I made a brief telephone call to both of them only to arrange a visit within the next couple of hours.

VI

One could not help but admire Fredrik Schelderup's equilibrium, or be deeply shocked by his indifference. I tended more towards the latter. Whichever it was, he certainly seemed to be extremely at ease as he lounged opposite me in the comfort of a velvet sofa in his spacious home in Bygdøy. He had graciously accepted my condolences on the loss of his brother, but showed absolutely no sign of grief.

I thought to myself that Fredrik Schelderup's home suited his personality: the house and furniture were of high quality, but their owner had done little to look after them. The room was dusty and untidy. The most striking feature was all the wine glasses and flutes that covered every surface, and the second most striking thing was the drinks cabinet that was larger than a fridge.

Within the last twenty-four hours, Fredrik Schelderup had lost a half-brother and seen his inheritance increase by millions. Neither of these things appeared to have made much of an impression on him. But the man was not entirely without social antennae. He quickly registered my surprise at his lack of interest and started to talk without being prompted.

'You must excuse my lack of visible grief. That is what happens when you grow up in Schelderup Hall and have more money than you deserve. Leonard had a mother I did not care for and paid no attention to, and I had a mother he did not care for and paid no attention to. The only thing we shared was a father whom neither of us cared for, but both always paid attention to. And not only were we born to the same father from different mothers, we also inherited different genes from him. We shared many of the same problems, but solved them in very different ways. Leonard chose to rise to Father's expectations by succeeding in arenas other than those Father had hoped for. And my choice to have no ambition whatsoever was even more provoking.'

I asked him to elaborate, which he immediately did.

'I have been extremely fortunate in terms of the money I have inherited, but perhaps not the genes. The only thing my mother ever did to ensure an easy life was to trick my father into marrying her. I did not have to lift a finger in order to live a comfortable life. And so I never have. You see, I am not stupid, just lazy and lucky. I only hope that my liver holds out longer than my mother's did. And here's to that,' he said, lifting the wine glass to his mouth. I suspected that it was neither the first nor would it be the last of the day.

The most important question in terms of my murder investigation was simply whether Fredrik Schelderup had visited his brother in his flat at any point over the past few weeks. His answer was a clear no. The last time he had been there was at least a year ago. Contact between the two brothers had been sparse in recent years. It was generally Leonard who got in touch for practical reasons, and a short phone call would suffice. I used this opportunity to ask whether they had been in touch by telephone the day before, but once again he shook his head.

Another question was whether Fredrik Schelderup knew of anyone who might have visited his brother. He immediately replied no to this as well. He and his brother moved in completely different circles, apart from family, and they had no mutual friends.

'If anyone in the family knows anything about Leonard's friends, it would be his mother. But I would not be surprised if she did not know much either. She of course worshipped him. But I was always under the impression that he kept everyone at a distance, even his mother.'

I sent him a questioning look. He continued without hesitation.

'Growing up as Leonard and I did can generate very different responses. In Leonard's case, it was obviously important for him to be able to go his own way, even in terms of his mother. His mother's greatest dream was always to move back to Schelderup Hall. If Leonard had ever been asked to stay there again, I think he would have set a new national record in his bid to get away.'

Fredrik Schelderup emptied his glass and poured himself some more wine. He was in a chatty, if somewhat pensive, mood now.

'There would be more atmosphere on the moon than at Father's Sunday suppers. It must have been unbearable for Leonard. I was always surprised when he showed up. As long as he lived, Father had an almost hypnotic effect on us all, and Leonard would never have confronted him as he disliked conflict so much. All the millions we stood to inherit must have been important even to Leonard, but they were without a doubt more important to his mother.'

Fredrik Schelderup sat contemplating something in between two glasses of wine. He lit a cigar, but it did nothing to lift his mood. Now he spoke finally in a voice that was almost sad.

'I have never believed that Leonard would ever be happy, and I don't believe that he did either. Regardless of whether he won gold or a stipend to do a Ph.D. All the same, in recent months it seemed as though his heart was lighter. What a tragic end to a short and no doubt challenging life.'

He looked sombre when he said this. It seemed that the gravity of the situation had finally caught up with him. However, when I asked if the reason for his brother's lighter mood in recent months was a woman, he shook his head with a disapproving look.

'One should of course never give a categorical no when it comes to women, as I have learnt from experience. But I have never seen Leonard with a woman outside the family home for years, and have no reason to believe there was a woman in his life now. And in any case, I have enough problems with my own personal life as it is, without having to worry about my brother's as well.'

His little joke cheered him up and he put his glass down on the table with purpose.

'And talking of my personal life, I am expecting a guest soon and she may actually be one worth holding on to. We are going to celebrate my inheritance and then discuss the possibility of using some of it on a trip to Brazil's balmy beaches, as soon as the investigation is over. So unless you have any more questions to ask today . . .'

I did not, and I longed to get out into the fresh air. I had started to realize that behind Fredrik Schelderup's play-boy image there might lurk a sadder story and a sharper observer than one might at first think. I did not trust him any the more for that, and though I doubted that a murderer would behave in this way, I felt uncomfortable sitting at the table with a man who, within hours of his only brother's death, would be celebrating his inheritance with wine, women, and song.

Leonard Schelderup's frightened voice from the evening before persisted in my mind like a bad conscience. As did the picture of his dead body and contorted face. So I quickly asked a final question as to whether Fredrik was aware of any changes in his father's health in the past couple of years. He replied that he was not, but would not have been told until it was strictly necessary. His father had never liked to share his weaknesses and came from the old school that kept any such worries secret even from their family for as long as possible. Following this answer, I decided that there was nothing more to be gained from talking any further to Fredrik Schelderup today.

VII

Who could tell me about Leonard Schelderup's life now that his father was dead, his mother was asleep and his brother knew nothing, proved to be a good question.

The head of the institute at the University of Oslo was not of much help. 'Young Mr Schelderup' had had very good qualifications and made a favourable impression, but he had only been there for six months and so had not yet got to know his more senior colleagues. As his supervisor had been abroad on sabbatical, the young Mr Schelderup had mostly worked on his own. The head of the institute thought that he seemed very nice, if a bit shy. I agreed with this conclusion, even though it did little to help. The conversation ended with the head saying that they had no doubt lost a great talent and that it would unfortunately mean a lot of work for the institute as the stipend would have to be advertised again.

The athletics club was my next port of call, but there was not much to be had here either. The chairman of the club expressed his sorrow and said what a loss it would be to the team only days before the annual Holmenkollen relay race, and then gave me the number of the man who had been Leonard Schelderup's trainer for many years.

Other than the dead boy's mother, the trainer was the

first person who sounded as though he would genuinely miss him. He said in a gentle voice that not only was Leonard Schelderup one of the greatest talents he had ever met, but also one of the greatest people. There was an incredible contrast between his iron will and competitive instinct on the track and his gentle, considerate nature otherwise. As far as the trainer could remember, he had never said no when the club asked him to do something. In the past couple of years, however, it had been generally understood that it was best not to ask without warning. They could see that it made him uncomfortable and they feared it might ruin his concentration in competitions.

The trainer had met Leonard Schelderup's mother on numerous occasions, and also his stepmother and sister a couple of times, but he only knew his father through the media. Leonard had been in the club since he was fourteen, but only his mother ever drove him to training in those early years. Then, when he was sixteen, he started to come on a bike and, later, when he had turned eighteen, in a car. But always on his own, as far as he could remember. It was not generally known in the club whether he had ever had a girlfriend. If I wanted, I could have the names and numbers of some of the people he had run and trained with, but it was unlikely that any of them had ever been to his home.

One of the youngest members of the relay team had once called Leonard Schelderup 'the lone horseman', obviously inspired by some boys' book about the Wild West. And the nickname had stuck, as a fond sign of respect. He had always been quite reserved as a person, but presumably that was in part due to his family background and wealth. In contrast to his son, the father was widely discussed and disputed, the trainer added.

I understood what he meant. Though he had never actually been there in person, Magdalon Schelderup had affected his son's life even in athletics circles. But to them, Leonard was simply the lone horseman, and apparently no one had tried to find out what was hidden behind his hero's mask.

Otherwise, the trainer agreed that Leonard Schelderup had had more of a spring in his step in recent months. The trainer had thought that this was perhaps in part due to his steadily improving performance and in part to resolving his work situation. I thanked the trainer for all his information and asked if I might call again if necessary. He replied sadly that of course I could ring, but he was unlikely to be of any more help to me.

Having put down the receiver, I sat in my office for a few silent minutes, deep in thought. Leonard Schelderup had, to an apparently alarming extent, been, if not a man without character, certainly one without a private life. He was someone towards whom no one felt any ill will but, equally someone whom no one, not even his brother, would miss. Leonard Schelderup had, to all intents and purposes, walked a lonely path through the inhabitants of Oslo, from his flat to his office to the athletics track, interrupted only by unwanted family gatherings. Even though he had not been willing to follow the path his father wanted, his short life had been deeply influenced by him. I thought about Patricia's concept about satellite people, and found it frighteningly fitting.

There appeared to be no conflicts outside family circles that would give anyone reason to want Leonard Schelderup dead. Yesterday's lady visitor was now even more mysterious and interesting, as was the unidentified man who had apparently visited him several times in the past few months.

VIII

The Wendelboes' house in Ski was more or less as I had expected it to be. Visibly smaller than Schelderup Hall, it was still larger than all the other houses on the street and most other houses in Oslo. There was only one car parked outside the house, but it was also quite possibly the largest and most expensive in the street. And it was a spacious white Volvo that I immediately recognized from outside Schelderup Hall. The car was newly polished and the lawn around the house had recently been cut.

I immediately felt more at home here than at Schelderup Hall. Petter Johannes Wendelboe opened the door himself and showed me into the living room. Having seated me in a comfortable chair by the dining table, he then said he would go and get his wife. I said that some of my questions were about the war and that we perhaps need not disturb her. He nodded and promptly sat down on the chair opposite me.

'That is very considerate of you. This tragic event has brought up many old memories that are still very hard for my wife to bear,' he told me.

I glanced quickly around the room. It was far more lived-in than the drawing room at Schelderup Hall. This was partly because the room was smaller. There were only eight chairs around the dining table. However, the main difference was all the family pictures on the wall. It is true that Wendelboe was not smiling in any of them but, photographed in shorts with his daughter and two grandchildren eating ice cream, he could be taken for a grandfather like all others. The sense of gravity was always there. The largest picture on the wall was an old black-and-white photograph of the couple in younger days, together with Ole Kristian Wiig. Mrs Wendelboe had one arm around her husband and one around her brother, but she was leaning most towards her brother.

He followed my gaze and cleared his throat.

'My wife is a kind-hearted good woman and she was exceptionally close to her brother. It was a great loss to her that touched her life deeply.'

It struck me that this loss had also greatly affected Wendelboe's life, but that he perhaps would rather die than admit it.

My initial questions about the recent events were quickly answered. He had heard about the young Leonard Schelderup's death on the radio. It made the situation even more tragic and had been yet another blow for his wife. Neither Wendelboe nor his wife could claim to know Leonard Schelderup well, but they had seen him regularly since he was a child during the war.

'We have talked about it many times. He was obviously a very talented young man, but quite unlike his father,' he observed.

'That nearly sounds like a compliment,' I ventured.

Wendelboe tightened his lips.

'Well, yes and no. They were, more than anything, incredibly different. Magdalon was a remarkably strong and successful man, but also a remarkably ruthless man. For a long time we have thought that his son seemed to be kinder, but also weaker.'

I nodded to encourage him on. He hesitated, but then continued.

'My wife and I were by chance sitting in the grandstand when he won the Norwegian Championship last year. Our eldest grandchild was taking part, but was far less successful. We commented then that Leonard must have inherited some of his father's willpower after all. My wife suggested that we wait for him outside the entrance after the ceremony, so we could congratulate him. And I am very glad now that we did. It was clear he was extremely grateful that we did.'

Wendelboe was not one to waste words, but it was easy to believe him when he said this. I suddenly understood what Leonard Schelderup had meant when he said that behind his mask Wendelboe had more human warmth than his own father.

However, Wendelboe did not have much more of any help to say. Neither he nor his wife had ever visited Leonard Schelderup in his flat. They had been at home together the evening before. Wendelboe had suggested inviting a couple to dinner, but his wife had not been up to it, he added, pointedly. I certainly found this to be believable, but noted down all the same that, in reality, the Wendelboes did not have an alibi.

It seemed to me that Wendelboe's eyes flashed as soon as I said that we now needed to talk about the war. His replies were concise and relatively unemotional as long as we talked about the Resistance group. What he remembered about the dead Resistance men was more or less what was written in the archives. Hans Petter Nilsen had been found dead in his home on 12 May and Bjørn Varden on 5 September 1941. He explained his excellent memory by saying that the death of friends during the war was not something one forgot. Furthermore, he and his wife had talked a lot about it later. Nilsen had lived alone and had neither siblings nor parents who were still alive. Varden had a young wife by the name of Mona, who, as far as they knew, still lived at the same address in 32B Grønne Street.

I made a note of this and swiftly moved on to talk about when Magdalon Schelderup had joined the group. According to Wendelboe, it had happened rather unexpectedly in the summer of 1941: in other words, between the two murders. Wendelboe had at first been rather sceptical and pretended not to know him when Schelderup contacted him. They had studied together for their university entrance exam and their families knew each other, but they were not close friends. The fact that his brother and sister were both members of the NS certainly did not play in Schelderup's favour. However, he was a man of action, the type of man they needed, and Wendelboe had somewhat reluctantly allowed himself to be persuaded by Ole Kristian Wiig to contact Schelderup again, who had been positively surprised and quickly proved himself to be trustworthy.

We sat looking at each other for a moment or two. He hesitated when I asked him in what way Schelderup had proved himself to be trustworthy.

I hastily added that the case would of course be time-barred and that I did not need any names, but had to know what happened. It could be of vital importance to the murder investigation and might even shed new light on the old war cases.

Wendelboe gave a brief nod to the former and a slower one to the latter. He leant forwards in his chair and continued in a hushed voice.

'It was a liquidation. An NS member with a lot of power and too many contacts on the German side, who we thought might be a threat to us and other people on the right side. He already had numerous arrests on his conscience, and several of those arrested later lost their lives or health in German war camps. He left behind no wife or children. I have not regretted that action one single day, only that we did not take him out before. We had spoken about it even before Magdalon joined us. I was interested to see whether he would oppose it; after all, it was someone he had studied with and who was a business contact. However, it was in fact Magdalon who initiated the operation. He first suggested it sometime in December 1941. I remember the case was discussed here under the guise of a Christmas dinner.'

'And the operation itself?'

Wendelboe hesitated for a moment again, but then carried on.

'It took place later on in the spring, towards Easter 1942.

He was shot when he was out skiing. I have promised never to say who was involved in those operations.'

'But it may be vital, in terms of Schelderup's role and his murder. I have to ask whether Schelderup was directly involved in the hope that you will either nod or shake your head?'

Wendelboe gave it a couple of moment's thought, then gave a curt nod.

'Ole Kristian Wiig?'

He nodded again.

'Hans Herlofsen?'

He shook his head.

'And yourself?'

He nodded. In that moment I believed his story and did not feel the need to press him any further. Certainly not at the moment. Instead I quickly changed the subject and threw down one of the trump cards that Patricia had given me.

'One might go to these Sunday suppers because one is forced to, or because one is in love with someone who is there, or because one wants to eat, because one wants to drink, or because one likes to hear oneself talk. No one could force you to go if you did not want to; you are a loyal husband, you did not need to go there for food and drink, and you never said anything when you were there. So you went there for another reason . . .'

Wendelboe looked at me, his eyes even more alert. I also thought I caught a glimpse of respect there.

'You went there to listen. And whatever it was that you hoped to hear was about the war, was it not?'

To my surprise, my strategy still worked. He nodded again.

'The mystery of our friends who were killed in 1941 was still unexplained and unsolved. But even more, it was the other incident that spurred me to go, the one from Liberation Day.'

I asked him to tell me some more about the alleged murder. A fleeting shadow crossed his face before he answered.

'Arild Bratberg was a well-meaning, if weak, man. We should never have taken him on. I can never forgive myself for letting us make that mistake. It would not have been easy to predict such a tragedy, but the link seemed to be clear enough. After all, he was caught with a smoking gun in his hand and a totally insane explanation of what had happened. So, in the end, I could live with it.'

'But your wife . . .'

He nodded and gave a quiet sigh. His gaze suddenly left me and moved over to the wall.

'I hoped that time would help to heal the wounds. But instead it seemed to get worse when the children left home and she had more time to dwell on the difficult memories. I could well have done without Magdalon Schelderup's parties. But my wife continued to hope, so I sat there with her and listened for anything that might provide an answer. For him to say something about Ole Kristian's death, or for her to say something about the others.'

I had to think for a moment before I understood what he meant.

'And by her, you mean Magdalena?'

He nodded again.

'She might know something about them?'

He coughed. 'This may sound strange. At first we all thought that the Dark Prince had to be a man. But if the Dark Prince was in fact a woman, then it was not unthinkable that . . .'

I gave Petter Johannes Wendelboe a sharp look. He looked directly at me and his eyes did not waver. And in that moment I felt a peculiar fearful admiration for him.

'We have for all these years hoped and believed that the member of the NS whom we shot in the spring of 1942 was the Dark Prince. There were no further murders later. Magdalena Schelderup was one of the few people who might have known enough about us to be the Dark Prince. Or she may have known who it was. Whatever the case, we listened well to what she said. But there was nothing new to be learnt there, certainly not as long as we or Hans Herlofsen were close by. Magdalon, on the other hand, said something very interesting during the previous meal . . .'

He stopped abruptly, but then continued when I sent him a quizzical look.

'He suddenly announced that he had been thinking about some questions from the past in recent months, and hoped that he would finally find some answers. It was, certainly for my wife and me, reasonable to interpret this to mean the war and the Dark Prince.'

He stopped there, with one of his ambiguous smiles. Then he added: 'We of course hoped that he would say more this Sunday.'

'Did you notice if any of the others reacted at the time?'

He shook his head.

'It was completely out of the blue and said in passing. We did not notice any reaction from Herlofsen or the former Mrs Schelderup, either then or during the meal. Both my wife and I looked at Magdalon first, then quickly over at his sister. She looked, as no doubt the rest of us old-timers did, first surprised and then tense. And then there was not much more to be gleaned.'

'And you did not ask Magdalon about it later?'

He shook his head.

'No. I realize that may seem strange. But it was impossible to raise the question there and then with eleven people around the table. And I knew Magdalon well enough not to ask later. I knew that he would not answer and he of course knew that I would not ask, for that very reason. If Magdalon knew more about the Dark Prince and other things from the war, he would let me and the others know as and when it suited him.'

'Let's go back to Liberation Day 1945. If I have understood correctly, the drama took place in the home of a former NS man who had been exterminated?'

Wendelboe nodded, and again I thought I caught a glimpse of admiration in his eyes. But it still took a few moments before I summoned the nerve to follow this up, and when I did it was again in anticipation.

'Do you remember when he was killed?'

Wendelboe nodded, but said nothing.

'On a skiing trip in spring 1942?'

He nodded again, and gave an appreciative shrug.

'That was why we went to his house on Liberation Day in

1945. We hoped that we would find some papers, weapons or anything else that might confirm that he was the Dark Prince and had been responsible for the death of our two friends. Then we could finally lay the case to rest. Instead the expedition ended in tragedy with us losing one of our men, and this time one we could ill afford to lose.'

'It is easy to understand that these things have deeply affected and your wife. Imagine if we were now, many years later, to discover something that in some way linked Magdalena Schelderup, or even Magdalon Schelderup, to any of these murders, how would you react?'

When I looked up, it was all I could do to stop myself from pulling back. Petter Johannes Wendelboe controlled himself well and remained sitting in his chair, his face directly in front of mine, and spoke in a hard, low whisper.

'We now live in a free country and a constitutional state, my young man, which was not the case during the war. I would immediately telephone you or someone else in the police.' His eyes were suddenly piercing and hard.

'But the first two murders are already time-barred, and the third will be so shortly. So let us imagine that for this reason or other formal reasons, a case could not be raised . . .'

'Then I do not know what I would do. But that has not happened.'

I nodded in agreement. To contradict Petter Johannes Wendelboe in his current frame of mind was not a tempting idea at all.

'No one is claiming that it has. But it is a possibility that you and your wife have discussed, is it not? That Magdalon

Schelderup might himself in some way have something to do with the deaths?'

He nodded and hurried to reply.

'We did not believe it, but did not dare to rule anything out. The cases were so extraordinary and you never knew what Magdalon might do.'

'Magdalon was a hard man to fathom.'

'We know of nothing that might link him to the deaths and we have no idea who killed him.'

'And the disturbed Resistance man, Arild Bratberg, have you ever encountered him since?'

He shook his head firmly.

'Never. I went to the trial after the war for a day, and he cut a pathetic figure. It only served to strengthen my belief that it must have been him who killed my brother-in-law. And I have never seen him since, nor wished to.'

This was said with intensity and absolute conviction. I believed him and he felt it. When I thanked him for his help and stood up a couple of minutes later, we were suddenly on an almost friendly footing again.

Wendelboe was once more his normal relaxed and controlled self when he showed me out. I liked him better than I had when I arrived. But I had also seen a glimpse of the other Petter Johannes Wendelboe. The one who had, once upon a time, taken decisions regarding life and death, and then ensured that those decisions were carried through. And in that moment I had understood what people meant when they said that Petter Johannes Wendelboe was perhaps the only person Magdalon Schelderup was afraid of.

At the end of the day, I did not think that Wendelboe had killed Magdalon Schelderup or had anything whatsoever to do with Leonard Schelderup's death. But if I had ever been in any doubt that he might under certain circumstances be capable of killing someone, I no longer was.

We shook hands by the front door. His handshake was warm, but I was also surprised by its strength. He said once again how grateful he was that it had not been necessary to disturb his wife and added that he hoped that what he had told me would be of some help.

Just as Wendelboe was about to unlock the door, I asked one final question that might be of significance.

'Do you happen to know the name of the man Magdalena Schelderup was engaged to, the one who broke off the engagement in autumn 1940?'

He stopped mid-movement and stood stock-still looking at me for a moment.

'Yes. There was a time when I knew Magdalena Schelderup's fiancé well. He died many years ago now.'

I nodded, but still did not understand the connection.

'I would still like to know his name before I go.'

He nodded, and it struck me that he seemed almost relieved.

'Magdalena Schelderup's fiancé was called Hans Petter Nilsen. He was an unusually good man, who deserved someone better,' was Petter Johannes Wendelboe's curt reply.

Then he opened the door for me. Outside, on the front step, I commented that it might perhaps be worth my while to speak to Mona Varden. He answered swiftly that it might be a good idea, but that I should also perhaps consider talking more to Magdalena Schelderup first.

I had to concede this point, but did not mention that there was in fact a third woman I definitely had to talk to first. I was very interested to find out what Patricia would make of all of this.

IX

Back at the office, I looked through the preliminary findings from Leonard Schelderup's flat. The pathologist was confident that the cause of death was a bullet to the head, fired at close range. The time of death was less certain, but he could say with 90 per cent certainty that the shot was not fired before half past twelve and with 100 per cent certainty that it was not fired before midnight. The ballistics expert could add that the bullet in Leonard Schelderup's head definitely came from the revolver that had been found lying on the floor in the hallway.

The report from the flat was hardly sensational and not particularly uplifting. There were no fingerprints on the gun. This fact, and the position of the gun in a different room from the body, precluded all theories of suicide.

· An examination of the living room and bedroom had thus far produced traces of only two sets of fingerprints. One naturally belonged to the deceased, Leonard Schelderup. The other, which was found on both the bed and the sofa, did not belong to any of the nine living suspects.

And so I had to admit to myself, if no one else, that my

theory that it was Synnøve Jensen who had paid a visit to Leonard Schelderup's bed had come crashing down like a house of cards. Without any great hope of a breakthrough, I asked if they could examine the other rooms and also start to compare the new fingerprints with those registered in our archives. The former would take another day, the latter possibly more.

The time was no more than three in the afternoon. For want of more clues to follow up in relation to Leonard Schelderup, I turned to the questions Patricia had given me regarding his father.

Finding Magdalon Schelderup's doctor proved to be as simple as finding his telephone number. I was given both in a two-minute telephone conversation with Sandra Schelderup. Getting through to the doctor was, however, not so easy. To begin with, the telephone was engaged for ten minutes, but the problems began in earnest when someone finally answered. It took me five minutes at least to convince the super-pedant of a nurse that I really was a detective inspector. Then it took a further ten minutes to persuade her that a murder investigation had to take precedence over a consultation with a patient, even when the patient was over forty-five and had a blood pressure that was several per cent more than average.

The doctor himself was a pleasant surprise when he finally came on the line. He was so unbureaucratic and informative with his answers that I almost made up for the time lost on the engaged signal and the pedant nurse. Yes, he had been Magdalon Schelderup's personal doctor for many years, twenty-one to be precise. Yes, Schelderup had been in generally good shape both physically and mentally. Yes, something dramatic had happened to his health a year ago. Again, to be precise, on 8 July 1968.

The doctor had noted the date partly because it was his best-known patient, and partly because it was the first time he had experienced a patient having a heart attack in his waiting room. The nurse had called the doctor when she discovered Schelderup sitting almost lifeless with his eyes closed on a chair in the waiting room, mumbling incomprehensible words. He had been treated quickly and the situation had not been life-threatening. At his own wish, Schelderup had gone home after only a few hours in hospital. The heart attack had, however, revealed serious heart disease which meant that Schelderup was not likely to live much more than two or three years longer, with the risk of a new and more serious heart attack within the next twelve to sixteen months.

Nor had the doctor ever known a patient to receive such grave news with such calm as Magdalon Schelderup showed. He had later come to several routine check-ups, but had never asked any questions or made any comments as to how he felt about the situation. He had not revealed who he had told about his heart, but the doctor had the impression that he had kept it to himself.

My final question to the helpful doctor was whether he had heard anything of what Magdalon Schelderup had said when he was semi-conscious after the heart attack. The doctor remarked with a merry little laugh that that was something that Magdalon Schelderup had also asked, a few hours after the attack. He could only tell me what he had told him – and that was that the name 'Synnøve' was the only thing that had been clear to anyone in the midst of all the incomprehensible burble. Schelderup had commented with an almost joking smile that it was, in principle, perhaps not such a good thing to mention your secretary rather than your wife, but at least no great secrets had been revealed.

In short, Patricia had once again been right. Something dramatic had happened in Magdalon Schelderup's life in the summer of 1968, which provided a credible explanation as to the origins of his first will. However, any deeper significance in relation to his dramatic death in May 1969 was still unclear to me, to say the least.

My ponderings on the cases from the war were suddenly interrupted by a heavy pounding on the door. A breathless constable came into the room and, obviously impressed, informed me that they had just received a phone call from the Ministry of Foreign Affairs. The foreign minister, Jonas Lykke, was leaving on a trip to Eastern Europe the following morning, but would take the time to see me this afternoon if I could go there immediately.

X

The foreign minister, Jonas Lykke, was smaller than he looked on the television, but otherwise more or less as I expected.

The former Resistance fighter and prime minister was what could be described as corpulent with greying hair. But his gaze was still intense, his voice was dynamic and his handshake was firm. Sitting behind a large desk in his office, Jonas Lykke radiated precisely the calm and dignity that one would expect of a foreign minister.

There were two tall piles of paper in front of him. To my surprise, they both appeared to be about the mandate possibilities in the up-and-coming general election, rather than the day's foreign policy issues.

'I must say that I am not entirely sure how I can be of use with regards to your ongoing murder investigation. But I will of course do everything I can to help you,' he said after a couple of moments, in his characteristic dialect.

I took the hint that the foreign minister's time was limited and promptly launched into a hastily improvised list of questions.

In answer to my first question about the treason trials after the war, the foreign minister apologized that he unfortunately knew nothing about them. He had spent the final years of the war in Sweden. He denied any knowledge of operations carried out by Resistance groups in Oslo during that time, and he had only heard about the 'tragedy on Liberation Day' after the event. From what he had read, there was something very odd about the circumstances surrounding Ole Kristian Wiig's death. But legally the case appeared to be cut and dried and had quickly been overshadowed by the trials against leading Nazis.

Lykke sat lost in thought for a few moments after he had mentioned this, but then quickly returned to the present. He concluded in a grave voice that he unfortunately could not be of much help to me with regard to the war either. He had met both Magdalon Schelderup and Petter Johannes

Wendelboe several times later, but did not know either of them particularly well and had never discussed with them what went on in the war. At the time, Schelderup had been more interested in the Cold War and contingency plans for a possible Soviet invasion. Even after fifty, he seemed to be a man who preferred to guard against possible future scenarios rather than dwell on the past.

Jonas Lykke became obviously more animated and informative when the subject turned to the Conservative parliamentary group after the war. In fact, I thought to myself that he was remarkably informal given that he was still a senior politician. He remarked with a quiet, dry chuckle that Magdalon Schelderup had come across as 'unusually intelligent, unusually clear-sighted, unusually conservative and unusually cynical, even for a Conservative member of parliament for Akershus or Oslo!'

I ventured to ask why, then, Schelderup's career in national politics had been so short-lived. Lykke answered with another gentle smile that that problem had in fact been Magdalon Schelderup's clear-sightedness. He quite obviously preferred to be in a position of power and was realistic enough to admit that it would be many years before the Conservatives would ever form a government. When he stood down in 1953 he was fifty-four years old and had decided to concentrate on his extremely successful business empire.

It had become standard practice that the war was not mentioned unnecessarily when Magdalon Schelderup was present. But the court case from 1945 had been mentioned now and again when he was not there. Lykke added with a dry laugh that the Conservatives had a habit of dealing with sensitive issues in this way. However, he did not remember the issue from the war being raised in connection with the question of Schelderup's renomination in 1953. Lykke had certainly never mentioned it himself at that time.

Continuing in this jolly and frank vein, the foreign minister added that he had not been sorry when Schelderup decided not to stand again in the general election.

'We needed a right-wing coalition, and he was not someone who promoted that. He was far too conservative for those on the left, and too urban for members of the Centre Party. And the Christian Democrats strongly disapproved his divorces.'

I understood what he was saying and had to reluctantly concur with Jonas Lykke that there was not much of relevance to the murder inquiry here either. As a politician, Magdalon Schelderup had been respected, but not liked, not even within his own party. He appeared to have left politics of his own volition, and if it was the case that he was pushed, it certainly seemed to have nothing to do with events during the war. I did not think that Jonas Lykke knew anything more of importance about the war, and was fairly sure that if he did, I would not be able to wheedle it from him.

So I thanked the foreign minister cordially for his time. He shook my hand and jokingly wished me luck with 'both the spring murder investigation and the autumn election'.

The final seat in Oslo was evidently very uncertain and could be decisive, according to the sheet on the top of the left-hand pile that I glanced at as I left the room. Jonas

Lykke had already turned his attention back to the papers by the time I closed the door behind me.

XI

The yellowing papers from the war were waiting on my desk when I got back to the office.

According to these papers, the NS member whose house Magdalon Schelderup and Ole Kristian Wiig had visited on Liberation Day 1945 was called Jens Rune Meier.

I quickly found the case in the archive for unsolved murders under 1942, and could thus confirm that Wendelboe had thus far proved to be reliable. Jens Rune Meier had indeed been shot when out skiing at the start of Easter 1942. The operation had obviously been well planned. The police found the tracks of the perpetrators, who had clearly been familiar with his route and lain in wait behind some undergrowth on a more deserted stretch. The ski tracks led back to the car park, and even though considerable resources were given to the case, not enough evidence was found to pursue it.

At the time of his death, Jens Rune Meier was unmarried. He was a thirty-two-year-old lawyer who lived in Kolsås; a Norwegian citizen from a good middle-class family, but his grandfather had been from Germany, so he had a German surname. It would appear that the occupying forces and the NS had had high hopes for him and, if rumour was to be believed, he was being touted as a possible cabinet minister in Quisling's government.

Jens Rune Meier glared at me from a black-and-white passport photograph dated autumn 1941, and from a report about the attack in the NS newspaper, *Fritt Folk*. I sat there for a couple of minutes looking him in the eye without finding the answer as to whether he had been the Dark Prince or not. Following liberation in 1945, no guns were found that in any way resembled the missing 9×19mm calibre Walther pistol. I sat there a little longer musing on where it might be today, as I wrote the short daily report for my boss. The report was not the best I had written, in terms either of language or content. My thoughts were preoccupied with what Patricia might be able to deduce from the new information about the case. In the end, I put the report to one side and drove over to see her a quarter of an hour earlier than agreed.

XII

Patricia listened while we ate the starter and I told her in detail about how Leonard Schelderup was found and the circumstances surrounding his death. She uttered a disapproving 'hmmh' several times. And this was clearly not with reference to the delicious vegetable soup.

But she really only got into her stride shortly after the main course had been put on the table and I finally told her about my visit to Petter Johannes Wendelboe. She then became so intensely interested that it took several minutes before she even touched the tenderloin on her plate. I had both expected and hoped that she would show greater interest in Magdalena Schelderup and her wartime fiancé. What instead fascinated Patricia was the chronology of her fiancé's death and other events that took place within the group.

'Hans Petter Nilsen was killed on 12 May and Bjørn Varden on 5 September 1941. Magdalon Schelderup joined the Resistance group in the summer of 1941, and the NS member, Jens Rune Meier, was executed at Easter 1942, following Schelderup's suggestion just before Christmas 1941 . . . The pattern is so striking that I do not for a moment believe that it is coincidence.'

I nodded and racked my brains to discover what this striking pattern might be.

'Did you ask Wendelboe if he could remember what date Magdalon Schelderup joined the group? Because that is one of the two key questions that I need to have answered before I can move on.'

I shook my head apologetically. Patricia's reaction was as instantaneous as it was surprising. She lifted her telephone from the table and held the receiver out to me.

'Then ring him and ask now!'

I looked at Patricia, astonished, and saw that she was deadly earnest and impatient.

'Please call Petter Johannes Wendelboe at once! This is extremely important, and will possibly determine whether my theory is correct or not. And if my theory is right, we will have taken a great leap forward.'

I was not entirely sure about calling the Wendelboes at this time in the evening, so tried to bide my time.

'And what date would Schelderup have to have joined for your theory to be confirmed?'

Patricia did not bat an eyelid and replied immediately.

'If I was going to give a date for when he joined the Resistance movement, I would say 23, 24 or 25 June 1941. But any time within a fortnight after would also fit. If, on the other hand, Wendelboe says that Magdalon Schelderup joined earlier, then my otherwise alluring theory falls apart.'

I understood nothing. Not a jot. Either about what kind of theory one might build around the chronology of these events, or where the dates 23, 24 or 25 June had sprung from. I sent Patricia a pleading look, but she continued to stare at me without touching her food. As I then continued to prevaricate, Patricia did the most extraordinary thing. She dialled the number from memory and quickly handed me the receiver. I had barely had time to put it to my ear when I heard an authoritative male voice say: 'You have called the Wendelboes, can I help you?' Patricia leant forward across the table to hear what he was saying.

I stammered an apology for disturbing him again, but assured him that I only had one short, straightforward question about the Second World War, which was of some importance, and that was if he could remember around what date Magdalon Schelderup had contacted him in 1941 to offer his services.

'The twenty-fourth of June.'

The date rang out in my ear. I had to put my other hand up to the receiver in order not to drop it in surprise. And above the telephone I saw Patricia sitting waving her hands triumphantly above her head in silence, like a footballer who has just scored a goal.

'And you are absolutely certain of that?'

I could hear the sceptical edge in my own voice, but there was no doubt whatsoever in his.

'Absolutely certain. I understand if you find that hard to believe. But 24 June was my brother-in-law Ole Kristian's birthday, and I was on my way home from his place when I was stopped by Magdalon. And given what happened later, we have always felt that it was a bizarre coincidence.'

I had to agree with him there. I thanked him and put down the receiver. Patricia had now began to eat her meat with gusto, an unusually smug smile on her lips.

'The cook really has found a perfect tenderloin this time. Sheer luck, of course,' she commented, after a few mouthfuls.

I gave her a deeply exasperated and admiring look.

'You would have been burnt as a witch in the Middle Ages for less, Patricia. How on earth did you manage that? And why on earth was 24 June 1941 significant, except for Ole Kristian Wiig's birthday?'

Patricia took pleasure in slowly swallowing a mouthful of meat before answering. Then she took the book about battles of the First and Second World War from the pile and put it down on the table between us.

'Fortunately we are not talking about the Middle Ages, but about the Second World War. Nothing special happened on the 23, 24 or 25 June 1941 but, as you know, that made what happened on 22 June all the more dramatic. Keyword: Operation Barbarossa.'

I inwardly cursed my lack of interest in history at school and waved her impatiently on.

'Germany invaded the Soviet Union, slowcoach, only the greatest military offensive in the history of the world. Three million soldiers marched in a line that was nearly 1800 miles long. And still it caught Stalin and his generals by surprise. The German military machine appeared to be indomitable. Some intelligent and far-sighted people in different parts of the world realized quickly what was about to happen – that Germany was going to bite off more than it could chew, that a great backlash would start in this confrontation with the Soviet Union's vast population and hard winters. And one of them was Magdalon Schelderup of Gulleråsen in Norway, who, when the opportunity arose a couple of days later, joined the side that he now thought would win the war.'

Patricia ate a few mouthfuls more, licked her lips and looked very pleased with herself when she continued.

'The balance of resources in the war definitely tipped in favour of the Allies when the USA was forced to join the war following the Japanese strike on Pearl Harbor on 7 December 1941. Once again, a technical military success that was also a huge mistake on the part of the Axis powers. A few days later, Schelderup contacts Wendelboe again, this time to suggest that he and the others should liquidate the NS member who they suspect is the Dark Prince. The chronology of the war and Schelderup's movements in Oslo is remarkable.'

'But was this Jens Rune Meier really the Dark Prince, then?'

Patricia shook her head, but took the time to help herself to some more meat before answering. There was certainly nothing wrong with her appetite any more.

'We're on less firm ground there. But lots of pieces fall into place if Jens Rune Meier had to die not because he was the Dark Prince, but because he knew who the Dark Prince was. Particularly if my theory of who the Dark Prince was is correct.'

Patricia chewed happily for a minute before looking up at me. I was still so confused by this sudden change in scenario that it was all I could do to ask who had killed Hans Petter Nilsen and Bjørn Varden then, according to her theory. The answer was like a punch in the stomach.

'Magdalon Schelderup, of course. You are forgetting to eat,' Patricia remarked. It was only then that I woke from my trance-like condition.

'What extraordinary reasoning. You have surpassed yourself. But we cannot be sure about that.'

Patricia nodded thoughtfully.

'No. But we are starting to get to know the quite remarkable Magdalon Schelderup rather well, following his death. He thought, as his sister said, more like a player than a normal person. He would sooner change the wind than his coat. But if the wind was not for changing, he would swiftly turn his coat. And it is quite obvious that this is what he did in 1941. Whether he went so far as to kill two members of the Resistance is, however, not so clear. There are other possible explanations.'

'That Magdalena Schelderup was the Dark Prince, for example?' I asked. It was a theory that I had found hard to dismiss, particularly given the information that the wartime fiancé who had let her down was one of those murdered. It was tempting to think that arresting her for the two old murders and two new ones would tie up all the loose threads in this extraordinary case.

Patricia nodded.

'For example, yes. Or Herlofsen. Or Wendelboe. Or even Mrs Wendelboe or Ingrid, Magdalon Schelderup's wife at the time. Keep a note of anything you find of interest when you speak to Mona Varden and others tomorrow. But in the meantime, Magdalon Schelderup is at the top of my list of suspects for the two murders. And I would double the odds on him. He obviously seems to have known who else was in the group when he contacted Wendelboe on the way home from Wiig's birthday. Again, the chronology fits suspiciously well. In spring 1941 there was great optimism on the German side, and the outcome was not yet clear. From a player's perspective, it makes perfect sense that Magdalon Schelderup engaged in a secret operation for the Germans. In autumn 1941, the campaign in the Soviet Union still looked unexpectedly promising for the Germans. This may have inspired Schelderup to carry out another murder and, for example, tell his contact that he had joined the group as a double agent.'

I had to agree to the logic in this, but still found it hard to accept that Magdalon Schelderup was the Dark Prince. We agreed to hold the option open in anticipation of further information.

'What about the other incident from the war, the mystery of what happened on Liberation Day?' I asked.

Patricia put down her cutlery and leant forwards across the table.

'That is also of increasing interest. There is a possible connection to the other murders in that it happened in the house of the liquidated NS man. There is also one striking detail that the police do not seem to have noticed. But let us wait with that and the other stories from the war until tomorrow. In the meantime, try to find not only Mona Varden, but also the mentally disturbed Resistance man, Arild Bratberg, who supposedly killed Ole Kristian Wiig. If you find Bratberg, and if he is not too mad to answer some questions, then ask him the same question that you asked Wendelboe: that is, whether Wendelboe or any of the others we know have contacted him in recent years. There were five people around the table who had been there during the war and all of them could have strong motives for murder if they, rightly or not, suspected Magdalon Schelderup of wartime crimes. So please try to find this Arild Bratberg.'

I promised to do that.

'And what about the murder of Leonard Schelderup?'

Patricia sighed deeply.

'It is a shame to bring it up now when we are having such a nice time, but it really is unavoidable. I think that we are closer to solving the mystery of what happened during the war and the murder of Magdalon Schelderup than we are to solving the new mystery of Leonard's death. I have a couple of theories about who might have visited him last night, but still lack the information to confirm or disprove them. The witness account from the lady next door is important, but at the same time so full of holes when it comes to numbers, time and gender that there is not much to build on. The only person we know for certain was there and had a key is the mother, but that can be dismissed more or less out of hand. It is highly unlikely, both rationally and emotionally, that she would have killed her only child, especially when she might have earned millions more by murdering him a year earlier. It is difficult to see a motive for murdering Leonard, especially when both the mother and daughter at Schelderup Hall have an alibi. And Synnøve Jensen and Fredrik Schelderup were both too happy with their inheritance to want to murder someone in the hope of gaining a few million more.'

'Or perhaps Synnøve Jensen, if she and Leonard were having a relationship and had conspired to kill his father,' I ventured.

Patricia heaved a heavy sigh.

'But they obviously were not,' she said.

'Even though I can see no reason why, could the murderer perhaps have been someone from outside the family, with no connection whatsoever to Magdalon Schelderup's death? The hairs and fingerprints show that someone else had been there recently. And the mysterious guest has still not been identified,' I added.

Patricia lightened up, and laughed her not entirely sympathetic laugh. Then she smiled secretively.

'I shouldn't laugh; after all, murder is a serious thing. Of course the person who was not only in the flat, but also in the bed, was an outsider. I don't know who it was, but I do know what happened. What is more, I think I know how you might get hold of this mysterious guest, if that is of interest. None of it is directly linked to the murder, though. But it might still be of interest to talk to the person who left the fingerprints and the hairs in the flat yesterday.'

I stared at Patricia in fascination and nodded eagerly. With what could have passed for a shrug, she picked up her notebook and wrote down a short text, the content of which was: 'The police request that the person who visited the deceased Leonard Schelderup in his home in Skøyen on Sunday, 12 May between 10 p.m. and midnight, please contact Oslo Police Station as soon as possible. This person is not suspected of being connected with his death in any way, but must be cleared from the case.'

'Ask for this to be read out on the radio tomorrow, and I would be very surprised if you do not hear from the person in question pretty soon thereafter. The person will no doubt be following news of the case closely.'

I looked at Patricia with some scepticism and pensively stroked my finger over the last sentence.

'But, my dear Patricia, the person who visited Leonard Schelderup yesterday will naturally not contact us if he or she was, despite what we think, party to the murder. The opposite is more likely to happen. The person will not contact us for fear of being unfairly suspected of being involved in the murder. And possibly for fear of a public scandal.'

When I said the latter, my head finally started to clear.

'Because we are talking about some secret lady love, are we not?'

Patricia sighed.

'I thought the situation would be clear to any intelligent

person under forty. But apparently that is not the case. Secret lady love or something of the sort is certainly an acceptable general description, yes. But that is only down to luck, really.'

I was not entirely sure what age or luck had to do with it, but nodded in agreement and took it to mean that we were talking about a lover. How Leonard Schelderup had met this lady was interesting enough in itself.

'But how can you be so certain that this outsider, who left proof of their presence in the flat yesterday, did not murder Leonard Schelderup?'

Patricia sighed again.

'Theoretically it is not impossible. But the very reason that Leonard Schelderup did not want police protection was clearly that he was expecting a visit from this person, and wanted it to go ahead as planned. He would hardly have done that if it was someone who might have a motive for killing him. It is of course possible to make mistakes. If any theory that it was an outsider with no connection to Schelderup Hall was to hold water, however, it would, to put it mildly, be hard to explain how this person managed to get hold of the revolver from the gun cabinet at Schelderup Hall.'

I had known that, just forgotten it – or so I hoped. Fortunately, Patricia was on a roll and promptly carried on.

'Here is something to cheer you up: the investigation may in fact uncover a criminal alliance. But if that were the case, it would not in any way be linked to the murder, and would not be something that you or anyone else at the police station would wish to pursue through the courts in the given situation. And if we return to things that are of greater interest, in terms of the murder, the most striking thing in this case is in fact the murder weapon,' she added, swiftly.

I felt somewhat at sea, but still made a feeble attempt to protest.

'But surely that is the most obvious fact? You yourself just said that the revolver found at the scene of the crime was the murder weapon and that someone had taken it there from Schelderup Hall?'

Patricia nodded.

'So far so good. But why on earth did the murderer leave the gun lying on the floor by the front door? If you can give me one credible reason for that, I am almost certain that I could promise to find out who it was within twenty-four hours.'

Unfortunately, I could not. I had not given the position of the revolver much thought until Patricia mentioned it now, whereas she clearly had.

'This was in no way a crime of passion. It would seem that the murderer stole the gun from Schelderup Hall with the intention of using it to shoot Leonard Schelderup. It might of course be smart to take the murder weapon away with you in order to avoid leaving any clues. Or, one could leave the weapon beside Leonard Schelderup's dead body, which would also open up the possibility of suicide. But why on earth did the murderer take the gun out of the room, only to leave it by the front door of the flat? Say, for a moment, that the murderer was very absent-minded and forgot to leave the gun behind and only realized this on reaching the front door, the most logical thing would then be to go back and leave it by the body. There are of course several possible motives here, that one or other of the inheritors wants to increase their share, or that there is an avenger out there who, having killed Magdalon Schelderup, has now started on his children. But neither of these alternatives give any reason to leave the murder weapon in such a peculiar place. So I simply do not have a clue what to make of the murder of Leonard Schelderup.'

The maid came into the room at this point and Patricia demonstratively kept her lips closed.

'Excuse me, but are you Beate or Benedikte?' I asked the maid as she approached with the dessert. I should not have done that. She looked questioningly at Patricia, who chose to answer on her behalf.

'That is most definitely Beate. And, may I add, she is the only one you will see here now, because if Benedikte was here you would have no problem telling them apart.'

Patricia sighed and shook her head in exasperation, while the colour drained from Beate's face and she looked as though she wished she was anywhere other than here. I could of course not help but ask what had happened to Benedikte. And I should not have done that either. Patricia immediately transformed into a gossiping teenage girl. And a rather self-centred and unbearable one at that.

'Well, would you believe what the ninny has managed to do now? She let the latest of her halfwit boyfriends get her pregnant and so will now be busy with the preparations, delivery and consequences of childbirth for the entire summer. It is very tempting to say that she made the bed so she could lie in it. But it is Beate and I who have to bear the brunt of it, Beate because she now has to work every day for the whole summer, and me because the help I get will not be so good!'

Sometimes I seriously doubted whether Patricia was actually joking or not. This was one such time. I sat there, waiting for the laughter that never came. Patricia composed herself and apologized for her outburst. But she still looked more irritated than self-deprecating when she added: 'It is all very inconvenient for me, just before summer. And I could never bear little children, not even when I was one myself. Excessive IQ is really not a problem in that family. Let us hope that Beate is smarter than her sister, though she barely knows what IQ is, all the same.'

Beate's face blanched even more and she made a hasty exit as soon as she had gathered up the plates.

There were times when I wondered whether Patricia was serious, but knew that she could be truly horrible. And this was certainly such an occasion. But at such a critical stage in a murder investigation, it would perhaps not be prudent to raise the issue. So I took the episode as another example of how self-centred Patricia could be, and how vulnerable she became when the order in her domestic universe was threatened. In order to lighten the situation as swiftly as possible, I quickly asked how she knew the Wendelboes' telephone number off by heart.

'I have memorized the numbers of all those involved. You have nothing to fear, though, I will most definitely leave all direct contact with them to you. I have always found it easy to remember numbers, and being able to keep

telephone numbers in my head has proved – as just demonstrated – to be very practical.'

I had to agree with her, yet again.

XIII

Around nine o'clock I went back to the police station to
finish my report. Once I had done this I wrote out Patricia's
suggested wording for a police bulletin. In the absence of
any new findings, I could think of no other means of solving
the murder of Leonard Schelderup. It was still a mystery to
me who of the possible suspects might want to kill Leonard
Schelderup and how it had come to pass. Even though I did
not place as much weight on the position of the murder
weapon as Patricia did, I had to admit that it was yet another
puzzling piece within the greater mystery.

The police bulletin that Patricia had written was relayed
to the national broadcaster at Marienlyst by phone, and they
promised to read it out on the morning news. I was still
somewhat sceptical as to whether Leonard Schelderup's
unidentified guest would contact us voluntarily, but saw
no reason not to try.

The switchboard informed me that the newspapers had
shown far more interest in Leonard Schelderup's death than
they had in his father's. Both news desks and sports desks
were on the story now. I hastily wrote a short press release
to confirm that Leonard Schelderup had been found shot
in his own home, and that the police were working on
the premise that there might be a direct connection with

his father's death two days earlier. I also left a message that I would like to receive the census files for Arild Bratberg and Mona Varden as soon as possible the following day.

I finally drove home at around ten o'clock. Tuesday, 13 May 1969 had been a long and demanding day. After having watched a short report about Leonard Schelderup's death on the evening news, I went to bed with one more murder investigation than I had had at the start of the day. Despite this, I went to sleep that night with a growing belief that the case would be solved within a few days.

For some reason, I fell asleep with the image of two young ladies playing on my mind. One was not surprisingly Patricia Louise Borchmann, and the other was Maria Irene Schelderup. It bothered me that both the possible motives for the Schelderup murders that Patricia had mentioned could also constitute a danger to Maria Irene's life.

DAY FIVE

On Overgrown Paths

I

When I sat down to breakfast on Wednesday, 14 May 1969, the only thing I could say with any certainty was that the anonymity with which Leonard Schelderup had lived his life, despite being the heir to millions and an athletics star, contrasted dramatically with the fame he achieved in death. The main story of the day was a major fire in the centre of Tromsø, but all the big newspapers reported on Leonard Schelderup's death in the sports pages, and most of them ran a headline on the front page. 'Olympic Flame Snuffed Out' was the headline across the top of *Dagbladet*'s front page. The papers all wrote that at the time of his death, Leonard Schelderup had been one of Norway's greatest hopes for the Summer Olympics in 1972, something I could not recall any of them having written before.

All the newspapers had pulled out photographs from last year's national championships. I was struck by how unruffled and earnest he looked both before and after he crossed the finishing line, and when he stood on the podium to receive his medal. Petter Johannes Wendelboe was not the only person involved in this case who never smiled. I had never actually seen Leonard Schelderup smile, in a photograph or in real life. With the exception of the carefree, partying older son, any smiles from Magdalon Schelderup's supper guests were few and far between. I thought to myself that what Patricia had said about how terrible the case was, and how cold and bleak it was out there in the spheres of the surviving satellite people, was entirely appropriate.

I opened the door to my office at nine o'clock on the dot, just as the telephone started to ring.

'Detective Inspector Kolbjørn Kristiansen,' I rattled off when I picked up the phone. The first thing I heard was a relieved sigh, followed by an unidentified man's voice.

'Thank goodness that I have managed to get hold of you. I have nothing whatsoever to do with the murder of Leonard Schelderup, but I am the person who visited him last night between ten o'clock and midnight. I would be more than happy to tell you what little I know, if that can help solve the murder. I would rather not come to the police station if at all possible. Could I meet you somewhere else later on today?'

It was my turn to be silent for a while. As he spoke, I finally understood the circumstances.

Just to make sure, I asked if he had by any chance visited the flat on other occasions through the spring, and if so, what he had been wearing. He replied immediately that he had been there several times and that he had been wearing a hat and a coat with the collar turned up. It occurred to me that I had heard his voice somewhere before, but I was not able to place it without seeing him.

I heard myself saying that I was a liberal young man under forty too, and did not wish to cause any problems for him. So I suggested that we meet in a cafe on one of the side streets off Karl Johan, the main shopping street, at midday, and added that there was a reasonable chance that his name could be kept out of the public eye if he answered all my questions. He assured me that he would do as much as he could to help solve the murder and promised to be waiting at a table at the back of the cafe at midday. Then he put down the phone.

Left alone with the dialling tone, I decided that I had managed to clear up some of the mystery surrounding Leonard Schelderup, but that I was still far from solving his murder. I sat there and speculated idly about where on earth I had heard his guest's voice before. But that was a mystery that would hopefully be solved soon enough. So in the meantime I let it go, having first gone through a quick elimination round to make sure that it did not belong to anyone I had met in the course of the investigation.

II

As there were no better clues to follow up in the Leonard Schelderup case, I turned to the overgrown paths from the Second World War for the rest of the morning.

The first thing I encountered was a setback. The census records for Arild Bratberg stopped with the note that he was registered dead on 14 March 1969. He was recorded as living at an address in Rodeløkka, but according to his file had also spent substantial periods in Gaustad Mental Hospital. He was last registered as leaving there in December 1968, following a sojourn of one year.

I finally managed to get hold of the head doctor who had been responsible for the ward where Arild Bratberg had stayed during his last periods there.

The doctor's voice on the other end of the phone was deep-frozen to begin with. Fortunately it then thawed somewhat when he realized that I was 'that well-known detective inspector from the newspapers', and that the case might also be connected to the 'much-talked-about and very interesting Schelderup murders'. By this stage he was almost friendly.

The doctor was willing, 'between you and me', not to make too much fuss about confidentiality, given that the person in question was dead and had no family. He could therefore tell me that Arild Bratberg's death had been long anticipated. He had for many years been a 'committed chain-smoker and heavy drinker', and had developed lung cancer. At his own wish, he had been discharged so that he could celebrate Christmas at home and then die. The doctor added that there might well have been a celebration at Bratberg's home in Rodeløkka, but it was not likely that there had been many guests. Both his parents were dead and his siblings had not been in touch for years. The doctor said, by way of explanation, that seeing Bratberg was often not a pleasant experience.

The only person who had visited Arild Bratberg in

recent years was a 'very caring' elderly neighbour from Rodeløkka, a widow by the name of Maja Karstensen. She had no doubt looked after him when he got home. His answer to my question whether Arild Bratberg had been seriously and chronically mentally ill was a definitive yes. His answer to my question whether the war had contributed to this was also yes, though it was very likely that there was something there from birth or childhood. The staff all knew about the judgement after the war and he had 'maintained repeatedly on many occasions and often with great intensity' that he had never killed anyone. However, all he could do was regurgitate his ridiculous explanation over and over again. In recent years it seemed that he had become less violent, though he could still be threatening if anyone mentioned the case or challenged him in this connection.

I thanked the doctor and then picked up the telephone directory. And sure enough, there was a Maja Karstensen listed who lived on the same street in Rodeløkka as Arild Bratberg. She was at home and would be happy to talk to me if it was of any help. It might perhaps be best if I could come to her, she said, with a small sigh. Her legs were not what they used to be and she had sold her bicycle. I suggested that I could be there at half past one, and she promised to have the coffee ready when I got there.

The next mystery from the war was in connection with the Dark Prince. According to the census records, Mona Varden was very much alive and still listed in the telephone directory as living at 32B Grønne Street. She picked up the telephone on the second ring, saying: 'Mona Varden, can I help you?'

I introduced myself as Detective Inspector Kolbjørn Kristiansen and apologized for disturbing her. I would be very grateful, however, if she could answer some questions regarding the unsolved murder of her husband.

'Finally,' she said slowly, her voice trembling.

After a couple of moments' silence, she continued.

'Please don't put the phone down. Every day for the past twenty-eight years I have waited for the police to call and ask about the murder of my husband. You can come here or I can come down to the police station, whichever suits best. I will answer all your questions.'

I felt a vague sense of guilt on behalf of the police. So I mumbled that perhaps someone should have called her before, but that I would very much like to meet her today, and that I was more than happy to come to her house if that was easier for her. She did not hesitate.

'I would gladly walk barefoot from here to the police station if it would help to clear up the murder of my husband. But it is perhaps best if you come here. Then at least you can see the room where he was killed. I have left it untouched for all these years, in case someone should ask about it one day. So you are more than welcome whenever you want to come.'

I heard myself asking if three o'clock would be suitable. She replied immediately that it would be fine and that she looked forward to meeting me.

I sat holding the receiver for a while after she had hung up. The feeling that I had had before ringing Mona Varden was now stronger than ever. It was true that Magdalon

Schelderup's death was unearthing more and more interesting stories involving other people's lives.

III

I arrived at the agreed cafe to meet Leonard Schelderup's mysterious guest at four minutes past midday, having first quickly changed into civilian clothes. I ordered a coffee and a piece of cake and then made my way towards the back. There was only one man sitting there, but I could not see his face as a waiter was standing between us. I had come just in time to see the waiter, a young man of around twenty, take back a piece of paper with an autograph on it.

I caught a glimpse of the name as the excited waiter dashed past me. But by then I had already seen who the guest was and realized where I knew his voice from. It was from the sports news on the radio, and the football pitch. He was still high on the list of top scorers in the Norwegian premier league, and had played a good many games in the past decade or so with the Norwegian flag on his shirt.

He gave a short, friendly nod as I sat down. His voice, which had been loud and jocular in his conversation with the waiter, was now quiet and serious.

'It was me who called you at around nine o'clock this morning, and I'm not sure that any further introduction is necessary?'

I nodded and held out my hand. His handshake was firm, but I noticed that his hand was clammy and trembling.

'I would like to thank you for your discreet handling of

the case so far. This has been a huge dilemma for me, as I very much want to help as far as I can to solve the murder of my dear friend, but must also confess to being afraid of causing a scandal and of being suspected of murder. It was very considerate of you to come in civilian clothing, and your announcement was so carefully phrased. The use of the word "person" and the wording "to be cleared from the case" indicated that you had understood the situation, but did not wish to blow our cover.'

I nodded and said that the words had been carefully chosen. Fortunately he accepted without further question that it was I who had composed the announcement.

'So I am the person who visited Leonard Schelderup late yesterday evening. We had agreed a few days earlier that I would come. I did call him earlier in the day to say that perhaps it would be better if I didn't come, given the situation. He said that he felt cornered and that he needed to talk to me. So I went as agreed, despite the additional risk that it now entailed. I cared a lot for Leo. More than for anyone else in the world.'

He said the latter very quietly indeed. I gave an appreciative nod and lowered my voice too when I replied.

'Then it is undoubtedly your hair and fingerprints that were found in the flat, and in the bedroom. Is that right?'

He gave a tiny nod. Even though we were sitting on our own, at a safe distance from the few staff and customers who were there, his voice was almost a whisper when he answered.

'Yes. But not a lot happened there yesterday. We lay with our arms around each other; that was it. Leo needed intimacy more than anything, and was too nervous and tense to do any more.'

Again I gave an understanding nod, as if we were discussing the football results. A couple of new, younger, customers who had just come in pointed, or rather, waved at us. The man I was talking to gave a friendly wave back.

'That is quite usual, and really rather nice,' he explained in a whisper. 'Both Leo and I were quite comfortable with our fame. But of course our already peculiar double life was all the more peculiar because of it. It was very odd at times, in the midst of our joy, to know the fear of rejection and what the reaction might be if our secret got out.'

'And how long had this been going on?'

'We have known each other for five years, but have only had secret trysts at his flat for the past seven months. We had met relatively frequently in various connections before we dared to admit it, even though we both felt more and more certain. In the end it was I who had to take the initiative, by dropping in at his place uninvited. He was extremely careful in public, more cautious than most. But he was all the more affectionate when I then came to him.'

It was easy to imagine the situation and I saw no reason to ask for more details.

'Since then, things have developed as quickly as secrecy permits. Our happiness within the confines of his flat was in stark contrast to our increasing fear and paranoia outside. I think it was even worse for Leo than for me. He was terrified of how his family would react if the truth came out, especially his conservative and more than slightly tyrannical old man.'

Again I nodded to show my understanding. It all sounded believable enough.

'So no one in his family knew about this?'

He shook his head, tentatively.

'Not as far as I know. Some of them may have had their suspicions, but Leo thought that they still knew nothing. He was afraid that someone might discover us, and that his siblings and stepmother might even use their suspicions to turn his father against him. And he was worried that his mother would find it hard to accept. I am absolutely certain that he told no one, not even his mother. It was largely because he could not bear the thought of the pressure from his family – he feared that more than losing the money.'

He gave a deep sigh, and looked longingly out of the window as he carried on. Suddenly, despite his size and muscle, he reminded me of a small caged bird.

'Leo commented only a few weeks ago that if he only inherited a third of the money when his father died, then we could let the world think what it liked and escape to a more tolerant city in a more tolerant country for a few months. Somewhere where we could walk hand in hand in the streets, like other couples who are in love, and not worry what other people thought of us.'

He still had a dreamy look in his eye when he turned back from the window. Then he recognized the danger and had to backtrack.

'Please don't misunderstand. I think it was never more than a romantic dream for him to comfort himself with when life got too demanding. If he had inherited the money, we could both have left our jobs easily enough, but it would still have been very hard to leave our families and sports, certainly if we ever wanted to return. I am absolutely sure that Leo did not kill his father. Off the tracks, Leo was the kindest man on earth. I remember the qualms he had after killing a wasp in the window last autumn. That is what I liked most about him. He was a good, kind man through and through, whose only wish was to be allowed to live his life in peace without creating problems for others.'

I slipped in a quick question as to whether, only hours before his own death, Leonard Schelderup had said anything about his father's murder. His guest shook his head in apology.

'I told him last night that I would always love him, even if it turned out that he had killed his father. But all he said was that it was not him and that he had no idea who put the nuts in his father's food. He stood there in the middle of his living room and repeated it again and again, for the last time just as I left. They were the last words I heard him say.'

He looked out of the window again as he said this. I was about to put my hand on his shoulder, but then changed my mind. The situation felt fraught enough as it was, without any physical contact.

'It's so sad that Leo is dead. I miss him terribly already and it hasn't really sunk in that he's gone. But in a way, it might have been worse if he had to live his whole life constantly having to hide who he was. On several occasions we talked about the possibility that maybe, towards the end of our lives, society might have changed so much that people like us could show our love without fear or shame. I am an optimist and believe that it will happen. Leo was not so certain. He could be quite the pessimist, no doubt thanks to his family and upbringing. There had not been much joy in his life. And now it's over. And I, the great love of his life, have nothing to remember him by. I don't even know if I dare go to the funeral.'

The tears were running down his cheeks now. He tried to disguise it with a shallow cough, and then dried his face with a light-blue handkerchief.

'So I sincerely hope that you will find whoever killed him. I think it must have been someone in his family, but have no idea who. His father would have been my prime suspect, had he not already been murdered himself. You only have to ask if you have any more questions, but to be honest, I am not sure that I have anything more to tell.'

He answered the remaining routine questions clearly and concisely. Leonard Schelderup had been frightened by the threatening telephone call, but had not said who he thought it might be. It looked as though he had had another visitor earlier in the evening, but he had not wanted to say who it was or what they had discussed. There had been cups and plates on the table when he arrived, and they were still there when he left.

In answer to my final question regarding his own alibi, the man opposite me said that his wife and perhaps his two older children would be able to verify that he came home at ten to midnight.

It was only then that I fully understood the absurdity of the situation. But I could also safely say that the man I was talking to had left the scene of the crime before the fateful shot was fired. I sympathized with his grief and pain. But the idea that he would be welcomed home that evening by his blissfully unknowing wife and children, who had not the faintest idea of his double life and betrayal, was hard to swallow. So I left what remained of my cake, thanked him for the information without shaking his hand, and hurried back out onto Karl Johan. It was nearly one o'clock and almost time for my next appointment.

IV

Widow Maja Karstensen was older and greyer than I had imagined. She must have been closer to eighty than seventy and used two sticks to walk the few steps across the floor of her tiny flat. But her smile was youthful and the coffee was ready on the table. When I asked her if she had known Arild Bratberg for a long time, she replied in a voice that was both friendly and helpful.

'Yes, I would say so. Arild was born in the flat next door, and I visited him and his mother the very same evening. She was my best friend, Mrs Bratberg. You see, I couldn't have any more children of my own, the doctors had told me so three years earlier when I barely survived the birth of my second son. So it was a real joy to have a little one on the stairs again.'

I nodded and let her take the time she needed to continue. Her progress was steady, if not fast.

'Arild was a bit of surprise. His brother and sister were about fifteen years older and his father was over fifty. He died just a few years after Arild was born, so things were often not easy for Arild and his mother. Arild was small and puny as a boy, never the strongest or the smartest. But he was as kind and helpful as the day was long. And he seemed to be doing all right for himself just before and during the war. He had got himself a job as a messenger boy down at the Schelderup office in town and seemed quite optimistic about the future. He had a bicycle and dreamt of buying his own car one day. But then . . .'

She suddenly floundered and fell silent, but found her voice again after drinking some coffee.

'But then there was that terrible murder on Liberation Day. There were so many awful things going on at the time, and so many good men found their lives turned upside down by some terrible thing that happened one day during the war. Arild was one of those whose lives changed most, and in the most inexplicable way. But it was the word of a rich man from the best part of town against that of a poor lad from the east end. So Mrs Bratberg and I quickly realized how the court case would end.'

I took the liberty of commenting that the version of events that Arild Bratberg wanted the court to believe was rather wild. She let out a sad sigh.

'Yes, indeed, it was a bizarre story. Even I doubted it until more recently, and there were times over the years when he really did seem slightly mad. But then, as time passed, I too became more certain that it did not happen in the way it was told in court. Arild had his clear moments when he was sober. And he always repeated that the court judgement from 1945 was wrong. He used to say, "I might well be mad now, but I wasn't back then."'

Maja Karstensen was not the quickest of people and perhaps never had been. But I suspected that for most of her life she had been one of the kindest. Her voice was still gentle when she continued.

'It was quite obvious that Arild did lose his mind. When he was released from prison he came back home and his mother looked after him as best she could. She had little time for anything else. He was never really himself again. At any time of the day or night he would suddenly start to rant and rave about the murder; he said so many strange things, even when he had not touched a drop. His mother left the flat to him before she died in 1955. She thought that his brother and sister could manage fine on their own without it. But they didn't like that at all, did they? So he was left completely on his own after the death of his mother.'

Maja Karstensen took another short pause. Suddenly her gaze fled out of the window, over the back fence. In a strange way, this grey-haired woman reminded me in that moment of the national football player I had met earlier in the day.

'I gave my own sons to Norway and the sea, and neither Norway nor the sea gave them back. The elder one was on a boat that was torpedoed, and drowned somewhere near Shetland on 5 April 1944. I was informed of it in a letter that I received one day after the war, when I still hoped that he would come back. My younger son was on a ship that sank in the Pacific, and after seven days at sea in a lifeboat he finally managed to swim ashore to Australia. He wrote to me that he would never dare venture out onto the water again. So he stayed there, on the other side of the world, and is still there today, as far as I know. I still send letters to his old address at Christmas and Easter, but the last reply I got was for Christmas in 1953. So after my friend died, I ended up looking after her son. It was not always easy, believe me. For many years he was unbearable when he was drunk, and very depressed when he wasn't.'

I nodded in sympathy. It was easy enough to imagine. Maja Karstensen had escaped her own loneliness by continuing in her best friend's orbit around her sick son.

Arild Bratberg's life was clearly a terrible tragedy. But I did not feel that I was any closer to solving the murder mysteries from 1969 – until Maja Karstensen suddenly uttered a couple of short, but very intriguing sentences.

'Despite being ill, Arild seemed to be calmer in the final few months of his life. I suppose it was in part because he realized that he was going to die and accepted it. And perhaps, more importantly, he had finally met a couple of people who seemed to believe him.'

I gave her my full attention and encouraged her to carry on. She gave another of her gentle smiles, but then shrugged and opened her hands.

'As far as I could understand, a man and a woman came to ask him about the old case, and it seemed that they both believed what he told them. But I am afraid that I don't know who they were. Whether they meant it or not, I am very grateful to them because they helped to ease his burden in those last few months.'

I of course immediately asked when these visits had been, and whether she could remember any more of what Arild had said about them. She hesitated for a while.

'It must have been in the winter or early spring. As I

understand, the man came first and the woman shortly after. He mentioned them separately, but I can't be sure. Arild was not the most orderly person and sometimes months could pass before he told me things. It is also possible that they never came at all and that in his despair he imagined they did. But I don't think that is the case.'

And neither did I. And I would have given my eye teeth to have seen the faces of the two people who had been there. I had a strong feeling that I would recognize them both.

I asked what had happened to Bratberg's flat. Maja Karstensen sighed heavily.

'I washed and cleaned it and removed all the empty bottles, but otherwise it is as it was when he died. It turned out that a few weeks before he died, he left everything to me in his will. So his brother and sister, who have not been here for nearly twenty years, have now sent a letter through their lawyer stating that the will is not valid because he was mad. Where the case will end, heaven only knows.'

I expressed my sympathy and said that I hoped that she would get the inheritance she deserved. Then I asked if it would be possible in the meantime to have a look at the flat. She nodded and then slowly, almost ceremoniously, unhooked one of the two keys on her key ring.

V

Arild Bratberg had spent his final years and died alone in a one-bedroom flat on the second floor of a building in Rodeløkka. The flat was not a particularly inviting place in which to do either. The walls were impregnated with smoke and the paint was flaking in several places. It only took a quick look to see that Maja Karstensen had done a very thorough job of clearing the place after his death. Any hope of finding fingerprints left by guests who had been there a few weeks or months ago was as good as zero.

Arild Bratberg had obviously not been a systematic man or writer. He had left behind a substantial collection of books, but only a small pile of handwritten papers. The writing was simple, with a mixture of small and capital letters. I found seven postcards with Christmas greetings on them, all addressed to Gaustad, all written by either his mother or Maja Karstensen. There were also four pages, torn out from magazines, of crosswords that had been abandoned halfway. The pile also contained three reminders for electricity bills, the last of which was very pointed. Then I found two rough drafts of a will that did indeed leave 'my flat and contents, 325 kroner in my post office savings account and the two ten-kroner notes under the coffee tin, and anything else of value that I might own, to my precious neighbour, Maja Karstensen'.

At the bottom of the pile lay a small, plain sheet of paper with nothing on it but a name and a date. It left me transfixed, however, for a couple of minutes.

Then I put down the rest of the papers in the pile and took the single sheet of paper with me. I went back to Mrs Maja Karstensen and asked if she recognized the name on the piece of paper.

She thought about it long and hard and, in the end, said that she could not recall ever having met the man, but that Arild had mentioned his name. Could it perhaps be someone who worked at the Schelderup office during the war? I nodded, thanked her for her help and rushed away.

I was very impatient to get an explanation as to why there was a piece of paper with only 'Hans Herlofsen, 12 February 1969' written on it in the late Arild Bratberg's flat. But I would have to wait for a few more hours to find out. It was already half past two, and I had agreed to meet a woman at three o'clock who had been waiting twenty-eight years for my visit.

VI

At first glance, Mona Varden looked younger than I had expected. She was fifty-two, but in a photograph could easily have been mistaken for a woman in her forties, with her black hair and pale skin. There was, however, something about her face and movements that was heavy and serious, which aged her when you met her in the flesh. She gave a small smile when she saw me. I got the impression that she had not laughed for years – perhaps not since the end of the war. Her hand was heavy and firm, and rested in mine for a few moments.

'Thank you so much for coming. I am so grateful that a young policeman such as yourself wants to make amends for the neglect of your seniors, even though I do realize that it is the more recent murders that have sparked this interest in my husband's death.'

I could not deny this. So I gave a friendly nod and

assured her that I would very much like to clear up the mystery surrounding her husband's death at the same time.

Mona Varden had a spacious and tastefully decorated two-bedroom flat from the early 1900s. The most striking feature was a door that was barricaded by a large bed.

The coffee and cakes were already on the table when I came into the living room. As was Bjørn Varden. The photograph was old, but his eyes were still clear. The picture showed a tall, fair-haired and handsome man in a dark suit on his wedding day. His wife's dress was a dazzling white, as was her smile.

She pointed to the picture and gave another fleeting smile.

'That was on Sunday, 13 October 1939, in Gamle Aker church. The war had already started in Europe, but here in Norway everything still felt very safe. We had to marry in a bit of a rush, but were thrilled to do so. We had been together for a little over two years and I had wanted to get married for as long. But Bjørn had had a hernia when he was younger and was afraid that he might not be able to have children. And in that case, he wanted me to be free to choose another man, or so he said. Even though I assured him time and again that he was the only one for me. Then on 1 October 1939, I told him that I was pregnant. He wept with joy and asked me to marry him on the spot. We ran hand in hand to the priest, who granted us dispensation and agreed to marry us two Sundays later. We were the happiest people in the world that autumn, even though we only had a room in my mother's flat and had to borrow money for the wedding meal.'

I nodded and waited patiently for her to continue. Mona Varden lost herself in her memories for a while, but came back to earth before the coffee got cold.

'When our love child was born, she was born into an occupied Oslo. It has plagued me since that I tried to stop Bjørn the first time he mentioned joining the Resistance. I thought that his primary duty was to make sure that his daughter had a father. He said that his duty was to ensure that all the brothers and sisters she would have later were able to grow up in a free country and lead valuable lives. And he was, of course, right. My saving grace is that I soon gave in and later supported him wholeheartedly.'

She looked slightly worried when she said this. I hastily commented that I was sure that he understood and appreciated that.

'We lived in constant fear. Especially after Hans Petter Nilsen was killed by an unknown murderer in his own home. We hoped that we would be safer because there were two of us.'

With a slowness in her body, she stood up and pointed towards the bed that was barricading the door.

'My daughter and I slept in that bed, which was pushed up against the door to the bedroom behind. The idea was that if a murderer broke in, he would stop either out of compassion or because he could not get past us without causing a commotion that would wake Bjørn. I have since realized that Bjørn thought differently. He knew that the window was the risk, and we would be safe on the other side of the door.'

She carefully pushed the bed to one side and waved for

me to follow her into the bedroom. I got quite a shock when I crossed the threshold, and only reluctantly went into the room.

Bjørn Varden's bedroom had been kept as a museum of his murder, and of the man who had died in the bed here twenty-eight years ago. Some photographs of him had been hung on the wall. But the rest of the room was exactly as it had been on the morning she came in and found him dead, his widow assured me. I believed her.

'My daughter and I had all the space we needed in the rest of the flat. For many years I could not face walking through this door and, as I said, I have waited until today for the police to come and ask questions.'

She took a couple of deep breaths before she continued.

'We did realize that the window might be a risk. It was easy to open from the inside in case he needed to escape, but it was equally easy to open from the outside if the person trying to get in knew what kind of window it was. We thought it would be safe, as we were on the first floor, but an intruder would need no more than a short ladder to get in. We truly believed that no one would do it, and that no one knew which window and bedroom it was. But we were wrong.'

I asked quickly who might have known about it. She let out a great sigh and then answered.

'Everyone in the group: the Wendelboes, Magdalon Schelderup and Hans Herlofsen, as well as the late Ole Kristian Wiig. They had been here for a meeting only three days earlier. And then there was, well, the one who I always thought . . .'

'In other words . . .'

'In other words my former friend, Magdalena Schelderup, who very conveniently happened to come by for a coffee only a few days before. We had just moved in, you see, so I played the good hostess and showed her around the flat when she asked. Of course, I did not mention the issue with the window, but goodness knows whether her eagle eyes picked it up.'

I nodded appreciatively, and felt my pulse racing. Once again, there seemed to be much to implicate Magdalena Schelderup. I asked if there had been any contact since.

'With Magdalena? No, nothing. Either she killed my husband, or understood that I suspected her of it. She was certainly wise enough to stay away.'

Mona Varden stood alone with her sad memories for a moment or two. Then a cautious smile slipped over her lips.

'The others were terrific. I got money from the Wendelboes and Schelderup, so that I could stay here for the rest of the war. One day after it ended, Magdalon Schelderup himself came to see how we were, my daughter and I, and to ask how much we would need for the years ahead. He spoke to Wendelboe about it, and since then, they have deposited all the money I need into my account in January each year. I received 6,000 kroner a year from 1946 to 1951, then it was 8,000 until 1958, and from 1959 I have received 10,000 kroner every year. I have always thought that Magdalon suspected his sister but was not certain, and that he therefore showed a generosity that was not seen by many. Whatever the case, it was incredibly kind of him.'

I had to agree. It was incredibly kind of Magdalon Schelderup. And not like him in the slightest. Out of interest, I asked how long the money had continued to come into her account. Mona Varden looked almost ashamed when she replied.

'I still get it. I wrote to them when my daughter moved away from home a few years ago, and said that I could now start to work again, but the money continued to come. It was around that time that Bjørn's first grandchild was born. So I simply accepted the money and used the time to look after my daughter's child.'

I could not think of any other questions, so I asked how life was for her daughter and grandchild.

'As well as could be hoped. My daughter did not suffer the financial difficulties that many other children without fathers did after the war. But she did grow up without a father and things did not go as well at school as I had hoped, even though I got a private tutor for her for a while. Bjørn was not here and I was here all the time. I suppose she is too much like me and too little like him.'

She looked serious when she said this, but then she brightened up again.

'She has a son who is three years old now. He is called Bjørn, and is so like his grandfather. Come, have a look!'

The boy in the photograph was very sweet and all smiles. However, other than the colour of his hair, I could see no noticeable similarity between him and the Bjørn Varden in the old photographs. But it was not relevant to my investigation and I trusted that Mona Varden was a better qualified judge of that. So in my friendliest voice I said that there was a remarkable similarity and that he was obviously a very intelligent little boy. She responded with a warm smile.

To get back on track again, I then asked if she had lived here alone with her daughter for all these years.

'Yes. I said before the wedding that it was him or no one, and there was no one after him. In the years after the war, there were a few not entirely unsuitable men who showed an interest. But I wanted to dedicate my life to Bjørn's daughter, and, well, when you find the person you love dead and never manage to find out who killed him, it breaks something in you that can never be fixed.'

That was understandable enough. But I had to ask whether any of those who had shown an interest were men she had known during the war.

'Never Magdalon Schelderup and never Petter Johannes Wendelboe, if that is what you mean. Both had married well, and when Schelderup later got divorced, he was married again within a matter of weeks. So the help that he gave me seems to have been with no strings attached. On the other hand . . .'

She hesitated, but then carried on when I indicated impatiently that she should.

'On the other hand, there was a time when I got the impression that the manager, Hans Herlofsen, was interested. It was in the period just after he had lost his wife, when life was no doubt difficult for him and his young son.'

She noticed my astonishment and promptly continued.

'It was completely harmless. He stopped by a couple of times after work, talked about how much time and money two single parents, each with their own child, might save by getting married. He was not someone I would have chosen anyway. And, more importantly, I still had nothing to give any man other than Bjørn, and did not think that I ever would. I helped him to understand this and he paid no more visits. It has always been pleasant enough whenever we have met again over the years. But I really do not see what that has to do with any of the murders.'

Neither did I, if truth be told. However, I noted down a new question for Hans Herlofsen, and reflected that he had obviously forgotten to tell me rather a lot.

I remarked that I had probably seen all that I needed to in the room where her husband had been killed and that she could now do whatever she wished with the room, with a clear conscience. She shook her head sadly.

'I would love to tidy out the room, but I am not ready for it yet. I hope that I will be able to start the day after you tell me who murdered my husband.'

I took the hint and stood up to leave. I heard my voice promise to do my best and said that I would let her know as soon as I discovered anything new. At the same time I thought to myself that, no matter who had killed Magdalon Schelderup, he had indeed left a sad collection of people and fates in his wake.

VII

When I left Mona Varden at around four o'clock, it was clear to me, given the day's findings, that I should pay another visit to one of the parties. It would be impossible to finish the day without having confronted Hans Herlofsen with the new information, in particular the piece of paper from Arild Bratberg's flat. I stopped by the office to see if there was anything new there.

Most of the staff had gone home for the day and, as I expected and feared, there were no new messages from the forensic department.

There was something that caught my attention, however, waiting all alone on my desk. It was a small, slim envelope addressed to 'The head of the investigation into the murder of Magdalon Schelderup'.

The typeface was the same as the letter that I had received the day after Magdalon Schelderup's death. This envelope also contained a single sheet of white paper. However the text was even shorter this time.

Here, now.

So one of the dictator's children has gone.
More may follow, if you do not soon find out which of us is doing wrong . . .

I sat there staring at the piece of paper. Patricia's preliminary conclusions about the first letter were certainly reinforced by the second. If the sender really was the murderer, he or she was without doubt a mediocre poet who for some reason or other felt the need to show off to the police.

But I was unable to glean any more than that from the brief letter. And there was one obvious and disturbing conclusion: that more dramatic deaths were to be expected.

The sender had, reasonably enough, not signed this letter either. I made a photostat copy of it and sent the original to be checked for fingerprints – without any high hopes. With the naked eye, I could see that it was the same type of envelope, addressed in the same way as the last letter.

But there was one small, strange difference. Whereas the back of the last envelope had been white and unblemished, I discovered a tiny mark from a green pen on this one. It was a straight line, not even an inch long. But somehow I could not bring myself to believe it was accidental. In a peculiar way that I could not even explain to myself, the short green line only increased my confusion and concern about future developments in the case.

VIII

Hans Herlofsen's house out at Lysaker was larger than I had expected. It was of roughly the same size as the Wendelboes' house, a spacious home spread over two floors, with a well-kept garden. Herlofsen's old Peugeot somehow looked out of place.

The front door was opened by a young woman with a small toddler dozing on her arm. She gave a cautious smile and said that her husband had not yet come home from work, but that her dear father-in-law upstairs was at home.

I found Hans Herlofsen in a large dining room, seated alone at a big table with the remains of an early supper in front of him. He immediately indicated that I should sit down on the other side of the table. His face took on a doleful expression when I complimented him on such a beautiful, well-kept house.

'It would be hard to find another man in this town who is more attached to his house than me. I was born on the ground floor and have lived here for all fifty-five years of my life. We have a wonderful arrangement now whereby the younger generation live downstairs, on the promise that I can live here until I die. I could not imagine my life without this house and my son. It is a small miracle that I have been able to keep them both. And to have acquired a daughter-in-law who is a good cook into the bargain.'

'The contents of the will must have been an enormous relief for you?'

He nodded.

'I am more than happy to admit that. It was as though a dead weight I had been carrying around for some twenty years had been lifted, when I heard the will being read. As long as there are no complications or anything like that, I can now forget my past and start saving my own money. I have learnt to live frugally, so with no more interest and down payments to make, I should be able to save around 4,000 to 5,000 kroner a year. With the current interest rate, that could amount to nearly 100,000 before I am seventy and can retire. Which means that I could leave my son and his family a house with no mortgage and a healthy bank account. I have never asked for more, after all that has happened.'

It seemed a shame to ruin his happy, carefree mood. But it was easier to do so now that I knew he had withheld important information.

'I apologize, but I am afraid that I have to ask you some more difficult questions. I am, after all, leading a murder investigation, and Magdalon Schelderup's death was clearly a great release for you.'

Hans Herlofsen wiped his brow with a look of concern.

'No one would deny that, but I have been perfectly open about it. There are at least three others who have gained considerably more than I did, before you even count the unborn child. I had no idea that the will had been changed and, had it not, his death would quite frankly have spelled my ruin. So I find it hard to see that as a motive and, in any case, I did not kill him.'

His reasoning was logical enough. But there were still some questions regarding issues that Herlofsen had not been so open about, and I was intrigued to see how he would react.

'I went to speak to Bjørn Varden's widow today. She told me that you courted her shortly after the war. She even remembered your calculation of how much you could save if the two of you got married.'

Herlofsen was thoughtful for a moment. A sad smile twitched at the corners of his mouth before he answered.

'And I still remember those figures too: the average financial outgoings of both households multiplied by 0.75 . . . That is an embarrassing episode that I had hoped she had forgotten, and I cannot see how it bears any relevance to the present murder investigation. It only illustrates how desperate I was for the first two or three years after my wife's death, both socially and financially. Mona Varden made it clear in a very considerate manner that she was not interested and I left without protest. I later realized that it was best for everyone. I had no money and was living under such enormous pressure that I would not have been a good husband to her or any other woman. And I have since understood that she is still deeply affected by the painful memories of her husband's death. So it would have been like the deaf leading the blind.'

'There are those who would see that as a possible motive for killing her husband – if it is assumed that the killer was in fact someone else in the Resistance group.'

Herlofsen looked at me with a sudden cold animosity.

'Well I sincerely hope that no one does. Bjørn Varden was a good friend of mine and I would never have harmed him. What is more, I was myself happily engaged when he died. It is of course not unthinkable that his murderer might have been one of the six surviving members sitting at the table when Magdalon Schelderup died. But in that case, it must have been one of the other five.'

I gave him a friendly smile, and intensified my attack on his crumbling defences.

'I want to believe you, but you will first have to give me a credible explanation for this document, which I found earlier today in Arild Bratberg's flat.'

Herlofsen looked at the piece of paper and pulled a grim face. He sat in silence for a minute, sighing heavily twice before starting.

'Both the name and the date are correct. I should have told you, but I feared that I would be unfairly suspected of murder and estimated that the risk of any traces being left of my visit was fairly slim. The truth is that I visited Arild Bratberg on 12 February this year. I had pondered on it for a long time, because I wanted to find the answer to one of the mysteries from the war. I had heard rumours that he was in a very bad way indeed and thought to myself, well, it's now or never. Which turned out to be the case. According to the notice in *Aftenposten*, he died thirty-two days after my visit.'

'And how was the visit?'

He shook his head sadly.

'Very difficult. Emotional conversations like that have never been easy for me. The man was very obviously dreadfully ill, slightly intoxicated and smoked incessantly. He struck me as being rather unbalanced. He repeated his story from the trial over and over again and swore on his mother's grave that it was Magdalon Schelderup and not he who had shot Ole Kristian Wiig on 8 May 1945. He wept as he spoke and, by the end, was almost on his knees, begging me to believe him. It was an extremely uncomfortable experience and I regretted ever going there.'

'But what did you say to him?'

He looked straight at me, without flinching.

'In the end, I told him the truth: that I believed him. It made him so happy. I still think the details of his version were incredible. But I knew Magdalon well enough to know that he was capable of doing more or less anything if his own interests were at stake. Arild Bratberg was so deeply unhappy and sincere that I estimated the likelihood that he was telling the truth to be well over 50 per cent.'

He pointed at the piece of paper.

'He seemed to recognize me as soon as I arrived, even after all these years. I did not say my name and was not sure that he knew who I was. Obviously he did. So even though he was confused about other things, it would seem that the events from the war were still very clear in his mind.'

I nodded in agreement. Hans Herlofsen was a logical man and obviously remembered more than just numbers. I thought I noticed a tremor and was even more ruthless in my attack.

'During the visit, did Arild Bratberg ask you to kill Magdalon Schelderup?'

I half expected that he would collapse in his chair. Instead, he straightened up. Again I caught a glimpse of the stronger, harder man behind the pleasant façade.

'No, certainly not directly. He repeated several times that Magdalon was a calculating killer who should have been shot after the war. But he never said a word about killing him now, and did not ask me to, either. He was a broken and resigned man.'

'Do you know if any of the others involved in the case have been to see him – before or after you?'

He shook his head firmly.

'No. He did not mention anyone, but he did say that I was the first person to visit him for years, other than the woman next door. I did not contact him again later and none of the others have said that they went to see him.'

We finished the conversation there, on a relatively civil note. I asked him to let me know if he had anything more to tell me. It seemed to me that he hesitated for a second, but then he replied that he had nothing more to tell or declare, as he put it with a small smile. He repeated that he had not murdered Magdalon and did not know who had done it.

We said goodbye fairly politely at five o'clock. His hand was definitely sweaty now.

On the way back into the centre of Oslo, I passed Lysaker station just as a train was pulling out. Standing alone on the platform was a young man in his twenties who had obviously run to catch the train, but not made it. He looked so lonely and bewildered that I hoped his life would not be off-kilter for more than an hour or so. But that image of a completely unknown young man at the railway station stayed with me as an illustration of the tragedy of the now-deceased Arild Bratberg's life. No matter whether he was guilty of murder or not, Arild Bratberg had been left alone on the platform as the train pulled out after the war with all the others on board. And no matter whether he was guilty of murder or not, his loneliness and confusion were so great that he stayed there for the rest of his life.

As far as Hans Herlofsen was concerned, I knew that he had not had an easy life either, and I did feel some sympathy for him. But all the same, I did not trust that he was not the murderer, in fact even less now that he had told me the truth. When I thought about it, the same was also true of several of those who were still alive. And I would meet one of them very shortly, as I was now on my way to Magdalena Schelderup's flat in Gulleråsen.

IX

'Why did you choose not to tell me that your fiancé in 1940 was none other than Hans Petter Nilsen, who was shot by the Dark Prince the following year?'

Magdalena Schelderup looked tired and fractious. It struck me that she appeared to be older and more bitter than when I met her five days ago. She defiantly lit another cigarette before answering.

'Well, first of all, because I did not think it was relevant any more. And secondly, because I assumed that either the Wendelboes or Herlofsen would have told you already, and that you would ask if you felt there was a need. It is not something that I am proud of. A broken engagement in 1940 with a man who left me because I was a member of the NS, and who then became a war martyr. I have talked about it as little as possible since.'

'There is much to indicate that the Dark Prince may well have been one of the others who were around at the time. There are no doubt some who might think that revenge on a man who let you down was a possible motive.'

Magdalena Schelderup blew some smoke out into the room and then crushed the cigarette in an already over-flowing ashtray.

'I know more than a few who would dearly love to believe that, yes. But it is pointless all the same. The very idea that it was a crime of passion founders on the fact that I never loved Hans Petter and that he did not leave me for another woman. I did not miss him after he broke off the engagement. But I did cry for several hours when I heard that he was dead. Even though I did not love him, he was a good man. The fact that he had been shot in the dark in his own home by an unknown killer did not make it any easier. After all, I had lain there in that very bed with him only a few months before. So I dressed myself up in black and went to the funeral and have since spent many an hour speculating about who might have killed him. But I have never found a sure answer.'

'But you had your suspicions about who the Dark Prince was?'

She lit another cigarette. And once again it crossed my mind that there was something odd about her hands.

'Yes, I have had plenty of time to think about it as I whiled away the hours here on my own. In fact I have had several theories over the years. But there is one that I believe in more than the others. I am going to keep it to myself, though. It is rather tenuous and I do not like spreading rumours.'

Her answer was absolute. So I moved quickly on.

'And then there was the strange coincidence with Bjørn Varden. As I understand it, you happened to be in the flat only days before he was killed. Is that right?'

Magdalena Schelderup stubbed out her cigarette in a burst of fury and then slammed her bony hand down on the table.

'My, everyone suddenly seems very keen to blame an old scapegoat. I won't even ask if it was the Wendelboes or Bjørn Varden's poor widow who told you that. I have always had nothing but sympathy for her. She lost her one true love

227

in a much more painful way than I did. Though to be fair, she still had a child to live for, which is more than I did.'

The fire in Magdalena Schelderup's ageing body flared up fast, but then died down again just as quickly. Her eyes were darker and her voice weaker when, after a slight pause, she spoke again.

'I knew Mona Varden through her sister, who was in my class in the final year at school. We got on well back then. Then one day we met on the street and, as I had no children of my own, I was utterly charmed by hers. So I accepted her invitation to come in. I did not just turn up on her doorstep, and I knew nothing about the murder of her husband. In fact, I don't think I ever met him.'

I had nothing more to ask her. But then, all of a sudden, I did, when I saw both of her hands on the table and realized what it was that was different.

'But tell me, what has happened to your first engagement ring, the one that you said you would never take off?'

My apparently harmless question triggered an unexpected reaction. Magdalena Schelderup sobbed and hid her face in her hands before answering.

'I wish I knew myself. I was wearing it when I drove to Schelderup Hall for the reading of the will on Monday. There was so much drama there that I did not notice until I was back home that I no longer had it on. The only explanation is that I took it off when I washed my hands in the bathroom before the will was read. I phoned immediately, but they claimed not to have found it in either the bathroom or anywhere else. So I just hope that it will turn up again somewhere, but it seems less and less likely. I have no idea who has taken it, but I am sure that it was one of the others who were there. They all hate me.'

I did not say anything. I had again hoped for an explanation but had instead uncovered another mystery. I remembered clearly that I had in fact noticed something odd about Magdalena's hands at the reading of the will. When I looked at her bony old hands without any rings on, they reminded me suddenly of an eagle's claws.

'I am so upset about it. I drove around all the pawnbrokers in the area today, but no one has offered them anything similar. They would hardly have got any money for it. But I would give everything I have to get it back again. The ring is the only thing I have left from my love. Without it, I have nothing to show that we were ever together. For years I have had the notion that the day the ring disappears, I am not long for this world. I am a lonely old lady now and I perhaps believe in fate and other supernatural phenomena more than you young people do today.'

We sat in silence following her outburst. She seemed to be very old and tired, and I just felt more bewildered. Magdalena Schelderup's missing ring was yet another mystery within the murder mystery. I promised her that I would keep my eyes peeled for the ring and would contact her immediately should it turn up.

She seemed to appreciate that and apologized as I left for being so emotional. New murders that unearthed old bodies were enough to rattle anyone's nerves, she said. And it was easy enough to believe her, especially when I heard the safety chain going on only seconds after she had closed the front door behind me.

Magdalena Schelderup was increasingly becoming the incarnation of a bitter, lonely old woman. But I had to admit that she still had a sharp mind and sharp tongue. And I was not at all sure that she was not also a sharpshooter.

X

It was now half past six in the evening. The starter and main course had been eaten and the day's events recounted. While we waited for the dessert to be served, Patricia sat in silence with a look of deep concentration on her face.

'I do not like this case in the least, no matter how interesting it is. We are getting closer to the heart of the mysteries from the war and the past few days, but the details are becoming ever more alarming,' she added after a pause.

'The new letter . . .'

Her nod was very grave indeed.

'That is one of the things I like least of all, yes. There may be a danger of more deaths. And what is more, the green pen mark on the envelope reinforces a terrible suspicion that I have and sends a shiver down my spine, even though I am sitting indoors in May.'

She was quite literally shivering in her wheelchair.

'The letter is extremely short and very like the previous one, but there is not much more to be learnt from it, other than that it is possibly the same person who carried out both murders, or is there?'

To my astonishment, Patricia was already shaking her head.

'This letter is very similar to the last one, but also very different. The same type of paper, the same type of envelope, the same type of stamp and the same type of typewriter. And both contain the same pretty useless rhyming. But whereas the first is very detailed in content, the second is noticeably vague. No date, no details of the murder, not even the name of the latest victim. There is nothing to indicate that the writer had even been to Leonard Schelderup's flat. So it is best that we keep all options open for the moment.'

Beate came in with the dessert, which today was a delicious chocolate pudding with whipped cream. As usual, Patricia did not say anything while the maid was in the room, but then quickly carried on as soon as we were alone.

'The disappearance of the ring is also ominous, even though I do not believe in fate or other such superstitious nonsense. Either Magdalena Schelderup is lying about why the ring has disappeared, or one of the others has taken it. Neither of which is accidental. So I am more or less certain that one of the parties involved now has the ring, and that he or she has a plan for it, though I have not the faintest idea of what that might be. And the fact that I have not the foggiest about something I need to know is very unnerving indeed.'

The latter was said with an ironic smile. But Patricia was serious again as soon as I asked my next question.

'What are your thoughts about Hans Herlofsen?'

'A lot of what he says may be true, but I doubt that it is the whole truth. The pot of gold left to him in the will, though overshadowed by the three main bequests, has been bothering me. It is not at all like Magdalon Schelderup to write off a debt as easily as that.'

I sent her a questioning look and she let out a patronizing sigh.

'Let's do a little thought experiment: you are Hans Herlofsen, you believe that Magdalon Schelderup was the Dark Prince, you owe him lots of money, you see that he is starting to get old and you have no reason to expect any generosity from his wife and daughter. What would you do?'

I thought for a while and had to admit that she had a point.

'First of all, I would hope for the best, but that would not appear to be very promising in the case of Magdalon Schelderup. So, the other alternative would be to confront him with it.'

Patricia nodded.

'Precisely – which is probably what I would do. Or discuss the case with Wendelboe, who I know Schelderup holds in awe. In fact, perhaps I would do both. Ask Wendelboe and Herlofsen about it tomorrow. When you speak to Wendelboe, ask him detailed questions about his wife's involvement too. I suspect that he comes from the old school who would rather not lie to the police, but that he reserves the right not to say anything about things he is not asked about.'

'The mysteries from the war, you mean?'

Patricia leaned forwards across the table.

'We are discovering more and more interesting details and personal stories. It has been a very successful day in that way. Both Arild Bratberg and Mona Varden have been unable to move on from events in the past and are thus human flies. But they are also satellite people. Mona Varden is still orbiting her husband, nearly thirty years after his death. Bratberg had a kind neighbour who circled around him while he clearly was still caught in an outlying orbit around Magdalon Schelderup. And as far as the story from 1945 is concerned, I am surprised that no more attention was given to one very interesting detail in court. Hint: in search of lost time . . .'

Now, I had heard the book title *In Search of Lost Time*, but I could not remember who had written it, or see its relevance here. Patricia waited with a teasing smile until I lost patience and demanded that she give me an explanation.

'It is incredible how often in court cases and investigations it is possible to overlook blatant problems in relation to time. It could be that there is not enough time for the given event to take place, or the opposite: that there is too much time. As is the case here. Magdalon Schelderup's account may appear to be plausible. But quite some time must have passed between him waving to the policemen outside and them coming up the stairs and into the room; say half a minute, if not a whole minute. Which is a long time in a situation like that. The young Bratberg appeared to be completely petrified. And yet they came in at the door just as Magdalon Schelderup took the gun from his hand. He would have needed nerves of steel to shout out of the window when he was standing with an armed man who had just shot his colleague. But what is even more peculiar is that he took such a long time to take the murder weapon from the paralysed man. That may of course be what happened, but it could not have happened in the way he described in his statement.'

It did seem strange that neither I nor anyone else had thought about this. Out loud I said that I would definitely have thought about it had I been investigating the case. Patricia did not look convinced, so I moved swiftly on.

'Whereas Arild Bratberg's apparently insane statement . . .'

She responded on cue.

'. . . given the time perspective, in fact works rather well, yes. It would seem that both the police and the court did not take the case seriously enough. The time issue is one thing. Another is that no one seems to have had intelligence enough to imagine that in some situations, apparently irrational behaviour is in fact the most rational.'

I must have looked puzzled, as Patricia sighed with exasperation again.

'Imagine the following situation: Ole Kristian Wiig and Magdalon Schelderup find something in the flat that constitutes a shocking revelation, and it would be a catastrophe for Magdalon Schelderup if it ever got out. The only way to avoid this, then, is to shoot Wiig immediately before he can tell anyone. Schelderup knows that Bratberg is mentally fragile and that an unexpected murder might paralyse him. But how then would he escape and prevent Bratberg bearing witness? If he shot Bratberg as well, he would clearly be guilty. What would you do?'

I eventually realized where she was going and had to admit that, true or not, it showed creative thinking.

'What I would have done, before it was my word against his, was perhaps to make up a simple and credible story

234

about the other person in the room being the murderer. And then also behave madly myself in the hope that he would become even more confused and come across as the less credible of the two, even when he was telling the truth.'

Patricia nodded slowly in agreement.

'Exactly. All of a sudden, the most irrational behaviour was the most rational. If that is in fact what happened, it demonstrates how terrifyingly quick-witted and cynical Magdalon Schelderup could be. So I am working on the theory that Bratberg's apparently incredible account is true and that it was Magdalon Schelderup who shot all three Resistance men during the war.'

I had seen it coming now and was therefore not so surprised when Patricia dropped the bombshell that Magdalon Schelderup himself was the Dark Prince. The idea that the Resistance hero Magdalon Schelderup could also be a double agent and triple murderer now seemed plausible. But I was yet to be fully convinced.

'The way you present it now, it all seems very plausible. But I would still like to keep the option open for the moment that it might have been one of the others, most probably either Hans Herlofsen or Magdalena Schelderup. Because that is equally possible, is it not?'

Patricia nodded somewhat reluctantly.

'I don't think that it is very likely, but yes, it is absolutely possible.'

'And if we move on from the war to the murder of Magdalon Schelderup . . .'

Patricia nodded, this time in clear agreement. Then she carried on herself.

'. . . then all options are still open, yes. However, if my theory is correct, it does not rule out that Hans Herlofsen or Magdalena Schelderup, for example, murdered Magdalon Schelderup. Thus far we do not know enough to rule out even one of his guests. They all have or could have strong motives, and the motives simply multiply and get stronger if he did commit one or more murders during the war. The real challenge . . .'

I had an inkling of what was coming, but it was unexpectedly fast and concise when it came.

'. . . is not to explain why anyone killed Magdalon Schelderup, because everyone around that table might have wanted to do it. The real challenge is still to explain why anyone would kill Leonard Schelderup. And also why in the world the gun was left by the front door.'

I nodded.

'Well, the mystery of the guest has been solved, at least. It would seem that you were right, that it has nothing to do with the murder.'

Patricia sat deep in thought again. It was obvious that she was struggling and more preoccupied with the murder of Leonard Schelderup.

'Leonard Schelderup's male lover definitely had nothing to do with the murder. The fact that Leonard Schelderup had a male lover may, however, be of some interest. I would be keen to know how much his father and brother knew. Do ask the brother about it next time you see him. But there is one thing that puzzles me, in connection with the will . . .'

She hesitated a moment, but then continued.

'It may be of no significance, but it is worth noting. In the first will, Leonard Schelderup was left ten times as much as his brother. In the second, they were equal. It would seem that something had happened to improve Fredrik's standing. So I would like to know whether Magdalon knew about Leonard's secret and, if so, when he found out.'

I promised to do my best to find out. My visits to Patricia had a tendency to result in both important new conclusions and new tasks.

She stopped me unexpectedly for a moment as I was about to go out of the door. When I turned around, her face was sombre and pale.

'I should perhaps say that I find this case more and more alarming. And if the theory that is forming in my mind is anything close to the truth, the case will be the epitome of human evil.'

The sudden gravity with which she said this took me aback, but reinforced my own feelings of danger and unease . I knew her well enough to understand that as there was still so much uncertainty, she was not ready to say any more about her theory. So I put my best foot forward and went off to carry on with the investigation.

XI

It seemed to me on the evening of Wednesday, 14 May that the case was becoming more and more intense. It was almost to be expected that the telephone would ring in the evening now, once I had come home. This time it was no later than a quarter past ten and I had just turned on the box to watch the evening's documentary about the slums of New York.

Once again it was Sandra Schelderup's voice I heard at the other end. At first I feared that there had been another death, this time involving Maria Irene. But there was no mention of catastrophe and no angry outburst. Her voice was controlled and in no way unfriendly.

She apologized for calling me so late. But she was suddenly unsure about something that was potentially of great importance, so she simply wanted to check whether we had found her husband's sizeable key ring, either in his pocket or his office.

I replied, as was the truth, that we had not found a key ring of any size, and that she would of course have been told if we had removed anything from the house.

There was silence on the line between us for a moment. Total silence.

'But . . .' Sandra Schelderup eventually said, when the silence became unbearable. Then she went on in a hesitant voice.

'But it is not here. So someone must have taken Magdalon's key ring. And it has keys to all the rooms, cupboards and cars here at Schelderup Hall on it, as well as keys to several other people's homes. Magdalon liked to have keys to the homes of as many of those close to him as possible; it was part of his need to control.'

I felt a chill spread through my body and straight away asked which other keys were on the ring. Sandra Schelderup said that she believed he had the keys to both his sons' homes, his sister's and his ex-wife's, possibly also Herlofsen's, but probably not to his mistress's and almost certainly not to the Wendelboes'.

I promised to follow this up immediately, and the first step in doing this was to ask Sandra Schelderup if she would like police protection at the house. She wavered, but then said that it was not urgent. It was perhaps more important to warn the others as soon as possible. I agreed with her and therefore finished the conversation. I did, however, add that she should give my regards to Maria Irene, which she promised to do.

I still did not trust Sandra Schelderup. Though she did seem to be getting better as the investigation went on. But I was by now already dialling the first number.

It did not take long to phone around. Mr Wendelboe confirmed that Schelderup did not have a key to his house – 'not even during the war did he have one'. He denied any knowledge of the missing key ring on the part of himself and his wife.

Synnøve Jensen stated simply that her dead lover had not had a key to her house. Magdalon had at one point asked to have a key, but had unexpectedly backed down when she explained that she only had one and reassured him that her door would always be open for him: all he had to do was knock.

Ingrid Schelderup was at home and sounded relatively calm when I spoke to her. She confirmed that her former husband had a key to her flat. He had asked for it shortly after their divorce and she had not wanted to say no. For many years, she had hoped that he would one day use it but, alas, that had never happened, she added with a mournful sigh. Ingrid Schelderup promised to put on the safety chain, and, if possible, to change the lock in the morning. In the meantime, she would be very grateful for police protection. She was still shaken by the events of the past few days, so I arranged for a policeman to go to her house before I phoned anyone else.

Magdalena Schelderup was, understandably enough, not so pleased to hear my voice, but thawed as soon as she realized that I had phoned to warn her that the keys had been lost. About which she seemed to be remarkably calm. Her door was already reinforced by a security lock and an extra latch and padlock. It would appear that Magdalena Schelderup was the only one who was cheered by the disappearance of the keys.

Hans Herlofsen was curt and bitter in his reply that Magdalon Schelderup had always had a key to his house. It was the symbolic subjugation that pained and frustrated him most, but he was sadly in no position to oppose it. He did not trust what Magdalon Schelderup might do in a crisis, and had also secured his door with an extra padlock. Now that his son's family were living on the ground floor, he reckoned the risk of any danger to be 'well under 10 per cent'. Even if you disregarded Leonard Schelderup and the murderer, he was still one of eight possible victims should there be any more attacks. And in any case, he could not fathom who would be interested in killing him, now that Magdalon Schelderup himself was dead. In short, Hans Herlofsen also seemed to take the news with relatively good humour, given the circumstances.

Fredrik Schelderup, however, was in a foul mood, even

given the circumstances. He sounded as though he had had a glass or three to steady his nerves already, even before I phoned. Whether it was the number of glasses, a late reaction to his brother's death, or whether it was because there was a threat to his own safety was hard to say – though I strongly suspected it was the latter. He certainly lost his self-control when I told him that the keys were missing. It was a violent and in part incomprehensible outburst, the gist of which was that the police should have discovered this before and that surely, in 1969, a man should be able to feel safe in his own home, especially in Bygdøy. There was a loud bang when he threw the receiver onto the table.

He was, however, more subdued when he picked it up again a few seconds later. Despite the alcohol in his blood, Fredrik Schelderup was almost his usual self-centred and relaxed self. When he heard my offer of police protection until he got a new lock, he immediately accepted, but then added that the policeman standing guard must not stop two beautiful young ladies who might drop by, as they had nothing whatsoever to do with the case. I mentioned that there were a couple of other things that I would like to ask him about, but that it would perhaps be better to talk tomorrow when he was more sober. He laughed and signed off with a cheerful, 'Here's to that.'

After I had arranged for a policeman to go to his house, I sat there deep in thought. It was not hard to understand that Fredrik Schelderup was under enormous stress following the murders of his father and brother. But it felt as though I had seen a glimpse of another even more egotistical and slightly less jolly Fredrik Schelderup on the phone. All of the nine remaining guests from Magdalon Schelderup's last supper had now been informed about the missing key ring. They had all denied any knowledge of its whereabouts. It seemed highly improbable that none of them knew. But when I eventually went to sleep around midnight on Wednesday, 14 May 1969, I was no closer to knowing who of the nine had the keys and what they planned to do with them.

DAY SIX

Long Day's Journey Into Night

I

My start to Thursday, 15 May 1969 was certainly far from the best. I had scarcely got into the office before the phone began to ring. It was my boss, who asked me to come to his office immediately. I knew straight away that something was wrong. As 17 May was Norway's constitution day, the day's newspapers were, in preparation for the national holiday, dominated by advance reports about the launch of Apollo 10 in the USA and the launch of Thor Heyerdahl's *Ra* expedition in Morocco. The short, concerned notices that stated there were still no developments in the 'difficult and important' investigation into the murders of 'multi-millionaire Magdalon Schelderup and athletics star Leonard Schelderup' did, however, warn that a possible media storm might be brewing.

Even though my boss was in the better of his two possible moods, this was, as anticipated, not a pleasant conversation. I understood that he and the rest of the station were, following the murder of Leonard Schelderup, under mounting pressure to get some concrete results. This in turn meant that there were others internally who were also increasingly impatient to have the case solved. The question as to whether there was anything new to report was therefore becoming urgent. If there was still nothing concrete, then there might be a need to increase the number of people involved in the investigation.

I told him the truth, that nothing decisive was imminent in the form of an arrest or the like, but that the investigation had made a number of important breakthroughs and that there was every reason to hope that both the cases would be solved soon. Yesterday's written report was hastily supplemented with some of Patricia's conclusions, without mentioning her name or the fact that I had been to see her, of course.

I finished by asking whether my boss, with his formidable experience and skills, could glean anything more than I had thus far from the available information. He smiled and shook his head pensively. The outcome was that I would work overtime on 15 and 16 May, and if no arrests were imminent then we would discuss the case again at some point on the 17 May holiday.

Once out of my boss's office, I heaved a sigh of relief. Now, if not before, it struck me that there were obviously plenty of colleagues who would only be too happy to challenge my position. And I stopped at none of the other offices on the way back to mine.

II

If the start of the day had been a bit troubled, the rest of the day was all the better for it. The first telephone call was from Schelderup Hall. It was Sandra Schelderup who rang. Her voice was still friendly and respectful. She wanted to thank me once again for leading the investigation so well, and added that both she and her daughter would be very grateful for an update on the situation if I was able to drop by in the course of the day.

I had no real plans for the day, other than talking to Herlofsen and Wendelboe again. So I replied that I also had a couple of questions that I would like to ask them, and hoped that I could be there around lunch. She said that they looked forward to seeing me.

I had just put the phone down when there was a knock on the door. An out-of-breath fingerprint technician was standing outside, as he wanted to tell me in person about the sensational find from Leonard Schelderup's flat. On a bureau by the door in the living room, they had unexpectedly found a single but clear and relatively new fingerprint that corresponded to that of one of the women who had been fingerprinted at Schelderup Hall following the murder of Magdalon Schelderup.

The faces of the women who could have been there flashed past me before he said the name. And it was the name that I hoped it would be. Two minutes later I was in the car on my way to Gulleråsen. I turned off before

Schelderup Hall. This time I was very interested to hear what Magdalena Schelderup might have to say in her defence.

III

I arrived at Magdalena Schelderup's flat with every expectation of solving the case. The result was nothing more than yet another depressing conversation. Either Magdalena Schelderup was a better actress than I thought, or she was genuinely distraught. Again and again she repeated that she had never learnt to tell the whole truth in time and that she should of course have told me this before. With tears in her eyes and desperation in her voice, she also repeated over and over again that Leonard Schelderup had been alive when she left his flat. And that she had no idea who might have killed him or her brother.

Her story was simple enough and, I had to admit, not entirely incredible. Following Magdalon Schelderup's death and her interview with me, she had guessed that the finger of suspicion was pointing at her and Leonard, in the first instance. For want of children of her own, she had always got on well with her nephew. So the day after, she had called him and asked if they could meet to discuss matters. He had said she was welcome to come over. She had gone there early in the evening and they had had a pleasant enough conversation, given the situation. She had urged him to confess if he had murdered his father, and said that both she and the others in the family would understand if that was the case. Leonard had been categorical: he had nothing to confess. His aunt had, at the time, not been sure whether she believed him or not. Which she did of course now, she added, with a pained expression on her face.

Leonard Schelderup had, if one was to believe Magdalena, been relaxed for much of the conversation, but had suddenly become very agitated after a telephone call from an unknown caller around nine o'clock. She had been standing beside him and had been able to hear the voice on the other end well enough to make out the words. The person was accusing Leonard of murdering his father, and threatened that he might soon be murdered himself if he did not lay his cards on the table. The caller then hung up as Leonard replied in desperation that he had nothing to confess. He had been extremely agitated and wanted to call me straight away after the phone call. So she had beaten a hasty retreat. He had locked the door behind her. And that was the last time she had seen her nephew alive, she said, with tears in her eyes.

'He liked you and hoped that you could solve the murder of his father,' she added swiftly.

It was without a doubt well intended. However, we were both struck by it. I had, three days later, still not solved the murders of either Magdalon or Leonard Schelderup. And in the light of today's conversation, she was now the prime suspect for both.

I asked why there was only one fingerprint in the flat, and why it was on the bureau by the door. The answer was that due to the gravity of the situation, she had not wanted to leave any traces in the flat of another suspect, so she had not smoked. She had been wearing gloves when she came in and had tried not to touch anything. Leonard had put out some coffee and biscuits, but she had on purpose not taken anything. She thought the fingerprint on the bureau was probably because she tripped on her way out and put a hand out to steady herself.

Magdalena Schelderup realized just how tenuous her situation was and asked me straight out if I intended to arrest her. The thought was tempting, especially given the conversation with my boss earlier in the morning. But I knew only too well how harsh the backlash could be in the event of hasty arrests, and had to admit that there was really still no evidence against her. And her explanation tallied with Leonard's telephone call to me and the statements from the neighbour and Leonard Schelderup's lover. It was of course possible that Magdalena Schelderup had returned sometime between midnight and three in the morning and then murdered her nephew. But there was no indication whatsoever that she had done this. So I concluded that any arrest would have to wait, but asked her to tell me immediately if she knew anything else of importance.

Magdalena sat and thought as she smoked her cigarette. Then she stubbed it out with determination.

'In that case, under duress and against my will, I will confide in you something I promised many years ago never to tell another living soul, which is a promise I have kept to this day. And it is the name of the person who got me to join the NS in 1940 . . .'

'And that is . . .'

She hesitated for a beat, and then launched into the story.

'My dear older brother, Magdalon Schelderup. He came

to my house one evening, put an already completed form down on the table and asked me to sign it. He had done the same with my brother. It would secure the family fortune in the event of a German victory and would be of no consequence should the Allies win. Fortunately we will never know if the first conclusion was right, but the latter certainly was not. I know that from bitter experience in the years after the war.'

Then she added: 'You don't believe me, do you?'

I thought about what Patricia had said about the chronology of events in 1940 and heard myself saying that I was not sure if it was of any importance to any of the murders, but that based on other discoveries I had made in the course of the investigation, I could in fact believe what she said about the NS membership.

Our parting was almost friendly. But my suspicion of Magdalena had only been strengthened by this latest failure to tell the whole truth. I had come there in the hope of a confession and left with the growing doubt that she actually had anything to confess.

IV

Even though I had more exciting things to ask both Herlofsen and the Wendelboes, I thought I might as well pop into Schelderup Hall as I was in Gulleråsen already.

Sandra Schelderup met me personally by the front door and looked as though she was in far better shape. She gave concise and clear answers to my questions. Following yesterday's conversation, she had searched high and low without finding the missing key ring. The lock on the outside doors would be changed within a few hours and once that was done, she would not need to use precious police resources. There had been no signs of any disturbance at Schelderup Hall for the past few nights and the dogs had been quiet.

She said she realized that it was a very complex investigation and that I might not be able to say much more here and now, but that she hoped we were making progress. I confirmed this and said that we had our suspicions. Sandra Schelderup trilled with relief to hear this and said that her daughter wished to speak to me and would no doubt appreciate this news too.

V

The door to Maria Irene Schelderup's room was closed, but was quickly opened when I knocked on it.

Her room turned out to be a combined bedroom and study. There was plenty of floor space, even though she had a separate corner suite with a television and stereo player, a large desk and a neatly made-up four-poster bed. In the doorway stood a smiling Maria Irene in an unexpectedly elegant outfit: a fitted black cocktail dress. The light caught the gold chain she was wearing around her neck and sparkled in the red diamond pendant.

Maria Irene had obviously been studying as some of her schoolbooks were lying on the desk, but she waved me in and closed the books. I commented that books on economy and law were not part of the curriculum when I took my exams. She laughed and replied that that was still the case, but that she was going to university in the autumn and, anyway, she was not an ordinary pupil.

I could not have agreed more, and queried whether such elegant working clothes were normal at Schelderup Hall. She laughed and replied with a quick wink that she only wore this when she was expecting very special guests.

I did not have much to tell her about the investigation, nor did I have many questions to ask her. As far as the ring was concerned, her answer was more or less the same as her mother's, as was the case regarding the key ring and the situation at Schelderup Hall. The only thing that she added was an apology for her mother's emotional outbursts in connection with the reading of the will.

We stayed sitting on the sofa all the same and time simply flew by. There was no doubt that Maria Irene still fascinated me more than any of the other parties in the case, despite the fact that as their pasts unfolded, their lives were far more gripping. There was something about the dignity and calm that she exuded, combined with her youth and beauty, which stood in sharp contrast to the outbursts from Magdalena Schelderup and the other older people who were nearing the end of their lives.

I allowed myself to say that it must have been very difficult for her to witness such tragedies in her close family at such a young age. Maria Irene assured me that she would cope, but admitted that the past few days had been very demanding. She thanked me with a very sweet smile for my concern.

Maria Irene placed her small hand on my shoulder as she said this. Her hand was softer and warmer than I had imagined. It was only now that I noticed that the top three buttons of her dress were undone, so that the upper part of her young bosom was visible.

I would later have considerable problems explaining even to myself what happened in the next few seconds. I seemed to leave my body in some peculiar way. I heard Maria Irene's voice saying that she had found the last days here at Schelderup Hall very difficult and lonely, and that it would cheer her up immensely if I would dance with her. I heard my own voice saying yes, that taking three minutes out of my working day must surely be allowed, and certainly if it was to help her. I saw Maria Irene smile, lean forward, put a single on the turntable and start the record. The movement meant that even more of her bosom peeped out from under her dress and the gold chain.

Then, suddenly, we were up and I was dancing with her to the tune of a hit from a couple of years back, Nancy and Frank Sinatra's duet 'Something Stupid'. Under the veil of the music, Maria Irene whispered to me that it was her favourite song and that it was kind of me to dance with her. I replied that the song suited her well. I thought that Nancy Sinatra's voice was very like Maria Irene's, but that Maria Irene was more beautiful.

Whether I actually whispered this to her or not, I could not say for certain later. I remember that I thought her body felt safer and firmer in my arms, that her smile was more beautiful, and that her red lips were even closer to mine. I could hardly avoid letting my eyes slide down her neck, and did not even try. First they rested on the spectacular diamond, but then they slid down even further to look at her spectacular breasts. I was struck by the dizzying and slightly absurd thought that I had been asked to dance by a very beautiful young heiress who was worth at least 40 million kroner, in her home, when no one else was there.

We seemed to glide in circles over the floor as though entranced, with a slightly unreal feeling that I had never experienced before on the dance floor. But then again, I had stepped out onto a very special dance floor with a very special young lady. We were over by the record player when, to my annoyance, the music faded out. To my relief, Maria Irene let go of one hand and deftly put the needle down again.

We continued to dance and circle round the room for another three minutes. Our circuit took us from the sofa to her four-poster bed. As the melody faded for a second time, Maria raised her red and breathy mouth to mine. It stopped less than an inch away. I looked down into her dark eyes. And in that moment I felt certain that she would not object in any way if I was to do the only thing in the world that I wanted to do. In other words, to lift her up and kiss her beyond all reason.

Suddenly I was at the point where the temptation was so overwhelming that the rest of the world and all its worries seemed to disappear. This time it felt as though I forgot not only time and place, but also age and planet. I looked down into Maria Irene's face, with an almost taunting smile curled on her red lips and a twinkle in her brown eyes, but still that bottomless calm. I felt a flash of teasing anger, and a deep desire to remove that taunting smile and peace from her face. In my ears I heard a kind of echo of Maria Irene's voice from our first interview, remarking that Synnøve Jensen was surprisingly voluble in bed for someone who otherwise was so quiet. And I was instantly overcome by an irresistible desire to find out what sort of sounds were hidden in Maria Irene.

I had just lifted her up the tiny distance that still separated us when we were quite literally brought back down to earth with a bump by a noise outside in the hallway. There was a knocking at the door and an extremely irritated maternal voice said: 'Maria Irene, if the detective inspector is still with you, please do not plague him with that terrible music of yours.'

It was the first time in the investigation that I had actually hated one of the parties involved. I would later be very grateful to Sandra Schelderup and shudder to think what might have happened if she had come a little later or, even worse, walked straight in. It is more than likely that ten seconds later I would have been standing there with my tongue in Maria Irene's mouth. And it was not unfeasible that a minute later, I would have been lying on top of her on the four-poster bed, the spell felt so strong. But thankfully it was broken by her mother's voice. I let go of Maria Irene instantly, as though she was burning – which in fact was perhaps not so far from the truth.

We each took a couple of steps back in our shared fear

that her mother would open the door. Within five seconds, Maria Irene had reached the record player and lifted off the needle. And she had already fastened the top three buttons of her dress, so that her bosom was hidden again. Then, in one lightning movement, she pulled off the gold chain and hid it behind her back.

I heard my own voice say very loudly that I was happy to have the music on, but I still had to ask about the missing ring and key ring. Maria Irene answered – also in an unusually loud voice – that she had helped to look for both those things, to no avail.

The danger passed quickly. Her mother left without even trying to open the door. But the magic had gone and the floor was firm beneath my feet. I was back in my body and had, to some extent, regained control of my mind. So I thanked Maria Irene and said rather loudly that I had now got the answers to all my questions, certainly for the time being.

Maria Irene smiled again and assured me – again in a voice that was perhaps louder than necessary – that I was welcome back whenever there was a need, if anything cropped up where she might be of help. She then added in a very quiet voice that she hoped she would be able to invite me back at some point later, once the case had been solved and the investigation closed.

I gave her a sheepish hug as we parted. It was then that I noticed that she had opened the top two buttons of her dress again. I mumbled that she should take care in the meantime and retreated swiftly.

Sandra Schelderup was waiting by the front door. I got a fright when I saw her, but then calmed down again when she said that she hoped that I had not found the music bothersome. She added that her daughter had a strong personality and her rebellious streak had become more apparent in the days since her father's death. I assured her that it was fine and that she had a super daughter and said they should take good care of each other until the case was solved.

Safely back in the car, I sped through the gate as I contemplated what had happened in those minutes in Maria Irene's room and wondered if it was real or a dream. My conclusion was that I had in reality been uncomfortably close to what could have been my life's worst nightmare. At the same time, it could also be the opening for a dream situation once the investigation was closed, if only we arrested someone soon. I promptly agreed with myself that this episode must under no circumstances be mentioned to Patricia. And that I would simply write in the daily report to my boss that 'both mother and daughter maintained once again that they had no knowledge of the missing key ring or the missing ring'.

VI

By the time I swung in to park outside the Wendelboes' house in Ski, I was more or less in full control again. The investigation was now my biggest and only passion. Contrary to the situation only half an hour ago, I was now deeply grateful to Sandra Schelderup because she had so inadvertently prevented what might otherwise have turned into a scandal. I could not bear even to think about what my boss and jealous colleagues would have said, or what the media might have written about the case. So I thanked my lucky stars that I had been stopped in time, and promised myself to be more careful in my personal dealings with the people involved. Certainly until the case was closed. And I hoped that the Wendelboes might help me to do this.

Petter Johannes Wendelboe once again opened the door himself. I asked him how he and his good wife were keeping and was told that, unfortunately, things were still much better for him than for his wife. This was the closest to humour that I had known Petter Johannes Wendelboe to come and I felt that it was a promising start. So I suggested that perhaps we two should talk on our own again, without his wife. He nodded and showed me into the living room.

I got straight to the point and told him what I had discovered about Herlofsen's visit to Arild Bratberg. Then I waited in anticipation for some kind of reaction, which never came. This reinforced my suspicion that I was onto something now. I reminded him that he had given a clear no to my question as to whether he had been in contact with Arild Bratberg or not. He immediately confirmed this. But to my question as to whether his wife had been in contact with him he replied, to my surprise, yes.

I looked at him askance, without eliciting any further reaction. I finally fathomed what the situation was, and asked the right question: in other words, whether Herlofsen had contacted them after his visit.

'Herlofsen came here one day in the middle of February and was unusually agitated. He had been to see Bratberg and heard the story as you told it just now. As a result, he was now inclined to believe that it was Magdalon Schelderup himself who had shot Ole Kristian Wiig and that he might even be the Dark Prince. He asked me to consider whether we should confront Schelderup or take some sort of action. But that never happened, of course.'

He fell silent. I was starting to get to know Wendelboe now, and had understood what was needed to prod him, which was a concise question.

'But you considered it enough for your wife to go and visit Arild Bratberg?'

Wendelboe nodded.

'She went on her own initiative, in fact, without asking me. Yes, it is true that she went to see him and that she returned with the same impression as Herlofsen. The possibility of confronting Magdalon Schelderup was discussed again later. But never realized. Certainly not by us.'

'Certainly not by us . . . So you think it is possible that Herlofsen may have acted alone?'

He shook his head.

'There is nothing to indicate that he did, but that is of course not to say that he didn't. He came here to discuss the possibility. And we dismissed it.'

Wendelboe's stony face closed again as soon as he finished speaking. It felt as if I was banging my head against a brick wall.

'When you say confrontation or action, could that possibly include an attempt on his life?'

'Herlofsen did mention that as an option. But he never acted on it, certainly not as far as my wife and I know.'

It frustrated me to admit that I was not going to get any further here and now. So I said to Wendelboe that I would unfortunately also have to confirm this with his wife. He got up without a word and went out into the hallway. I stood beside him as he called up to her that she had to come down.

She appeared from one of the rooms almost immediately, visibly frail, but dressed and on her feet. We sat at the table and I asked her the same questions as I had asked her husband, and was given the same answers.

Yes, Herlofsen had come to see them and talked about the possibility of either confronting Magdalon Schelderup or taking some form of action. Yes, she had gone to see Arild Bratberg on her own initiative and she also believed his version of the story. Yes, the three of them had discussed the possibility of how to tackle Schelderup afterwards. But no, nothing had actually been done. At least, not as far as she knew.

The atmosphere in the room during this conversation was sombre, but not unfriendly. I regretted that I had not asked Mrs Wendelboe to be there from the start, but had little reason to believe that it would have made any difference. The extent to which the Wendelboes' version was true or not was not easy to say. But it struck me that whatever the case, it was watertight before I came to see them. So I asked them to stay at home for the rest of the day and not to contact Herlofsen. Then I drove across town to see him.

VII

I found Hans Herlofsen where one might expect to find him at half past three on a working day: in the office in the centre of town, hidden behind a pile of papers full of figures and columns. He remarked in a quiet voice that work was the only thing keeping him going.

I assured him straight away that that side of the case was clear-cut and fine, but that some other important issues had cropped up that we needed to talk about. He nodded and reluctantly pushed the accounts to one side.

'You told me that you had not contacted the Wendelboes after you went to see Bratberg,' I started.

The expression in his eyes hardened.

'No, and they should not have told you that I did. I would not want in any way to cast a negative light on old friends from the war, and I was 100 per cent sure that they had nothing to do with Magdalon's murder. But if they are trying to lay the blame on me, then I am now no more than 50 per cent sure. And, of course, I should have told you yesterday,' he added swiftly, in his own defence.

My patience with the people who were only telling me half-truths in this investigation was starting to wear seriously thin. I remarked curtly that he should definitely have told me before. Then I ordered him, in his own interest, to tell me everything he knew that might be of relevance, regardless of whether or not it involved old war comrades, or anyone else for that matter.

He nodded, and started to talk. Unfortunately, his revised

version was now very much in line with what the Wendelboes had told me. He admitted that he had contacted them in the middle of February, or 16 February to be precise, and mentioned the possibility of taking some sort of action vis-à-vis Magdalon Schelderup. They had resisted, but twelve days later called him back, after Mrs Wendelboe had also been to see Bratberg. They had then sat round the table and concluded that Magdalon Schelderup was guilty of killing Ole Kristian Wiig, but that the circumstances were so unclear that they did not feel confident enough to confront him in any way. So nothing was ever done. 'At least, not as far as I know,' he added, with some hesitation.

I felt a growing anger with the main players in the case. It was clear that it was the Wendelboes and Herlofsen who had been in contact with Bratberg, and that they had then discussed the possibility of killing Magdalon Schelderup. The Wendelboes denied any part of it, but did not rule out the possibility that Herlofsen had acted on his own. Herlofsen denied any part of it, but did not rule out the possibility that the Wendelboes might have acted on their own. And I had no evidence that any of them had anything to do with poisoning him. Once again it felt as though I had come up against a brick wall just when the solution was within arm's reach.

I asked Herlofsen if he had any reason to suspect Mr Wendelboe. He waited a beat and then replied that he had once, twenty-eight years ago, heard Petter Johannes Wendelboe threaten to kill Schelderup, in connection with him joining the Resistance group. Wendelboe had been most sceptical about letting him join, and at Schelderup's first meeting had said to him directly: 'Welcome to the fight for the liberation of Norway. But if it ever transpires that you have betrayed any of us, I will kill you. And if you betray me, I will have made sure that someone else will kill you.'

Herlofsen then commented that it was not entirely unthinkable that he might have carried out this threat many years later. He added that it was the only time in all these years that he had seen anything resembling fear in Magdalon Schelderup's eyes.

I noted this down with interest and promised both Herlofsen and myself that I would ask Wendelboe about it. Then I carried on with my offensive and said pointedly to Herlofsen that he still had things to explain, and that my conversation with Wendelboe might indicate that he himself had confronted Schelderup with his discovery.

'Impossible, because . . .' he exploded spontaneously.

His face suddenly flushed red. We sat in silence for a short while. Then I finished his sentence for him.

'Impossible – because you had not told them. But you did, didn't you? And that is why he changed his will.'

He nodded sheepishly. He put his hands down on the table in an attempt to calm himself.

'It rode me like an obsession and I was starting to get desperate. I was more and more sure of my case, but Bratberg was dead and Wendelboe did not want to take it any further. They were all right financially, so I was the only one who could do it. So, having stopped at the last moment eight times, on the ninth day I went in to talk to him in his office. It was on 4 April, before I went home.'

There were sparks in Herlofsen's eyes. I waited with bated breath for him to continue.

'It was both the greatest and the worst moment of my life. No one could know how Magdalon would react to blackmail. But I felt more and more confident. My hate for him grew ever stronger and my frustration with my financial situation intensified. So one day I just marched in and said it straight out. That I had talked to Bratberg before he died and that I now believed that Magdalon was the one who shot Ole Kristian Wiig. Then I said that unless we could finally resolve the issues that continued to hang over me, I would be forced to share my suspicions with Wendelboe.'

'How did he react?'

Herlofsen gave a bitter smile.

'There was no reaction whatsoever. That was when I was convinced I was right. He just sat there in his chair and looked at me with complete calm. I have to admit that I was not telling the whole truth when I said just now that the only time I had seen Magdalon Schelderup show any fear was in 1941. To begin with, he sat in silence. Then he said it was, of course, all nonsense and speculation, but that one never knew what Wendelboe might believe, and it was perhaps time to draw a line under the past. So he took the promissory note and confession out from his drawer, handed them over to me and added that he would specify in his will that my debt to him was cleared.'

It looked as though Herlofsen was reliving the emotions he felt in his meeting with Magdalon Schelderup as he told me about it. His face lit up, but one could also see a shadow of fear in his eyes and a faint trembling in his hands. It crossed my mind that it only went to show that Magdalon still wielded enormous influence over the lives of those closest to him, even after his death.

'I did not dare to take his hand. So I just accepted them and assured him that I would not make any more fuss. I added swiftly that if anything should happen to me, both Wendelboe and the police would be sent a letter informing them of my conclusion. He nodded and then turned back to his work, while I returned jubilant to my office and burnt both the promissory note and my confession to cinders over a candle.'

Hans Herlofsen smiled, but he was still trembling.

'That was the greatest moment of my life since the war – greater even than when I saw my first grandchild. But then afterwards, a deep uncertainty came creeping over me as to what he might do. Even though I had warned him, I was on guard for the following weeks. I did not feel home and dry until the will was read out. He might not have done what he said he would, and he might have kept copies hidden somewhere of the documents I had burnt.'

'But you did not leave any letters ready to be sent to Wendelboe in the event that you were killed, as that was not necessary. Because if you only confronted Magdalon Schelderup once Bratberg was dead, it was already several weeks after you had informed Wendelboe.'

He nodded.

'Absolutely. I went to see them sixteen days before I went to see him. I would undoubtedly have been willing to take some form of action against him. But only if I could be sure that my financial situation was secured in this way and only if they were willing to be part of it. Once I had the papers I wanted, I would not have been opposed if the Wendelboes had murdered him. I have no idea whether they did or not. I only know that I had nothing whatsoever to do with his death.'

This conclusion was a disappointment that I should have expected. It had felt as though Herlofsen was in free fall. But he still categorically denied any involvement in the murder. There was no evidence that pointed to him as a more likely murderer than either the Wendelboes or Magdalena Schelderup.

I felt no need to thank Herlofsen, despite the fact that he had provided me with some very interesting information. So instead I reprimanded him for not having told me this before. It was already dawning on him just how vulnerable his position was and he was now visibly nervous.

Just as Magdalena Schelderup had done a few hours earlier, he now asked if he was under arrest. After a short pause for thought, I replied that he was still free for the moment, but that he was a suspect and that he had to remain available for further questioning over the next few days. He repeated that he had nothing to hide with regard to the murders. As I left the office, he withdrew into the world of numbers again with a faint smile on his lips. I felt rather uncertain as to whether the smile was connected to the numbers or to the way in which the meeting had gone.

VIII

Fredrik Schelderup and I definitely had a lower percentage of alcohol in our blood today. He was almost totally sober when I arrived, and had even tidied up the table since I was last there.

The first thing we talked about was the missing keys. He apologized for his outburst the night before and said that he would be happy to accept the offer of a constable to keep watch. He remembered his father's large key ring well: it had always been a symbol of his power and control. His father had had a key to his door for years, but had never used it. Now that he was sober and had the safety chain on, Fredrik was relatively calm about the missing keys.

I used the opportunity to ask him directly whether he knew that his brother had a lover, but that it was not a woman. He was undecided for a moment or two, but then nodded.

'I might perhaps be lazy, egotistical and generally of no use to society, but I am not a criminal and I do not lie to the police. Yes, I have known for many years that Leonard was happiest in the company of men. I asked him about it when he was nineteen. I had had my suspicions for a while by then. Leonard was good at not saying anything, but was hopeless at lying. He admitted it straight away. He was terrified and asked me never to tell anyone. I promised that I would not. Then I added that I would be happy for him to keep it secret for my part too. It would hardly benefit my reputation as a party animal if people knew that I had a brother who slept with men. The ladies tend to think it is contagious and, what is more, hereditary. That is to say, a number of the ladies I socialize with do.'

I sent him a stern look. He caught it and quickly carried on.

'We never spoke about the matter again. We both knew what he was and neither of us wanted anyone else to know. So I know nothing about his boyfriends. But I do not imagine there were many. I happened to drive past a restaurant last year and saw him sitting outside chatting to a well-known sportsman. It would not have been noticeable to many others, but there was a kind of intimacy between them that made me guess that my brother had a lover. It also explained why he was in unusually good humour over the next few months.'

'And how did you feel about it?'

He shrugged.

'In terms of my own opportunities, I hoped that it would not get out, but I was happy for Leonard to get his pleasure with whoever he fancied as long as I did not need to witness it.'

'Did your father know?'

Again, there was silence for a while, and this time it was definitely more protracted. Fredrik Schelderup swallowed twice before answering. I registered with some glee a faint trembling in his voice when he did.

'I hope you appreciate my honesty and openness now. Yes, my father did know. He heard it from me some days after the episode last year that I just mentioned. I thought that it might be of interest to him to know what his son got up to . . .'

Now I really did give him a very stern look indeed and could hear the indignation in my voice.

'And the reason that you broke your promise to your brother was that you believed that it might be beneficial that your father knew this before he wrote his will?'

He looked down and nodded. When he spoke again, his voice was definitely shaking.

'As I hope you understand, I am a greedy but honest good-for-nothing. Yes, I feared for my own position in terms of the will and reckoned that young Leonard would do well regardless. He has always been so determined and conscientious. And I have never been either, so have to get by as best I can with what I was born with: family money and a degree of intelligence.'

I did my best to show restraint and asked Fredrick Schelderup when this might have been, and how his father reacted. He thought hard, his brow furrowed.

'I cannot remember the exact date, but it was late in the autumn, around November–December possibly. Father was a man of exceptional self-control. All the same, it was obvious that he was affected by the news and that he disliked it intensely. He said "thank you for the information", and I cannot remember him saying anything like that since I came home from school with an unexpected top mark for one of my exams some twenty years ago. I have no idea if he ever talked about it with Leonard, nor if it was one of his reasons for changing the will. I certainly did far better in the second will than I did in the first, but fortunately that was also true of my brother.'

I noticed that Fredrik Schelderup was suddenly being very familiar with me, and I was not flattered by it, given the conversation.

'So you broke your promise and let your brother's greatest secret out of the bag, all to increase your own share of the inheritance. Not only that, you then went on to inherit millions more when your brother was shot. I hope you understand that these developments in the case now make you a prime suspect.'

His temper flared up briefly and there was indignation in his voice.

'I understand that you have to regard everyone as a suspect, and that inheriting vast sums of money when both your father and brother are murdered may give rise to some suspicion. But other than a fatter bank account, there is no evidence that would point the finger at me more than any of the others in the case. There is absolutely nothing to link me directly to either of the murders. And I have just demonstrated my honesty by telling you something that I am not proud of in any way and that shows me in a very bad light.'

I assured Fredrik Schelderup that he was only one of several suspects in the case and had not yet been given any official status. He immediately calmed down again and said that he was happy to hear that. We parted without falling out, but also without shaking hands.

It was tempting to believe that he was a greedy but honest good-for-nothing. However, I was more certain of his greed than his honesty. A couple of times over the past day or two I had seen a glimpse of a far less jovial Fredrik Schelderup, who seemed to make an appearance whenever his interests were threatened. Despite all other apparent differences, he suddenly reminded me of his Aunt Magdalena. I could appreciate that living in the shadow of Magdalon Schelderup could not have been easy, even if in purely financial terms they had not a care in the world. But I still could not bring myself to like either Fredrik or Magdalena – and I dared even less to trust them.

IX

There was no news of any importance waiting for me when I returned to my office around four. I still had more questions for the Wendelboes, but they were the only ones, and after what had so far been a turbulent day, I desperately wanted to talk to Patricia before doing anything else. So in the end I called her and suggested that we had our daily meeting earlier than usual at five, to which she agreed. In the meantime, I wrote a short report which I left in my boss's pigeonhole on the way out.

My meeting with Patricia was shorter than usual, and we agreed to limit the refreshments to coffee and cake. I omitted to tell her about my visit to Maria Irene, and mentioned only briefly my conversation with her mother at Schelderup Hall. On the other hand, I told her the day's other news in great detail. Patricia nodded in appreciation.

'The investigation is continuing to make significant breakthroughs. We now know who went to see Bratberg, and we have confirmation that the Wendelboes and Herlofsen did speak and may have had some form of plan to deal with Magdalon Schelderup. So now more than ever, all parties have some kind of motive to murder Magdalon Schelderup, but we lack any evidence that someone actually carried this through.'

She said nothing for a moment, but then carried on forcefully.

'But we do know one thing for certain: the circumstances and incidents are so numerous that none of the guests could have acted alone. All of them could have committed one or more murders, but no one could have done it all.'

I could not follow her.

'Maria Irene and Sandra have alibis for Leonard's death. But the others, well, alibis are still sorely lacking . . .'

Patricia shook her head.

'For the murders, yes, but not for other things. All of them could have put the powdered nuts in Magdalon Schelderup's food, and all of them could have posted the threatening letters. But all of them could not have phoned Leonard to scare him. It would have been impossible for Magdalena to do it, as, according to the neighbour, she was already there. Hans Herlofsen was sitting in a meeting at the office when the phone call was made. And I think we both agree that Ingrid Schelderup could not have killed her son.'

I was increasingly bewildered.

'What about the Wendelboes then? Either of them could have called him, or they could have phoned together, and committed both murders?'

Patricia gave an impatient shake of the head.

'Yes, in theory, but they could not have slashed the tyres on Magdalon Schelderup's car. They were still in Bergen when he telephoned you about that.'

It slowly dawned on me that this was not only true, but that it could also be of considerable importance.

'So, what you are saying now is that it must be a conspiracy between two or more of the guests who are still alive?'

Patricia nodded pensively.

'That is absolutely a possibility. It may also be that there was no organized conspiracy, but that it was more a case of out-of-orbit satellites crashing into each other. Which I think is just as likely. But it is definitely worth bearing in mind that there are obviously several people who have committed a crime here.'

Patricia helped herself to a piece of cake, but sat with it in her hand for a while before she started to eat it slowly.

'I still think that Wendelboe would find it hard to lie to a policeman. Ask him about his wartime threat, ask if they discussed any concrete plans with Herlofsen about how to bump off Schelderup, and ask Mrs Wendelboe if she telephoned Leonard Schelderup on the evening he was murdered. I hope that they will give you answers that can help us progress. Otherwise . . .'

Neither of us said anything for a moment. I unfortunately had a good idea of what she was going to say when she continued.

'Otherwise, we know quite a lot, but not what you should do tomorrow. I do not think there is much hope of squeezing out any more information and it is not obvious where else we might look. So we still lack a catalyst that will help to wind up the case.'

I nodded in agreement and believed that Patricia was thinking the same as me. In other words, that yesterday's letter had implied that there would be another murder, and that was not the catalyst that we wished for in the investigation.

I left 104–8 Erling Skjalgsson's Street with an uneasy feeling that a new catastrophe was imminent, but I did not know where, when or whom it might impact. With a pang of anxiety, my thoughts turned to Maria Irene, who only a few hours earlier had been so soft and warm and trusting in my arms during our interrupted dance at Schelderup Hall.

X

I arrived at the Wendelboes' house in Ski once again at around seven o'clock. This time it was Mrs Wendelboe who opened the door with a brave smile and showed me into the living room, where her husband was already seated. The atmosphere was tense, though they both said that they perfectly understood my situation and apologized for not having told me things before that they perhaps should. The tension eased a little when I said that there were perhaps also questions I should have asked sooner.

It was inevitable, however, that my new questions would ratchet up the tension again. As regards his sharp warning to Magdalon Schelderup during the war, Wendelboe immediately admitted to it. They had been in a very difficult situation and he had doubted Schelderup's loyalty. Mr Wendelboe had, only in our last meeting, admitted that he would have considered direct action against Schelderup if it could be proved that he was guilty of killing his brother-in-law. He did not believe it was certain that Schelderup was guilty, and so had dismissed the idea of doing anything now. Herlofsen had outlined various possibilities and had mentioned times and weapons that might be used. The Wendelboes claimed that they had not wanted to go ahead with any plans. Neither of them had heard Herlofsen mention anything about poisoning, and certainly not in connection with powdered nuts or the Sunday suppers. That is, if one was to believe their joint explanation.

But the real drama happened when I turned abruptly to Mrs Wendelboe and asked her directly if she had telephoned Leonard Schelderup on the night that he was killed. She burst into tears. Her husband looked at me intently, but I also caught a small glimpse of respect in his eyes. Once again, it was he who answered.

'My wife has had to live with a heavy burden and it has been weighing on her even more in recent days. We hope that it will not be necessary to tell Mrs Ingrid Schelderup about this episode. My wife and I had nothing to do with Leonard Schelderup's death. But it is unfortunately the case that my wife phoned him and made a threat in the hope that he would confess to the murder of his father. We have obviously realized with hindsight that he had nothing to do with it, and that this does not have anything to do with his death. But it has been hard for my wife to live with the knowledge that she unjustly made such a threat to a young man who only hours later was killed himself.'

I looked questioningly at Mrs Wendelboe. She was still sobbing, and nodded three times before she managed to find her voice.

'What my husband says is true; it is terrible, and he knew nothing about it. I knew that we had nothing to do with Magdalon Schelderup's death. But we had only days before sat here with Herlofsen and discussed the possibility of murdering Magdalon Schelderup. I was terrified that Herlofsen would let it slip and that we would become suspects. The thought of how awful that would be for our children and grandchildren was unbearable. And given the situation, it seemed most likely to me that the poor young Leonard had killed his tyrannical father. I wanted to frighten him into a confession, but instead added to the burden of an innocent man in what were his final hours on earth. The world came crashing down around my ears when I heard that he too had been murdered.'

Mrs Wendelboe was so inconsolably distraught that it was impossible to be angry with her. I patted her on the shoulder and thanked her as kindly as I could for her explanation. She asked for permission to go and lie down and left the room with a bowed head. Her husband and I remained sitting and listened to her footsteps as she dragged herself up the stairs.

As he showed me out, Wendelboe thanked me in a quiet voice for my understanding.

'As you have no doubt understood, my wife has been in a terrible state over the past few days. In a way, she has continued to circle round her dead brother for all these years. And recent events have just brought it all up again. She did not tell me that she had called until afterwards and I immediately said that I wished it was undone.'

I could not help but ask what he had thought the next morning, when he heard that Leonard Schelderup had been found dead. He gave a heavy sigh; things had obviously been difficult for him too.

'I have to admit that I was actually quite relieved when I heard that young Leonard had been murdered. My wife and I were not involved in any way and the desperately unfortunate phone call was obviously of no relevance to his death. But the steps I had to take as I approached my wife's bed that morning to tell her about his death felt like an interminable journey. As I entered the room, I thought that the worst thing would be if Leonard had committed suicide and it later transpired that his father had been killed by someone else. I think my wife's fragile mental health would then have cracked and I would have had to watch over her day and night to ensure that she too did not take her own life.'

I nodded and then shook his hand. I felt sorry for Mrs Wendelboe. And I definitely felt that Petter Johannes Wendelboe was more reliable than Hans Herlofsen. But after the day's revelations I did not trust either of them, particularly when it came to the death of the much-maligned Magdalon Schelderup.

XI

After my second visit to the Wendelboes that day, I felt empty, both physically and mentally. On my way home, I had to face up to the fact that I had no more leads to follow, either this evening or tomorrow. Following the day's revelations, I now believed that the murderer was either Hans Herlofsen or Magdalena Schelderup. But I had no idea whatsoever how I would manage to get any evidence or discover a crack in the defence.

And, on top of all the other problems, I felt a physical exhaustion creep over me, which made it even harder to think clearly. I got home around seven, set my alarm for nine and lay down for an hour or two. I fell asleep almost immediately, but did not sleep well. The surviving guests disturbed my sleep. And then I finally slipped into a very pleasant dream where I was dancing with Maria Irene in her room at Schelderup Hall. Just as I bent down to kiss her, we were interrupted – this time by my alarm clock.

As I lay there for a few extra minutes, half awake, I had to admit to myself that I was more than fascinated with Maria Irene, I was in fact in love with her.

I felt sure that this had nothing to do with her money and property. The diamond on the gold chain, which symbolized her wealth, was no more than an insignificant detail in my memory from Schelderup Hall. The image that had burnt itself into my mind was her red lips, only a breath away from mine, and the glimpse I had seen of the tops of her beautiful young breasts. As I lay there in bed, I made a pact with myself that I would make a serious attempt to see the rest of them as soon as the case was over. In my dozing daydream, I lay with her for a few moments more in her four-poster bed at Schelderup Hall, with her mouth gasping for mine, her naked, moaning body under mine. She was no longer relaxed and in control, but quite the opposite; unexpectedly wild and passionate.

This dream was definitely the highlight of the day so far. But one absolute requirement was that the murder case had to be solved before I could even begin to follow up on the dream. At half past nine, I got out of bed alone and moved into the living room. I spent the next hour in an extremely frustrating state where I could not think of anything other than the case, but at the same time was unable to make any headway.

XII

For a change, my phone rang at half past ten in the evening on Thursday, 15 May. This time it was Synnøve Jensen's distraught voice that I heard at the other end.

'Maybe this is silly . . . But Magdalon said something to me not long before he died, something that I don't understand. And I also have something I think I should show you. I should probably have done so before. It is all very peculiar and I may have done something wrong without knowing it. Would you be able to come here first thing tomorrow morning?'

I hesitated a moment and then asked if she had received

some kind of threat. She immediately replied no, and then added that it was probably not so urgent I needed to go there now, straight away. But I felt more and more uncertain. There was something about the intensity of the case and the memory of Leonard Schelderup phoning me in the evening and then being found shot before I could meet him the next day. So I pushed my tiredness to one side and said in a determined voice that I would come immediately.

It took no more than two minutes from the time that I put down the receiver until I had my coat on and was out through the door. But all the same, I felt reasonably calm as I left my house.

It was while I drove through the night alone in my car, heading towards Sørum, with no means of communication with Synnøve Jensen, Patricia or anyone else, that I was overwhelmed by a sudden unease.

This was probably due to a combination of the anxiety I thought I detected in Synnøve Jensen's voice, the fact that Leonard Schelderup had been shot only hours after he called me and yesterday's letter warning of another death. Whatever the case, I felt a rising anxiety and put my foot to the floor. Visibility was good and there was very little in the way of traffic. In a strange way, the great silence and loneliness of the road only served to heighten my fears. My thoughts were preoccupied with what it was that Synnøve Jensen thought was so important to show me, but I could find no sensible answer.

I had been driving well over the speed limit, and at five past eleven I parked the car and made my way up to

Synnøve Jensen's little house in Sørum. The rain was pelting down so I dashed through the dark towards the front door.

XIII

There was no doorbell. I knocked hard on the door three times, without any response from inside. And yet I could see through the small windows that the light was on in the living room.

I called out to Synnøve Jensen, but still heard not a sound from inside. I hammered on the door for a fourth time. Then it occurred to me that it might not be locked. In the same moment, an icy-cold feeling told me that something was wrong, very wrong, and what is more, dangerous.

I knocked on the door for a fifth time. Then I opened it and went into the living room.

The sight that met my eyes was at first an enormous relief. Synnøve Jensen was sitting on the sofa facing me, wearing a simple blue dress, and there was no sign of anyone else in the small room. Her eyes were wide and they met mine.

Another even stronger feeling of danger flashed through me in those few seconds. Synnøve Jensen sat looking straight at me, but did not move. It was a relief when she opened her mouth. But this immediately turned to horror when the blood spilled out. I then noticed that blood was pouring from a bullet wound in her chest. The bullet had clearly been fired too high and missed the heart. There was a pistol lying on the floor by her hand. I vaguely registered that it looked rather old-fashioned, but I was more concerned about the woman on the sofa.

Her staring eyes were wide and frightened. The will to live still burnt bright in them. They told me one thing loud and clear, and it was important: Synnøve Jensen had not shot herself.

I grasped her hand. It was burning. The pulse in her wrist was still there, but barely.

Thoughts tumbled through my mind – that the murderer must have left by the door only shortly before I arrived. But I could not leave the fatally wounded Synnøve Jensen. Her hand held desperately onto mine, as though she was trying to cling to her life through me. Again she tried to say something, but was prevented from doing so by the blood. Her right hand clung to mine. She waved her left hand towards the back of the room, without much force. I instinctively looked up but could see no sign of anyone there.

'Was it Hans Herlofsen who shot you?' I asked.

Her eyes met mine, but I could not see any affirmative or negative response. The same happened when I asked: 'Was it Magdalena Schelderup?' I could not work out whether Synnøve Jensen did not want to confirm or simply could not.

Synnøve Jensen waved her left hand towards the back of the room again, with even less force. Her eyes looked into mine with a deep desire to tell me something, but she was unable to express what. Her free hand crept slowly up and stopped on her belly. Then her eyes closed.

For some reason, as soon as her eyes closed, I started

to count the pulse in her wrist. I felt four slow beats. Then Synnøve Jensen's pulse stopped.

I sat for a few seconds with her hand in mine before slowly releasing my hand from her dead body, which sank down onto the sofa with no resistance. I was gripped by a violent rage, in part with myself, but mostly with the faceless person I was pursuing. Synnøve Jensen was dead, and her unborn child was now dying in her womb. I had come a few minutes too late to prevent the murder and perhaps only seconds too late to hear Synnøve Jensen say who it was who had shot her. I had no idea what to do now. I had seen no sign of another living soul out there in the dark. It was most likely that the murderer was over the hills and far away by now.

I went over to her telephone and called for an ambulance. Then I rang Romerike police station to let them know that there had been a murder, and that I was already at the scene of the crime.

Then I dialled Patricia's number.

I was worried that she might already have gone to bed. It was a great relief when I heard her voice after only five rings. I explained very quickly where I was calling from and what I had seen.

There was silence on the other end for a few seconds. Complete silence. It felt as though neither of us dared to breathe.

After a few breathless seconds, Patricia let out a deep sigh before starting to speak.

'You said that you had just come in through the door, which was unlocked, and found Synnøve Jensen who had been shot and was dying, but still visibly alive with her eyes open. A pistol lay on the floor beside her. She could not speak but waved her hand twice towards the back of the room before she died?'

'Yes,' I confirmed.

'But . . .' she started.

There was silence again for a moment, before she mustered the courage and continued.

'But then the shot cannot have been fired more than minutes before and it is unlikely that the murderer would dare to leave while she was visibly still alive. So then the most feasible explanation is without a doubt that the murderer was standing there waiting for her to die and when you knocked on the door, dropped the gun onto the floor and ran upstairs to hide in one of the rooms. In which case, he or she will still be there.'

Neither of us said anything. I turned around quickly and looked up the stairs. There was no sign of movement up there. However, the logic in what Patricia had just said was undeniable. Synnøve Jensen had tried to say something when she waved her hand around and she had indicated the stairs, not the door. There was a considerable chance that the murderer was still upstairs.

'As the murder weapon is still there and as it is unlikely that the murderer would want to be caught with the weapon after the murder, it is likely that he or she is unarmed now. But one cannot of course be certain of that. As you have not heard any noises, you may assume that there is only one person. But of course, one cannot be certain of that either,' Patricia's voice said, with a sudden worried undertone.

I thanked her and promised to call back as soon as I had a chance. Then I put down the phone.

I sat still for a brief moment, my eyes moving between the dead Synnøve Jensen and the empty stairs. I did think about calling the police station again to ask for reinforcements. But I was not sure that there was anyone upstairs and the risk that the intruder might escape through a window or over a balcony would only increase in the time that it would take to get any backup here. And what is more, I had no idea how long it would take to get more men here so late in the evening.

So I sat there, staring at the gun. With a pounding heart, I realized that it was an old Walther pistol, the same type that the Dark Prince had used to shoot his two victims during the war. The thought that the Dark Prince might be hiding upstairs made the possibility of an arrest even more tempting. So I made a hasty decision that there were not likely to be any fingerprints on the gun in any case, and picked it up with my handkerchief. Then, armed with the murderer's own weapon, I mounted the stairs to the first floor. I vaguely registered that my watch showed that it was a quarter past eleven precisely when I started my ascent.

XIV

The stairs swayed and creaked alarmingly under my weight. But all was quiet on the first floor. There were three doors and I had no reason to choose one rather than the other.

So the most obvious thing was to start with the door

closest to the stairs. It was unlocked and there was no light to be seen through the keyhole. I rapped on it twice. Then I opened the door with the gun raised.

There was no sign of life in the room. But I did see something that made my stomach lurch – I was in the deceased Synnøve Jensen's bedroom. Her bed was made up for the night and by the head was a small cradle, standing ready for the baby.

I turned away from the cradle and could quickly ascertain that there were no hiding places in the room. Nor were there any possible escape routes. The room did not have a window, only a small air vent in the wall.

So I went back out onto the landing again and over to the middle door. When I looked through the keyhole, this also appeared to be dark and unlocked. Again I knocked on the door twice, without any response. With all my senses alert and the pistol at the ready, I opened the door.

This time I stepped into a tiny bathroom. There was evidence here too of how happy Synnøve Jensen was about her baby. She had made a small nappy-changing area ready by the very ordinary sink. There was not a trace of the person who had killed both the mother and her unborn child only minutes ago. And again, the bathroom did not have a window, just an air vent in the wall that you could scarcely get a hand through.

Only one door remained. If the murderer had run up the stairs, then he or she must have disappeared through that door. I could feel the tension bubbling in my body when I noted that the third door was locked, and that the key was on the inside.

I knocked hard on the door and shouted that I was armed and willing to kick the door down. There was not a sound from inside.

I squatted down in front of the keyhole and managed to push out the key that was in there with the help of my car key. There was no light on in this room, either, but I caught a movement in the dark all the same. My heart was hammering violently. All that separated me from solving the case and finding the murderer was the door and a few steps.

I knocked hard on the door again twice and called out that I was armed and could not be held responsible for the consequences unless the murderer now unlocked the door and came out with their hands above their head.

There was still not a sound from within.

I stood up and threw myself against the door. That was when I suddenly heard a very clear sound from inside the room. What it was, I could not discern. But the murderer was in the room and was doing something. This only served to strengthen my determination and agitation. The door looked rickety and one of the hinges was loose. When I threw my weight against it the first time, it shook noticeably. On the third attempt it burst open with a bang.

I managed to keep my balance, quickly stepped back and pushed the remains of the door to one side as I shouted: 'DO NOT MOVE!'

The third room on the first floor of Synnøve Jensen's house was a small storage space. There was not a person to be seen here either.

But there was a window in the room that was now wide

open. Just as I charged into the room, I heard a thud on the ground below. The drop was no more than ten feet. Through the window I saw someone in a raincoat, with the hood up and gloves on, struggle to their feet and then run up the slope behind the house.

I tasted blood and my hunting instinct was stronger than ever. Only seconds later I hit the ground myself, and fortunately managed to stay on my feet.

XV

'STOP!' I shouted as soon as I had regained my balance from the jump, and fired a warning shot into the air over the head of the raincoated person.

This made no difference. The person in front did not even turn their head, let alone slow down. For a second I lowered the gun and aimed at the running legs. But at the last moment I remembered the order to use firearms only in situations where it was strictly necessary, or in self-defence. The fact that it was not a service weapon hardly made the situation any better. So instead I started to run up the slope. There was a fair distance between us now. However, it seemed to me that the person ahead was not running at a speed that made this discouraging. And the pace did not get any faster as the slope got steeper.

For some reason that was wholly inexplicable to me, I started to think about the deceased Leonard Schelderup as I chased after Synnøve Jensen's killer. In my mind, I was back at Bislett Stadium, watching him audaciously catch up with all his competitors until, only yards from the finishing line, he overtook the final one. It felt as though Leonard was showing me the way in the dark, running in front on his light feet, his fair hair fluttering on the wind, as I pursued the person I assumed was his murderer up the slope. We were getting steadily closer.

I had almost halved the distance between us when the person up ahead reached the top and I got even closer when they stumbled and almost fell as the ground levelled off. Even though it was dark, I could see that the person was smaller than me, and thought gleefully to myself that I would easily catch up with them once I too reached the top.

That was when I heard a sound that made me swear out loud into the night: the impatient revving of a car engine starting up.

I reached the brow of the hill in time to see the car disappear. Synnøve Jensen's murderer was still impressively cool-headed. He or she drove with the pedal to the floor and without lights. What I saw was the movement of the car as it rounded the farthest bend into the dark.

I found two unclear tyre tracks where the car had been parked, under the shadow of some trees where the ground flattened out. The footprints of the person I had been chasing were very light and would soon be washed away by the rain. It looked as though the shoes were a good few sizes smaller than my own. Not that that helped much. I could not rule out any of the remaining guests on the basis of those tracks and an unclear picture of the person I had pursued.

I had never felt so alone and such a loser as I did around

midnight on 15 May when I walked back through the dark night and rain to the body of Synnøve Jensen. I had only been a matter of feet away from her murderer and from solving the whole mystery, but had failed to use the chance either to grab hold of the murderer or to discover their identity.

XVI

I called Patricia as soon as I was back in Synnøve Jensen's house. She picked up the phone on the second ring and I thought I detected a light sigh of relief when she recognized my voice. I told her quickly what had happened since we last spoke. She exclaimed that I should have shot the murderer in the foot, but added hastily that I of course could not do that, given my orders. I agreed with both statements. She suggested that I should come to see her as soon as I could the following day, and assured me that she would be happy to welcome me any time between seven in the morning and midnight.

Right then I heard sirens and footsteps outside, so I wished Patricia a good night and put down the telephone. It was only later that I realized I had forgotten to ask her who she now thought had sent the mysterious threatening letters.

The case was becoming more and more of an obsession and my adrenaline levels were rising. Even though it was now past midnight, I could not leave the scene of the crime where Synnøve Jensen had been killed until the place had been searched.

The only thing we found of any significance was in the pocket of Synnøve Jensen's coat – but the discovery was so sensational that my thoughts dwelt on it until I finally fell asleep around two. But the only conclusion I came to was that I had to talk to Patricia as early as possible the next morning.

DAY SEVEN

Satellites in Fast Motion

I

'So, what do you think we found in the late Synnøve Jensen's coat pocket?'

It was five past seven in the morning of Friday, 16 May 1969. I had slept for no more than five hours, and then jumped into the car without eating breakfast. A clearly sleepy Beate had just put down a selection of rolls on the table at 104–8 Erling Skjalgsson's Street. Patricia was sitting opposite me with a cup of steaming black coffee, wearing only a dressing gown, as far as I could see. However, she was looking at me with eyes that were as bright and alert as ever, and answered in her usual sharp tone.

'A letter very much like the last one you received in the post. I have to admit that I cannot remember the exact words, but I would be very pleased to know.'

I pulled out the letter and almost threw it across the table in disbelief. The message was short, and that it resembled the last one I had received was undeniable.

Here, now.

So, the dictator's sister has also gone.

More may follow, if you do not soon find out which one of us is doing wrong . . .

Patricia had read the text in a flash and then looked up at me again.

'I only have one question, but it is a very important one. Was the envelope containing this letter sealed?'

'The envelope was sealed, as it was with the other two letters, with the same typed address.'

I really did not understand the significance of the question. But Patricia obviously did, as she nodded with satisfaction and even uttered a quiet 'ha!'

'And—' we suddenly both said at the same time. I stopped and let her finish.

'*And* perhaps there was a small mark on the back of the sealed envelope? Not green this time, but most probably blue.'

'Red,' I told her, giving her an impressed nod all the same.

Patricia shook her head, obviously annoyed.

'Hopefully just arbitrary. Red is less usual than blue, but a common enough pen colour that might be found in any office or home without drawing attention. And I must say it tallies very well with my theory. We are nearly there now, the case will soon be closed.'

I nodded, slightly in awe, but most of all in delight that we were close to anything.

'In fact, I have every hope that I will have a solution in

the course of the day. Certainly to some of these apparently inexplicable deaths and events. But for that to happen, you have to carry on doing all the things that can be done today, while I sleep, think and preferably put on a few more clothes.'

I nodded and helped myself to a roll. Seeing the plate of food had reminded me how hungry I was.

'I will do. And I suppose I should talk to the surviving guests before we meet again? I had thought of gathering them all at a meeting at Schelderup Hall to fill them in on our progress so far, no matter how unpleasant that might be.'

Patricia nodded and finished her coffee. She suddenly looked as though she had got up too early.

'A splendid idea. I had thought of suggesting that myself. It could very interesting to see who says what once they are together again. And let me know immediately if any more letters pop up. Now, is there anything else I can help you with before you go?'

I took the hint, quickly finished the first half of a roll and hastily grabbed another to take with me.

'There is one thing that I have been wondering about. If the murderer was still there when I knocked on the door and Synnøve Jensen was so clearly still alive, why did the murderer not shoot her again? I initially thought that perhaps the shot was fired seconds before I came in, but then I would have heard the bang.'

Patricia immediately livened up. She leant forwards over the table and looked at me so solemnly that it almost felt like an accusation. Her voice was unusually brisk and passionate when she spoke.

'I will tell you right away. Because the person who shot Synnøve Jensen is a particularly cold, intelligent and egotistical person. It is a heartbreaking story. The plan was to make the murder look like suicide, by leaving the pistol beside the body. However, something unexpected happened: the shot was not aimed well enough, so Synnøve Jensen was left to die slowly on the sofa. The murderer could have curtailed her suffering, but then the suicide plan would not work. So instead the murderer chose to stand patiently and wait until the victim died from the first bullet wound. It is likely that we may never know how many minutes this took. What we do know, however, is that this heartless plan would have worked perfectly if you had not responded so swiftly to Synnøve Jensen's telephone call, and therefore arrived while she was still alive.'

Despite the lack of sleep, Patricia's face was alert and engaged. She hurried on.

'It is a truly despicable act to watch a person who is suffering die like that. And it becomes inhuman when you then think that it was a young, pregnant woman who was killed in her own home.'

I had to agree with her and put down the half-roll that I had been holding, uneaten.

'It is, as you said, the epitome of human evil.'

Patricia waved a hand in irritation.

'I was not talking about this crime when I said that, and it is highly unlikely to be the same perpetrator. But I cannot decide which is worse: what I was thinking about then, or this. It really is a grotesque case.'

Her voice was verging on livid and I suddenly noticed that she had goosebumps on her bare arms. I leant forwards spontaneously and put my hands on them. This touch of human warmth seemed to help. The goosebumps vanished and Patricia's voice was friendlier than normal when she carried on speaking.

'The big question with regards to last night's murder is what happened in the minutes before the shot was fired, when the murderer first came into the house and then aimed the gun at Synnøve Jensen? It is true that Magdalon Schelderup's key ring is still missing, but the key to Synnøve Jensen's house was not on it. Right now, I can only think of one logical explanation, but there may of course be several.'

'So . . .' I started.

'So, even though this is a very pleasant way to start a Friday, we should now both work separately for a few hours. I think the best division of labour is that you continue to gather information while I work with what we already have. But do give me a call if you come up with any questions later on in the day.'

I took the hint, withdrew my hands and stood up.

II

The last papers before the weekend were favourable, given the circumstances. The Labour Party conference had now finished but still dominated the news, and all the papers, with the exception of the Communist rag, *Friheten*, praised the party's clear yes to the renewal of Norway's membership of NATO. On the other hand, opinion was divided with regard to the Labour Party's prospects in the autumn general election, and what significance the national conference's unexpected vote in favour of demanding the introduction of abortion in Norway might have. The murder in Sørum last night was not covered by any of the papers. But the press had got wind of the news and the switchboard reported an increase in enquiries. I wrote a five-line press release in light of the ongoing investigation, stating that there would be no further comment.

At five minutes past midday, a police constable came running in to tell me that a witness from the night before had just come forward. He also warned me not to expect too much, certainly if one was to believe the witness himself.

I understood what he meant as soon as I saw the witness. He was a grey-haired, thin elderly man in a plain brown coat, who kept his eyes fixed to the floor as he twisted a cloth cap in his hands. When we shook hands, his was feeble and trembling.

'I hope you'll forgive me if I'm wasting your time, but . . . I don't imagine that I have anything of much import-ance for you. But you see, I was up on the hill behind poor Synnøve's house last night, and saw a car parked there. It was the wife who told me that they'd announced on the radio that anyone who was nearby was to report to the police immediately. I think I was the only one there;

I certainly didn't see anyone else. But I don't really have much more to tell, so perhaps I should not have come.'

I assured the witness that he had done the right thing by coming. After a few minutes more, however, I also had to concede that he really did not have much of interest to add. He lived on a smallholding nearby and had been out walking his dog on the hill behind Synnøve Jensen's house. The witness had passed the house at around half past eleven and was surprised to see a car parked up there in the dark. He had thought that it was perhaps the police or some other important people and so had taken a detour rather than pass too close to the car.

The witness had not seen anyone there, and could not give any further details as to the make or colour of the car. He knew very little about cars in general. He apologized and explained that his lack of interest was due to the fact that there had never been any real possibility of him ever owning one. The car he saw had a roof and wheels, but he would not dare to describe it in any more detail than that.

The conversation depressed me, but it seemed to be even more painful for the witness. It ended with him sitting with his face buried in his hands.

'After seventy-two years working in the fields, without ever having achieved much, I have to witness my poor neighbour being killed in her own home. And I was close by and didn't check on her. It's terrible, may the Lord forgive me,' he lamented.

I tried to comfort the man and asked a bit about his neighbours, but there was not much to be gained here either. Both he and his wife had realized that Synnøve Jensen did not have an easy life. Her father was a drunkard and her mother was depressed. But the neighbours had enough problems of their own and had not wanted to interfere. No one had a word to say against Synnøve herself, but then no one knew her very well either. She had worked very hard and in recent years had really only come home to sleep.

I eventually asked the witness to wait a few minutes and went to call Patricia from my office. I did not think that there was anything more to be had from him, but could not let him go until I had checked with her.

Patricia was obviously wide awake now and listened thoughtfully to my brief update.

'I have only one question for the witness, but it is potentially extremely important. Was the door on the driver's side open when he passed the car?'

I did not understand why this was relevant, but I went out and asked the witness. He looked up at me in surprise, but quite noticeably livened up.

'No, I am absolutely certain of that, I could swear to it – I would have noticed if the driver's door was open. I would have gone to see what had happened then. There's no doubt about that!'

Suddenly the man was upbeat, almost cheerful. He repeated a couple of times that he was certain that the car door had not been open and then asked promptly if it was important. I still did not understand why it was significant, but replied that it was likely to be of considerable potential importance, and I thanked him profusely on behalf of myself and the entire police force. The man shook my hand in delight and more or less flew out of the room.

The door slammed shut behind him, but was opened again half a minute later. He had come back to offer me a written statement that the car door had been closed, if that would be of any help to the investigation. I assured him that a spoken statement would suffice for the moment, but that we would contact him later should we need a written statement. He gave a jovial salute and promised that he would stay at home and get up early until the case had been solved.

So in the middle of all the horror, I sat with a gentle smile on my lips until well after the witness had left the station. Whatever Patricia had meant by her curious question, it had certainly saved the day and the mental well-being of a well-meaning witness.

III

It was with a pounding heart that I went to meet the constable who had been on night watch at Schelderup Hall at around lunchtime. His report gave no cause for concern, however. He had been awake at his post all night and had seen no sign of anyone trying to get into or out of the building. The dogs had barked furiously for a few minutes around half past ten, and then again at about one o'clock in the morning. It would seem that this was entirely unprovoked on both occasions, and the night had otherwise passed without drama.

Afterwards, I rang Schelderup Hall and suggested that

everyone should gather there at three o'clock. Sandra Schelderup immediately said yes to this.

I was unable to get in touch with one of the eight remaining guests by phone. I felt my heart beating faster as Ingrid Schelderup's telephone rang again and again without being answered. However, I soon realized what might have happened and called the hospital, and was informed that she had been taken in the same morning. The constable who had been on guard outside her house overnight had driven her there only an hour before in a very unstable condition. Once he was back at the station he could tell me that she had appeared to be in relatively good humour the evening before, and that the night had passed without incident. But the news of Synnøve Jensen's death in the morning had affected her with such unexpected force it had caused another collapse. Mrs Schelderup had been given tranquillizers when she got to the hospital and was now expected to sleep until early evening. This was not hard to believe. And in any case, from what the constable had told me, it could be ruled out that it was Ingrid Schelderup who had murdered Synnøve Jensen last night.

The others were easy to get hold of, but hard to fathom. The Wendelboes had been at home together all evening, and Herlofsen had been at home alone. His son and daughter-in-law could confirm that he had been there, as they had had an evening coffee together around ten, but they could not be certain that he had not left the house later.

Magdalena Schelderup claimed to have been at home but there was no one to confirm this. She was extremely upset about being without an alibi for yet another murder.

As for Fredrik Schelderup, he had had a visit from his girlfriend, but had asked her to leave around half past ten, as he did not feel up to it. And from then on, until the morning, he had been seen by no one other than 'the drinks cabinet and his bed'.

Everyone was clearly affected by the ongoing case and they were further shaken by the news of Synnøve Jensen's death. They all categorically denied knowing anything about it.

Once I had called everyone, I sat and thought about what I was actually going to say to them. One thing that I was not going to mention at the moment was the existence of the letters. These could be an important lead, but where they might lead I still did not know. Either the murderer had left the letter in her pocket, or Synnøve Jensen was responsible for the letters herself, and in that case might also be behind the first two murders.

I could not quite bring myself to believe in the idea that the murderer had left the letter in Synnøve Jensen's pocket. It seemed highly unlikely that the murderer would do that while she was still alive. This possibility was also thwarted when the fingerprint report came back: the only prints on the envelope were those of Synnøve Jensen herself.

It did seem to fit rather well that Synnøve Jensen had killed Magdalon and Leonard Schelderup. If she had known about the will, she had a possible motive for both murders. And a copy of the will had been kept at her house in the metal box to which she had a key, in an envelope with her name on it. But who had killed Synnøve Jensen was then an even more burning question.

IV

Understandably enough, the seven guests sitting in their usual places around the table at Schelderup Hall at three o'clock were very sombre indeed. They listened to my account of the situation following Synnøve Jensen's death. I ended with the conclusion that there had been some important breakthroughs in the investigation, but no one had been arrested and no one had been named as an official suspect.

Following my update, there was silence. I had been prepared for loud diatribes against me and my investigation. It was six days now since they had sat at this very table and witnessed the death of Magdalon Schelderup, and his murderer had still not been caught. Instead, two further guests had been shot.

Fortunately, it seemed that none of those present wanted a confrontation of any sort with me. Maria Irene smiled almost imperceptibly when my eyes met hers. The others showed no reaction when I looked at them, but did show increasing animosity towards each other. Herlofsen scowled at the Wendelboes, and Mrs Wendelboe glared back at him. Every now and then, all three of them sent spiteful sideways glances at Magdalena Schelderup, who was smoking even more than usual and had a dark expression on her face. Sandra Schelderup looked alternately from her sister-in-law, Magdalena, to her stepson, Fredrik, but never with a pleasant face. Fredrik Schelderup sipped his glass of white wine and, for the moment, seemed rather unaffected by it all.

I was interested to see who would be the first to speak. Slightly unexpectedly, Magdalena's rusty voice was the first to be heard. Her defence was offensive.

'We all fully understand that this is an extremely difficult case. But when those who have been killed are my brother and two of his four heirs, then there is every reason to consider who stands to gain most from this.'

And so all hell was let loose. Only two people sat quietly with inscrutable faces. And it was the two whom I now liked best: old Petter Johannes Wendelboe and young Maria Irene Schelderup. All the others were suddenly making a noise. Sandra Schelderup snarled that she was not standing for any such insinuations, when all the time she and her daughter were the only two who could prove that they did not commit the two most recent murders.

Magdalena retorted that she had not mentioned any names, but reminded everyone that alliances were a possibility and that no one had an alibi for Magdalon's death. Then, for good measure, she added that there were those who still harboured grudges from the war. Herlofsen's face flushed red and he pointed out that there were three candidates in the room and demanded to know who Magdalena meant. The otherwise careful Mrs Wendelboe waded in too, with tears in her eyes, and said that Magdalena must of course mean Herlofsen, but that she, if anyone, should be wary of raking up old sins from the war. Sandra Schelderup snarled again and snapped that it was easy enough to see who would gain from the will, but a good place to start might be someone who had inherited an unmerited amount without having an alibi for anything.

At which point, things boiled over for the until now calm Fredrik Schelderup. He shouted that he did not think it was any more respectable to screw your way to a fortune than to kill for it.

The electric atmosphere in the room meant that everyone rather bizarrely turned against Fredrik Schelderup following his angry outburst, despite the fact that he quickly regained control and only seconds later tried to apologize. Herlofsen and Mrs Weldelboe turned away from each other and now glared at him. Even Petter Johannes Wendelboe had turned discreetly towards Fredrik Schelderup. I noticed with a small shard of jealousy that Maria Irene had finally turned her eyes away from me and was now looking at her half-brother. Magdalena Schelderup was puffing furiously on her third cigarette and through the smoke blew out a question as to whether a statement like that might not constitute a confession.

With this, the pressured and slightly intoxicated Fredrik Schelderup let his mask slip completely. He roared his innocence, slammed his glass back down onto the table with such force that the stem broke, and added that he was the only one around the table that he could guarantee had not killed his father.

There was complete silence in the room for a moment. Six pairs of venomous eyes watched Fredrik Schelderup as he poured himself another drink and drained the stemless glass. Then he crashed the remainder of the glass demonstratively down on the table, stood up and asked if he could now consider himself arrested.

I replied that his outburst and behaviour had been noted. I would not arrest him, but that from now on he would only be allowed to move between Bygdøy and Gulleråsen with my permission. This was obviously seen as further provocation. He came and stood right in front of me and howled: 'You can see for yourself the situation I am in. My father and brother have been killed, I am being accused of killing them, and all the people in this room can be trusted to try to kill me too. So tomorrow you can either arrest me or let me go to South America. Prison or Brazil are the only places I can now feel safe from these monsters!'

Before I could answer, he stormed out of the room and the building. Six pairs of eyes watched me in silence as I let him go. I wrote in my notepad with exaggerated movements to demonstrate that his behaviour would not be forgotten.

Sandra Schelderup had regained much of her composure, but her voice was still sharp as a knife when she demanded a continued police presence to safeguard her and her daughter until an arrest was made. Magdalena echoed this demand. I agreed to both on the spot. Magdalena Schelderup's face called to mind an old owl when she gave a curt nod. She shook my hand briefly in passing and left the building without gracing the others with so much as a look.

Mrs Wendelboe leant forward and whispered something in Hans Herlofsen's ear, who responded with a brief nod. I sent them a questioning look, and asked if there was anyone else who would like police protection overnight. Mrs Wendelboe looked at Mr Wendelboe, who shook his head. And, like a strange echo, Herlofsen did the same. All three of them got up to leave.

I followed them out into the hallway and asked Mrs Wendelboe what she had said to Herlofsen. She claimed that she had simply apologized for her outburst. Herlofsen confirmed this, but asked her somewhat curtly to repeat what else she said. She blanched, sent him a withering look, but then told me what she had said: 'It must be either Fredrik or Magdalena.' Herlofsen nodded his confirmation, said clearly that he believed this to be the case, and left the house in a rush.

I stood on the steps for a moment with the Wendelboes. I repeated my offer of police protection. This provoked the first comment of the day from Petter Johannes Wendelboe.

'No, thank you. We will definitely not be going out, either this evening or tonight. And if any of the others should decide to pay us an unexpected visit, which is highly unlikely, they will receive a warm welcome.'

I thought I caught a shadow of a smile on Petter Johannes Wendelboe's face when he said this. It occurred to me that he, unlike all the others, seemed to be enjoying the dramatic situation. But I was not able to discern if that was due to anything other than reliving some of the excitement of the war. A moment later, his face wore its usual stony mask. Both he and his wife shook my hand and then left without further words.

I loitered for a minute or two in the hall, apparently to think things through, and what I hoped and expected might happen did. Maria Irene came almost dancing down the stairs, smiling her mischievous smile, and apologized that the atmosphere at Schelderup Hall was unfortunately not at its best at the moment.

'But let us hope that it will improve in the future, when this whole nightmare is over,' she added, with a broader smile. 'Do you think it will take long?' she asked in a whisper. I replied that I hoped and thought that there would be a resolution within a couple of days.

Maria Irene nodded and looked up at me questioningly, but then nodded again with understanding when I just gave her an exaggerated stern look. I was given a brief hug before she tripped silently back up the stairs.

I stood there, looking up, for a few seconds after she disappeared. Then I went out on my own into the May day.

I left Schelderup Hall feeling remarkably unsettled. Following this gathering of the remaining guests from Magdalon Schelderup's last supper, I understood better than ever Patricia's description of them as satellite people in a universe that had lost its point of gravity. The situation still felt very unstable and unclear, no matter which way I looked. And it became no clearer when I returned to the office and discovered a new finding from the deceased Synnøve Jensen's house waiting for me on my desk.

V

'So, what do you make of these? A blue line on the back of the first envelope, and a black line on the back of the second.'

I put the letters down on the table in front of Patricia.

The letter with the blue line read:

Here, now.

So one of the dictator's wives has now gone.
More may follow, if you do not soon find out which of us
is doing wrong . . .

And the text in the letter with the black line was:

Here, now.

So one of the dictator's friends has now gone.
More may follow, if you do not soon find out which of us
is doing wrong . . .

Patricia sat and pondered for a while, but then gave a cautious smile.

'This really is very depressing news, but does tie in rather well with my theory about how it all fits together. So these were hidden between the pages of two different books on Synnøve Jensen's bedside table? And both envelopes were sealed?'

I nodded, without fully understanding the significance of this. Patricia fired her next technical question.

'And the letter in Synnøve Jensen's pocket, you only said that her fingerprints were found on the envelope? Were they on the letter as well?'

'Only on the envelope. There were no fingerprints on the letter itself.'

Patricia nodded sagely, but also let out a heavy sigh. I asked her, anxiously, if that did not fit with her theory. She replied that it in fact fitted well, but pointed to a very depressing conclusion. I was slightly flummoxed as to what she meant by that in a situation where I myself would be more than happy with any conclusion to any of the three murders. In my mind I counted my lucky stars that there were no newspapers on 17 May, but was not overly optimistic as to how my boss would assess the status of my investigation.

Patricia looked at me for a few seconds without saying anything. Her expression was unusually friendly, almost affectionate. She just sat there looking at me. For some reason or another, I thought about Maria Irene. It was not a comfortable situation. So I broke the silence with a question.

'A penny for your thoughts, Patricia?'

The answer was swift and unexpected.

'Just wondering why you are still alive!'

No doubt I looked rather stunned at this. She carried on immediately.

'Do not get me wrong, I am very glad that you are still alive. But has it not struck you as rather odd? Just imagine the situation the murderer found themselves in last night when you arrived. The murderer who had just shot Synnøve Jensen was standing behind her with a loaded gun in their hand when you rather inconveniently knocked on the door. Given that this is clearly an exceptionally intelligent and callous person, one might assume that the most obvious solution was to shoot you as soon as you opened the door, and then escape afterwards. Instead, the murderer carried through the suicide plan at ridiculous risk, leaving the gun beside Synnøve Jensen and then barricading themselves in upstairs, unarmed. Understandable if the murderer did not know who it was knocking on the door, or had reason to believe there was a large muster of policemen outside. But undeniably strange if the murderer knew that it was only you who was standing there.'

I had actually not thought about how strange it was that I was still alive. But I took her point when she put it like this and immediately asked if she had a theory about the connection here. To my relief, she gave a measured nod.

'I really only see one possibility. And that fortunately falls into place with my overall theory of how everything fits together. But I am still not absolutely certain, and it is without a doubt a very serious step to accuse someone of murder when you have no concrete evidence.'

She hesitated, then asked abruptly: 'What do you make of the situation yourself?'

I realized that Patricia was not willing to divulge her theory without knowing what I thought, and I had little to lose by revealing this in such a closed and highly unofficial space. So I launched myself out into the unknown waters.

'I have to admit that I am not certain about anything. I think you are right in saying there is more than one person involved here. Yesterday, I was very close to arresting Hans Herlofsen. Today, my main theory is that Magdalena Schelderup was the Dark Prince and killed the two Resistance men during the war, but that Synnøve Jensen wrote the letters and killed the Schelderups, both father and son. Synnøve Jensen had planned several murders, most immediately Magdalena, who then beat her to it.'

Patricia stared at me wide-eyed for a moment.

'You surpass yourself,' she remarked, apparently serious.

My joy lasted for all of ten seconds. Because when she continued, it was far less pleasant.

'I would not have believed it was possible to get so much wrong in two sentences, and at such a late stage of a murder investigation. Magdalena Schelderup is neither the Dark Prince nor the person who killed Synnøve Jensen. Synnøve Jensen did not kill either the father or the son, she never planned to murder anyone, and nor did she write any of the letters. And just to be clear about it, the person who killed Synnøve Jensen is not the Dark Prince, either.'

It was indeed quite a salvo, even for Patricia. Fortunately, I still had a trump card up my sleeve, and decided to play it straight away.

'Are you certain that Synnøve Jensen's murderer was not the Dark Prince? That it was not the same pistol that was used?'

Patricia shook her head vigorously.

'Don't be ridiculous. It would be an incredible coincidence if it was the same kind of gun, or demonstrate a rather warped sense of humour on the part of the murderer.'

Triumphantly, I pulled out a sheet of paper and threw it down on the table between us.

'Well then you are very wrong yourself, my dear Patricia, and I can prove it. I took this written report from the ballistics expert with me, just in case. It is 100 per cent certain that the bullets that killed Hans Petter Nilsen and Bjørn Varden in 1941 came from the same Walther pistol that was found lying in Synnøve Jensen's house yesterday. The registration number has been filed off, so we will not be able to trace it, but it is definitely the same weapon.'

I later regretted that I did not have a camera with me. In a flash, Patricia's face was transformed into the most surprised woman's face I have ever seen. It was the face of a person who has suddenly seen their entire perception of the world, their whole view of life, crumble before their very eyes.

Then, just as suddenly, a relieved grin spread over her face.

To my astonishment, Patricia whooped loudly in triumph: 'EUREKA!'

Then she started to laugh, a loud, coarse laugh. It was almost a minute before she had composed herself enough to talk again.

'Please excuse my somewhat eccentric behaviour. But thanks to you, the final, most important, piece of the jigsaw puzzle has now fallen into place. It is incredible just how ironic fate can sometimes be.'

I looked at her, nonplussed. She chuckled a bit more, but was then suddenly serious again.

'No more sympathy or other unnecessary luxuries. There really is only one detail left in connection with Leonard Schelderup's death. Drive over to the hospital to see Ingrid Schelderup, and ask her as soon as she wakes up where the revolver was before she left it on the floor by the front door. When you have found out, come back here, then I will explain to you how this fits in with the other two murders.'

I looked at her again with a mixture of surprise and scepticism.

'I thought we both agreed that Ingrid Schelderup could not possibly have anything to do with her son's death?'

'No one is saying that she had anything to do with her son's death. However, the revolver which was used to shoot her son was lying somewhere else when she got there that morning. And where it was lying when she came in is of vital importance to the question of who shot Leonard Schelderup. And when I have my theory confirmed as to who shot him, I can hopefully quickly fill you in on how everything fits together, including who sprinkled the powdered nuts on Magdalon Schelderup's food and who shot Synnøve Jensen!'

This was definitely too good an offer to say no to, particularly given my last conversation with my boss. So I got up and made ready to leave.

Patricia stopped me with a final brief remark as I stood up.

'To misquote Sherlock Holmes ever so slightly, from one of Conan Doyle's best novels: the point to which I would wish to draw your attention is what the dogs did in the night-time.'

I was totally lost.

'But . . . if you mean the guard dogs at Schelderup Hall, they did absolutely nothing on the night that Leonard Schelderup was murdered.'

Patricia nodded smugly.

'Precisely.'

I must have looked very bewildered, but Patricia was all secretive and jolly, and just waved me out of the door.

Three minutes later, I was in the car driving to the

hospital. On the way there, I pondered Patricia's mysterious parting remark, and could find no connection to the fact that the guard dogs at the Gulleråsen mansion had been quiet on the night that Leonard Schelderup had been shot in his flat in Skøyen. But in a strange way, I felt secure in the knowledge that Patricia had seen something that I could not, and that her explanation and solution were just around the corner.

VI

Ingrid Schelderup had slept heavily, but had just woken up when I arrived at the hospital. I had to wait a little while until she was in a fit state to talk to me. So I sat waiting for a very long half hour indeed, before being shown into her room at around half past eight. By then I had worked out the connection between who shot her son and the importance of where the revolver was placed. And I had to admit that it seemed highly plausible, to the extent that anything in this case did.

Ingrid Schelderup kept her dignity well in the face of the greatest tragedy of her life. She was sitting in an armchair, slightly slumped, but fully clothed. Her face was dead and her movements delayed. She looked at least six years older than she had done the first time we met only six days ago. I thought I could even see more grey hairs in amongst the black. Throughout our short conversation, her body seemed to be hanging off the chair. Her head sat atop her thin neck and moved very gently back and forth and her eyes were still alive. They stayed fixed on me from the moment I came through the door. She nodded faintly, but did not say anything or make any other movement.

I sat down with care on the chair that had been put out in front of her table, so that we were only a few feet apart.

'I do apologize that I have to disturb you. We all sympathize with your grief over the enormous loss of your son, and we have no reason to believe that you have anything to do with any of the murders . . .'

She nodded almost imperceptibly again, but still did not say anything. Her tense, fearful eyes were fixed on me.

'However, we do now have reason to believe that you have given us some false information regarding an important point which may be vital to the investigation.'

Everything in the room stood still for a few breathless moments. I still feared an outburst of anger. But all I got was another small nod. This time, barely that.

'The revolver that was used to shoot your son was on the floor by the front door when you left. But it was not there when you arrived. Where was it then?'

I saw a ripple down Ingrid Schelderup's neck, while her face remained blank. I realized soon after that she was in fact trying to speak, but could not find her voice. In the end, I saw no other solution than to assist her.

'It was on the floor beside your son, wasn't it?'

She nodded.

'And the reason that we did not find his fingerprints on the revolver was that you had wiped them off.'

She nodded in silence one last time. Then she finally found her voice. It was still not much more than a whisper, but it was a pleasure to hear it break the tense silence between us.

'I didn't know what I was doing, and then later could hardly remember what I had done. The boundary between life and dreams was so hazy. And now everything is just a blur. But yes, I must have.'

And suddenly there was no more to be said. The truth about Leonard Schelderup's death was painfully clear, both to me and his mother. She was the one who spoke first.

'But you really must not believe that . . . Leonard did not kill his father. Quite the contrary, it was the death of his father that killed him. Leonard's life was never easy, but he was the kindest boy in the world. He would never have hurt anyone other than himself.'

I nodded to reassure her.

'I believe you. But no matter how confused and grief-stricken you were, you obviously understood what would happen – that if it got out that he had shot himself, everyone would believe that he shot his father and then regretted it. And you understood the importance of removing his finger-prints.'

She nodded.

'I apologize,' she said suddenly, her voice thick with tears.

I got up to leave, when she rather unexpectedly asked me a question.

'The poor secretary who was shot last night . . . I didn't really know her that well; she came from a different background, after all. But I hope for her sake and for mine . . .

that things would not have been any different for her if I had told you the truth before?'

I desperately wanted to answer no. But I had to be honest, so I said that at the moment no one could answer that, and it was possible that no one ever would. At last there was some movement in the sagging body in the chair. With surprising speed, she lifted her hands and hid her face.

I quickly thanked her for her help and left the room as quietly as I could. I had thought of asking Ingrid Schelderup formally whether she still denied having sprinkled nuts in her ex-husband's food, but I was now certain that she had not. And I had feared that I might have to ask her what she knew about her son's secret love life, but that was obviously no longer of any importance.

'We have nothing left to say to each other that matters any more,' a seventeen-year-old summer love once told me at Åndalsnes train station many years ago. And rather oddly, this remark echoed in my ears as I closed the door to the sixty-year-old Ingrid Schelderup's hospital room on Friday, 16 May 1969. I had the same feeling that we would not see each other again and that we would never have anything more of any significance to say to each other anyway.

It was only when I was on my way back that I realized how much I dreaded telling Petter Johannes Wendelboe. He would now have to take those seemingly endless steps into his wife's room to tell her that Leonard Schelderup did in fact take his own life only hours after she called and threatened him.

I still could not fathom who had killed Magdalon

Schelderup. But I thought to myself that whoever it was had started a chain of events that was claiming ever more victims, including some of the living. Then I thought about Patricia's comment that all of the ten guests at Magdalon Schelderup's last supper were satellite people. Two of them had now definitely crashed and two others were so out of orbit that it was uncertain whether they would ever find their paths again. And hidden in their ranks was still one, if not two murderers. And as I drove back to 104–8 Erling Skjalgsson's Street, I was more unsure than ever about who this might be.

VII

'So there you have it. You have solved the mystery of who shot Leonard Schelderup. The answer is Leonard Schelderup himself.'

Patricia nodded glumly and took a deep breath in preparation for one of her longer speeches.

'I should have dared to draw that conclusion earlier, but was uncertain because of the gun. The problem was not so much where it was lying, but where it was not lying. I did not want to risk accusing poor Ingrid Schelderup unnecessarily. The answer was really very logical to anyone with a minimal understanding of psychology. It would hardly be surprising if Leonard Schelderup had had suicidal thoughts earlier, given his great secret and his troubled relationship with his father and family. Poor Leonard was, as his sister said, strong on the tracks where he felt at home, but weak where he did not. And then he was forced out of orbit, into a highly vulnerable and unpredictable position in space. He clearly considered suicide as an option when he took the revolver from Schelderup Hall. What finally pushed him totally off course was the series of events later on in the day. First of all, his aunt urged him to confess, then he was threatened by a stranger on the telephone. We will never know for certain what was the final straw. I think it is quite possible that his conversation with you helped him through the first crisis after the telephone call, and that it was in fact his lover who quite unintentionally gave him the final, fatal push later on in the evening. Despite all his talents, Leonard Schelderup had been a very lonely person all his life. After all those years, he had finally found his love. Imagine the disappointment, then, when the only person he truly trusted and loved also urged him to confess. Who on earth would believe him then?'

Patricia gave a sorry shake of the head and concluded sadly: 'His lover of course knew no better. Even though Leonard Schelderup pulled the trigger himself, it still feels as though he was murdered. In part by a conservative society that would not allow him to live the way he wanted, simply because he was different. And in part by the evil person who intentionally and in cold blood put him under impossible pressure by means of the well-staged poisoning of Magdalon Schelderup.'

I vaguely noted that Patricia had an unexpectedly liberal view on homosexuality, despite her conservative family background. However, I was so focused on developments in the investigation that I did not stop to discuss the topic.

'There is, alas, not much that we can do about the former, but there is definitely something we can do now about the latter. Who was it who sprinkled the nuts on Magdalon Schelderup's food?'

Patricia finished her coffee and then sat in contemplation.

'That is, if possible, the most depressing part of the whole thing. Over the past few days, I have come to realize that the two who have lost their lives were perhaps the kindest of the guests round the table when the man they all orbited died. The murder of Synnøve Jensen was, as I have already said, cold-blooded in the extreme. The powdered nuts in Magdalon Schelderup's food and the plan behind it are, even so, the peak of human evil and the work of an extremely devious and egotistical person.'

I waited in suspense for the name of Magdalon Schelderup's murderer. But instead, Patricia started to reflect on his nature.

'I understood very early on that the guests sitting around the table were all satellite people who orbited Magdalon Schelderup. But I did not fully understand to begin with how inseparable his dominant and extremely distinct personality was from the solution. You should always be wary of making psychological diagnoses of dead people. However, there can be no doubt that Magdalon Schelderup, behind his mask, suffered from severe narcissism. It is a condition suffered by many famous geniuses throughout history, including the philosopher Nietzsche. The symptoms are an exaggerated ego that often results in an equally exaggerated lack of consideration for others, and a pathological need for control. Life for Magdalon Schelderup was simply a matter of asserting himself, the line between the play and the player becoming ever more diffuse. And this is where the key lay to the mystery of his death.'

Patricia was silent for a long time following this introduction. I realized that she wanted to wait a little longer before revealing the name of the person who had killed Magdalon Schelderup, so asked instead what clues she had followed.

'There were various factors that all pointed in the same direction. But the most important thing was the letters. One thing was the question as to why the murderer had taken the trouble to send them to the police. And the other was just how different they were. The first letter was very detailed; the second one that came in the post and the others that were found in Synnøve Jensen's house were remarkably general and vague. They contained nothing to indicate any knowledge of the later deaths. In fact, we would probably have dismissed them as the work of a mad person, had it not been for the first letter and the few similarities. There was also the strange fact that the first letter was posted before Magdalon Schelderup's death, whereas the second was not posted until after his son's death.'

I looked at her with some scepticism.

'So are you saying that the first letter was written by someone different from the others?'

Patricia shook her head.

'I did consider that possibility. But gradually I came to favour the alternative possibility, based on the obvious technical similarities between the letters, and the fact that no one had seen the first one. This was that the letters were written by the same person, but that he or she for some reason knew more about the first death than the subsequent ones. Now that we know that Leonard Schelderup committed suicide, it seems reasonable enough that no one else could know the details before or after.'

'But if the letters were written by the same person then, judging by the circumstances, they must have been written by Synnøve Jensen? How else would you explain the fact that the last letters were found at her house with only her fingerprints on them? Were the letters planted there by the person who murdered her?'

Patricia shook her head again, but only briefly.

'The murderer could in theory have planted the letter in her pocket, but not the others in her books. She is the one who posted the letter after Leonard Schelderup's death.'

I felt increasingly baffled.

'I am sure that when we discussed my theory earlier on today, you were quite clear that Synnøve Jensen had nothing to do with the letters?'

'I did not say that Synnøve Jensen had not posted one of the letters, or that she would not post any more. However, she did not write them. In fact, circumstances would indicate that she had not even read them.'

'So it was not she who posted the first letter?'

Another shake of the head, but this time more definite.

'No. If she had known anything about the first letter, she would no doubt have informed you straight away. Magdalon Schelderup's death was a shock for his lover, and she probably knew nothing about how much she stood to gain from the will. The first letter, and that one alone, was posted by another person. By the very same person who, the day after, according to his fiendish and cunning plan, sprinkled nuts onto Magdalon Schelderup's food.'

Patricia paused for effect and drank another full cup of coffee. The expression on her face was the grimmest I had seen. I had to prod her to continue.

'So you are saying that the murderer is a man and that he wrote all the letters, but posted only the first one. The second one was posted by Synnøve Jensen, who had no idea what it said.'

Patricia nodded and released a deep sigh.

She pulled the Russian book about chess from the pile and put it down on the table.

'When analysing a complex chess position, one first has to try to figure out several possible moves ahead. One then has to consider how the pieces will respond to the various moves. This can be extremely difficult, particularly when the moves are complicated and not obvious. The man who posted the first letter and who gave the remaining letters to Synnøve Jensen was in just such a position. He could to a certain extent predict possible future moves, but could not know for certain what would happen after the first death. People are by nature more unpredictable than chess pieces, so the possible future moves in this game would be even more uncertain. Which is why the letters are more vague. And why Synnøve Jensen was given several letters, which she was to send according to who had died. There were several possibilities, so Synnøve Jensen, simple and loyal woman that she was, made small pen marks on the back of the envelopes so she could remember which letter to send under which circumstances.'

'So the man who gave her the letters was the same man who put the nuts on Magdalon Schelderup's food?'

Patricia nodded.

'He is the only one who could have got her to post the letters and she is the only one he could have trusted with such a task.'

'This man was then perhaps also the real father of her unborn child?'

Patricia gave a bitter smile.

'Without a doubt.'

I racked my brains. The only remaining male candidates were Fredrik Schelderup, Petter Johannes Wendelboe and Hans Herlofsen – and of course the now deceased Leonard Schelderup. One of them must have had a relationship with Synnøve Jensen. But I could not understand who.

'The man with the powdered nuts knew about Magdalon Schelderup's heart condition?'

Patricia sent me a puzzled look.

'Of course, it is perfectly obvious that he did.'

'But why did this man need to write the letters beforehand and then give them to Synnøve Jensen? Why could he not wait and see what happened and then send them himself?'

I definitely made myself vulnerable with that question. Patricia now looked at me with mildly patronizing eyes, as if I was a small child who could not understand anything.

'For the very good reason that he himself would be dead!'

The truth punched home as she said this. And the impact was brutal. This was indeed a terrible truth.

'So the man who planned it all, posted the letter, slashed the car tyres, put on the recording of the fire alarm and then with devastating precision sprinkled the nuts on Magdalon Schelderup's plate was in fact . . .'

Patricia nodded.

'Magdalon Schelderup himself.'

We sat in silence for some seconds. It felt as if the air itself was trembling with fear. Patricia's thin arms were certainly shaking. She pulled out a handkerchief and dabbed her eyes before she continued.

'As Sherlock Holmes so aptly said: "When you have eliminated the impossible, whatever remains, however improbable, must be the truth." But this is perhaps not so improbable when you consider Magdalon Schelderup's distinctive and egotistical character. His whole life was about self-assertion and attention. He loved only himself and did not give a hoot about his family and friends once he was dead. Quite the contrary: he would have liked to kill some of them, if he could avoid being caught and having to face punishment. The man had a perverse need for control and power over other people. His secrets and the things that he had done in the past were starting to catch up with him. Herlofsen posed a threat, and behind his mask Magdalon Schelderup was still more frightened of Petter Johannes Wendelboe than of anything else. The danger that he would be found out was growing. The thought of suicide must have been tempting once he found out that he did not have long to live. His collapse in the doctor's waiting room had given him a shock and he did not want to risk a more serious attack on the open street or at a dinner party. Magdalon Schelderup became a hunted man and was terrified of saying something that might give him away.'

I had nothing to say. So I just nodded to Patricia for her to continue.

'But Magdalon Schelderup did not want to die with the disgrace that suicide so often entails. It would be far better to die as the victim of murder, whether it was left unsolved or someone was accused of doing it. He planned a suicide that was camouflaged as a murder, and that would at the same time cause the murder of some of the people he hated and scorned most in his closest circle. Magdalon Schelderup wanted to go down with his colours flying; he wanted to continue to exert influence on the lives and deaths of those closest to him even after he was gone. But most of all, he wanted to fool everyone, including the police, as he had done during the war. This was his final game and charade. Last Saturday, he was finally ready to set the wheels in motion. Having first punctured the tyres on his own car, he started the ball rolling by calling you. Then the following day he continued as planned, first by putting on the cassette recording and then, in the ensuing chaos, by sprinkling the powdered nuts on his food.'

Patricia stopped abruptly, looked at me, and then carried on.

'He needed an assistant to ensure that the game continued and of course chose his loyal and dependable secretary, Synnøve Jensen, who was the only person who really cared about him. She continued to orbit him even after his death and loyally posted out the letters as instructed. Presumably, he had also told her that the letters might be important to the police investigation should more people than just himself be killed. She would never understand the danger in which her dead lover's game placed her. But she sensed after a while that something was not right, and rang you to tell you about the letters. Unfortunately she was a bit slow on the uptake and ended up calling you just minutes too late to save her own life.'

I had finally regained the power of speech and felt the irritation and wonder growing.

'So I have been leading a murder investigation for five days when in fact there has been no murder, in a legal sense. Now, do not come here and tell me that Synnøve Jensen's death was not a murder and that it was not a murderer whom I chased that night?'

Patricia shook her head and was deadly serious.

'Absolutely not. Synnøve Jensen was without question murdered and you were chasing a cold-blooded and egotistical murderer that night; a person who, without knowing the truth about Magdalon Schelderup's death, had seen an opportunity and taken the chance in the chaos that ensued. And while we do not need to fear any further action from the man who sprinkled the nuts on Magdalon Schelderup's food, there is a considerable danger that the person who shot Synnøve Jensen might strike again. There is in fact every reason to fear that this person is planning to strike again tonight, again at one of the remaining guests. I cannot of course be 100 per cent certain, as the risk is enormous. But the gains are so great and the chances of getting away with it so good that I believe the murderer will take that risk tonight.'

I stood up without thinking.

'That's terrible,' I exclaimed, spontaneously.

Patricia looked up at me with absolute calm.

'Yes and no. It is terrible, but it could also be perfect. You may have another chance to do what you nearly did yesterday: that is, to catch the murderer in person at the scene of the crime. Even though I am fairly certain of who it is you are chasing, there are still potentially two people who might turn up tonight. However, you should get in touch as soon as possible with the person who is at risk of being murdered.'

I nodded earnestly.

'In which case, where should I hide tonight?'

There was no turning back now, so Patricia did not hesitate for a moment.

'In Fredrik Schelderup's flat. Ensure that there are no policemen visibly standing guard and conceal yourself somewhere inside.'

'Please excuse a silly question, but how will the murderer get in?'

Patricia gave another of her bitterest smiles.

'Perhaps pure luck, but that is in fact not such a silly question. They will in this case come through the door, using the key from Magdalon Schelderup's missing key ring. So check first that Fredrik Schelderup has not changed the locks, and make sure that he does not put the safety chain on. It would be rather a shame if the murderer could not get in to be arrested.'

I agreed and got ready to leave. However, Patricia waved at me to stop.

'Just a couple of quick final things. We have already seen how cold-blooded the person who killed Synnøve Jensen is, so beware, and please keep your wits about you. And get some rest first. I can guarantee that nothing will happen before a quarter past eleven at the earliest, and possibly not until a few hours later, so you still have plenty of time.'

I nodded. My trust in Patricia was without limit following the day's performance and her concern for me gave a touch of warmth in what was otherwise such a cold, cynical case.

'And the second thing?'

'I will keep the telephone within easy reach tonight. Call me if you have to during the night, but if you can wait until tomorrow morning sometime after eight, it would be preferable. I tend not to sleep very well during murder investigations.'

She had my full understanding for that and I promised to call her as soon as the night's mission had been accomplished.

VIII

I ordered a constable to guard Fredrik Schelderup's home at a discreet distance and in civilian clothes until eleven o'clock that evening, when I would myself take over.

Then I rang Fredrik Schelderup and fortunately this time was greeted by his easy-going, jocular self. I gave the situation a positive slant and promised that I would grant him permission to travel to South America tomorrow if there had not been an arrest before then. In the meantime, we would guard his home and I would myself spend the night in his flat. I joked that he would no doubt rather have a beautiful young woman to stay overnight, but hopefully the fact that she would instead be allowed to travel abroad with him tomorrow might be acceptable compensation. He immediately agreed to this and said, before putting down the phone, that in that case he had better call her and tell her to start packing.

I myself went to bed around seven for three hours' kip, with the alarm clock set for ten. This went unexpectedly well. Only a couple of times did an image of the remaining candidates flicker through my mind, but I was still none the wiser as to who it was that I had chased the night before, or who I might meet in Fredrik Schelderup's home that night. I fell asleep at ten past seven, strangely secure in the knowledge that a solution was close at hand.

IX

At a quarter past eleven I took over from the constable outside Fredrik Schelderup's home, and rang the doorbell. My host was far from entertaining company now. He complained of getting a headache after his first glass of the evening and that he drank a couple more without it helping much. He went to bed around half past eleven, which, according to him, was the earliest he had gone to bed for several years – that is to say, when the intention was to sleep.

To begin with, I managed only too well without his company, but soon time started to drag as I sat at my post behind the door in the living room. By one o'clock, I was very sceptical of Patricia's prediction, and by two I was thoroughly bored of the whole thing. The cigarette smoke that impregnated the walls made me more and more drowsy. At half past two, I caught myself dozing off for a couple of seconds.

But then at a quarter to three, I found myself wide awake on hearing a muffled sound by the front door. All my senses were on full alert by the time the door was opened with great caution a couple of minutes later.

A person about half a head shorter than me, dressed in trousers and a shirt, with a nylon stocking pulled down over the head, tiptoed in. I caught a glimpse of a key ring in the person's left hand. The figure then glided silently across the floor towards the door to Fredrik Schelderup's bedroom. The intruder was holding a small pistol in their right hand, but he or she appeared to be otherwise unarmed.

I was unable to identify the person in the pitch-dark. It was only when I slipped up behind the intruder and put my hand round their right upper arm that I knew that it was without doubt a woman.

I did not have time to think any more. The pistol fell onto the floor with a thud and then slid under a chair when I grabbed her arm. I had obviously instinctively thought that the drama would then be over, as the intruder was a woman who was not only smaller, but also slighter than me. However, the next shock was greater for me than for her. In her fright, she let out a piercing scream and with a furious movement managed to twist out of my grasp.

For a few seconds we stood facing each other, unarmed, in the middle of the dark room. Then there was a flash as she pulled a sharp kitchen knife from a pocket.

The woman with a nylon stocking over her head stood dancing on her toes in front of me, holding out the knife threateningly. We stayed like this, the one measuring up the other in tense animosity and fear, for a few moments. I did not dare to take my eyes off her for a second.

Suddenly she made a lightning thrust towards my chest. I quickly sidestepped and managed to move back at the same time. She did not follow up on this attack, but instead took a couple of steps back. With her left hand, she fumbled behind her for the door. Despite a dangerously high pulse, I took a couple of steps towards her. I got so close that I could see that her hands were shaking, but not close enough to recognize her, and not close enough to apprehend her.

Then she made another unexpected lunge, this time towards my throat and face. One moment I saw with horror the knife coming through the air towards my eye, and in the next I felt it slice cold and hard past my cheek.

A second later she lost her balance. This was precisely what I needed to kick her right leg from under her. She fell, but was cool-headed enough to keep a firm hold of the knife. There was another struggle, with her on her hands and knees on the floor, and me above her with my hands round her upper arms. Again she twisted and turned, with the strength of a desperate animal.

We continued to struggle on the floor. I had managed to

get a firm hold of her right arm, but her fingers were tight around the handle of the knife. The small woman on the floor was stronger and had more stamina than one might expect on first seeing her. In the dark and heat of the struggle, it felt as though I held her right wrist forever before she eventually let go of the knife with a quiet groan.

Even without a weapon, my opponent's furious fight to escape was not over. She lashed out, bit, clawed and kicked blindly and wildly with a panicked intensity. Her sharp nails scratched my bare underarms several times. A small eternity seemed to pass before I eventually managed to get out the handcuffs and snap them shut round her right wrist. She was such a wild, feral beast that she continued to kick and hit out, and I felt another searing scratch down my arm, until I finally managed to cuff her left wrist as well.

Following her first scream, she had been impressively silent throughout the whole struggle. It was only when the cuffs were on both her wrists that she spat out 'NO, NO!' a couple of times, then seemed to hiss. I sat with all my weight on her legs, initially in shock and with a racing heart, as she slowly stopped flailing.

My first attempt to pull the nylon stocking off her head provoked a new furious outburst. And my self-discipline broke. I manhandled her onto her back and straddled her stomach, leaving her legs to kick as much as she liked. Then I ripped the nylon stocking from her head in anger.

Just as I was unmasking my prisoner, the door to Fredrik Schelderup's bedroom opened and the light was switched on. He stood swaying and squinting in the doorway in his dressing gown, with a wine glass in his hand. Fredrik

Schelderup took one look at my prisoner on the floor, rolled his eyes and exclaimed: 'It's a good thing you were here on guard to stop her, Detective Inspector. She is not only a little too old, but also too difficult for me to want her in my bedroom.'

No more was needed to provoke another burst of rage from Sandra Schelderup. She screamed barely comprehensible swear words at her stepson, and kicked and flailed so furiously that I was almost frightened that the handcuffs might give way. Fredrik Schelderup looked down at her with scorn and fetched a length of nylon rope from a cupboard.

He remarked: 'I wish you a continued goodnight, despite the unfortunate female company. It has happened to me more than once.'

With a slightly exaggerated yawn and no further comment, he retired back to bed.

I still did not like Fredrik Schelderup, but had to admit that he had a point. This hissing, hateful version of Sandra Schelderup that I was now alone with was certainly not one I would want to take home.

Once the nylon rope had been tied around her legs, she calmed down. I found the pistol, the knife and the large key ring on the floor. I felt another mysterious small metal object in her pocket. This turned out to be Magdalena Schelderup's missing ring. It was such a cynical detail that I certainly did not look at Sandra Schelderup with kinder eyes.

At a quarter past three in the morning of 17 May 1969, I stood in the living room of Fredrik Schelderup's flat with an almost trussed Sandra Schelderup. I felt enormous relief that an apparently inexplicable murder case had suddenly been solved.

At the same time, I suffered for the first time in my life what can only be called a panic attack. It came over me in the form of a bizarre fear that if I left the house, I myself would be shot or attacked in the few steps that it took to get to my car. The fear was so paralysing that to begin with I could not even go to the window to look out.

I had to convince myself that the fear was completely irrational and due to being overtaxed. I had no reason to believe that Sandra Schelderup might have an accomplice out there in the dark. In the end, however, I called the police station and asked them to send two constables over in a Black Maria as quickly as possible. The official explanation was that someone needed to continue to stand guard over the place while I took the suspect in.

When I finally had Sandra Schelderup in the back of the car and was driving to the station, I had to admit to myself that all the drama had taken its toll.

We drove for the first five minutes in grim silence. Now and then, I glanced over at my passenger to make sure that she was not planning to try anything, and could see that she was calming down.

'If I confess, is there a possibility of mitigating circumstances, even if I have been arrested and am accused of murder?' she asked in a controlled voice, just before the police station loomed into view.

I replied that that was something that the court would have to decide, but it was a possibility.

'In that case, I hereby confess to the murder of Synnøve

Jensen and the attempted murder of Fredrik Schelderup. But I do not know who shot Leonard Schelderup or who killed Magdalon Schelderup,' she stated, after a pause.

I smiled to myself in the mirror and assured her that both those deaths had now been solved.

'My poor daughter is fast asleep in her bed, gloriously unaware of all of this. I did it without her knowing, but I did it for her sake and the inheritance. She is the only one of my husband's children who is suited to carrying on his work. Every mother has the right to fight for her children,' she said, from the back seat.

I bit my tongue and said nothing. I detested Sandra Schelderup and had no wish to talk to her. But her next attempt to excuse herself made my blood boil.

'I now regret what has happened, though I did it through sheer desperation and almost in self-defence. I did not kill Leonard. I would never do that. He was not a parasite and his mother is still alive. Both Synnøve Jensen and Fredrik Schelderup were parasites who were just waiting for my husband to die. Neither of them were of any benefit to anyone and neither of them had parents who were still alive. So Synnøve Jensen's death was no great loss to the world, and nor would Fredrik Schelderup's have been.'

I felt my anger rising and suddenly hated the very sound of Sandra Schelderup's voice with intensity. I turned around and remarked with force that Synnøve Jensen had in fact been the mother of an unborn child that had died with her. Sandra Schelderup looked away as soon as our eyes met. The remaining minutes of the journey were spent in silence once again.

When the Iron Curtain Falls

I

I disliked Sandra Schelderup more than I could ever remember having disliked a woman. However it was difficult not to be impressed by her willpower. In sharp contrast to her violent behaviour the night before, and despite her bleak future prospects, the woman who gave a confession and explanation to me in one of the interview rooms at the main police station on the morning of 17 May 1969 was focused and calm. She had been offered legal assistance, but had declined as she did not see what help that would be at the moment. So she sat there alone with me and a prosecutor, and answered all my questions clearly and concisely.

Her husband's death had been a shock. As had the shooting of his son two days later. She knew nothing about these deaths. The reading of the will had been a nasty surprise that made her furious on her daughter's behalf, and the tense situation had caused her to have increasingly wild thoughts in the days that followed. She had seen an opportunity when Leonard Schelderup died. The number of heirs had been reduced to two and she had every hope that any new murders would be attributed to whoever was responsible for the first two. She had first hidden her late husband's key ring and then reported it as missing. And she had kept Magdalena Schelderup's ring so that it could later be planted as a red herring, as she had intended to do the night before. She admitted that she had taken the ring before Leonard Schelderup was killed, but claimed that she had kept it 'just in case' after the reading of the will, though at that point she had no concrete plans. I reserved some doubts, but moved on to the murder of Synnøve Jensen.

The details of Sandra Schelderup's confession were both clear and convincing. She had sneaked out late that evening and driven to the top of the hill behind Synnøve Jensen's house in one of the company cars, which was kept in a parking place relatively close to Schelderup Hall. She immediately identified the key on her late husband's key ring. She had been prepared to change her plan at any point, but then the temptation was too great when she got there without meeting a soul and was let into the house. Her hatred for her husband's mistress had been overwhelming. She had shot the secretary and waited for her to die in the hope that she could camouflage it as suicide, but then fled when she heard me coming.

Sandra Schelderup's description of the ensuing chase was exactly as I remembered it. She had asked for police protection at Schelderup Hall to ensure an alibi for a possible murder, and then given in to temptation. The fight for her innocent daughter's legacy had become an obsession and she saw an opportunity to secure an undivided inheritance for Maria Irene and to get away with it. Fredrik Schelderup had always hated her and she had nothing but scorn for him. He was a man without a family, who would just squander the money if he got it. So she had decided to carry out her plan when she saw that there were no policemen guarding the house, only to be outwitted by me.

To my question as to how she had managed to get in and out of her own home unseen, she replied that there was a concealed passage from the cellar. Magdalon had once mentioned briefly that he had built a secret passage after the war as a combined hiding place and escape route in case of a crisis in the future. He had, however, asked her never to look for it until after his death, unless there was a crisis situation. The night after her husband's death she had gone to find it, as she no longer need fear her husband's reaction and she wanted to see if he had hidden anything of value there. And she had found a collection of gold and dollar bills, a valuable diamond and three guns in a cavity in the wall. She had guessed that the gold, money and diamonds were easily transportable valuables in the event of a crisis. In the 1960s, Magdalon had on a couple of occasions quite exceptionally mentioned his fear of a Soviet occupation.

She discovered that all the registration information had been filed off the oldest and largest pistol. So she had taken this with her and left it behind after she had shot Synnøve Jensen. The second gun was the smaller pistol with which she had intended to kill Fredrik Schelderup. Her plan was to leave the gun at Magdalena Schelderup's house later, if necessary. She had also taken the ring for this very reason, and had thought of leaving it behind as a clue. Magdalena was obviously in a vulnerable position and she was a cold-hearted old woman with no children, and in any case did not have many years left to live.

It was not a story to be proud of but, unfortunately, it was true, said Sandra Schelderup, wringing her hands without looking me in the eye. I had to agree with her, but assured her that the confession was registered and would be considered by the court. She thanked me with a wan smile, and then unexpectedly apologized for the situation this had put me in. She had been treated with distrust by the others in the family and their circle of friends and had come to hate them all, but she had nothing against me and only wished me well in my career. Her daughter had also expressed great sympathy and admiration for me, she added in a quieter voice. She now realized that what she had done was not fair on her daughter, and she hoped that she would be able to explain herself to her as soon as possible. I found this a suitable point to finish the interview.

It was by now nine o'clock in the morning of 17 May and I felt an enormous relief settle over me. I telephoned my boss, who was very pleased indeed that the case had been solved and looked forward to hearing more details tomorrow. I was just about to compose a press release when I realized that some details were still missing, and that I had to inform Maria Irene Schelderup of the night's dramatic developments as soon as possible.

II

To my relief, all was calm outside Schelderup Hall. The policeman on guard had stayed awake all night. The dogs had barked loudly and been restless for a few minutes around midnight. However, no one had tried to get into or out of the house. I could rest assured that Maria Irene had been there. She had obviously slept badly and had been seen at the window two or three times during the night.

Inside Schelderup Hall, a forensics team was in full swing with an investigation of the cellar, where they had found a well-camouflaged door into the secret tunnel, as described by Sandra Schelderup. The cavity that she had mentioned had also been found and I was given a list of the remaining contents, which tallied well with her account.

Maria Irene had sought refuge in her room. I was nervous about how she would welcome me this time, but soon found that that my fears were ungrounded. She embraced me as soon as the door was closed behind us. She had slept badly and had therefore got up several times during the night, and was very concerned to discover in the early hours of the morning that her mother's room was empty.

But the eighteen-year-old's equanimity was impressive. She listened with concentration to my account of the night's dramatic events, including my tussle with her mother. There was a touching moment when she cried: 'You weren't hurt, were you?' She added that I must not think ill of her, even though her mother had done terrible things. I felt a great relief wash over me and happily assured her that children could not be held responsible for the actions of their parents.

I remarked that her mother had expressed a wish to talk to her as soon as possible. Maria Irene replied coldly that she would no doubt have to visit her mother in prison one day, but that it would not be for a good while after this. On the other hand, she hoped that I would be kind enough to come and see her again as soon as the official investigation was over. 'After this, I need someone I can talk to and lean on more than ever,' was her sad conclusion. 'And this time, I can at least promise you that my mother will not disturb us,' she added with a quiet little smile.

I gave her a cautious hug, and was very pleased with my situation as I left Schelderup Hall. I thought to myself that I had never had a better reason to celebrate Norway's national day. It was only when I was in the car on my way back to the station that I realized that I had not phoned Patricia following the arrest of Sandra Schelderup.

III

Patricia listened with great interest to my account of the night's arrest, but then became more and more agitated as I told her about the interview and the visit to Schelderup Hall. When I eventually enquired if there was anything else she thought I should have asked Sandra Schelderup, her reply was fast and hard.

'Yes, definitely. The simple and crucial question from a

classic Simenon novel: what was the colour of the dress worn by the woman she claims to have killed?'

I must have seemed utterly astounded, as Patricia certainly lost all patience with me.

'You ask your oh-so-suddenly cooperative arrestee about that, and then call me as soon as you have the answer!' Patricia snapped, and put down the phone with unusual haste.

I called her up again ten minutes later. She answered the telephone after the first ring and appeared still to be angry.

'She said that the dress was blue, which it was. And what is more, she gave a detailed description of the room and the sofa where Synnøve was sitting when she died. It all sounded fairly convincing to me.'

I had hoped and thought that this would make Patricia calm down. But instead she became even more vexed. First there was a deep sigh at the other end, then an explosive: 'Buggeration!'

'What is that supposed to mean?' I asked.

Then I anxiously enquired if in some mysterious way this entailed problems with our understanding of the deaths of Leonard Schelderup and Magdalon Schelderup. The voice at the other end of the phone sounded no more cheerful.

'No, both those deaths have definitely been solved. But this does mean that there are still problems in connection with solving the murder of Synnøve Jensen. Come to see me as soon as you can, and I will explain why.'

I hesitated. She noticed and carried on swiftly.

'On your way over here, ponder the problem of timing

from 8 May 1945, but this time in connection with 15 May 1969. This time there are not too many seconds, but too few. Something that is even harder to explain. If it was Sandra Schelderup you chased up the slope behind Synnøve Jensen's house, if you were only fifteen to twenty yards behind her, and if the door to the car up there was still closed . . . how on earth did she have time to open the door, get in, start the engine and drive off before you got close enough to see her?'

I felt the blood rushing to my head and the floor heaving beneath my feet, and then what felt like an icy-cold hand tightening round my throat. I finally heard my own voice say that perhaps she had a point, and that I would be there as soon as I could.

Patricia simply said 'good' before abruptly putting down the phone. It certainly did not sound like she meant it.

IV

'It might perhaps have been possible if the car engine was running and the door was open. But impossible if the door was closed, which it was, according to the witness. And you heard the car starting. Ergo, Sandra Schelderup is lying. There must have been two people out under the cover of dark that night. One who committed the murder and was chased by you. Another who was sitting waiting in the car and who opened the door and started the engine as soon as they heard footsteps. And there is only one person who could possibly have been there with Sandra Schelderup, and

Sandra Schelderup is now willing to be punished in order to protect her.'

Her reasoning was idiot-proof; I had understood this finally, better late than never, as I was on my way into Patricia's library. I had a fervent hope that Patricia would have worked out another solution, but it was thus not entirely unexpected.

'So what you are now saying, in plain language, is that you think Maria Irene Schelderup was driving the car when Sandra Schelderup went to murder Synnøve Jensen?'

Patricia looked even more dejected and shook her head.

'No. Unfortunately it is far worse than that. What I am saying, in plain language, is that Sandra Schelderup was driving the car when Maria Irene went to murder Synnøve Jensen. And it is not just something I think, but that I know.'

I had not expected this, and it was definitely worse than anticipated. I sat as if paralysed and stared at Patricia.

The steaming cups of coffee remained so far untouched on both sides of the table. Patricia now emptied her cup in one go.

'It is the only possible solution, sadly. I have in fact had my suspicions all along. Remember that there was no key to Synnøve Jensen's house. Synnøve Jensen would never in her life have let Sandra Schelderup in, because she both hated and feared her. But she might well have let Maria Irene in as, naive and trusting as she was, she liked her and thought of her as an innocent child.'

The bottom of my world, my triumph and my future dreams fell out and came crashing down. I made a feeble attempt at protest.

'But surely there are other possible explanations . . . for example, that she opened the door for Sandra Schelderup in the belief that it was me.'

Patricia poured herself another cup of coffee and drank it, then shook her head mercilessly when she was done.

'Possibly, but highly unlikely. Synnøve Jensen did not even have a doorbell. She no doubt looked out of the window when someone knocked on the door, as she did on your first visit. But there are several more grave issues here. What Synnøve Jensen in her desperation was trying to tell you when she waved her hand towards the stairs and then patted her tummy was, first, that the murderer had gone upstairs, and second, that the murderer was the child. The reason that you suddenly thought of Leonard Schelderup as you ran up the slope was because the footfall of the person in front subconsciously reminded you of his, because, as you noticed earlier in the investigations, his sister has the same light step.'

We both sat there in sombre thought. Patricia lifted the coffee pot again to see if there was anything left, but then threw up a hand in exasperation when she found it empty.

I tried to ask Patricia how she had worked out the exist-ence of the tunnel. She answered in a distracted and distant voice that she had developed that theory from quite early on. It did not seem likely that a former Resistance fighter of Magdalon Schelderup's character would live in a house without a secret escape. This was confirmed by the times at which the dogs barked on the night that Synnøve Jensen was killed, as it chimed well with when the tunnel would have been used if the murderer came from Schelderup Hall.

The dogs had registered sounds and movement even if the policemen on duty had not seen anyone.

'I have to say you are right again, and that really does make this an incredibly depressing story,' I eventually conceded.

Patricia gave an even sadder sigh.

'But the most bitter pill is yet to be swallowed . . . namely, that we can sit here and know who the murderer is, but have no evidence to prove it in court. And legally that is not sufficient to pass a judgement; in fact, it will barely suffice to keep someone on remand. Sandra Schelderup's confession is plausible, and, as far as I have understood, you have submitted a written report in which you state that you could not recognize the person you were chasing. The issue of the time it takes to open a car door thus becomes our word against hers. I can already hear the lawyer objecting to the hand on the stomach. Could that really be called evidence, that a dying pregnant woman instinctively puts her hand to her stomach . . . ?'

Patricia took my cup of coffee and drank it straight down. Then she sat there as if all the energy had drained from her body. I heard my own voice quivering with emotion when I tried to sum it all up.

'You are right about everything. We know who the real murderer is, but unless we find some technical evidence, we simply have to let her go – with an enormous inheritance.'

Patricia nodded almost imperceptibly. Despite her massive intake of caffeine, she sat as though otherwise dead in her wheelchair. Only her eyes showed that she was alive.

'And that despite your enormous efforts, the like of which I have never seen,' I added.

But Patricia was definitely not in the mood for more flattery today. She sat passively in her wheelchair for a few seconds more. Then she suddenly slammed her fist down on the table with unexpected strength.

'So close yet so far. A thoroughly cynical, egocentric and evil person who shot a young, pregnant woman in her own home and then stood there and watched her and her unborn child die a painful death. And she may get off scot-free, with an astronomical inheritance into the bargain.'

I thought quietly to myself that the problem was even greater than that. Patricia was about to lose the battle with a young woman of the same age, who not only could walk, but also had the world as her oyster. This feeling was re-inforced by her next comment.

'Now I feel as you did when you were chasing after the murderer. I can see her in front of me, I can see her face and even call her name, but I still cannot catch her.'

There was not much more to say. So we sat there in silence for a while longer.

Patricia had tears in her eyes when she eventually threw up her hands.

'But there really is no more that I can squeeze from this lemon now, so no one else will be able to either. She has been both ingenuous and lucky. The known facts give no evidence against her. So perhaps you should just leave me alone to weep bitter tears over this tragedy. I am sure that you do not need Beate to show you out any more.'

I was reluctant to leave Patricia alone in such a despairing mood. But her voice was forceful and clear, and there was nothing I could say to cheer her up.

It was only after I had closed the door behind me that a new thought occurred to me.

I stopped for a moment, then turned around and went hesitantly back into the room with cautious steps.

I had not anticipated the sight that met me. Patricia was lying over the table with her face down. There was no movement or sound whatsoever, and with a cold blast of fear, I worried briefly that she too had lost her life in some mysterious way. But then, fortunately, I heard her sobbing.

I tiptoed out again as silently as I could, and knocked on the door. It took a few seconds before Patricia whispered that I should come in. When I entered again she was sitting up in her wheelchair, but looked broken and very gloomy. I thought I could see a redness to her eyes, and stood waiting by the door.

'There was a small episode involving Maria Irene at Schelderup Hall that I have not wanted to mention before . . . but perhaps I should now, even though I am not sure how much it might help.'

I looked away as I said this and prayed that I was not blushing like a schoolboy. When I turned back, Patricia's body language had changed entirely. She was now sitting up straight and as near to on her toes as she could be in a wheelchair, as though ready to jump over the table.

'Well, sit yourself back down and tell me, then,' she urged me.

So I sat down and told her.

It felt a little odd to start with the sentence: 'I have danced with Maria Irene . . .'

Patricia rolled her eyes, but fortunately all she said was: 'In principle, dubious but of very little practical use. Tell me as precisely and in as much detail as possible what she said, how she looked and what happened otherwise.'

Patricia listened in deep silence and concentration while I told her the story. Then a slow smile slid over her face.

'It only remains to be seen whether that is sufficient evidence for a judgement. However, there is one very interesting detail in what you just told me, which certainly justifies another round of questions,' she said.

'Now I have her within reach again,' she added, rubbing her hands with glee. 'If she falls now, she truly is a victim of her own excessive ambition,' Patricia remarked, with a cackling and wholly unsympathetic laugh.

V

'Thus far it is all very understandable, if tragic and deplorable. My mother has murdered one person and attempted to murder another out of a misconstrued love for me and a desire to increase my share of the inheritance. I am obviously extremely upset about it. But why on earth should I be called in here; what more do you expect me to say?'

Maria Irene looked at me across the table of the interview room with pleading, nonplussed eyes. As did her lawyer, Edvard Rønning Junior, who was sitting beside her. The prosecutor, who was sitting beside me, also sent me a questioning look.

'The problem is, first of all, that your mother cannot have committed the murder alone, as she describes. We have an eyewitness who confirms that the car door was shut. And it would not have been possible for the person ahead of me to open the door, get in, start the engine and drive off before I got there.'

All three slowly seemed to understand this. Maria Irene nodded thoughtfully.

'You really have thought of everything in this investigation. But I am afraid that again I cannot help you. Now that you say it, I do not doubt that my mother had an accomplice who drove the car, but I have not the faintest idea of who that could be. As far as I know, my mother has no secret lover, nor any friends who would be willing to help her with something like this.'

'Precisely,' I said.

The silence in the interview room was becoming ever more oppressive. Maria Irene had understood the significance, but was holding out for as long as possible before admitting it.

'So what you are now implying is that I was with her and drove the car? But that is absurd, as I do not even have a driving licence.'

'That is correct, my client does not have a driving licence,' Rønning Junior repeated emphatically.

I ignored the lawyer and looked straight at Maria Irene.

'I am not saying that you drove the car. I am in fact saying that your mother drove the car and that you committed the murder.'

This time the reaction from both the defence and the prosecution lawyers was instantaneous. Maria Irene, on the other hand, sat there just as calmly for a few seconds before pulling a somewhat exaggerated face.

'This is becoming more and more absurd. I have never committed a crime of any sort in my life.'

She was convincing and I saw the look of disbelief on both lawyer's faces, so hurried on.

'It is perhaps true that you had never committed a crime before the evening in question. But that evening you committed a murder. I was close enough to recognize your tread, which is remarkably similar to that of your late brother. And what is more, you are the only person Synnøve Jensen would have let in. You knocked on the door and were admitted, you pulled out the pistol and shot her, you stood there waiting for the poor woman to die, and you cunningly dropped the pistol, then ran and hid when I knocked on the door.'

Six eyes were staring at Maria Irene with increasing interest. Her gaze was steadily fixed on me, as calm and irritatingly self-assured as ever.

'With all due respect, this is all nonsense, unfounded speculation. I was at home in my bed at Gulleråsen when this terrible tragedy took place at Sørum. I was obviously on my own, so the lack of witnesses is hardly surprising.'

Rønning Junior rushed to his client's aid, in a long-winded way.

'May I be permitted to say, Detective Inspector, that you

are now making very serious accusations indeed on rather flimsy evidence. We seem to be caught in a classic situation of one person's word against another's – in this case yours against my client's – as to whether she was at the scene of the crime or not. And according to the fundamental principles of law, her word carries as much weight as yours. I would therefore like to ask why my client has not been confronted with this charge before, when you claim to have identified her already on the night of the murder?'

I nodded.

'A very timely question, sir. The answer is that there was still a good deal of uncertainty regarding the involvement of your client's mother, and that we were waiting for stronger evidence, which we now have.'

All three stared at me in silence, Maria Irene with an apparently genuine look of surprise and slightly raised eyebrows.

I produced the pistol and showed that there were six bullets left in the magazine before putting it down on the table.

'This is the murder weapon. The two bullets that are missing are the one that killed Synnøve Jensen and the warning shot that I fired over the murderer's head. You and your mother found the weapon hidden in the secret passage in Schelderup Hall. You used it without knowing that this was the gun your father had used to liquidate two other members of the Resistance group he was in during the war.'

Maria Irene shook her head resolutely.

'I did not know that my father had shot anyone from the Resistance during the war and have never seen that pistol before now. And I knew nothing about the secret passage until this morning.'

I hurried on as soon as she had closed her mouth.

'It is quite probably the case that you did not know about your father's crimes during the war. But it is not true that you have never seen this pistol, or that you have never been in the secret passage.'

I took a short, dramatic pause.

'You will perhaps remember that at an earlier stage of the investigation I danced with you briefly in your room?'

Both lawyers were once again taken aback. Maria Irene nodded, with a hint of a smile tugging at the corners of her mouth.

'This breach of normal investigation standards was made solely in the hope of securing evidence in the case. Which I did.'

I opened my briefcase and took out another object which I then placed on the table. The red diamond and gold chain sparkled in the light.

'You can, I presume, confirm that you were wearing this diamond?'

Maria Irene suddenly understood the connection. She looked first at the diamond, then at me, then back at the diamond, her eyes darkening as she thought. Her voice was still impressively controlled when she answered.

'No. You must have remembered wrong. I have never seen that necklace before and have certainly never worn it!'

The silence in the room when she finished speaking was breathless. I stared at her with a thrilled awe. The eighteen-year-old Maria Irene Schelderup lied without so much as a flutter. Just as I hoped she would.

So I continued to follow Patricia's plan and swiftly carried on.

'Neither you nor your mother perhaps knew that this is an extremely valuable diamond that has been missing since 1915, when your grandparents were paid a considerable sum in insurance because they claimed that the necklace had been stolen. But you do know, all too well, that you were wearing this diamond when you danced with me. It was hidden in the secret passage, along with the pistol that was used in the murder. You had taken the diamond from there without your mother knowing.'

Maria Irene shook her head again. Her voice was still controlled and her cheeks were still dry.

'I can only repeat, absolutely no. I had never seen the pistol before you put it down on the table, I have never been in the secret passage, and I have never seen that necklace before.'

Her lawyer's voice was slightly more uncertain, but still firm when he again offered his services.

'We are, without a doubt, still in a situation where it is one person's word against the other's: that is, that of the detective inspector against that of my client, as was the case before. My young client's word is still no less credible than your own.'

I nodded blithely.

'Of course not. Providing that your young client can give a credible explanation as to why her fingerprints are then on the necklace.'

The expression 'deadly silent' suddenly seemed appropriate. Three pairs of eyes were trained on Maria Irene. She was completely still, almost as if dead, on her chair. I tried to keep an eye on the second hand of the clock on the wall behind her. Every second felt like a minute. After forty insufferably long seconds, Maria Irene turned to her lawyer and asked: 'Do I have to answer that now?'

'No. You are in no way legally obliged to answer the detective inspector's question here and now.'

It was Rønning Junior who broke the electric silence between her and me.

'I am, however, obliged to inform you that with regard to any future trial, it would clearly be considered a major issue in terms of evidence if you are not able to give a credible answer now to the detective inspector's highly relevant question.'

The clock on the wall ticked on for another fifty seconds. Maria Irene moved her mouth twice as if she was about to speak, but then stopped both times without making a sound.

I should have had ample time to prepare myself for an explosion. I had previously discovered that incredibly calm people often erupt violently under extreme pressure. And I already knew that Maria Irene had a mother with an explosive temperament. But she sat there, apparently still calm and composed, and with such a relaxed face that it took us all off guard when in a furious rage she swept the necklace off the table and grabbed the gun. I only vaguely registered that both lawyers dived under the table, from either side.

Maria Irene leapt up and took three feather-light steps

back, keeping her eyes trained on me. Her eyes were glittering so fiercely that for a second I was seriously afraid that they would fire splinters out into the room.

For a brief moment I felt once again the same strong desire for physical contact with Maria Irene that I had experienced a couple of days earlier in her room. But everything had changed in the intervening forty-eight hours. She had not only killed another young woman, she had also lied to me in cold blood. When I was now confronted with her true egotistical and heartless self, all I wanted to do was to strike the pistol from her hand and twist her arms hard up behind her back.

I relived for a second the moment in my last case when I suddenly found myself staring down the barrel of a loaded gun. Despite the instinctive feeling of unease, I also felt a deep sense of satisfaction and triumph. Maria Irene's soft iron mask had finally shattered. Her eyes were burning and her slim hand trembled dangerously with the weight of the pistol. When she broke the silence, her voice was also trembling dangerously.

'I did not think you were that intelligent!' she said, with a delightful undertone of desperation.

I relished the apparently menacing situation, and mentally thanked Patricia for her meticulous preparation before I answered.

'In which case you have underestimated me again. Because I was certainly smart enough to replace the bullets in the murder weapon with blanks before putting it down within your reach,' I told her, with hard-won composure.

And in the most incredible fashion, all the tension in the

room dissolved into what could almost be described as a relaxed peace in the course of a few seconds. I remained seated and observed the threatening spark die in Maria Irene's eyes. Then I got up and reached for the pistol. She stood and hesitated for a moment before she slowly gave it to me. Her hand was no longer shaking, and for a moment I thought I caught the hint of a smile.

Then I sat back down, impressed by my own self control. I did have a burning desire to throw myself over Maria Irene and twist her arms up behind her back, but instead I kept my calm and enjoyed my triumph in silence as I watched Maria Irene sink back down onto her chair.

It was only then that I discovered that the prosecutor was also back in his chair. Rønning Junior peeped over the edge of the table and said in a remarkably level voice: 'Based on this latest development in the case, it might perhaps be beneficial to all parties if I had a brief consultation with my client in private.'

I gave him a friendly nod, picked up the gun and waved to the prosecutor to follow me. The gold chain and diamond were still on the floor by the door. I bent down discreetly and picked them up as I passed.

The prosecutor and I stopped outside the door. He congratulated me on my successful investigation. To begin with, I said simply that it had been a complicated and tragic affair, with many pieces that had gradually fallen into place. When he then congratulated me for a fourth time, I allowed myself to say that I was extremely pleased with my own performance. At that moment, the door opened and Rønning Junior waved us in again.

'In order to avoid any further misunderstandings in this case, I would just like to confirm that the outcome of the current murder investigation is naturally of no importance to the question of Magdalon Schelderup's will. It is clear that my client had nothing to do with the deaths of her father and half-brother. Synnøve Jensen was not an heir, and the foetus had no legal status prior to birth.'

I looked at the defence lawyer with horrified fascination. Then I looked at the prosecutor, who gave me a short nod. Which I then returned, though reluctantly.

'Now that the framework is clear, my client is willing to confess to the murder of Synnøve Jensen and to cooperate with the police with regard to resolving the final details of the case. She will plead guilty to the murder. We will, however, cite several mitigating circumstances. In addition to the confession, these include my client's age, family wealth and her rather unusual upbringing, as well as the emotional shock and grief triggered by the sudden deaths of her father and brother. Her version is that it was her mother who planned the murder and persuaded her to carry it out, and we have every hope that a revised statement from her mother will support this interpretation.'

My initial sense of triumph was now giving way to far more complex feelings. There was something about the combination of the lawyer's voice and Maria Irene's expressionless face that made me want to scream out my frustration at her shocking lack of grief and other human emotions, and her inhuman treatment of Synnøve Jensen.

The lawyer's voice droned on without cease, as if he were already in court.

'The defence will accordingly request seven years' imprisonment, with the hope of parole after four for good behaviour.'

My feelings of revulsion at Maria Irene's lack of humanity in no way diminished, but did have to give way to a reluctant admiration in the face of her renewed composure. It was she who held out her hand when we stood up to leave, and congratulated me on carrying out such a thorough investigation. She added quickly that she did not hold a personal grudge against me and that the pleasure would be hers entirely should we meet 'under more favourable circumstances later in life'.

Her hand felt dry, cold and hard in mine. I withdrew my hand rather sooner than usual and in a strange way found the cigarette smoke outside the interview room rather refreshing.

VI

'What a turniphead she turned out to be after all!'

Patricia smiled her smuggest smile, and paused demonstratively before helping herself to some cauliflower. The clock on the wall had just struck eleven. It was late evening on 17 May, the day we celebrate Norway's constitution, but more importantly now, the day we celebrated the conclusion of another successful murder investigation. The adrenaline was still pumping in our veins and we were now well into the main course of a truly celebratory meal.

'Her critical mistake was to deny any knowledge of the

necklace instead of the pistol. Had she instead admitted that she had taken the diamond necklace from the secret passage and worn it during the meeting with you, it would hardly have been possible to link her to the pistol and the murder. But I guessed that she was not that intelligent, and it had been luck so far.'

I nodded. Tonight I would accept practically anything that Patricia said.

'You should be very happy with what you have achieved, it really is quite remarkable. Not only did you solve three apparently inexplicable murders from the present day, you also solved three murders from the war,' I told her.

Patricia's smile was even broader.

'*And*, please do not forget an almost fossilized case of insurance fraud,' she added. 'The diamond case was so old that it is unlikely that anyone from the insurance company is alive to remember it, but the truth will always out, even if it takes decades.'

I nodded, but said nothing.

'You do not seem to be overly happy, despite the fact that the investigation is now closed and all the murders are solved,' she commented, after a pause.

I shook my head.

'When I do a headcount of the ten guests from Magdalon Schelderup's last supper, there are now two dead, two in prison and two on the verge of a nervous breakdown . . . The host's Machiavellian plan to spread fear and chaos amongst his guests has worked alarmingly well.'

Patricia gave a pensive shrug and waggled her head at the same time.

'Yes and no. It was a truly Machiavellian plan that took the lives of some of his guests and ruined the lives of other. It remains to be seen how Mrs Wendelboe and Ingrid Schelderup will cope with life after this. But the others from the war who are still alive, including Mona Varden and Maja Karstensen, did finally get an answer as to what actually happened. Herlofsen will certainly have a better life for however long remains, and that may also be the case for Magdalena Schelderup and the Wendelboes. Fredrik Schelderup perhaps does not deserve it, but he will have an even more carefree life than before. The Schelderup mother and daughter have to take full responsibility for their egoism and greed. So tragedy really only applies to the two young people who died. We were in the nick of time to save the useless Fredrik Schelderup's life and inheritance, but not to save his far nicer brother, Leonard, or the hardworking and honest Synnøve Jensen. Unfortunately, the lot of a murder investigator is that one can do no more than solve frightful crimes and bring those responsible to justice. It is normally very difficult to solve a murder before it has happened.'

I was well aware of that, but still could not force myself to be pleased. She realized this and continued quickly.

'As for Magdalon Schelderup, it can only be said that he did to a certain extent succeed in his final great gamble, but he did not succeed in his great act. If Magdalon Schelderup, against all odds, could see us now, be it from heaven or hell, I can promise you that he would curse us from the bottom of his heart for having unmasked him. In a matter of days, the whole of Norway will know not only that Magdalon Schelderup committed suicide, but also that he was a criminal and a traitor during the war, and that he wanted to spread death and destruction amongst his family and friends. His true character will eventually be revealed and he will be publicly condemned as the callous man that he was. And as for you, you will hopefully get all the honour and recognition you deserve for your achievement.'

I have to confess that the last thing Patricia said did manage to raise my spirits a little.

'Yes, thank you, I have to say it is overwhelming. Congratulatory messages are flooding in already, despite the fact that it is a public holiday, and the weekend newspapers will no doubt make pleasant reading. But remember that for the past week I have been out there meeting these people, including Maria Irene. It frustrates me immensely that the person responsible for such a grotesque crime should get away so lightly. Synnøve Jensen and her unborn child are gone for ever, whereas Maria Irene will be released before she is twenty-five, and has earned tens of millions from the murder.'

Patricia nodded in agreement, but smiled all the same.

'Of course, it is a paradox. She will naturally be punished far too lightly in the end and will have far more money than she deserves. But you will have to comfort yourself with the knowledge that you did all that you could and she did not get away with it. I can assure you that every day in prison is hell for human predators like her, and she is not likely to enjoy the company in Breitvedt Women's Prison. It will be a long and hard road should she ever want to find a good husband after the court case has been reported in the press. But, most importantly, her plans to inherit all the money and run the business single-handedly are in ruins because we prevented the murder of her half-brother.'

I had to say that Patricia was right in her reasoning, but I was still not happy with the situation. She was not put off by this and carried on after a pause for thought.

'In the midst of all this tragedy, it is actually quite amusing that Maria Irene fell victim to her own absurd ambition to such an extent. She tried to lay a trap for you, and ended up being trapped herself!'

Patricia burst out laughing, then attacked her ice cream dessert with a healthy appetite. It struck me that she was a very complex young person. And behind the mask, she had invested some powerful emotions in this case.

I personally was too relieved by the outcome of the case to want to pursue the topic any further. Instead I asked Patricia if she had found the answer to her question as to why I was still alive. She suddenly became very serious, but it did not last long, and soon a mischievous smile crept over her lips again.

'That was in fact one of the things that convinced me that it was Maria Irene who had killed Synnøve Jensen. I saw no reason why Sandra Schelderup would not have shot you in that situation. On the other hand, there were two possible reasons why Maria Irene Schelderup instead put down the gun and ran. One was that she found you so handsome and attractive that she could not shoot you, and perhaps still even hoped that she would get all of the inheritance and all of you.'

I nodded. The explanation was neither reasonable nor unreasonable.

'And what was the second possible reason?'

Patricia swallowed the last spoonful of ice cream and leant back.

'I am tempted to say, don't pretend to be more stupid than you are . . . The second reason is of course that she considered you to be so naive and gullible that she thought you would not understand what had happened and that she would manage to escape without being seen.'

This was a far less attractive option, but sadly it was equally neither reasonable nor unreasonable; I had to admit that.

'Which of those theories do you believe to be true?'

Patricia shot me a delighted and teasing smile.

'My friend, when will you understand that more than anything I hate to make mistakes, and therefore would rather not give my conclusions before I am as good as 100 per cent certain that they are correct. It might even be a combination. I believe more in one explanation than the other, but only Maria Irene could tell us which one is right. And my guess is that you would not want to ask her.'

I most certainly would not. It struck me as I sat there that Patricia, despite her obvious mood swings, was both physically and mentally more mature than she had been the previous year. If I had not realized this before, I certainly did at a quarter to twelve when Beate suddenly appeared with a bottle of superb vintage French wine. I took only a small glass, whereas Patricia drank two generous glasses and became increasingly gregarious. After the first glass, she laughed and remarked that she would dearly have loved to have been in the interview room and seen Maria

Irene with 'her mask and trousers finally down'. I could not remember having heard this expression before and strongly suspected that Patricia had made it up.

It was around half past midnight by the time I got up and went over to Patricia to embrace her goodbye, and discovered something that was indeed different this year. Patricia had not unbuttoned her blouse as far as Maria Irene had two days ago. But she had undone the top two buttons. And I saw that, despite her handicap, she had become a beautiful young woman. My cheek touched hers briefly, and as I pulled back our eyes met for a moment. And I got the same feeling that I had at Schelderup Hall only days before when I was dancing with Maria Irene Schelderup. I somehow instantly knew that if I had tried to kiss Patricia she would not have protested, but rather would have kissed me passionately back. The tension and opportunity lasted for a few breathless moments. This time no one knocked on the door. I turned to the side at the last moment, and so it was a light kiss that I planted on her cheek rather than a passionate kiss on the mouth.

When I think back to this episode now, it is still unclear to me whether it was the strange similarity with the situation with Maria Irene, Patricia's handicap, the age difference between us, or something else I do not understand that made me hold back. What is clear is that I did. Then I left the room, somewhat more hastily than planned. I felt an urgent need to get out into the night and to think things through by myself.

Patricia, of course, stayed sitting where she was, on her own in the wheelchair by the table. When I looked back briefly on my way out, her smile was more inscrutable than ever. Then, with a discreet little yawn, she wished me a good journey home, and in closing said that I should not hesitate to contact her again if I worked on any more interesting murder cases where she might be of help. But by then I was already rushing through the door and out into the safety of the dark night.

Epilogue

No new interesting murder cases landed on my desk in 1969. For the rest of the year I could rest on the laurels of the Schelderup case. The story continued to cause a stir in the media, especially during the major court case in the autumn. To my deep frustration, but in line with what the defence had claimed, both Maria Irene and Sandra Schelderup were sentenced to seven years' imprisonment.

My frustration had peaked before the trial even started, however. On 7 October 1969, I awoke to the headline: 'Eighteen-year-old accused of murder now Oslo's richest woman'. Underneath was a photograph of Maria Irene. The report stated that her brother, Fredrik Schelderup, had been killed in a crash, in an excessively large car with excessive amounts of alcohol in his blood, on the way from a bar to the beach in Rio de Janeiro. And with that, several months after the main event, another of the satellite people from Magdalon Schelderup's last supper bit the dust.

Ingrid Schelderup was admitted to hospital again when the court case caused the circumstances surrounding the deaths of her former husband and her son to be splashed across the front pages of all the newspapers once more. When I called her sometime later, I was informed by the hospital that it was not the best day to disturb her. But when I offered to call another day, I was told that it was not the best week or month either. So I took the hint and never rang back.

To my surprise, Petter Johannes Wendelboe was in the courtroom on 3 November, the first day of the trial. He looked exactly as he had before, and shook my hand with the same firmness. When I asked after Mrs Wendelboe, he replied shortly that she had unfortunately gone from 'bad to worse'. She had, as had Ingrid Schelderup, been exempted from appearing as a witness for health reasons. I could not help but ask if he had been in touch with Magdalena Schelderup. He told me curtly that he had apologized on behalf of his wife and himself, and that this apology had been accepted. So Petter Johannes Wendelboe was himself to the last, and a remarkable man in my eyes.

Hans Herlofsen told me, when I called one day to ask some routine questions, that he had never been better. He had resigned from Schelderup's company and had found himself a far better-paid job with a company car, thanks to all the coverage the case had been given in the press. The balance of his personal account was already 17,782 kroner. So some of the satellite people from Magdalon Schelderup's last supper had managed to find themselves a better orbit in the new universe that opened up when the circumstances surrounding his death had been established.

I received a letter from Mona Varden thanking me wholeheartedly for the 'somewhat late, but remarkable' unmasking of her husband's murderer. There was also a sentence to say that she had now, finally, been able to clear his room. She enclosed a photograph of the grandson who was apparently the spitting image of his grandfather. A few days later, I received a postcard from Maja Karstensen in Rodeløkka, to thank me for redeeming Arild Bratberg's 'honour and memory'. There was a PS to say that Bratberg's siblings had dropped their claim on his flat, following all the coverage of the case.

On 10 November 1969, I myself stood up in court to bear witness against the Schelderups. And I rather reluctantly had to admit that Maria Irene played her part very well from her place in the dock. She was surprisingly convincing as the remorseful and bewildered offender who had been led astray by her mother. The press even managed to photograph her with tears in her eyes as she spoke about the murder. But when I passed Maria Irene on my way to the witness stand, at barely an arm's length, I saw the shadow of a lioness's smile on her lips. Our eyes met a moment later. And I am certain that I detected something that she herself would never admit – that despite the discomfort of the court case and prison, it had been worth it, now that she had the whole inheritance and would have more than enough time to use it when she got out.

It somehow felt unnatural for me to contact Patricia without an ongoing murder case to discuss. Through the autumn I increasingly pondered over how early on Patricia had realized the truth about how the father and son had died, and how different the story might have been if she had confided in me before the murder of Synnøve Jensen.

As far as Maria Irene was concerned, I was eternally grateful to Patricia for revealing her egoism and ruthlessness to me in time. There were occasions later on in November when I even suspected that Patricia might have held back the explanation of the earlier deaths on purpose, in the hope that Maria Irene would commit a murder.

I never considered asking Patricia about this. I was too grateful to her for all the help she had given me with my first two murder investigations, and too conscious of my own dependency in the event of future investigations. For reasons I have often speculated on without drawing any conclusion, Patricia never contacted me on her own initiative. Our somewhat hasty and confusing goodbye shortly after midnight on Sunday, 18 May 1969 was therefore the last time that we saw each other in the 1960s. It was not until seven months into 1970 that a sensational new murder investigation, which had a very dramatic start for me, brought us together again.

Author's Afterword

This novel, written thirty-five years after her death, is my homage to Agatha Christie, the world's greatest crime writer, who gave us the most original plots. Without any illusions of having achieved the level of Agatha Christie's best mysteries, I have tried in 2011 to capture her style and spirit in terms of the plot, time structure and characters. In doing this, I have based the book on Christie's views of the good and evil nature of human beings, even though this only in very specific cases tallies with my own personal views.

I have also, as I did in my first novel *The Human Flies*, tried to find my own literary crime niche by taking inspiration from three classical crime writers of bygone years. This time, once again, I have written a plot inspired by Christie, with a detective duo who are more akin to Sir Arthur Conan Doyle's tales about Sherlock Holmes and Dr Watson. And again, I go beyond the realms of the British crime tradition of Christie and Doyle, and follow in the footsteps of the great Belgian writer, Georges Simenon, in trying to combine an exciting crime mystery with an engaging story about people's different fates and histories.

If my crime novel, *The Satellite People*, is successful in these endeavours, then it is to a large extent thanks to my good advisors who have worked with me on the manuscript. My editor, Anne Fløtaker at Cappelen Damm, has once again been my most important advisor, but I have also benefited greatly from the input given by Anders Heger and Nils Nordberg. I would also like to give two thousand thanks to my invaluable group of personal advisors, which this time includes my good friends Mina Finstad Berg, Ingrid Baukhol, Ellen Øen Carlsen, Synne Corell, Lene Li Dragland, Anne Lise Fredlund, Kathrien Næss Hald, Hanne Isaksen, Bjarte Leer-Salvesen, Torsten Lerhol, Espen Lie, Ellisiv Reppen, Kristine Kopperud Timberlid, Arne Tjølsen, Katrine Tjølsen and Magnhild K. B. Uglem, as well as my sister, Ida Lahlum. This time, Mina deserves to be mentioned before all others for her enthusiasm from the drawing board to the finished manuscript and for her many important comments on the language and content.

And finally, I would like to offer a more symbolic thank you to someone I have never met, namely the highly successful singer Lena Meyer-Landrut, who came to Norway last year. Her song 'Satellite' has kept me company for many an hour while writing this novel and was in part the inspiration for the title.

My articles on this book and other literary topics are freely available (in Norwegian) to those who might be interested on Cappelen Damm's blog page: www.forlagsliv.no/hansolavlahlum.

Any readers who have questions or comments about the book are welcome to contact me via Facebook, or directly by email: hansolahlum@gmail.com.

If you enjoyed Satellite People *you'll love*

THE CATALYST KILLING

the third instalment in the K2 and Patricia series
from Hans Olav Lahlum

1970. Inspector Kolbjørn Kristiansen, known as K2, witnesses a young woman desperately trying to board a train only to have the doors close before her face. The next time he sees her, she is dead . . .

As K2 investigates, with the help of his precocious young assistant Patricia, he discovers that the story behind Marie Morgenstierne's murder really began two years ago, when Marie's boyfriend Falko, the charismatic leader of a politically active group of friends, vanished without a trace.

But were the relationships between this group of friends and comrades all they appeared to be? What did Marie see that made her run for her life that day? And could both mysteries be linked to Falko's discovery of a cell of Norwegian Nazis he suspected may still be active?

It soon becomes clear that Marie's death will act as a catalyst in a dark set of events, and K2 and Patricia must work hard to unravel the clues before Marie's killer can strike again . . .

An extract follows here . . .

DAY ONE

The woman on the Lijord Line

I

I saw her for the first time, rather suddenly and unexpectedly, at nine minutes past ten in the evening of Wednesday, 5 August 1970.

Later that evening, I would find out the young woman's name. But over the next seven dramatic days I would continue, in my mind, to call her 'the woman on the Lijord Line'. Had I understood the reason for her behaviour there and then, it might not only have saved her life, but also the lives of several other people.

I had finished my evening shift a few minutes earlier with a fairly routine callout to a hotel by Smestad. If the manager there had been somewhat tense before the Soviet invasion of Czechoslovakia in 1968, he had definitely become a touch paranoid since. He reported a new potential terrorist threat at the hotel roughly every other month. This time he had called about a guest whose behaviour was 'suspiciously secretive', one of the manager's favourite expressions. The guest in question was a man who was possibly no more than thirty, though it was hard to say for certain because of his full beard and apparently suspiciously dark sunglasses. He was well dressed, spoke perfect Norwegian and had been politeness itself when he asked for a room with a balcony on the first floor. He had, however, not reserved a room in advance and did not give a postal address. The guest had said that he was not sure how long he would stay, but paid in cash for the first ten days at least. He did not want his room to be cleaned, and asked for a breakfast tray to be left in the hall outside his room every morning at nine o'clock. As long as the empty tray was put back out in the hall again, one could safely assume he was still there. And this had been the case for the past six days, but no member of staff had seen any other sign of life from the guest.

I dutifully put my ear to the wall in the hallway for a minute or two, without hearing anything suspicious, of course. I ascertained that there was no evidence of criminal activity, and said that there could be many explanations for the guest's undeniably unusual behaviour. Then I promised to check the name he had given – Frank Rekkedal – in the police records, and asked them to contact us should there be any more grounds for concern.

For purely practical reasons – the axle on my police car had broken earlier in the day – I had taken a local train to Smestad. So, at nine minutes past ten, I boarded the train back into the city centre. It was a very quiet summer's evening in Smestad. I had been the only passenger waiting on the platform.

It was just as I sat down that I saw her for the first

time. She emerged very suddenly from the darkness on the road leading up the platform. And she was moving fast, extremely fast.

My first thought was that she must be a top athlete, as I could not remember having seen a woman run so fast before. Then I imagined that I might soon see a man with an axe or a scythe running after her. But there was no sign of any pursuer, even though I could see a good twenty to thirty yards behind her. In fact, there was no one else to be seen out there. And yet the woman ran even faster, despite her extremely tight jeans, hurtling towards the last door of the last carriage. It dawned on me that she might in fact be a madwoman as, despite her speed, she was running in a very odd way. Twice she hopped to the left at full speed, and once to the right.

Despite her tremendous exertion, she did not manage to reach the train in time. The doors slid shut right in front of her. It felt as though the entire carriage shuddered when she ran into them. For a couple of seconds, we stared at each other through the glass windows in the doors. I could see that she had long blonde hair and guessed that she was in her mid-twenties and slightly taller than average. It was, however, her face that struck me. It was a frozen mask of fear. The blue eyes that stared into mine were as wide as could be.

The doors did nothing to stop the young woman's desperation. She hammered on them with her fists in despair and then pointed a trembling finger at me, or at something behind me.

I turned around automatically but could see no one else

in the carriage. It was only once the train had left Smestad station that I realized she had been pointing at the emergency cord on the wall.

I sat and thought about this strange encounter with the woman on the Lijord Line all the way back into town. The trains were still running every twenty minutes, so it could surely not have been such a disaster that she missed it. By the time I got off at Nationaltheatret, I had dismissed the whole incident, having convinced myself that she was obviously a few sandwiches short of a picnic. I did not regret that I had lacked the sense to use the emergency brake, and thought to myself it was just as well as I would probably never see her again.

But I did see her again – that very same evening, in the very same place. At five to eleven, to be precise, only moments after I had jumped out of a police car borrowed from Smestad police station.

In my somewhat feeble defence, I did immediately realize what had happened when I got a telephone call from Holmenkollen at a quarter to eleven to say that the train that left Smestad station at twenty-nine minutes past ten had run over a young woman on the tracks.

When I returned, the woman on the Lijord Line lay immobile and lifeless on the tracks, in sharp contrast to the energy and sheer speed she had displayed in her mad dash to catch the train when I left Smestad only an hour ago. It was without a doubt the same woman. I recognized her jeans and her fair hair.

The driver was understandably beside himself. He repeated over and over that the woman had been lying on the tracks when he ran over her, and it had been impossible to see her in the pitch black until the train was almost on top of her, and by then it was technically impossible to stop. It had all happened so fast and been so terrible that he could not say whether she had been alive or not before he hit her. Fortunately, he seemed to calm down a bit when I assured him for the fourth time that no one suspected him of negligence or any other criminal act.

According to the student ID card she had in her purse along with three ten-kroner notes, a fifty-kroner note, a monthly travel pass and two keys, the woman on the Lijord Line was called Marie Morgenstierne. She studied politics at the University of Oslo and had apparently celebrated her twenty-fifth birthday four weeks earlier. That was all we found that might be of any interest. If she had had a bag with her that evening, it had been lost before her dramatic flight ended on the tracks.

It struck me immediately that I had heard the name Marie Morgenstierne before. But there and then, I could not recall where or under what circumstances.

The train had been coming to a halt when it hit her, but her upper body was so badly injured on impact that it was impossible to establish the cause of death at the scene. Her face, however, was intact. She stared up at me with the same frozen expression of fear that I had seen through the train window scarcely an hour earlier.

Again I wondered whether she might simply be a disturbed woman who had thrown herself in front of the train, or whether there was something else behind this. And then I promised myself that I would not let this case go until I found out. Fortunately I had no idea how many days this would take, or how complex the search for the truth about the death of the woman on the Lijord Line would prove to be.

II

It was with some trepidation that I dialled the home number of my boss at ten minutes past midnight. I knew that he was a night owl who lived on his own, and he had granted me permission to take advantage of this in the event of 'murder or suspicious circumstances until just after midnight'.

My boss listened carefully to my brief account. Then, to my relief, he immediately said that given my first-hand impressions of both the victim and the scene of the crime, I was obviously best qualified to head the murder investigation.

'Do you know who Marie Morgenstierne was, by the way?' he then asked, with great seriousness.

I had to say no. I still had the uncomfortable feeling that I had heard the name somewhere, but could not remember in what connection.

'Marie Morgenstierne was Falko Reinhardt's fiancée,' my boss said, pensively.

There was silence on the line for a few seconds, before he swiftly added: 'She was one of the small circle around him, one of the anti-Vietnam activists in the revolutionary youth movement. And she was sleeping in the same bed as

Falko Reinhardt on the night that he went missing. She was the first to discover that he had disappeared. A good many people in the police and the public in general, I am sure, would be extremely grateful and impressed if you managed to learn what happened to Falko Reinhardt on that stormy night in Valdres, at the same time as solving the new case. I will have all the papers from summer 1968 sent to your office first thing tomorrow morning.'

I thanked him and put down the receiver.

Then I went to bed, but was unable to sleep. In the course of one and a half hours on what I had assumed would be a quiet Wednesday evening, I had been given responsibility not only for a new murder case, but also the division's strangest and most talked-about missing person case of the past decade.

Only one thing was clear to me when I finally fell asleep on 5 August 1970 after an unexpectedly dramatic day, and that was who I needed to call before doing anything else when I reached the office the next morning. The telephone number for the disabled professor's daughter, Patricia Louise I. E. Borchmann, was still written between the emergency numbers for the fire brigade and Accident and Emergency department on my telephone lists, at home and in the office.

extracts reading groups
competitions books new
discounts extracts extracts
competitions discounts
books
new events
events books
extracts reading groups
new titles
interviews
events extracts
discounts events
new books events interviews
events new
discounts extracts discounts
www.panmacmillan.com
extracts events reading groups
competitions books extracts new books